THE CYCLE OF THE
RED MOON

THE CYCLE OF THE
RED MOON

BOOK ONE:
THE HARVEST OF
SAMHEIN

José Antonio Cotrina

DARK HORSE BOOKS
Milwaukie, OR

Cover design by Patrick Satterfield and Jen Edwards, and Amy Arendts
Cover painting by Fiona Hsieh
Translation by Katie LaBarbera with Gabriella Campbell

Special thanks to Davey Estrada, Jenny Blenk, Ervin Rustemagić, Tina Alessi, Gabriella Campbell, Annie Gullion, Cara Niece, Judy Khuu, and Christina Niece.

Neil Hankerson *Executive Vice President* • Tom Weddle *Chief Financial Officer* • Randy Stradley *Vice President of Publishing* • Nick Mcwhorter *Chief Business Development Officer* • Dale Lafountain *Chief Information Officer* • Matt Parkinson *Vice President of Marketing* • Vanessa Todd-Holmes *Vice President of Production and Scheduling* • Mark Bernardi *Vice President of Book Trade and Digital Sales* • Ken Lizzi *General Counsel* • Dave Marshall *Editor in Chief* • Davey Estrada *Editorial Director* • Chris Warner *Senior Books Editor* • Cary Grazzini *Director of Specialty Projects* • Lia Ribacchi *Art Director* • Matt Dryer *Director of Digital Art and Prepress* • Michael Gombos *Senior Director of Licensed Publications* • Kari Yadro *Director of Custom Programs* • Kari Torson *Director of International Licensing* • Sean Brice *Director of Trade Sales*

Published by Dark Horse Books
A division of Dark Horse Comics LLC
10956 SE Main Street
Milwaukie, OR 97222

DarkHorse.com
SAFComics.com

Library of Congress Control Number: 2020932892

First edition: September 2020
ISBN 978-1-50671-680-0

Printed in the United States of America

1 3 5 7 9 10 8 6 4 2

TABLE OF CONTENTS

This one's for my sister.

Cities, like dreams, are built on fears and desires; though the thread of their discourse is secret, their rules absurd, their perspectives deceptive, and everything hides something else.

—*INVISIBLE CITIES*, ITALO CALVINO

VORTEX

The city was restless.

It was an auspicious night, harvest time, and the crackling of magic filled the air. A bolt of lightning flashed high above, and thunder exploded a second later; it echoed in the darkness like the roar of an immense beast.

The hour had come.

Thousands of winged shadows became lords and masters of the heavens, forming shifting clouds that squawked senselessly as they swerved in a frenzy across the sky.

In the castle windows moved the silhouettes of its inhabitants. Some appeared for just a fleeting glimpse; others remained longer in the windows, contemplating the comings and goings of a figure outlined at the top of the tower.

It was a tiny man who walked huddled against the storm. He looked so fragile that it seemed as if the wind might carry him off at any moment. The battlement of the tower where he walked was dotted with coat racks, each of them draped with a single coat. He went from one to another, humming all the while.

High above the tower, a patch of intense red shone through a crack in the sky. Most of the winged shadows gathered around this tear in the sky, twisting and turning like sinister whirlwinds.

The little man raised his eyes toward the crevice. He shook his head and hurried over to the nearest coat. He stroked it from top to bottom as he chanted. Suddenly, the garment straightened up on its stand and waved its sleeves in front of him, as if it expected a hug. The little gray man grimaced from exhaustion and moved on to the next coat. Shortly after, another clap of thunder resounded in the heavens, an explosion that echoed throughout the cliffs for a long time. The break in the sky changed color from red to blue, and then from blue to an intense black. The little man closed his eyes, tried to control his breathing, and raised his arms. The time had come.

All at once the coats abandoned their coat racks and flew toward the crack, their sleeves and coattails flapping frantically in the storm. They entered the crack and disappeared, devoured by the darkness on the other side. Every last one of the shadows flying over the mountains followed suit. A veritable flood of darkness poured through the crack, screaming incessantly. The screams soon became words:

"Samhein! Samhein! No rest! No respite! Samhein! Find them! Until death takes us and we're condemned to oblivion! Find them!"

The gray man lowered his arms and staggered from side to side, sapped of his strength. He leaned against the edge of the battlement and turned his gaze to the sky. The tear in the sky still gleamed in the night, but not a trace of the winged shadows or coats remained.

Further beyond the castle and the mountains, the city in ruins awaited. Its winding streets made their way among dilapidated buildings, towers at the verge of collapse, abandoned squares and mountains of rubble. The storm, which until then had hovered in the mountains, spread its cloak and covered the entire city. Total darkness ensued. Several voices began to whisper in the blackness; they sounded muffled, as if they came from the depths of the earth.

"Fly, fly, little birds, fly to the world of men . . ." chanted one of them. It was a haggard, musty voice, a voice from which poured forth maggots and decay. "Bring us joy. Bring us hope. Bring light to the darkness."

"Or bring us howls," said another. "Massacre and destruction. Death and horror. Bring us the smell of fear and the hissing of spilled blood."

"Yes, please . . ."

"Bring us something that's worth being dead for."

SAMHEIN

It was Halloween, the last night of October, and a vast harvest moon floated high in the evening sky. Midnight had arrived, and silence was gaining a foothold on what had been a night of endless uproar. Most children were already back at home, but there were still a few stragglers walking through the snowy streets, disguised as magicians, vampires, and trolls. The spiders and skeletons that adorned the houses' façades swayed in the breeze, which carried with it a flurry of snow. From the windows jack-o'-lanterns kept vigil with twisted smiles and ghoulish, wide-open eyes.

Two siblings walked through the town's main street: Hector, with dark, disheveled hair, and Sarah, a petite girl dressed as a witch who clutched a bag full of candy tight against her chest. The young boy walked a few steps behind with his sister's broom in hand and a furrowed brow. He'd been down in the dumps all day and his mood hadn't improved as the hours wore on. He'd spent the past week waiting for Halloween night, but not to go trick-or-treating from house to house like a baby; he wanted to watch the horror movie marathon showing on TV. His parents were the ones who'd thwarted his plans: Sarah decided she wanted to go trick-or-treating, and according to them, her brother was responsible for going with her, whether he was fifteen years old or not. Things took a turn for the worse when, in order to keep her happy and to comply with tradition, he had to put on a costume. It didn't do any good to protest. His mother dragged him up to the attic and rummaged through a chest until she came up with last year's disguise.

"No, it won't work," she said as she held a Batman costume up in front of him, one that had already fit him poorly the year before. "You can't wear this. It'll be too tight. You've grown so much in the last few months."

Hector sighed with resignation. He had gained weight recently and the fact that he couldn't wear the costume was proof of it—proof that, of course, did nothing to improve his state of mind.

"Mom, I haven't been growing," he said, to dispense with euphemisms. "I'm getting fat."

In the end his mom improvised a vampire cape out of an old black sheet. Hector had managed to avoid wearing makeup, but even so he felt so ridiculous in that getup that when an old woman asked him what he was dressed up as, he answered (not very nicely) that he was a circus tent. His little sister had to resort to her best smile to convince the woman to give them some candy.

"Hector, look! A monster!" the girl yelled behind him. He turned around without stopping, thinking that his sister must have seen someone with a good disguise, not like the foolishness he was wearing. But Sarah pointed to something in the air, high above the rooftops. He looked in that direction and was shocked by what he saw: a human silhouette, somewhat deformed, flying to and fro through the air. His surprise lasted a mere instant, the time it took to distinguish what it actually was.

"No, silly," he said. "It's a jacket. It must have been hanging on a clothesline and got carried away by the wind."

"It's not a monster?" asked Sarah, disappointed, without taking her gaze away from the brown object that flapped around above the rooftops.

"Well, it's a pretty ugly jacket." It was true: even at that distance it was clear that the fashion was out of date, with leather-covered sleeves and large, shiny metal buttons. "I'm sure it's the type of coat a monster would like."

For a moment, the two siblings contemplated the jacket's movements in the sky, until Hector realized that Sarah, clutching at the bag of candy, was shivering.

"Hey! You're freezing to death! Why didn't you say something?"

She looked at him with very wide eyes and shrugged her shoulders. Hector sighed.

"Climb up on my back and hold on to my neck, evil witch. We'll go faster that way."

"What about the candy?"

"I'll hold it. You just hang on to your broom."

The little girl climbed onto his back and put one arm around his neck. Hector made sure she was comfortable and started to walk, trying to ignore the sporadic cry of "Giddyup!" that came from behind and the broom gently hitting his hip. Despite himself, the boy smiled. The magic of Halloween still captivated his little sister. Hector didn't regret making sure that the girl didn't notice how angry he was. It wouldn't have made sense to ruin the party for her as well.

The snow tinted their walk through the town with silver. The shadows they projected on the ground looked like ghosts that kept following them. Hector picked up the pace, thinking that he might still have time to catch the beginning of the second film in the marathon. The church clock sounded twelve thirty, and if he remembered right, it was just about to start.

High up above, the dark coat kept dancing among the white clouds.

They lived in a tiny white two-story house with a black roof and a fenced-in yard just on the outskirts of town. On turning the corner and seeing the porch light, Hector realized that he could forget about the movie. There stood his mother in the doorway, with her hands on her hips.

"Do you realize what time it is?" she asked him. She wore her thick dark green coat and a stern look. Hector bit his lower lip. Yes, without a doubt: so long, movie.

"Sarah didn't want to miss the houses downtown because they give out more candy. That's why we're late," he explained. From his back his sister solemnly agreed.

"And of course, that's why you stayed out so late despite how cold it got . . . Sometimes I don't know where your head is, Hector. Inside, let's go." She moved to one side to let them through and closed the door behind them.

"Are they back yet?" asked his father from the living room. Hector heard a scream coming from the TV and let out a pained sigh.

"Yes, they're here—both of them frozen to death," answered his mother.

Sarah turned around on Hector's back to get down. To make matters worse, just as she set foot in the hall she let out a sneeze so forceful that it blew her witch's hat off her head.

"Well, what do you know. She caught a cold."

"I did not catch a cold!" she insisted. She sneezed again and took off running toward her mom, shaking her broom in the air. "I got so much candy and I gave lots of people a fright! And we saw a flying jacket! And . . ." Sarah continued rambling while she pulled on her mom's skirt for attention, but her mother was too busy scowling at Hector.

"I told you twelve o'clock at the latest," she began.

"If it were up to me I'd have been home by ten," groaned Hector, "but, like I told you, Sarah wanted—"

His mother wouldn't let him finish. It was clear she hadn't the slightest intention of discussing it with him; she only wanted to lecture him. Hector sighed deeply and prepared for a barrage of reprimands.

"It's not the weather to be wandering around all over the place, as cold and snowy as it is out there," she was saying. "And besides, think about the people that had to get up out of bed to answer the door. No, Hector, no. That's not the way it works. You've got to have more sense than that . . ."

His ears were ringing. Sarah sneezed again. A new scream came from the living room, even more spectacular than the first. His mother continued her tirade, her voice getting louder and louder, with one hand on her hip and the other gesturing with disapproval. He took a step backward, and his right foot got caught in the folds of his cape. After flapping his arms in a desperate attempt to regain his balance, he fell to the ground. The candy went everywhere. Hector got up with a snort.

"You see? I can't even stand up right!" he yelled. "I'm sick of this! I'm going to bed!"

He ran up the stairs, deaf to his mother's yells, with his cape gathered in his arm so he wouldn't trip on it again. He went into his room and slammed the door. He let the cape fall to the ground, took off his shoes, and collapsed on the bed, huffing and puffing. He didn't really know who he was actually mad at, his mom or himself, which made him even madder.

Above the town's rooftops, the jacket continued its twirls and pirouettes; more than once it almost crashed into a house or got tangled in the branches of a tree, but at the last minute it would avoid obstacles with amazing agility, as if jumping through the air. It wasn't the wind that moved it: it was its own will. The jacket was alive. And it kept watch over the town.

It soared over the top of a tree, moving its empty arms. As soon as it got close, two twisted claws made of wire and black string appeared beneath its shirttails. The jacket used them to grab on to the tallest branch, and there it sat, bolt upright, contemplating its surroundings.

It let out a mournful howl and the sky filled with wings. Dark, threadbare wings that clove the air without making the slightest sound. A swarm of creatures appeared out of nowhere, cutting through the clouds and making themselves lords and masters of the town. They posed on rooftops, on the arcs of streetlamps, on treetops. They were enormous crows with wings made from rags. In their eye sockets danced marbles and buttons, burning bright. Their feet were made of wire, their beaks were soles of shoes, and the feathers covering them were cut from black paper.

On such a special night, even the birds appeared to be disguised as monsters.

"House by house, don't miss any!" croaked one from the top of the village church, perched on the weathervane that adorned the steeple. "Find them, find them. House by house, door by door! Samhein! Samhein! Samhein!"

They repeated their cry as they flew from building to building. As they neared the houses, they flapped their fake wings and hovered in front of doors and windows. Their poorly cut leather beaks twitched as if they could smell what was inside. They didn't spend much time hovering: as soon as they determined that what they were looking for wasn't there, they flew to another building, leaving behind a trail of paper feathers.

"Find them, find them!" sang another, as it glided through the air at such a speed that it lost one of the buttons it used in place of an eye. It didn't stop to look for it. There wasn't time. The hour of the harvest had come and there wasn't a moment to waste. "Samhein! Samhein! Samhein!"

It wasn't the first place they'd appeared in. On that long night the birds made of rags visited thousands of cities and towns. They searched and searched without rest or pause, since they had been made for that sole purpose, and for that night alone. Once the sun rose, the life they'd been granted would vanish with the dawn. They knew it, they accepted it.

The only thing that mattered to them was to fulfill their mission. The false wings beat the air in silence. It was magic, the magic of the last night of October. The magic of the harvest.

For the moment, they hadn't had any luck. Not in this town nor in the other cities where they'd searched. But they didn't lose hope, simply because hopelessness wasn't included in the small catalog of emotions that their creator had instilled in them. The only thing they knew was the longing of the search, the need to find the energy that they'd been taught to detect and that, up until now, remained elusive.

One of the strange birds flew over the tree where the jacket had rested moments before. It sniffed the air with total concentration and, unlike the others of its kind, worked in absolute silence. It had found such a promising clue that it had completely forgotten the chant. Its crystal eyes shone with a pearly brilliance. Yes, without a doubt: it was a mystic trail, it could see it ahead like an emerald ribbon among the sparse snowflakes that drifted from the sky. The creature flew faster. Little by little others detected the same scent and delved into the search, as silent as the first.

Soon they all followed suit, heading in the direction of that same two-story house with the white walls and the black roof. They landed on it where they could, clutching one another. Their wire claws clung to the shingles, to the gutters, to the stairways, to the windowsills . . . The house was swallowed up by the winged creatures. For a while the only sound in the night was their collective sniffing, faster and stronger by the minute. Until finally all the creatures burst into flight and screamed one word in unison:

"Samhein!"

Hector awoke suddenly. He opened his eyes in the darkness with a knot in his throat. Never in his life had he woken up with such a start. He was taken aback. He noticed his mouth was dry and his head was heavy and stuffy, as if he had a fever. He sat up in bed. He was still dressed in his blue jeans, shirt, and black sweatshirt. A dense odor permeated the air; it was a spicy smell that reminded him of the day when Sarah emptied a whole jar of oregano into a pot of soup because she wanted to see what "pizza juice" tasted like. He felt around for the bedside lamp, and it took him a while to realize that he was looking on the wrong side of the bed.

In that time, his eyes adjusted enough to the darkness that he made a surprising discovery.

There was someone sitting on his desk.

He could see him in the milky light of the streetlamps. He was a small man, barely five feet tall, dressed in a white robe with black stains on it. He sat on the table and contentedly smoked a pipe, from which arose a dense green smoke. His face, narrow and angular, was turned toward the window, contemplating the evening and the snow that now fell in droves. He smiled.

Hector's first thought was that this strange character seemed very friendly. He didn't wonder how he got there, nor did it cross his mind to yell and alert his parents. He still felt a heavy sensation in his head, but at the same time he noticed that he was able to think with incredible speed and clarity. The more he breathed in the smoke that unfurled from the pipe, the braver and more confident he felt.

"Who are you?" he asked as he turned on the light, with the same authoritarian tone that his mother used to get his attention. "How did you get in my room?"

The intruder at the desk gave a little snort and almost fell to the floor. Hector smiled. He had caught him by surprise.

"You frightened me, boy. I thought you were asleep," he said, looking at him tenderly. His eyes were tiny and black, his voice soft and melodious, like a barely whispered lullaby. Now that he could see him better, Hector discovered that the little man was an ashen gray color. His face was lined with hundreds—no, thousands of wrinkles, which combined to make his smile even bigger. This person definitely struck him as a friendly sort. "It is my utmost pleasure to make your acquaintance. My name is Denestor Tul, and I've been looking for you for some time." He jumped off the desk and approached the bed. Hector could see that what he'd thought were stains on his robe were actually words written in tiny letters.

"Looking for me?" He attempted to brush a strand of hair away from his forehead but somehow failed to do so. The entire room had turned green. "Looking for *me*?"

"Of course," replied the one known as Denestor. "You're different from everyone else. I know, I know . . ." He smiled kindly. "I'm not saying anything new. You've always known." The little man held his pipe in the left side of his mouth while he blew emerald smoke out of the right side. "You're different, yes. What you don't know is how different."

"Well, I . . ." Hector felt embarrassed. Of course he was different. He was . . . he was . . . He shook his head, disoriented. For a moment he was afraid, terribly afraid, but then the gray man breathed green smoke in his face and everything made sense again. It was obvious. "I am different . . ." he agreed vehemently.

"Different," emphasized Denestor. "Special, miraculous. Dare I say, unique." He pronounced each word with extraordinary affectation. "But *they* don't understand, isn't that right? Not your parents, not your sister, not even those who say they're your friends. Nobody sees what you're hiding on the inside."

"They don't understand me . . ." Hector assured him in a thin voice. It was so unfair that in his whole life no one had taken the time to try to understand him. Would it have cost them so much? Was it so difficult?

"I understand you," said Denestor Tul, and at once Hector felt a tremendous relief. The little man sat on the edge of the bed. He smelled like sandalwood. "I know your emptiness; I know your anguish. Throughout the years I've come across many like you. This world will never understand you, will never, ever understand you. And do you know why?" He blew out another mouthful of green smoke before answering his own question. "Because this is not your world. This is not where you belong. I have come to offer you the possibility of escape, of coming with me to the only place in all of existence where you can be who you really are. I've come to invite you to Rocavarancolia."

"Rocavarancolia," Hector whispered. It was a beautiful name, musical, a word that dissolved on the tongue like a sweet dessert. It was a name that could only belong to a beautiful place. A place where he could be who he really was. Anxiety and suspicion awoke once again in his chest. He was living a cliché; he and the little man were acting out a scene that he'd read and watched in the beginnings of dozens of books and movies, one that could be summarized as *You're special, and you must come with me.* Hector shook his head. Something about this wasn't right, something about Denestor, about his own thoughts. "I've never heard that name. No . . ." He felt lost, dazed. "No, no . . . What do you mean, this isn't where I belong?" he asked. "This is my home."

"I want you to listen to me carefully, Hector," Denestor said through the green smoke. The words on his robe were moving. They moved at different speeds on the garment, some in one direction and others in the opposite. "The first thing you must know is that no one is going to make you do anything you don't want to do. Whether you come with me or not is entirely your decision, only yours. But before you decide, let me tell you something."

Hector nodded, calmer than before. It wouldn't hurt to listen to him. Besides, he was beginning to suspect that it was all just a dream. Things like this didn't happen in reality. Ash-gray people that visited with crazy propositions in the wee hours of the morning didn't exist in real life.

"Like many other stories that seem impossible, this story is real," said Denestor Tul. "I'm from a faraway land, a land that, just like you, is not of this world. I come from Rocavarancolia, the kingdom of miracles and marvels." His eyes shone and his words were filled with such passion that it was difficult not to get drawn in by his excitement. "It was a marvelous place, full of magic—a place inhabited by beings so powerful and wise that many abandoned their own worlds to learn from them. In Rocavarancolia they taught arts and sciences that mankind had long forgotten."

"Did they teach magic?" asked Hector.

"Of course. But not just magic. They taught ways of facing life that would surely have surprised you. They also taught not to fear that which lives in the darkness. And possibly the most important lesson: they taught that there are more paths than those which mere mortals see and that those, my friend, are the ones worth taking."

"That sounds great," murmured Hector. He reached out his hand to trap a cloud of green smoke that slid through his fingers.

"Without a doubt. Rocavarancolia was glorious, magnificent . . ." Denestor's smile disappeared. He lowered his head in sorrow. "Until a terrible tragedy destroyed it."

"What happened?" Hector asked hurriedly.

Denestor Tul sighed.

"The king of Rocavarancolia lost his mind. He wanted more power than he could handle and his ambition destroyed the kingdom. Little is left of its former glory, little is left of the land of miracles and marvels." He shook his head in sadness. "But we do not surrender," he said, "and we will not as long as hope remains alive. That's why I'm here, Hector: because this night is the night of Samhein, the one time of year when the doors that the mad king helped destroy are opened and we can access this world in search of people like you. People to help us recover our past glory. We need you, Hector. Rocavarancolia needs you. Will you come with me?"

The young boy, on an impulse, was about to accept. He was more convinced than ever that it was all a dream. At the last second something held him back.

"But why me? What makes me special?" he wanted to know.

"What makes you special?" Denestor Tul opened his eyes very wide, as if he weren't expecting that question—as if, in fact, he never expected any question. "What makes you special? Many things! Let me explain." He sat down on the bed and puffed furiously on his pipe. He exhaled the smoke in a quick burst, then continued speaking. "Everyone is born with a certain amount of energy inside. You can call it magic if you like, although that's not the exact term. Most people spend their whole lives ignoring the power they possess, and that potential is wasted. And even if they were conscious of its existence, they wouldn't know how to use it. In Rocavarancolia they taught how to make use of that energy, how to channel it to achieve all kinds of feats. And all they asked in exchange was that a part of it, a very small part, be used for the good of the kingdom. We need this magic, Hector, we need it desperately."

"Magic," he whispered. His head was spinning. "I have magic inside me."

"So, will you come with me?" asked Denestor with a concerned tone that made it sound as if his life depended on the response.

Hector hesitated. He was almost persuaded to accept the gray man's offer, but there was something inside him that told him that, despite what he might think, he wasn't dreaming.

"No, no . . . I'm sorry, but I can't go . . . It's not . . ."

He broke out in a cough so severe that he lost track of what he'd been saying. Denestor had blown so much smoke in his face that for a few seconds the only thing he saw was an immense green spot. The smell of spices was so strong his eyes watered.

"If that's your final answer, there's nothing left to say," said Denestor, getting up from the bed. "It's been a real pleasure chatting with you, Hector. Forgive me for bothering you." He began a slow walk to the window. He was stooped over, like a man who'd lost everything. "I'll go now. It's going to be a long night ahead, and there's a lot of ground to cover." He sighed bitterly. "I hope to have better luck than I did here. Goodbye, Hector, we will not see each other again." He took a small bow and turned to open the window.

"I . . . it's . . ." Hector shook his head. Why was he so worried about it? It was a dream, nothing more than a dream. "It's not that I don't want to go, I'd love to, it's just that my parents," he whispered, "they would never let me leave like that."

Denestor Tul rubbed his eyes with the palm of his hand. Then a magnificent smile stretched across his face.

"I can promise you that if you come with me, they won't find out that you've gone. Nobody, absolutely nobody, will find out that you've left."

"If I accept, if I go to this place, how long will I be gone?" He was searching desperately for reasons not to go, or, maybe, for more reasons to surrender to the dream and accept Denestor's proposal. He wanted to be very sure of what he was doing.

The gray man smiled again. It was a conciliatory smile, as if he noticed Hector's interior struggle and was sympathetic.

"If it were up to me, you could leave Rocavarancolia whenever you like," he said, "but, as I've told you, the door to your world only opens once a year: during the night of Samhein, what you call Halloween. I can assure you that if in a year you want to leave, you can do so freely. No one in Rocavarancolia will stop you. As you can see, you'll have everything you need. We want you to feel very comfortable with us. What do you say?"

And in that moment, bewildered, fully convinced he was dreaming, yet at the same time with the absolute certainty that it was real, he spoke the words that would seal his fate:

"I'll go with you."

"You have no idea how happy it makes me to hear that!" Denestor almost raced to the bed. "How wonderful! You've made me so happy!" he continued, nodding his head ceaselessly. "Now we just have a couple of details to iron out and we'll be off!" Denestor grabbed a corner of his robe, and all of the words that hovered there moved toward it in a flock. When the last word arrived, he gave a tug and the robe ripped.

Denestor shook the torn remnant and then rolled and unrolled it several times before unfurling it before Hector. Not a single word remained on the robe; they were all on the piece of cloth, lined up neatly and very still.

"We have to put it in writing," he said. "It's nothing, just a trivial formality. Read it carefully"—he handed him the scroll and a large quill pen that appeared like magic from his sleeve—"and if you agree, sign it."

Hector had to blink more than once to center his vision. It took almost ten minutes for him to read the text:

I, Hector S. W., fifteen (15) years old, born on Earth, in the country known as the United States of America, hereby attest:

I have agreed of my own free will to accompany Denestor Tul, demiurge and guardian of Highlowtower, city of Rocavarancolia, capital of the kingdom of the same name. At no point was I coerced, or obligated in any way. All my questions have been answered and my doubts put to rest.

In Rocavarancolia I will be taught to make use of my potential and develop all of my power, and as compensation I promise to help reconstruct the kingdom, to the best of my abilities.

Every year, on the night of Samhein, I will be offered the possibility of returning home or, as I desire, remaining in Rocavarancolia.

Signature:

"The words won't change suddenly, will they?" he wanted to know. He recalled how cheerfully they moved before on the robe. "They won't rearrange themselves so that I'm signing something completely different?"

"No, they won't change." Denestor didn't seem surprised by his question. "I give you my most solemn promise that there is no deceit in my words or in this scroll. By oath and by law we cannot lie to our candidates," he added in a tone so serious that Hector knew, without a doubt, that he was telling the truth.

The young boy touched the tip of the pen to the cloth; the moment had arrived to set the dream in motion. He'd begun to print his name when he felt something move underneath the pen. He raised an eyebrow, looked anxiously at Denestor, and a second later a sharp pain in the fingertip of his index finger made him yelp and drop the quill. It remained upright over the paper as if held in place by an invisible hand. Two drops of blood spilled from his finger onto the cloth. The pen, imitating Hector's handwriting to perfection, signed his name in ink and blood.

"It bit me," he said, looking back and forth between the gray man and the cut on his finger. "The quill bit me."

In Denestor's eyes he glimpsed a sparkle of tremendous satisfaction. He raised his hand and the scroll and quill sailed toward it. One went in his left sleeve and the other in his right.

Hector, dazed, still thinking of the quill's bite and that nothing good is signed in blood, noticed a mob of silver spiders hanging from the torn part of Denestor's robe, spinning and spinning to reconstruct the torn corner. Only they weren't spiders, but rather dozens of sewing needles that emerged from tiny thimbles.

"Look how much work you've made for me," said Denestor. His voice had changed. It was no longer calming; now it sounded like a chorus of rusty bells. "I didn't think I was going to manage it. The regent will be satisfied. Very satisfied." He raised his hands as if getting ready to clap, and just then there was a yell at the bedroom door.

"The monster's coat is in my window!" said Sarah from the hallway. Sometimes she had nightmares and Hector let her sleep with him. "It's coming for us! Hector! Hector!"

"Don't come in, Sarah!" he yelled. "Stay outside!" He turned toward Denestor Tul, furious. The pain in his finger had cleared his mind. This was real, he wasn't dreaming. "What have you done to me?" He held his breath. Now he saw clearly. "The smoke! The pipe!"

"You're full of the bite of Morpheus," explained Denestor with his new voice like a broken skull. He still held his hands up, in midclap. "When you breathe in the smoke, it dulls your senses and makes you think that you're dreaming."

"Hector!" screamed the girl behind the door. In the distance he could hear his parents, woken up by the racket. "Who are you talking to? Who's in there?"

"Don't come in!" he yelled to his sister. "You tricked me!" he yelled at Denestor.

"Not at all," he answered. "Everything that I told you is true. Absolutely everything. My pipe only made you more receptive to my proposal. Rocavarancolia can't afford the luxury of losing a specimen like you."

"A specimen?"

Sarah chose that moment to open the door. As soon as she saw the gray man enveloped in green smoke, she began to scream. From the hallway came an alarmed voice that asked what was going on. It was his mother.

"Don't worry, child." Denestor raised his voice to be heard above Sarah's screams and the hurried footsteps in the hallway. "I didn't lie to you: no one will ever know that you left." And Denestor Tul, finally, clapped his hands. "Because no one will know that you existed."

The windows opened wide and a torrent of winged creatures entered the house, like a tornado of furious bats. Their fake eyes shone like embers. They kept screaming:

"Samhein! Samhein!"

"No!" yelled Hector when he saw a large flock of the creatures rush toward Sarah. The girl disappeared from his sight, surrounded by a curtain of flying horrors. They were everywhere. Sarah screamed. Hector heard his parents shouting at the door but he couldn't see them. Denestor Tul remained impassive in the middle of the room, with his robe twisting this way and that from the wind created by so many flapping wings. It rained paper feathers.

Hector got down from the bed. He wanted to make it to the door, but the chaos of the creatures coming and going made it impossible to move. One crashed into his chest and almost knocked him down. Two others flung themselves against the poster of Middle Earth hanging from the wall and began to devour it, bite by bite. Hector caught one by the wing and ripped it apart with his hands. All that remained in his fist was a felt sandal, with a broken button that appeared to look at him with fury. He dropped the shoe and tried to make his way through, shielding his face from the attack of the creatures summoned by Denestor.

"Samhein! Samhein!"

Dozens of the frightening birds surrounded his desk, completely covering it in ragged wings. When they flew away a moment later, not a trace was left of the furniture, not even marks on the floor. Hector's mouth dropped open. The creatures were eating his bedroom.

"Sarah! Mom!" he yelled as he tried to reach the door. Claws made from wire, rope, and wood tangled in his hair and pulled him backward.

"Oblivion," whispered Denestor Tul, with his eyes open wide and his arms outstretched. "Bring oblivion to the world. May every last memory of this child disappear from the face of the earth. Let nothing remain."

This was the new mission of the creatures belonging to Denestor Tul, demiurge of Rocavarancolia and guardian of Highlowtower: to erase every last trace of Hector. They erased him from the photo albums that his mother kept in the living room; from the mind of his sister, who screamed and screamed, beating at the air in a vain attempt to escape the horrors that lodged in her hair; from the memories of his parents, who looked around, terrified, with no understanding of what was going on. Wherever the slightest trace of Hector's existence remained, the rag birds went, ready to erase. And they didn't stop at his house.

They deleted him from his school records, from the memories of his teachers and classmates. Every last of his friends and acquaintances received a visit from the horrifying creatures, wherever they were. Distance meant nothing to the servants of Denestor Tul. They could cross continents with one flap of their wings. Nowhere was out of their reach. They peeked into minds and swept away memories with even the tiniest relation to Hector. He'd once been part of a live studio audience with his classmates; they erased every recording. They removed him from the background of another family's photo at an amusement park, where he appeared by chance. Within minutes, Hector ceased to exist in the world.

"Mom!" he yelled when he finally reached the door. The rag birds seemed to have calmed, and most of them remained perched on the ground or hung upside down from the ceiling, happily ruffling their paper wings. Only a few still pestered his family, erasing the last remaining memories of Hector. The boy shook his arms and shouted to try to scare them, but his parents no longer noticed him, neither him or the creatures that flew around them. They were dazed and looked around as if they'd just woken up from a dream. Sarah clung fiercely to her mother's leg, but suddenly she jumped up, rubbing her eyes. She yawned.

"Mom?" she asked, unsure. "What am I doing here?"

"You gave us quite a scare," the woman answered. She adjusted the girl's shirt collar and gave her an anxious look. "We're going to have to tie you to the bed so that you don't get up at night. Such awful screams! Did you have a nightmare, sweetie?"

Sarah nodded uncertainly.

"Mom! Can't you see me?" Hector yelled. "I'm right here! Sarah! Sarah!"

"It was a horrible dream," the girl explained to her mother, completely ignoring her brother's screams. "An evil jacket wanted to get in the house and was scratching at my window . . ."

Hector felt the strength rush out of him, and he fell to his knees. He didn't even have the luxury of hoping he'd wake from this nightmare at some point. What was happening seemed impossible, seemed like a dream, but it was real. Terribly real.

His father shook his head and looked in Hector's direction, without seeing him. He could almost feel his glance go right through him.

"Dad?" he called, faintly.

"They can't see you," explained Denestor, behind him.

"Forget, forget, forget," chanted the rag doll horrors, in a low voice, rocking from right to left.

"My creatures are altering their perception. As soon as they see you, they forget that they've seen you. They see no one in the room. If you try to touch them, they won't know that you're touching them. If you call to them, they won't hear you."

"We have to do something with this space," said his father, looking into the room overflowing with black birds that he couldn't see. "It's a shame to leave it empty."

"Why?" Hector asked, his voice broken. "Why me? What have I done?"

"Nothing, child," answered Denestor Tul. This isn't because of anything you've done; this is because of what you may become."

"A toy room!" pleaded Sarah. "I want a room full of . . ." She quieted, all of a sudden, with the feeling that something was missing. She squinted. For a moment she thought she saw someone on their knees in the doorway. A figure enmeshed in green smoke.

"Mom, Dad, please . . . I'm right here." Hector, in desperation, began to cry. "I'm here . . ."

"Sarah, get back to bed. It's very late."

Hector watched them walk away. Several rag birds still flapped around their heads, pecking here and there.

"It's time to go." Denestor rested the palm of his hand on Hector's shoulder. The teenager abruptly jerked away.

"Undo what you've done!" he screamed. He found the strength to jump up. Denestor retreated, surprised by the sudden movement. "Undo it!"

"It's too late for that. There's no turning back."

"I told you to—"

The ragged birds fell upon him and stopped his words with a wild clamor. Hector screamed in turn and began to hurl blows left and right, trying to defend himself from the whirlwind of feathers that surrounded and suffocated him. Through the cracks he could see his empty room, and, as if one image were superimposed upon another, he saw another place, a somber place that became clearer and more detailed as his room faded away. They were going, Hector realized. They were snatching him from the world. He suddenly felt the air go out of him. He couldn't breathe. He raised one hand to his throat and fell to the ground amid the beating of thousands of wings. The last thing he saw was his bare room, vanishing in the darkness.

Only Denestor Tul remained in the room. He looked around slowly, as if he wished to retain every detail of his surroundings and preserve a perfect image of the place in his memory. Then he shook his head.

Then, he vanished.

THE ROYAL COUNCIL

Hector felt weighed down in an extreme lethargy. He wasn't asleep, but he wasn't awake, either. His head throbbed immensely, and his arms and legs felt dense and heavy, as if they were covered in lead. Although his eyes were half-open, he could only percieve shadows.

He heard voices getting closer. They spoke in a language that was entirely unknown to him.

Suddenly, two hazy faces emerged through the darkness: one of them was big enough to be human, the other somewhat like Denestor Tul's face, although he couldn't be completely certain. The faces were engaged in a heated conversation and Hector, despite not being able to understand a single word, sensed that they were talking about him. After a few moments, the one that resembled Denestor left, shortly followed by the other. There was something strange in the way that he moved—an odd, lurching motion.

Little by little, the shadows in Hector's mind began to clear. Wherever he was, it was a cold and dismal place, and he was lying on an uncomfortable cot. He could barely move. It was pouring rain outside and from time to time he heard the rumble of thunder.

He suddenly became aware of something crawling up his forearm. For a second he thought it was an enormous mosquito, but then he realized that it was a wooden syringe, over two inches long, with a short glass needle at one end.

It moved up his bare arm like a worm inching up the stem of a plant. He tried to move to scare it away, but his body didn't respond. The syringe raised slightly as it reached his elbow joint, pitched forward, and plunged its needle into a vein. Hector didn't feel any pain, only a cold, unpleasant sensation spreading out from the puncture site. The syringe remained poised above his flesh for a long minute. Then, it sprouted two transparent wings and took off, swaying from side to side, as if moving were a difficult chore.

It's full of my blood, he thought, in a daze. He tried following it with his gaze, but eventually that became impossible without getting up, and his body was still stubbornly determined not to obey.

It was all so absurd that it couldn't really be happening. A little gray man had tricked him into abandoning his world. And, if Hector believed him, his creatures, those horrible crows, had erased every trace of his existence on Earth. It was insane. Completely insane. He had to do something: get out of there, find help.

He tried to get up and rolled over, falling from the cot. He hit the floor pretty hard but barely felt it. His senses, his nerves, everything in his body seemed completely anesthetized. Could it be an effect from the smoke of Denestor Tul's pipe? Maybe. Or maybe they gave him some kind of narcotic to keep him sedated. With a good deal of effort, he managed to get up. He felt weak and dizzy. He looked around, with one hand on the simple wooden bed for support. The room was small and damp, without any furniture or decorations, and was lit by a pair of dying torches. The floor was made of rough-hewn stones and the walls were constructed from boulders. Hector thought that the place looked like a dungeon. He took a slow breath. There was a wooden door reinforced with iron plates in the wall to his left. It was open partway, although not enough for him to see what was on the other side.

He took a tentative step toward it, leaning against the wall. His vision was blurry, and he had a vile taste in his mouth. They had definitely given him something to keep him unconscious, but whatever it was, its effect was wearing off. He peered through the gap in the door. It led to a shadowy hallway with a long and narrow arched ceiling. He saw in front of him a door identical to the one he was standing behind, and another a few yards ahead.

He didn't see anyone, and heard nothing, apart from the sounds of the storm. He took a chance, opened the door a little, and went out.

"This can't be happening," he whispered.

The floor was covered with puddles. He moved slowly, glued to the wall and alert to the slightest noise. He was barefoot and rocks jabbed into the soles of his feet with every step, but this didn't deter him. He had to escape. The darkness swirled in the hallway like something malevolent and alive. The place couldn't be any gloomier.

When he reached a bend in the hallway, he heard footsteps coming in his direction. Hector froze, terrified. Then he remembered that he'd just passed a door that was slightly ajar. He quickly backed up, opened it, and slipped inside. A current of cold air enveloped him at once. He scarcely had time for a quick look around, but luckily the room appeared empty.

He slowly closed the large door, trying not to make a sound. He heard the footsteps getting closer and closer, and they sounded so erratic and exaggerated that it was hard to tell if they belonged to two people or only one. He held his breath, his forehead pressed against the door and his eyes closed. A few seconds later he heard the footsteps on the other side and a mumbling voice that seemed to be talking to itself. Soon both sounds dissolved in the distance. Hector breathed a sigh of relief, opened his eyes, and, after making an effort to calm down, looked around him. The room that he'd entered was identical to the one where he'd woken up, except for one important detail: a good part of the wall opposite the door had collapsed, revealing the outside. The night and the storm stretched out before him; he saw the shadows of several buildings, crouching like immense beasts.

Hector moved slowly toward the opening. The rain instantly soaked him to the skin, but he did his best to ignore it. He leaned out cautiously. The façade led to a poorly paved alley. Although the ground was no more than ten feet down, a sudden surge of panic forced him backward. He'd suffered from vertigo for as long as he could remember. He'd never found a way to overcome it. It was simply beyond his ability. He bit his lower lip and forced himself to examine the wall that led down to the street.

The gaps between the bricks were more than adequate to allow a reasonably physically fit person to climb down easily. He frowned. Even if he could overcome his vertigo, which he doubted in no world, including this one, could, he be considered "reasonably fit." He was so out of shape that he'd never make it, especially with the storm. He was convinced that if he so much as placed one foot on the wall, he'd slip and crack his head open on the ground below.

He had no choice but to find another exit. He turned toward the door, gathering courage to go back out into the hallway. It was then he discovered that he wasn't alone in the room. There was someone in the cot next to the wall across from the opening. It was a dark-haired girl with a pale complexion, wearing a full black dress. She lay on her side, and her hair spilled over the bed like a pool of dark blood. He could barely make out her features in the semidarkness, much less tell if she were asleep or dead.

He took a tentative step toward her just as a flash of lightning strobed the room. Hector's heart leapt in his chest. She was beautiful. He'd only seen her for an instant, but her small, round face with its delicate features had been etched in his mind.

Had Denestor Tul tricked her as well? Was she also a prisoner here? It was absurd. Who in their right mind would shut someone in a cell with a crumbling wall? He then remembered that the door to his own dungeon wasn't locked either. Were they so confident that what they gave him would keep him asleep? Or was there something else? He didn't know what to do. A drop of water fell on the girl's forehead, and Hector saw her lips gently quiver.

He looked at the door, undecided. What should he do? Escape and leave her here? Wake her up? All at once, suddenly and absurdly, the tale of Sleeping Beauty came to mind, and he imagined himself waking her up with a kiss on the lips. He felt stupid for such a thought, but he couldn't help it. The girl looked exactly the part: like a character right out of a fairy tale, a princess dressed in black who had succumbed to an evil spell.

Lightning illuminated the dungeon once more, the flash highlighting the girl's face was filled with light. Without knowing very well what he was doing, Hector stretched out a hand to her cheek. He had to touch her, he had to find out if she was real.

"Who are you?" he whispered.

Just then, the door to the dungeon was flung open. Hector shouted and turned so quickly that he almost fell to the ground.

For a moment he didn't see anything in the doorway. Then something entered the room slowly, but from above, walking on the ceiling. It struggled to cross the threshold with difficulty. First one leg came through, then another, and a third, and a fourth. And an arm. And another. And two more.

Hector took a step back. From within that chaos of extremities, a head covered in long greenish hair watched him as it hung upside down from the ceiling. He couldn't believe what he was seeing. It was a giant spider with human features sporting a patchy gray frock coat. It wore a different monocle in each of its eight eyes.

"A gentleman never enters a lady's chamber uninvited," whispered the thing swaying from the ceiling. It blew into the palm of one of its furry hands, and at once a cloud of iridescent dust engulfed Hector.

Not again, he managed to think before he fainted.

The storm had broken out more than ten hours before, just as Denestor Tul's creatures left Highlowtower on the way to the vortex that led to the human world. Their search there didn't end until the sun rose in Rocavarancolia and the doorway to Earth began to close. Only then did the flocks of rag birds begin their return, squawking contentedly after having fulfilled their mission. Shortly after the last one went through the vortex, the breach disappeared as if it never existed, and the only brightness left in the heavens was the flash of lightning.

The great wooden gate to Highlowtower opened with a sinister rumble of pulleys and chains. Denestor Tul appeared, staggering across the threshold, supporting himself momentarily against the doorway. He could go no further; he was exhausted. The night of Samhein required so much effort and concentration that it took an eternity to recover. The previous year, as a matter of fact, he passed out just after dawn and spent three days submerged in a deep sleep. And that was a night they hardly required his presence on Earth. Not like this time.

"In thirty years there has never been a harvest night like this," murmured Denestor. He took a breath and went out into the storm. From the shadows of the tower emerged a black umbrella, its ribs twisted and rusty, that hovered over the little gray man, shielding him as best it could from the rain.

Denestor descended the stairs and walked toward the narrow wooden bridge that connected the tower with the rest of the fortress. The storm howled around him and was so violent that, despite the umbrella's efforts, he was soaked within seconds. He slowly crossed the footbridge, clutching the rope that served as a handrail and avoiding looking down. It was a drop of over two hundred yards. At the other end of the bridge was the castle, so enveloped in darkness that it was hard to distinguish it from the mountains upon which it was built.

The metal gate of the fortress was flanked by two imposing guards. They were nearly seven feet tall, but their ostentatious, tarnished gold armor made them look even bigger. Their helmets were shaped like dragons' heads, jaws half-open. They were armed with red-tipped halberds, the traditional weaponry of the castle guard.

As soon as they saw him, they moved to one side. The iron gate creaked as it opened slowly, very slowly, leaving a groove in the muddy earth. A howl echoed from beyond the entrance. An enormous shadow passed quickly through the gate and was lost in the darkness of the courtyard and gardens. Another howl cut through the storm. More shadows lurked among the trees and shrubs, weaving back and forth. The pack was restless.

They can smell it, thought the demiurge. They smell the children's power.

Denestor followed the cracked stone walkway that crossed the garden. One member of the pack walked alongside the edge of the path, growling with menace. Another climbed onto a dead tree stump and crouched there, watching him. A bolt of lightning flooded the skies right as he set foot on the steps that led to the main gate. The double doors swung wide open.

Denestor ran smack into one of the pale servants of the castle, who stood motionless in the middle of the hallway. He was dressed in stark black and was so thin that it looked like his clothes had nothing inside of them. Two large, expressionless eyes jutted out from the servant's frail, haggard face.

"They're waiting for you in the throne room, Master Denestor," he announced.

The demiurge nodded and entered the fortress. The umbrella remained in the hallway. It closed with a snap and fell to the ground in a corner before the servant's listless gaze. Denestor Tul was capable of bestowing life to any inanimate object; that was the magic power that had made him demiurge of Rocavarancolia so many years ago. He limped through the corridors of the castle, panting with every step. Harvest night had depleted him more than he liked to admit. If he was still conscious at all, it was only because of the energizing potions that Lady Spider gave him.

Without a doubt, Denestor thought bitterly, I'm as withered and gray as all of Rocavarancolia.

His footsteps gave rise to dusty echoes throughout the fortress. The rusty and twisted suits of armor of the great warriors of yesteryear studied him from their pedestals. A gauntlet had fallen from the armor of Vladimir the Soulbreaker, and it appeared that a small creature was using it for a den. Hardly anything remained of the castle's grandeur. Not a window was left unbroken; all the tapestries were moth-eaten. Ruin and filth ran rampant.

He climbed the carpeted staircase that led to the throne room. Another servant stood guard, identical to the one who stood in the entrance. He opened the door as soon as he saw Denestor gasping on the stairs.

The little gray man caught his breath and entered the hall. It was spacious, with a tall ceiling. At one time the walls were adorned with colored tapestries, mosaics, and banners, but now it was only bare stone, cracked and black from the dampness. On the western wall, a score of narrow windows faced a dark and dreary precipice. The black drapes that covered the windows shook like furious ghosts facing an onslaught of wind. A glacial cold permeated the room, but the low temperature hardly mattered to those gathered around the meeting table. They were all well protected from the inclement weather, some thanks to magic and others due to their peculiar nature.

Monsters, thought Denestor as he moved toward them, feeling all eyes on him. *That is what we are. Monsters and demons. Freaks and phantoms.*

Almost the entire Royal Council of Rocavarancolia was present. It was the most well-attended meeting that the demiurge could remember in years. Either they sensed that it had been a special night or they finally understood how little chance remained of saving the kingdom.

He saw the Lexel twins, seated facing each other; the twin on the left was dressed completely in black save for a featureless white mask, while the twin on the right was dressed in immaculate white with a featureless black mask. Both masks covered their faces, leaving only their mouths exposed. There was also Lady Serena, the only attendant who remained standing, with her hands laced behind her back, slowly rocking back and forth. Next to Lady Serena he saw a gauntlet floating in the air, grasping a glass of wine: there was Rorcual, Rocavarancolia's alchemist, who accidentally made himself invisible more than twenty years ago and still hadn't been able to find a way to make himself visible again. All in all, there were eight of them arranged around the great table.

"Look who finally decided to show up!" exclaimed one of the Lexel twins as he mockingly applauded the demiurge's arrival. "It's been more than an hour since dawn, Denestor!"

"Thank you for the information. With the storm I hadn't noticed," he grumbled as he sank into his chair. The enormous armchair at the head of the table was empty; it was the spot reserved for the regent of Rocavarancolia, whose grave illness prevented him from attending the meeting. *Thirty years without a king and soon we'll be without a regent,* thought Denestor bitterly.

He then directed his gaze to the dais at the head of the room. There was the Sacred Throne of Rocavarancolia, so covered with cobwebs that it was impossible to make out its form. For more than three decades the throne had no master save for the spiders who wove their webs over it.

"Well? How did it go?" Lady Serena asked. Her large, beautiful green eyes watched him with interest.

"Better than anyone could have hoped," announced the demiurge. "I've collected twelve children."

His words caused a commotion. Not surprisingly, given that the best harvest in the last thirty years hadn't yielded even half a dozen kids.

"Mmmm mmmmmmmmm grmmmm," mumbled Old Belisarius, seated to the left of the place reserved for the regent, a privileged spot in honor of his age. His words were incomprehensible, as they were pronounced through a thick layer of bandages that covered his mouth. His whole body was covered in yards and yards of dirty and threadbare dressing that made him look like a tattered mummy. He was Rocavarancolia's oldest resident. If what he claimed was true, he was almost seven centuries old.

"The noble Belisarius says that the number is impressive, but it means nothing if their essence is weak." It was Lady Serena who translated the ancient man's words. "So tell us, Denestor, are they strong? Will they be of use to us?"

"Get out your marbles at once, demiurge!" blurted out the white twin, waving a glass of wine in his direction. "Let's see what you've brought us!"

Denestor reached his right hand into the left sleeve of his robe and began removing, one by one, the twelve metallic spheres that he kept in the folds of his clothing. Each one of them was engraved with a different symbol, and each had a tiny button on its surface. As he took them out, he passed them around to those present. He saved two for himself.

Lady Spider had analyzed the magic essence of the specimens that Denestor obtained in the human world. As tradition demanded, first a sample of blood and then a pinch of soul were extracted from them to test the quality and quantity of the essence that they possessed. The results of the analysis were collected in the little metallic balls.

Rorcual's gauntlet took one of them, pressed the small button, and was immediately enveloped in a glowing sphere about six inches in diameter. It was a transparent pulsation with a soft, golden hue. Lady Dream, who sat next to Denestor, activated hers, and a new sphere, somewhat bigger than the first, appeared in front of her. The golden glow bathed the old woman's face. She had her eyes closed and was snoring softly, although she gripped the ball firmly in her hand. This was her normal state: sleeping.

"Hee, hee, hee," she laughed, deep in a dream. "Essence of blackberry and shadow. The darkness walks, facing the wall, and only she can see it."

Soon all of the marbles that Denestor passed around the table were surrounded by their own golden sphere. There were three that stood out among the rest, but all had more than worthy levels. Most of the attendees were satisfied.

"It's an excellent harvest," the twin clothed in black delightedly agreed. "Congratulations, demiurge. It was a favorable night."

"I'm not finished," asserted Denestor, and he showed them the first of the two marbles that he'd saved for himself. "This belongs to a boy I found on the streets of São Paulo. A petty thief, living out of cardboard boxes. I didn't have to exert any influence at all to convince him to come to Rocavarancolia. His life had been so miserable that once I gave him the chance to change it, he accepted without a second thought." He rolled the marble between his fingers, first to the left and then to the right. "He's dangerous," he added. "Life has punished him so much that he's full of rage."

"Excellent!" exclaimed Ujthan, the great warrior seated across from him. "That's just what we need here! Character!" He pounded the table with his enormous fist. He was covered in tattoos from head to toe, and every last one of them depicted a weapon; his skin was hardly visible through the swords, bows, knives, and axes.

"I can assure you, my dear Ujthan, that what we have in our hands is more than just character," said Denestor as he pressed the button on the marble. The sphere of brilliant light that emerged almost entirely surrounded the demiurge. The young man's level of mystical essence was ten times greater than the best one they'd seen yet.

An incredible uproar arose from the table. Everyone seemed to talk at once. Enoch the Dusty, a skeletal man dressed in black and covered in dust from head to toe, stood up from his spot and caressed the sphere that represented the boy's energy. His round red eyes shone with excitement.

"Oh. Delicious . . ." he murmured as he ran his tongue over his lips, revealing two sharp fangs.

Denestor silenced them all with a gesture and turned off the sphere. He tossed the last marble in the air and caught it with a flourish.

"That's not all." His tone caused them to look at him expectantly. Only Enoch remained distracted, still impressed by what he'd just seen. "There's another specimen that is even more promising," continued the demiurge. "I have never seen anyone resist the smoke of Morpheus to such a degree. Ever. And according to what Lady Spider has just told me, the boy in question woke up less than an hour ago and began exploring the dungeons. He needed a second dose of sleeping powder in order to stop him so we can finish our examination."

"What a fascinating young man," murmured Enoch, once again taking his seat. His voice trembled with excitement. "May we see his essence, esteemed Denestor? May we?"

The demiurge nodded, placed the little metallic ball before him, and rolled it across the table after pressing the button. An immense sphere of golden light was projected into the room. It was so enormous that it reached the ceiling, crossed the floor, and almost touched the walls to the left and right. All of those present were immersed in the great circle of light.

"It's . . ." began the white twin.

". . . impossible," finished his black counterpart.

"There must be an error in the analysis," said Rorcual, the invisible alchemist. He grabbed the marble in his gloved hand and the light that surrounded them trembled slightly. It seemed as though they were submerged in a yellow sea. "There can't be anyone with that much essence. No one."

"Mmm mmmm. Mmmmmm!" pointed out Belisarius, leaning forward, so excited that the ends of his poorly tied bandages flapped in the air. "Grmmm mmmmmmmmm arggghh!"

This time it wasn't Lady Serena who translated his words. A hard and cold voice broke in from behind the curtains.

"Belisarius says that the last time he saw something like that, soon afterward a new king was seated on the throne of Rocavarancolia. What you're seeing is the essence of kings."

A dismal figure entered through the window, so drenched with rain that it glistened. Two deep red wings shook the air between the curtains, causing a sudden shower on the tile floor. It was a tall being with human form and black skin speckled with what looked like tiny diamonds embedded in its flesh. It folded its wings and walked resolutely to the table. Soon it too was inside the gigantic sphere of golden light. Its oval, hairless face, with its small ears and almond-shaped eyes, displayed an unidentifiable expression, something in between apathy and scorn. It was Esmael, the black angel, Lord of Assassins of Rocavarancolia.

Denestor frowned. He deeply disliked Esmael and had felt relieved to see that he wasn't at the meeting; he should have known that he was not far off. At least Lady Scar wasn't present. Sparks flew whenever those two creatures were in the same place, sometimes literally. Both wanted to hold the regent's position once he died, and would stop at nothing to get it.

"Are you spying on us, Esmael?" Rorcual asked. The invisible alchemist's gauntlet tensely gripped the table. It was no secret that he was not fond of the newcomer.

"Mostly on you, Rorcual. It's always a pleasure not seeing you." He smiled, showing two rows of sharp teeth. The alchemist snorted, but Esmael paid no attention. His eyes traced the curve of the sphere projected by the marble.

"Can you see it, black angel?" asked Enoch, who'd been licking his lips repeatedly, in ecstasy over the glow that surrounded them.

"I see it," he replied. "And even so I can hardly believe it. What is this boy endowed with so much essence like?" he asked, looking at Denestor Tul.

"Fragile," the demiurge had to admit. He leaned back in the chair. He was exhausted.

"So forget about it, Belisarius. There won't be a king on the Sacred Throne," Esmael pronounced. Unceremoniously, he took the marble from Rorcual's invisible hand. "The boy will die, and this fire will die with him." He turned off the sphere. The light had been so bright that, for a moment, Denestor thought he'd gone blind.

"It doesn't have to be that way," pointed out Lady Serena. "I hate that habit of yours of digging graves ahead of time, Esmael."

"How many have survived in recent years?" he asked.

Those present knew the answer all too well. In the last thirty years, not a single child had lived long enough to prove useful. In fact, the two children collected by Denestor in the last harvest had died as soon as they arrived in Rocavarancolia. Roallen the troll had hidden in the dungeon and eaten them while they slept. As punishment, Roallen was exiled from Rocavarancolia. It didn't seem to bother him much. "We're finished," he'd told them, before taking off into the Malyadar Desert. "We all are and you know it. At least I had the pleasure of enjoying one last feast before dying."

"It's not a king that we need, Esmael," said Denestor. He rubbed his forehead, trying to clear his thoughts. He could hardly stay awake. "Rocavarancolia is dying. Our only chance is that one of these children will survive, whether or not they have royal essence. If we want to save ourselves, we need at least one of them to remain alive when the Red Moon comes."

"Save ourselves? It's kind of late for that, demiurge," said the black twin. He picked up the glass in front of him and downed it in one gulp. "There's no chance of salvation for us. You say that Rocavarancolia is dying, but you're wrong: Rocavarancolia is dead. It died thirty years ago when we were defeated, when all of our power and glory was snatched from us in a single blow."

"Mmmmmmmm!" The ancient Belisarius nodded his bandage-covered head.

"And what do you propose, Lexel?" asked Denestor. "That we surrender? That we have one last feast like Roallen did?"

Now it was Enoch the Dusty who nodded energetically, his red eyes open wide. "No. I won't surrender. At least not while there's still hope . . ." He slumped back in his chair. That last phrase didn't sound very convincing;

exhaustion was taking over. The effect of Lady Spider's elixirs was already starting to wear off. He would be out cold before long.

"*Hope* is an empty word," said Esmael. "It can't feed us or return us to greatness."

"But hope is the only thing we have left, black angel," said Lady Serena. "There are twelve of them. One will survive, I'm sure of it. They can't all die. We can't be that unlucky."

"Oh, yes, they can," said Ujthan. "Rocavarancolia is cruel."

"Only one," muttered Denestor Tul. His eyes closed. "We only need one. If the others die, so be it, but one must survive. It is essential."

The demiurge of Rocavarancolia and guardian of Highlowtower looked around at the cold, damp room, the cracks in the walls, the Sacred Throne covered in spiderwebs, the dust and filth . . . Everywhere he looked he saw corruption and decay.

"Once we were great . . ." he murmured with sorrow, and let his gaze fall on all of those present. "At one time, the name of Rocavarancolia was feared and hated from one end of creation to the other. Now look at us: we dress in rags and we live among ruins. This has to end, one way or another . . . It has to . . ." His eyes closed as he finally gave in to fatigue, and he collapsed forward.

"Carry him to his tower, Ujthan," ordered Esmael. "It's been a long night and our demiurge is exhausted."

The tattooed warrior nodded, got up from the table, and took the demiurge in his arms, as if he were a small child. Denestor's head bobbed, though he did not wake, and his face came to rest on Ujthan's chain mail.

He was dreaming. In the dream, an army of monsters bellowed at the castle gates and at the foot of the mountains. He'd had this dream hundreds of times over the years. In it, rows upon rows of monsters of all species brandished their weapons, their gazes fixed on the balcony of the castle's great tower. There the king of Rocavarancolia appeared to give the final orders before the horrific army left for battle. Everyone waited expectantly. Denestor and the other demiurges, mounted on the backs of iron and stone dragons, flew over the castle turrets. The sky was infested with flying creatures: there were flesh-and-bone dragons, manticores, vampires, winged sharks, Harpies, hippogriffs, and chimeras . . .

The land boiled over with monsters. The growls of the wolf pack and the howling of werewolves could be heard everywhere. Giants pounded their clubs against the ground. Legions of the undead waited, motionless, for their marching orders. Trolls danced and exchanged blows, eager for combat. The entire kingdom was a clamor of voices, screams, and growls.

The balcony doors opened. Denestor knew what would happen next. He had dreamed it hundreds of times. Now the king of Rocavarancolia would come out onto the terrace, massive and terrible in his red armor, and the crowd would cheer. Then the monarch would give the order to advance and would take off on the back of his gigantic black falcon.

But this time it didn't happen that way. It wasn't a monster that came to the balcony, but a chubby boy, badly dressed, with curly black hair. The young man raised his arms in greeting to the armies gathered before him and they responded as a single being. The crowd's roar was so loud that it shook the mountains.

And Denestor Tul, in the arms of Ujthan the Warrior, smiled in his sleep.

ROCAVARANCOLIA

Wake up, kid, you're going to miss the speech.

Hector awoke to a voice inside his head that wasn't his. He jerked up on the rickety cot in an instant, his eyes wide and his heart in his throat. The light of day came flooding in through the demolished wall in front of him, but it was a faint, dim light, not enough to blind him despite his sudden awakening.

He looked around to see who'd spoken to him in such an extraordinary way, but there was no one, no voice inside his head other than his own thoughts. He was in a different dungeon, as dirty and decrepit as the one from the previous night. This one was not only missing a wall, but a good part of the ceiling as well.

Hector climbed out of the cot and got as close to the collapsed wall as his vertigo would allow. He saw a glimpse of a narrow alleyway, and on the other side, four identical buildings with narrow façades and large, uneven bricks. One of them had been through a devastating fire, as its blackened and battered stones attested. Two were in relatively good shape, and as for the fourth . . . Well, something had taken a big mouthful out of the fourth. There was no other way to describe it. Most of the roof and third floor had disappeared, and the marks left on the rock were identical to what you'd expect in a sandwich after someone took a bite. He gasped, unable to imagine what type of monster could have caused such damage. Those marks, more than anything, made it abundantly clear that the normal world was long gone.

He looked up. His building was the largest in the area, and also the most ravaged. The façade was riddled with holes and covered in cracks, many of them charred around the edges, as if whatever caused the havoc were red hot. It gave the impression that someone had firebombed the place with cannons.

Denestor Tul had told him that his kingdom was in ruins. That much was true, he had to admit.

Hadn't he sworn as well that he couldn't lie to Hector? The boy grimaced. Maybe he hadn't lied, but it was obvious that he hadn't told the whole truth. He hadn't told him, for example, about the rag birds that would supposedly erase all trace of his existence from Earth, nor about the pipe smoke that made him "more receptive" to his proposal.

All of a sudden, he heard footsteps in the alleyway and instinctively took a step back. A figure dressed in black walked with caution down the street. Hector strained his neck in order to see better.

It was the girl he'd encountered during his nighttime escape. He recognized her, but only glimpsed her for a moment before she turned the corner and disappeared from sight. He was tempted to call her, but finally decided it wouldn't be wise to do so. He didn't know who else might hear if he cried out. He approached the door of the dungeon, which, like the night before, wasn't locked. He opened it slowly, and after making sure no one was around, stepped through.

He wasn't sure if the hallway he entered was the same as the night before; in the daylight it all looked different. He discovered several stairways to his left and went toward them. They led to a wide foyer, and from where he was he could see an arcade that led to the street. He descended carefully, using the wall for support. The steps were in such bad shape that he was afraid of tripping and falling. The foyer was larger than it seemed from above. In another era it must have had a tile floor, but the only evidence of the tiles were the marks drawn in the dust by their outlines.

Hector neared the exit and stopped a couple of steps from the threshold, as afraid of leaving as he was of staying inside any longer. In his imagination he thought he saw eyes spying on him from every window and every alley. The memory of the monstrous spider that left him unconscious the night before was still fresh in his mind.

He finally gathered his courage, took a deep breath, and stepped into the street. It was badly paved and walking on it in socks was torturous. Every five minutes a cobblestone would hammer him in the sole of his foot; sometimes it was so painful he had to bite his lower lip to keep from yelling out. Even so he moved as fast as he could, pressed up against the building's façade.

When he reached the corner where the girl had vanished, he stopped and peered around to see what he might find on the other side. The street ran down a steep hill and ended in a red brick wall. The only way she could have gone was to the right, so it seemed logical to think that she'd taken that direction. Hector didn't immediately resume his course; now that he'd turned the corner he had a wider view of this place where Denestor Tul had brought him.

In front of the enormous building where he woke up there was nothing but mountains of rubble. Farther away he could see other structures, crammed against each other in a disconcerting fashion. There were towers and one-story houses, large pavilions, walled-in areas, shanties and mansions, all in varying degrees of disrepair. The streets that lined the area were narrow and twisted, which gave it a labyrinthine appearance. Hector got the sense that he'd gone back in time to a medieval town that had been devastated by an earthquake. And he couldn't be absolutely sure that wasn't what had happened.

He thought he saw movement beyond the ruins to his right. He squinted his eyes and scanned the horizon. Yes, there it was: amid the rubble he could make out a small square with people in it, at least two of them. It was hard to tell among the ruins, but it seemed like they were kids, no older than himself.

He started to walk toward them. He hadn't taken two steps when something bumped into him, knocking him over. The fall left him dazed and breathless. He caught a glimpse of an open door, a silhouette in the doorway, scarcely a shadow, and a second figure tottering in the distance. He tried to get up, but before he could manage it, he was hit in the forehead. It was a sharp rap that sounded like the crack of a whip and made him see stars. A second later the shadow in the doorway pounced on him and pinned him against the ground.

He heard a scream and time stood still. Hector shook his head. Someone sat astride him, a girl with short dark hair and a wild look, grasping a wooden staff. She wasn't paying attention to him; she was looking out of the corner of her eye at the boy who'd just screamed. He was leaning against the wall and rubbing his stomach, in visible pain.

Hector squirmed on the ground to get free of the girl pinning hi, down. The sudden movement threw her off balance, but she didn't fall. She jumped away from him with a start. She shot him a look like daggers, turned toward her companion, and said something Hector didn't understand. It seemed like it was in Russian or some similar language. The other kid shrugged his shoulders and responded in the same language, but with the uncertainty of one speaking a language not his own. They both looked at him at the same time.

"I can't understand a word you're saying," he gasped. "I don't have the slightest idea."

"You and me, accident," tried the boy in English. "I go out, I no see you, and we crash," he added with a smile while he nodded his head in the direction of the doorway.

"I didn't see you either," Hector assured him, still stunned. He sat up on the ground. It was just a random mishap. The girl must have thought that he was attacking them and reacted accordingly.

Hector touched his hand to his forehead and withdrew it with a moan. It hurt terribly. There was no bleeding, but he was sure he'd get a nice bump.

The girl still regarded him with suspicion. Her deep dark eyes seemed made to always look angry, and the soot that blackened her face only enhanced her dismal, sullen look. The boy, on the other hand, looked at him with a warm friendliness, despite still being half in a daze from the blow. He came closer, still rubbing his stomach, with a smile on his lips. He was tall and athletic, with chestnut hair and brown eyes.

"Did Denestor bring you here?" Hector asked, as he accepted the boy's outstretched hand.

The other nodded and lifted him up effortlessly.

"Denestor Tul. He said I be very important here." He gave a small wave as he said, "My name is Ricardo."

"I'm Hector."

"Denestor Tul," murmured the young girl next to them as she stabbed at the air with her stick, as if she wanted to make it perfectly clear what she'd do if she ran into the small, gray-colored man. Then she raised her eyes. "Hector," she said, and after a lengthy phrase in Russian, she pointed to herself and said, "Natalia Denisova-Shalikov."

"She is sorry for hit you," Ricardo translated. "Denestor bring her as well. She no like this place. She want... she want leave and go home."

"I want to leave as soon as possible myself," he insisted. "Denestor tricked me into signing the contract. He smoked that pipe incessantly while he talked and talked. I was so dazed that finally I didn't know if I was dreaming or—"

"Talk slow or I no understand," the boy interrupted. "I no speak your language very well. I am Spanish."

Hector nodded and began to speak in a slower voice, but he hadn't uttered more than a couple of words before Natalia interrupted harshly and pointed to the square among the ruins, where Hector had been headed before the collision. He saw a blond boy perched at the edge of some sort of fountain; he was wearing blue pajamas with a white pattern.

"The others," said Ricardo. "Did Denestor Tul bring them? Or did they live here already?"

"I don't think the kid in pajamas is from here," commented Hector. Those kids seemed as out of place as they were.

"Should we go over there?"

"That would be best," he answered. "Maybe they know more than we do about all of this."

Ricardo nodded, and after exchanging a few words with Natalia, they began to walk toward the square. It was rectangular and very spacious, with a large circular fountain in the middle. The two kids that Hector had seen earlier shared an animated conversation with the one on the fountain. The girl in the black dress was there too.

Hector was wondering if it was a good idea to yell to make himself seen when he realized that Ricardo and Natalia were lagging behind. He turned around to see what was going on and he froze, as astounded as they were. Now that they weren't closed in between the alleys and walls of the dilapidated building, they could see what lay beyond. Such was the vision that it took their breath away: an enormous mountain range towered less than five miles from them, filling most of the landscape in their view. The actual city was situated in the foothills of a gigantic, hulking dark mountain that shot up toward the sky, far taller than any of the others. Its top looked like a broken spearhead.

And if the mountain range was impressive, the structure that rose up on the outskirts of the city was even more so. It was a building over thirty stories tall, in the style of a gothic cathedral. Surrounding it were an endless number of pointed towers attached to the main edifice by narrow buttresses covered in what appeared to be metal spines. The entire building was a strange color, a dirty red hue, as if it had been constructed entirely of metal which had oxidized with the passing of time. Hector had never seen such a chilling structure in all his life.

Natalia whispered something, without taking her eyes off the rusty cathedral. By the expression on her face it was clear that she liked the place about as much as he did.

"It's horrible," Ricardo said with a furrowed brow.

"I don't like this place," whispered Hector. And he wasn't just talking about the cathedral, but about the city as a whole. Even the mountains were monstrous; they looked more like the skeleton of a dead animal than a real mountain range.

They heard sudden shouts from the square. The others had finally seen them. The boy in the pajamas gestured in Hector's direction. He waved his arms and jumped from the edge of the fountain in such a wild way that Hector feared he would fall in. He didn't understand a single word that the boy said. He spoke in a foreign language, musical and abrupt at the same time. It resembled no language that Hector had heard before, and yet at the same time, it reminded him of all languages.

The other two boys remained alert. One was a black teenager, so tall and muscular that for a moment Hector took him for an adult. He'd never seen anyone with such dark skin. The other was a kid of medium height with big gray horn-rimmed glasses and short curly brown hair. The girl in the black dress drew closer to the others when she saw the newcomers appear.

"Did Denestor bring you here?" asked Hector, cupping his hand over his mouth to amplify the sound, throwing caution to the wind.

The one in the pajamas nodded emphatically, said something in that incomprehensible language, and jumped from the fountain. He seemed about ready to run toward them, but the other teen put a hand on his shoulder and firmly stopped him. They talked for a moment, then the blond boy turned toward them once more and gestured for them to come closer. Hector could see that the white pattern on his pajamas was of little lambs.

They went over to them, with Natalia and her stick in the lead.

"Denestor Tul," said Ricardo when they entered the square. He put his hands up, as if to show they had no bad intentions. "Denestor Tul bring us."

The black kid agreed and pointed to the fountain behind him. Then he gestured with his hands, as if bringing an invisible glass to his lips and taking a long drink. He pointed to the fountain again and gave them a big smile.

Ricardo looked at Hector out of the corner of his eye.

"He wants... we drink," he said.

He nodded and looked at the fountain suspiciously. In the center was a sculpture over fifteen feet tall of a tangle of snakes, entwined with each other in a confusing disarray. Only their heads and necks stood out from the chaos. The water that filled the fountain's basin flowed from their open jaws.

"Do you speak my language?" Hector asked. No one responded; they only looked at him and gestured for them to drink from the fountain.

Ricardo took over and addressed them in three different languages, but after each of his phrases they only repeated the same gesture, each time with more insistence. The blond boy in pajamas opened his eyes wide, as if surprised that they couldn't understand something so simple. He approached Ricardo, grabbed him by the forearm, and pushed him toward the fountain, talking all the while in that strange gibberish.

As they got closer to the pool, Hector managed a sidelong glance at the girl in the black dress. She had beautiful eyes, clear blue with hints of violet. For a moment, Hector felt as if her gaze could lift him from the ground and hold him suspended above the square. He shook his head, dazed by the strange sensation, and kept walking. His heart pounded in his chest.

Ricardo finally gave in and drank from the fountain, cupping the water with his hands. He opened his eyes wide when he took the first drink, as if the flavor caught him by surprise. He took a step back. Then he said something in a shaky voice. And this time it wasn't in Russian or in English: he spoke the same language as the others. The boy in the pajamas celebrated the event by clapping him on the back and uttering a long phrase in the same language. Ricardo agreed, his lower lip trembling softly.

"Magic," Hector said to himself as he looked at the water in the fountain. His face's reflection returned his stare. *If I drink, I'm playing along with Denestor's game*, he thought. *It will be like signing another contract.* Natalia was the second to drink. She did it in an irritated way, as if she wanted to finish a tedious chore as soon as possible. She dried her lips on the sleeve of her sweatshirt and spoke her first words in the new language. Hector couldn't make out what she said, but by the others' expressions it must have been something quite shocking.

He sighed and approached the fountain. He had to drink; there was no way around it. To put it off was to delay the inevitable.

He put both hands in the water. It was cool without being too cold. He took his hands out and let the water run between his fingers. He reached toward the stream of water that flowed from the mouth of the closest snake and then, unsure of whether he was doing the right thing, he finally drank. It felt like the liquid not only ran down his throat, but spread in concentric waves throughout his body. He took two steps back. Something was happening to his thoughts. He stopped thinking in his native language and started thinking in the new one. He turned around, surprised. The words that the others spoke began to make sense to him. He was impressed, even though he'd known what would happen. This was magic. True magic.

"Take it easy," the black kid was saying. "It's a little strange at first."

"Strange? It's incredible," said Hector, so stunned by speaking these words in a language unknown to him only seconds before that he covered his mouth with both hands. He took them away slowly and repeated, "It's incredible, incredible! This is impossible, it can't be . . ." He was almost in shock.

"Of course it can," shouted the blond boy in pajamas as he gave him a slap on the back. "We're in Rocavarancolia, the most magical of the magic kingdoms! Didn't Denestor tell you? We're going to help him turn this place into a marvelous city! And we'll become great wizards!"

"This place stinks." Natalia struck him down with a look. "Denestor tricked us. And if you don't see it, then you're as dumb as you look."

"Hey," he blurted out, "what's with you?"

"It's your pajamas, Adrian," said the other teen. He crossed his arms and smiled amicably. "They look kind of silly."

"That's not my fault, is it? They were a gift from my grandmother. And Denestor didn't give me time to change."

"I forgot all of the languages I knew," said Ricardo suddenly. His face was contorted and he wrung his hands nervously. "I . . . I can't remember a single word of them. Not a single word."

"It appears to be a side effect from drinking the enchanted water," explained the kid with the horn-rimmed glasses. He spoke slowly and pronounced each word with great care. "When one acquires the language of the fountain, all of one's knowledge of other languages seems to disappear. It may be that this new language takes up the space in the brain that previous languages occupied."

"He always talks funny like that," whispered the boy in the little lamb pajamas to Hector.

Hector tried to think in English, but he couldn't do it. The only thoughts that came to his mind were words in the new language. "I've forgotten them," repeated Ricardo in a thin voice. He looked around, anxious, as if he hoped to run into his lost languages fleeing the square. "They're gone, lost."

"It happened to all of us," said the girl in black, looking at Ricardo with a shy smile. She spoke in a very low voice, almost a whisper. She moved slowly toward him. "Look at me. I knew French, English, and some Spanish, and now I don't remember a single word of any of them." She extended her hand with an exquisite elegance. "My name is Marina," she said.

"Ricardo," he said, shaking his head and paying no attention to the extended hand, which the girl quickly retracted, embarrassed. "It's incredible! Even my name sounds different from before! I don't remember what it sounded like, but it wasn't like this!"

"Well, there's nothing you can do but get used to it," advised the blond boy in the pajamas. "I'm Adrian, from Copenhagen. And this one here is Bruno. I think he told me he's from Rome." He signaled to the boy in the horn-rimmed glasses, who almost stood at attention on hearing his name. "I found him not long after I woke up, and he gave me a good scare! He was standing motionless at my door, still as a statue." He gave them a smile that stretched from ear to ear. "And who are you? Where are you from? What did Denestor Tul tell you? Geez! I'm sorry, I'm so excited!"

"I'm Hector," said he, and in keeping with the trend that Adrian started, added the name of the small American town where he lived. "And the nice girl with the stick is Natalia."

"Natalia Denisova-Shalikov," she hurriedly finished, without much enthusiasm. "Russian."

"My name's Marco, Marco Kretschmann." The tall teenager was the last to introduce himself. "I'm German. I was born near Munich, although I've lived in Berlin my whole life."

"You're French, right?" Adrian asked Marina.

"Yes, I'm from Paris. Is it that obvious?"

Before he could answer, Natalia interrupted, "All right, we all have names and we know where we're from," she grumbled. "What matters now is that we find out where we are and how to get out of here."

"We're in Rocavarancolia! The most magical of the magic kingdoms!" repeated Adrian, elated. The constant displays of euphoria were beginning to bother Hector. "And leaving here? How dumb is that? Who wants to leave here?"

"If you scream in my ear again, I'll show you who wants to leave with my stick," warned Natalia, with an annoyed gesture.

"Can I just say that you're starting to annoy me," interjected Adrian, his arms crossed. "I think that Denestor made it pretty clear, right? We have a tough job ahead of us! To rebuild the kingdom and become wizards!"

"Did he ever tell you that we were going to become wizards?" Ricardo asked.

"No . . . He talked about the possibility, and of—"

"He talked nonsense!" interrupted Natalia.

"Then why are you here, know-it-all?" asked Adrian with contempt. "How did he convince you to come?"

Natalia huffed but didn't answer his question.

"The smoke from his pipe has a stupefying effect," said Hector, and everyone turned toward him. He had never liked being the center of attention, and he blushed to the tips of his ears, even more when he realized that Marina was looking at him with interest. "And, well, I don't know about you, but with me he never stopped smoking. I thought I was dreaming, that what was happening wasn't real. I don't know where my head was at. I agreed to go with him, but I didn't understand what I was doing. Then my sister came in, and Denestor summoned those rag birds."

"Rag birds?" asked Ricardo with a furrowed brow. "When Denestor Tul and I disappeared, I thought I saw a flock of black birds approaching my window."

"They're his. He conjured them."

Hector told them how Denestor had used those winged monsters to erase all the memories that anyone had of him.

"They've forgotten us?" asked Marina. She brought her hand to her chest. She turned pale. "My parents don't remember me?"

Bruno stepped in before Hector could respond.

"It's only logical to assume that if Denestor did that to him, he did the same to the rest of us. I suspect that the flock of birds that Ricardo saw before he disappeared was preparing to erase all trace of his existence."

"They erased us," whispered Marco. He tapped his upper lip and looked up pensively. "How weird . . ."

"Okay, okay, okay. If you think about it, it's not that strange," said Adrian. He jumped down from the fountain again. "I'd rather that my family not remember me while I'm here," he said. "That way they won't be worried, and looking for me everywhere. Poor guys; that would be horrible. I'm sure that when we return home everyone's memories will be back to normal."

Hector wasn't convinced of this; Denestor's words and attitude when he conjured the birds made him think that traveling here would be something permanent, with no going back, but he decided it would be wise to keep his opinion to himself. Mentioning it would only make everyone more nervous. Adrian's explanation sounded convincing and seemed to reassure them a little.

"One thing is clear: this is not how I imagined it would be," commented Marco. The German boy was huge, tall and athletic. He made even Ricardo look small. "No," he went on, "far from it. And besides, they dropped us here in the middle of nowhere. If we're as important as he said, why do that? Shouldn't there be someone with us? Someone from his organization or something?"

Then Hector remembered the voice that woke him up. It had said something about a speech. Or was that just a dream?

"There seems to be movement in the castle," announced Bruno.

"Castle?" asked Hector. "There's a castle?"

"In the mountain." Marco pointed in that direction. "They turned a light on in one of the towers."

Hector had a hard time distinguishing the building, since the color of the walls and turrets was identical to the color of the mountains.

The castle loomed in the lower third of the road leading to the top. It had four towers, three in the first building and a fourth situated so far away that it may not have been part of the structure; it even stood on a different ledge.

At the top of the main tower of the fortress they could see a green spark that swung from left to right. Everyone looked in that direction.

"Could it be a sign for us to come closer?" asked Adrian in a low voice.

"I do not know," answered Bruno. He looked closely at the glimmer, barely blinking.

"If it were a sign, it would be something more obvious, don't you think? Not some makeshift light," said Marco.

"It's moving!" yelled Natalia.

It was true. The emerald glimmer had started to circle around the tower, faster and faster, until it suddenly flew out to the left, toward the city. In just a few minutes it left the mountain behind and soared over the ruins of the desolate town, nearing the square. Soon they could see it more clearly: it was a huge, translucent sphere with a pale green hue.

"That's definitely magic!" Adrian jumped down from the fountain once again. He was as excited as a kid going to an amusement park for the first time.

"There are people inside," whispered Ricardo.

Hector lifted his hand to shield his eyes. Ricardo was right. There were two people inside whatever that thing was. They had a better view of them when the sphere finally arrived at the square and came to an abrupt stop above a half-destroyed turret, located about twenty-five yards from the fountain with the snakes. A splendid emerald light bathed the turret and most of the square, lending the scene a mood that seemed both phantasmagorical and underwater. The kids approached one by one, slowly, never taking their eyes off the bubble and its inhabitants. A mixture of anticipation and fear filled the air.

Two women traveled inside the sphere. One was slender, with an oval face and a sweet but melancholy expression. She was dressed all in green: she wore a green evening gown, and even her long, luxurious hair was in the same tone, the color of the sphere. The second woman looked nothing like the first. She was short and plump, and her dress was but a rough tunic that looked more like a sack than proper clothing. Her chestnut hair clung to her head like a dying fern. She had a prominent square jaw, a flat nose, and uneven eyes: one was enormous, while the other was a narrow, malevolent crack.

"What an ugly woman!" shouted Natalia.

Hector looked at her, horrified. He'd only known her for fifteen minutes, but it was clear that Natalia didn't stop to think of the consequences of her words or actions. Luckily, the occupants of the sphere either didn't hear her or pretended not to.

"Listen, all of you!" exclaimed the short woman in the language they'd just learned. Her voice resonated and bubbled as if she had a mouth full of hot tar. "I am Lady Scar, commander of the kingdom's armies and guardian of the Royal Pantheon, and I'm here to welcome you to Rocavarancolia! Our beloved regent should be addressing you, but unfortunately his fragile health prevents him from being here. I will be brief because I don't have much to add to what Denestor Tul has already told you.

"The first thing I must say is that you're here of your own free will. No one, absolutely no one, was obligated to come! It may be that you harbor doubts in that respect; perhaps you think that Denestor Tul influenced your decision in some way. However, those are only stupid attempts at denying the truth. You're here, in Rocavarancolia, because you want to be."

Natalia was about to interrupt her when Ricardo firmly covered her mouth with his hand. He whispered something in her ear, a few quick words that made her furrow her brow and nod her head. When the boy withdrew his hand, she remained still, observing the sphere with a somber air.

"This devastated city will be your home from now on," the horrible woman continued, speaking in her bubbling voice. "Face your life here as best you can. Stay together if you desire or seek your destiny on your own, without counting on the others, it doesn't really matter. The only advice I can give you is very simple: stay alive as long as you can. And it's hard advice to follow, I assure you. Because this city will do everything in its power to kill you. And no, it won't do it out of cruelty. It will do it because it must."

"Kill us?" asked Adrian, tugging at Marco's sleeve. "Did she say the city wants to kill us?"

Marco quieted him with a gesture. Lady Scar kept talking.

"Harvest time is over. Now is the time for sifting, the time to separate the wheat from the chaff. And this is where Rocavarancolia comes in. Only those worthy of serving the kingdom will survive. The rest will watch as their bones become bleached by the sun in this ruined city. In thirty years, no one has been deemed worthy of the supreme honor of serving Rocavarancolia. In thirty years, no one has lived long enough to see the Red Moon."

Hector couldn't take his eyes off Lady Scar. Her words were hypnotic; their gurgling viscosity permeated everything.

"There was a time when the harvest meant something . . . Hundreds of young people crowded together in the squares and streets of the city, eager to begin the long journey that would lead them to glory or to their death. Hundreds, I tell you. Brave and ready for anything." She made a disgusted face that distorted her features even more. Her enormous eye opened so widely that it gave the impression that her eyeball might fall from its socket. "And now . . . what do I have before me? Twelve brats who are scared to death."

"Twelve . . ." whispered Ricardo and Marco at the same time. There were seven of them in the square. There had to be five other kids somewhere else.

"And they say that we should be happy, that the harvest hasn't been this fruitful in years. They say we should be hopeful." She let out a laugh with no trace of humor. Her head seemed to bounce lightly, as if it weren't completely attached to her neck. "Fools," she spat.

"Her throat," whispered Marco. "Did you see her throat?"

Hector squinted his eyes. A large scar stretched across the woman's neck from one side to the other. And it wasn't the only scar; many others marked her hands, arms, and legs.

"Lady Scar," whispered Hector, with a knot in his stomach. Her name certainly did her justice.

"Fools, yes," continued the scarred woman. "Because only fools cling to hope when all is lost. For years, not one of Denestor's pups has lived long enough to prove useful. Why would it be any different now?" She sighed, and the sound of her sigh was like the groan of a tired beast. "But what I think isn't important. What's truly important is that you're here: in Rocavarancolia.

"There are only three places that are forbidden to you: the red building on the outskirts of the city, the cemetery in the hollow, and of course, the castle in the mountain. The rest of the city is yours: you can stay where you like, and use what you find as you see fit.

"But be careful. Rocavarancolia is riddled with dangers. There are active spells that remain in the most unexpected places, lethal curses that will kill you on the spot or insanity spells that will turn your brain inside out. And even we don't know what strange creatures might lurk in the ruins. Here death has a thousand faces—don't you ever forget it. Don't trust anything or anyone, or you'll be lost. This city may be your home, but it will never be your friend. It's here to test you."

"A charming place," whispered Ricardo. His voice trembled.

"Rocavarancolia is situated between the mountain range behind you and the cliffs to the east. The only way to leave is by crossing the tortuous mountain passes. They're the only path out of the city. And if anyone wants to take that exit, no one will try to stop you. Although I should warn you that you'll only be exchanging a probable death for a certain one. Because beyond the mountains lies the Malyadar Desert, where no one can survive for very long. It's a wasteland that stretches for days in every direction, a vast hell which even dragons would avoid . . . You'd have the same chance of surviving if you jumped from the cliffs."

Lady Scar is so dramatic . . . A voice in Hector's head suddenly spoke up, the same voice that had awakened him in the dungeon.

The boy jumped and looked around, startled.

I'm in the sphere. I'm the pretty one, the one that's not all cut up.

The woman in green seemed to be looking directly at him. She was pretty, but her beauty had a sad aura to it, an air of sorrow that neither her lips nor her smile could soften. Hector mumbled something that sounded like a half burp and took a step backward, colliding with Ricardo, who was so absorbed in the speech that he didn't bat an eye.

Calm down, Hector. No one knows that I'm in your head, and for our own sake, no one must know. So just relax and listen.

He looked around at the rest of his companions. They all remained focused on the scarred woman's speech, completely clueless about the person that spoke in his mind. Hector was so nervous that his teeth chattered.

I'm Lady Serena, consort to absence and nothing, specter of the twenty-sixth queen of Rocavarancolia, said the voice by way of introduction. *And, although it's strictly prohibited, I'm here to help you. You're the most important thing to happen to Rocavarancolia in thirty years. And if the kingdom is to survive, we need you alive.*

So we're going to cheat.

Hector's throat was dry. Lady Scar kept talking, but he no longer heard her; he could only pay attention to the voice that filled his mind, that voice that said it was a ghost, more or less. And he had no choice but to believe it. The figure of the emerald woman shimmered lightly and seemed less solid than it should be. Lady Serena was in constant movement; her hands traveled slowly over the entire surface of the sphere, caressing it. The young boy realized it was she who created the bubble of green light that transported them from the castle.

But keeping you alive is going to be a difficult business, projected the voice in his head. *It will take a lot of effort on your part. And unfortunately my help will be minimal, but not because I want it that way, I assure you. If anyone finds out what I'm doing, we're lost. They'll kill you and banish me from Rocavarancolia. It's the law. And therefore, you must keep absolutely silent. Do not tell anyone, absolutely no one, what I'm about to do. Because in this city even the wind has ears.*

Someone snorted next to Hector, startling him. It was Adrian.

"Enough, enough already!" he yelled, taking a step forward. He gestured angrily at the sphere of light. It was clear that he was terrified, but Hector couldn't help but admire him for overcoming his fear and taking a stand.

Lady Scar looked at him from above with an expression of amused curiosity.

"I want to go home, do you hear me? I want to go home!" shouted Adrian in the voice of a child who's not used to being contradicted. "This isn't fun anymore! Denestor didn't tell us that we might die!"

Lady Scar smiled the most disturbing smile Hector had ever seen. A purplish tongue darted quick as a snake's between her lips.

"He didn't tell you that?" she asked mockingly, imitating Adrian's voice. The effect was horrific, the hair-raising gurgle of a sick monster. "Everything that's alive can die, my young friend. Absolutely everything. Denestor didn't warn you that you might die here, just like he didn't warn you that you might get wet if it rains, or that you have to breathe to stay alive."

Adrian mumbled something incomprehensible and took a step back. His lower lip trembled uncontrollably; he looked like he was about to cry. Someone put an arm around his shoulders.

Don't get too close to your companions, said the voice in his head. *Just as Lady Scar says, most of them will die before long.*

But we must hurry. For the spell I'm going to perform I need visual contact with the target, and we don't have much time. My companion will finish her speech soon, and then it will be time to return to the castle.

"What are you going to—"

Silence, the voice cut him off. *I'm going to perform magic. A spell only for you. It's risky, but necessary. In the city there are creatures so sensitive to magic that they're capable of detecting the most minuscule enchantment. However, today their perception is affected. The opening of the vortex that united our worlds has created a mystical storm of such magnitude that right now Rocavarancolia is seething with magic in every direction.*

So take a deep breath, Hector, because what happens next is not going to be pleasant.

"I look at you and see nothing but weakness and fear," Lady Scar was saying, in what seemed to be the final words of her speech. "I look at you and see nothing but corpses who don't know that they're dead yet. I hope I'm wrong. I hope you achieve the impossible."

Something invaded Hector's mind. It was a dense, overpowering wave, a glowing shadow that filled his head like a gust of oily smoke. For a moment it was difficult for him to think. A second later he no longer knew who he was. His identity, his being, every last one of his thoughts was lost in the black fog that filled his brain. Until suddenly, the invading darkness began to gather and take form. Hector regained his sense of self, and at the same time, felt like his consciousness was leaving him.

No. No. No . . . Please. I can't faint yet. . .

SHADOWS

. . . Again.

He opened his eyes, startled. At first he saw only sky, an unending stretch of faded blue that hung above his head. He thought he was floating in space, lost in the heavens thanks to the ghostly woman's arts, and the vertigo made him gasp. Then Marina's face came into view, and reality pulled him back down again. He wasn't flying; his entire body was flattened on the ground of the square where he had fainted. He sat up slowly and made an inventory of the various pains he felt, in case he'd hurt himself in the fall. But all he noticed was the bump that Natalia had given him on the forehead.

Marina and Adrian were at his side, one squatting, the other standing up. The folds of the girl's black skirt fell over his elbow, partially covering it. Hector pulled it away with a start, as if the contact with the fabric burned him.

"That was quite a fall. You fainted," Adrian said. "Are you okay?"

"I . . ." He swallowed. He still noticed Lady Serena's spell moving around in his mind. It had been reduced to several thin, black spirals that spun inside his skull. "What happened?" he asked, uneasily. "I'm still a little dizzy."

"I lost my mind for a while too, believe it or not," said Adrian, and he gave a nervous little laugh. "I look at you and see nothing but corpses." He pretended to shudder, a shudder that wasn't as fake as he tried to make it.

"Is he awake?" asked Ricardo, approaching them.

"I'm not really sure," Hector answered for himself. The dark tentacles were dissipating from his mind, but the dizziness remained and his vision was blurry, images appearing before his eyes with wavy lines like on a very hot day. He decided that the best thing to do would be to stay on the ground until he was fully recovered. "How long was I out?"

"A few minutes," answered Ricardo as he sat down next to him. "You still look a bit pale."

"I just need to rest a little." He looked toward the spot where Lady Scar and Lady Serena's green sphere had been. No sign of it remained.

"They left shortly after you fainted," said Natalia as she followed the direction of his glance. "That horrible woman said that you'd probably be the fir—"

"Forget what she said." Ricardo cut her off abruptly. "Forget all of the foolish things she said. The part about how we were all going to die was just to scare us."

"Well, it worked on me," admitted Adrian.

He'll probably be the first to die—that's what Lady Scar had said when she saw him faint. And Hector couldn't help but agree with her, even though his fainting was because of the spell and not because of weakness or a panic attack. It was all a lot for him to take in. It was one thing to imagine living through dangerous adventures and a very different thing to see oneself actually wrapped up in them. And he had enough common sense to know that he was not prepared to face whatever lay in wait for him here.

But Lady Serena had seen something in him, something that seemingly set him apart from the rest. She'd said he was the most important thing to happen to Rocavarancolia in thirty years. He remembered the flying syringe in the dungeon. Was the answer in his blood

He wanted the spell that Lady Serena used to turn his mind inside out to have a purpose. As of now, all it had done was make him lose consciousness and leave him even more confused than before.

"What did the woman in the sack say at the end?" he asked.

"Stupidity and nonsense," groaned Natalia. She was the only one still on her feet. The rest of the group had sat down around Hector and Ricardo.

"She said we would have no issues with provisions," declared Bruno. "Apparently there are various locations in the city where they shall leave supplies for us." He had removed his glasses and was cleaning them with a tissue that he then folded carefully and placed in the pocket of his plaid shirt. "She also told us that any interaction with the city's residents would be useless. It is against the law for them to interfere in our affairs. They will not help us, but they will not actively seek to harm us, either."

"According to her it's likely that we won't see anyone the entire time we're here," added Marco. The German sat across from Hector, and when their eyes met, he smiled such a radiant and sincere smile that Hector felt a deep current of affection for him.

"Even better! I hope I never run into Lady Scar again in my life! She's horrible!" exclaimed Adrian, and he fell backward on the cobblestones.

"The other woman was beautiful, though," said Marina. "But she seemed very sad, did you notice? And the green color she wore wasn't a happy green. It's the color of fields that are starting to wither, as if from one minute to the next they'd begin to turn gray . . ." She suddenly realized that everyone was looking at her. She lowered her eyes, blushing. "I'm sorry, sometimes I talk too much."

"I hardly noticed her," said Ricardo. "The other one was more striking, with all those scars and marks everywhere."

"This place is a nightmare," said Hector.

"Well, we're not going to wake up just sitting here like this." Natalia gave them all a reproachful look. "What we have to do is get moving and find a way to return home."

"There's no way to return home," said Marco.

"You don't know that!" exclaimed Adrian. It was shocking to see the change that had come over him since Lady Scar's speech. Little remained of the enthusiasm that he had shown in the beginning.

"You're right, we don't know that," said Ricardo. "And that's the issue: we don't know anything. We have a mountain of questions, but no one to ask. Why did Denestor bring us here? What makes us special? What do you suppose we have to do here?"

"The answers to your inquiries must be located in some part of the city," said runo. "All we have to do is find them. From Lady Scar's speech we can conclude that our presence here is hardly a coincidence; it's part of a tradition that goes way back in time. And if that's the case, it shouldn't be too difficult to find information on such a matter." He spoke in a slow, weary manner. "There might be books, illustrations, paintings, inscriptions, or similar clues. Besides, since we know nothing about this city, any information we may find will prove helpful."

"Before we set out to look for books, I think we should try to find the rest of the people that Denestor brought," pointed out Marco. "If what Lady Scar told us is true, there are five other kids running around here."

"They could already be dead," whispered Marina.

"Don't say that!" yelled Adrian, frightened, sitting bolt upright. He had turned pale.

Hector sat up again, more upright this time. He was no longer dizzy and his vision was momentarily clear. He ran his hand over his neck as he looked around. His gaze rested on a building that stood beyond the square. It was a three-story dwelling with gray walls, ending in a small, pointed, and somewhat singed roof. Besides the damage to the roof, the house was in good condition. But what got his attention had nothing to do with the structure itself or the state of the building, but rather the column of dark mist that floated in front of the door, a hazy thread that reached up to the second story.

He blinked several times, thinking the mist was some kind of optical illusion, something in the atmosphere, or simply a result of his fainting spell. He was about to point out the column to the rest when once again he heard the voice that wasn't his in his head.

The black mist. You can see it, right? Well, avoid it always. It marks places that you should stay away from, cursed places or parts of the city where nothing good can happen. Flee from it. But be careful. With my spell you can distinguish the places in Rocavarancolia that I know for certain are dangerous. The problem is that even I don't know all of the dangers that this city holds. Don't ever forget this: just because a place is free from the mist, that does not mean it's safe.

Hector scanned the square and the buildings beyond it and discovered other dark marks. He found almost a dozen in only a few seconds. One of the columns of smoke was so immense that it almost completely obscured the building behind it: a brick tower surrounded by a garden in ruins, located at the other end of the square.

He shuddered. Right now, he couldn't begin to imagine how the spell could be useful to him. His only thought was that the black mist was everywhere. The feeling of danger was so palpable that he wanted to scream. He ran a trembling hand through his hair. His confusion only grew. There was so much he needed to know, so many questions. . . And, contrary to what Ricardo had said, he knew who to ask.

Do you hear me? Can you hear me? he said mentally. *Why did you bring us here? What do you want from us?*

He did not get a response. Either communication was only possible in one direction, or Lady Serena was ignoring him. He wrinkled his forehead. The ghost had made contact with him as soon as he discovered the black mist. In some way she had known what he was seeing. He closed his eyes, pursed his lips, and came up with a new question:

Why are you helping me? He concentrated on each of the five words until he could visualize them in his head, drawn in characters made of fire.

"Are you okay?" he heard Adrian ask him. "You look like you need to go to the bathroom."

"What? No!"

The voice returned, but not to respond to his question.

You're going to have to be very careful with the information the spell provides. You can't reveal that you know more than you should or you'll arouse suspicion. And if anyone finds out that you're getting help, I hate to repeat this, but I must make myself clear: they will kill you. It's the law.

And now I must leave you, Hector. I'll try to speak with you again later, while the magic storm still hovers over Rocavarancolia and I'm able to link to your mind.

At that the voice abandoned him, leaving behind only space for his own thoughts.

"We also have to find the spot where they'll leave our food," said Marco in that instant. "I'm starting to get hungry."

"Me too," said Adrian softly. He sounded surprised.

Hector agreed. The last thing he'd eaten had been a couple of candies during the outing on Halloween night with Sarah, and he didn't know how much time had passed since then. He trembled to think of his sister. He was so far from home that the distance didn't even make sense; Rocavarancolia was another world, a world that had nothing to do with Earth. Here magic was real, here it was possible for a ghost to slip inside your brain and bewitch you so that you were aware of the evil that surrounded you. It all made him dizzy.

Around him they were still discussing what to do next. Hector, lost in a thoughtful silence, hardly paid attention. His gaze was fixed on the enormous column of black smoke which hid the brick tower from view. He looked up. The sky above his head wasn't the same sky as on Earth, as he now saw. The shade of blue was too light, almost white. And the sun wasn't the same sun. It looked much smaller and paler than Earth's sun. He thought again about his sister, his parents, his friends, and that he'd probably never, ever see them again. A lump formed in his throat.

"I saw a spider," he said suddenly, interrupting the conversation. They all looked at him, worried. "It was bigger than me, it wore a frock coat and had a monocle in each eye . . . I passed out when it blew some foul-smelling dust on me. And I saw a house that someone took a bite out of. And a monster in a green bubble that told us we were going to die . . ." He looked at them, one by one. "I'm tired of this. I want to get out of here. I want to go home."

There was a long silence, finally broken by Ricardo.

"Let's get moving right now." He stood up in a determined way. "Let's see what we find in this marvelous city."

The spyglass, a beautiful silver-plated antique, flapped its wings and descended in a spiral till it landed with the rest of its kind on the banister of the terrace. There were about a dozen of them, all different types and colors. A long white one with delicate dragonfly wings took flight as soon as the silver spyglass landed next to it. Another, a shiny black one with bat wings, left its spot at one end of the terrace to land next to the new arrival. There were spyglasses scattered throughout the entire castle, perched on the windows and terraces, wandering among the turrets, flitting from one place to another.

Lady Serena watched as the silver spyglass pressed gently against its black mate, like a tired creature looking for a friendly shoulder to lean on. The ghost wondered, not for the first time, what degree of intelligence the creations of the demiurges possessed. Could they feel? Did they make the mistake of falling in love with each other? Did they have arguments like other living creatures? She'd once asked Denestor Tul these questions; the ancient wizard had given her a mysterious smile before answering concisely, "That's something only they know." Demiurges were wizards who were very protective of their art and its mysteries.

Most of the spyglasses on the banister were Denestor's handiwork; only the silver one had been created by another demiurge, who'd died decades earlier. This was why she'd chosen it to spy on Denestor's kids:

she didn't feel comfortable using something created by someone who was still living.

A flock of spyglasses flew over the tower's terrace, toward the castle's main entrance. Their lenses sparkled in the sun. She was still listening to their fluttering echoes when she heard a wizened voice behind her.

"Splendid and radiant, as always, Lady Serena. Your presence is a balm for the soul."

The ghost turned around. Someone was watching her from the shadows. She recognized the lean shadow of Enoch the Dusty. The vampire was hunched over with his arms crossed, far from the open door and the light of day.

"Your soul is withered, Enoch," she said, and with an elegant movement of her hands she conjured a swath of deep, dark night around him. "But even so, you're welcome here."

Enoch smiled happily and went out to the terrace under the shelter of the dark shadow. He stretched a skeletal hand toward the balustrade, and the spyglass with the bat wings immediately flew toward him. Lady Serena somehow wasn't surprised that it was this spyglass that flocked to his call. The spyglass hovered in front of Enoch's right eye, eagerly flapping its wings. The vampire cleared his throat and brought his head forward, half closing his left eye.

"They're so full of life," he whispered, after a few moments, with the tone of someone praising a well-prepared table. "That's him, isn't it? The boy with the dark curly hair?"

"That's him," said the specter. "And he's as weak as Denestor warned us he would be. He fainted during Lady Scar's lecture."

"Oh . . ." The vampire shook his head remorsefully. "What a tragedy. That such power comes in such a fragile container."

"At the end of the day they're all fragile, Enoch. Rocavarancolia will make them stronger or will kill them in the process."

"The Lexel brothers have placed bets on them," he said. "The white twin is sure that the majority will die before nightfall. The black one, on the other hand, says that it will be less than that, between two and six. That's his bet. Can you believe it, my dear friend? How frivolous! Playing with the lives of those poor children, toying with our hopes . . ."

"What's at stake?"

"Apples from Arfes. Ten pieces each."

The specter smiled. It had been thirty years since the portal that united Rocavarancolia with the rich world of Arfes had closed. Arfes was the only source of that fruit, and since then the value of the apples that remained in the kingdom had multiplied enormously. There were few delicacies that could compete with their exquisite flavor, and besides, they possessed the unique characteristic of never going bad. It didn't matter if they were picked centuries before being eaten; their flavor remained the same, identical to the moment when they were picked from the tree. Even Lady Serena, who for many years now had neither needed nor enjoyed food, hoarded a small quantity of them. For the living residents of Rocavarancolia those apples represented an oasis of sorts, taking them back to better times.

"Lady Scar is with our beloved regent, correct?" asked Enoch suddenly, with a distracted air, without taking his eye from the spyglass.

"Yes. She's waiting for him to wake up so that she can fill him in on the situation."

"I'm sure he'll be happy to know that the harvest was so magnificent this year. Hopefully it will bear fruit . . . And hopefully he'll be here to see it," he whispered. Then, after a languid gesture to dismiss the spyglass, he turned to Lady Serena. The black shadow that surrounded him quivered as it molded to his new position. "My dear, don't you think that Lady Scar spends too much time with the regent?"

"No," she answered unequivocally. "I don't think so. Especially considering that she's one of the main reasons he's still alive. Without her care and Lady Spider's potions, Huryel would have left us long ago."

"Oh." Enoch the Dusty raised his hands in a gesture of complete surprise, as if he'd totally overlooked such an important detail. "Of course, of course. Without Lady Scar's attentive care, the regent would no longer be with us. So much kindness and compassion from someone who aspires to take the place of the dying man, hmm?" He ended his statement with a smile full of evil intent. His fangs flashed in the bubble of night that surrounded him.

"Be careful, don't bite your tongue or you'll poison yourself with your own blood, dear Enoch."

The vampire laughed.

"Evil and hatred run through my veins, it's true," he said between his giggles. "But you know as well as I do the real reason why our commander goes out of her way to keep the regent alive."

Lady Serena didn't reply. Enoch was right.

Once Huryel died, the council of Rocavarancolia would vote to elect his successor. Tradition mandated that only two possible candidates could occupy the regent's place: the commander of the royal armies and the Lord of Assassins, a position held by Esmael, the black angel, for forty years.

It was well known that Lady Scar had very few supporters on the council. To tell the truth, the woman had never aroused much sympathy in the kingdom. But neither did she arouse the intense hatred that many felt for Esmael. And therein lay her chance at being regent. The council was divided among those who supported the Lord of Assassins and those who would do anything to keep him from rising in power, including voting for her as successor. For the moment, both forces were balanced. And that was what kept Huryel, the current regent, alive. Once the balance tipped clearly in favor of one of the candidates, his life would come to an end. If Lady Scar was the winner, she would neglect her care just enough that he would die without anyone being able to accuse her of causing his death. If, on the other hand, Esmael won, he would take advantage of the skills that made him the Lord of Assassins to make a final and lethal visit to Huryel's dwelling, and no one would blame him either for the regent's death. The natural order in Rocavarancolia was always governed by cruelty and blood, but when it involved the upper echelons, a certain amount of discretion was necessary.

"Lady Scar's motives for acting the way she acts are her own, Enoch. And I don't know them," said Lady Serena.

"How do you still not know who you're going to support when the time comes to choose a successor?" he wanted to know.

The specter smiled.

"The fact that I'm not shouting it from the rooftops doesn't mean that I haven't decided yet."

Although the council's vote was secret, the majority of its members had already announced which of the two candidates they preferred. Lady Serena was one of the few who opted to keep her decision a secret. Enoch the Dusty, on the other hand, was a declared supporter of Esmael. Which made sense, since the position of Lord of Assassins would be his once it became vacant.

With a wave of his hand, Enoch sent the black spyglass away. He looked at it silently for a couple of minutes. Lady Serena watched as his lips parted several times. She couldn't tell if the vampire was licking his lips or trying to find a way to tell her something.

"The black angel would be very generous if you decided to support him," he said finally.

"Esmael has nothing that could interest me."

"Oh. No, no he doesn't. That's true. But at some point he might."

"Don't beat around the bush, Enoch. Tell me what you've come to say."

"Esmael has obtained a certain book," explained the vampire after a calculated pause. "A powerful, ancient grimoire that contains long-forgotten spells. And among them, my very dear departed friend, is the Call to Reincarnation." He looked away from the spyglass and turned toward her. "Pay attention, Lady Serena: Esmael is in a position to promise you resurrection. He could bring you back to life, restoring your soul in a body identical to the one you had before."

If the ghost had owned a heart, it would have leapt in her chest. The expression of shock on her face made the vampire smile.

"But in order to achieve such a feat he'd need sources of power that he would only have access to as regent of Rocavarancolia," added Enoch.

"He'd need the Jewels of the Iguana," whispered Lady Serena. These were the royal jewels that were presently in the regent's power and which only he, as regent of the kingdom, could use.

A body, again, to touch and be touched. The opportunity to once more feel the wind in her face, the warm blood in her veins, the ground firm beneath her feet. Life, in short, in all its splendor. This was what Esmael offered, according to Enoch. But was this what she longed for?

She floated toward the balustrade, confused.

She'd heard talk of the Call to Reincarnation; it was a mythical enchantment, one of the many spells that fairy tales were made of. From what she'd heard, it used the essence of a spirit to reconstruct the body that the spirit once inhabited, and then fused them together. However it supposedly worked, it was considered to be a lost spell. No one had known about it for centuries.

"What book are you talking about?" asked Lady Serena.

"He didn't tell me."

The ghost was quiet. Her dress, a reflection of her favorite clothing in life, shook as if it had a soul of its own. It wasn't the wind that moved it, but rather her own anxiety. She felt anything but serene in moments like this.

"Well? What would your answer be?"

"My answer? Fine, I'll give it to you: tell him that I don't deal with messengers or servants. If your lord and master has something to tell me, he can come tell me himself," she replied in a curt tone. She didn't like the idea of talking to the black angel, but she needed time to clarify her thoughts.

"Oh." The vampire shifted uncomfortably in response to the ghost's frostiness. "I'll deliver your message to Esmael without delay."

He left the terrace with long strides, taking his darkness with him. She made sure that the vampire closed the door before turning her attention to a different presence that awaited on the terrace.

"My apologies for not greeting you sooner, Rorcual, my friend, but I guessed that you didn't want Enoch to know that you were following him," she said. She managed to keep the agitation that she felt out of her voice.

After a few moments of silence she heard an uncomfortable cough from a corner of the terrace.

"I didn't mean to disturb you, Lady Serena," the alchemist assured her, completely invisible without his glove. "I discovered Enoch snooping around the corridors and decided to follow him to see what was going on. I hope . . . I hope you're not contemplating even for a second the possibility of accepting the contract that he proposed. You know as well as I that Esmael cannot be trusted."

Nor you, invisible leech, nor Lady Scar, nor anyone, she thought.

"The end is coming for Rocavarancolia," she said instead. "Does it matter who's at the helm of the ship when we're drowning?"

She heard the alchemist's steps as he approached.

"What about Denestor's children?" he said vehemently. "Who can say that this will really be the end? If even one child survives there will be a new beginning. You know that! And do you really want the black angel to be leading us when that happens? If we rise from our own ashes, do you really want to be under the command of such a bloodthirsty, abominable creature?"

Lady Serena didn't answer. She remained pensive, her gaze lost in the chaos of ruins that was Rocavarancolia. She thought of the black angel, how in all of the years she'd existed, alive or dead, she had never met anyone as monstrous as him. Esmael was capable of committing the most terrible atrocities without thinking twice; there was no aberration or crime he was not willing to undertake. That was how he earned the position of Lord of Assassins, the position given to the most ruthless being in the kingdom. They said that only the spider kings and Hurza the Eye-Eater, first Lord of Assassins, surpassed him in cruelty. Handing the reins of Rocavarancolia over to Esmael was to plunge the kingdom's government into total darkness, into limitless evil.

"Lady Serena?"

"Esmael can return my life to me, Rorcual," she said, simply.

"Only to snatch it away from you as soon as he's returned it!"

"Alchemist . . ." she said, deliberately. "You've expressed my greatest desire with clarity: I wish to die. And for such an achievement, I must be alive."

"What the hell is that?" Natalia made a face as she pointed at the gray stain they found on the ground as soon as they opened the door.

"It looks like a rotten rug," Ricardo responded, after a couple of moments of hesitation. "At least I hope it's a rotten rug."

"I hate this place," groaned Natalia.

"You've said that before," commented Hector, looking inside the room. It was in as bad shape as the rest of the building.

"I just hate it!" she insisted. "I hate it so much!"

Hector nodded in a listless manner and entered the space, careful not to step on the stain on the ground. He had wrapped his feet in various rags that he'd found in a cupboard on the first floor. It wasn't very comfortable, but it was better than walking around with no shoes. So far those rags were the most useful thing he'd found.

Ricardo followed him in while Natalia guarded the door with her usual scowl.

The place was in pieces. There was destroyed furniture all throughout the room, most of it stacked up in a corner.

Hector squatted down to pick up one of the many books strewn on the ground among the remains of a bookshelf. It was a good size, with a cover so ruined that he couldn't make out the title or the drawing on the front. The pages had stuck to one another, forming a grayish mass.

He let it drop and approached the window, paying no mind to the other books scattered at his feet. He needed some fresh air.

The window looked out over the now-deserted square. They'd finally decided that the best option would be to split up; one group would investigate the buildings surrounding the square, on foot; the other would explore the streets nearby, without going too far from the first group. Only Marco seemed to have an issue with the plan, but in the end he had to give in.

From the window, Hector could see the façade of the tower covered in dark fog. He had to find a way to prevent them from entering the building, and furthermore, he had to do it without arousing suspicion. No one could know that he had help; Lady Serena had made that very clear. But what if the ghost's help wasn't what it seemed? How did he know he could trust her? And what if the mist were nothing more than a trick to throw him off track, keeping them out of places that were actually useful? The only solution he could think of was to enter one of the marked areas, and he didn't like that option very much.

Ricardo walked through the hall, carefully examining everything.

"That's strange," he mumbled, thoughtfully.

"What?"

"All this mess . . . It's weird. Look—look closely."

Hector looked around. Everything was turned upside down. He didn't know what Ricardo was talking about.

"All I see is a room torn to pieces."

"Yes, but the destruction follows a pretty clear pattern. Look." He walked backward toward the window where Hector stood, first pointing toward the trash on the floor and then toward the corner, covered in broken furniture. "Most of the junk is piled up there, you see? It's as if something threw everything in this room against the wall, and whatever it was had a temper. There are even shards of wood embedded in the stone."

Hector nodded.

"You're right. I see it. Something picked up the room and threw it to the other side. So what?"

"Give me a hand," Ricardo said and went to the window.

He grabbed a piece of wood from the pile, causing most of the rubble to come crashing down. Ricardo jumped, surprised by the sudden avalanche. Then he let out a laugh and kept clearing away bits of broken furniture, covered in a cloud of dust. Natalia moved closer to him, leaned her stick against the wall, and started to help him remove the debris. Ricardo hummed, and she grumbled.

"You guys are crazy, you know?" said Hector.

"You don't want to help us because you're a slacker," Natalia scolded him.

"I'm not a slacker. I just don't want to waste my energy doing things that don't make sense. It's stupid. And tiring."

But he started toward the rubble, reluctantly, biding his time so they could do the worst of the job before he lent a hand. Just as he was about to begin, another avalanche cleared the corner almost completely.

"I guess you didn't need my help after—"

Something fell to the ground with a crash and pushed away the last bits of wood stacked against the wall. A huge cloud of dust arose and a sudden wave of fetid air enveloped the three of them. Hector and Natalia stepped back, coughing. Ricardo, however, remained glued to the spot, an expression of shock and surprise on his sooty face. Among the shards of wood and broken beams was the skeleton of a humanoid creature, in a dented gray suit of armor. It measured about three feet tall and had short limbs. Its skull was snub nosed and pointy, with a prominent jaw full of sharp fangs. The armor had holes on the back plate to allow for the creature's wings. Only one wing remained, a mess of broken cartilage, and it was enormous compared to the rest of the body.

"The wall," Natalia whispered.

The cadaver's silhouette was visible on the uncovered wall, outlined sharply on the stone. And off to the right, fully extended, lay the missing wing.

"You were right, everything was thrown on top of it," said Hector with a knot in his throat. "It was pinned to the wall."

Ricardo nodded and crouched down next to the cadaver. The armor was in very bad shape, so damaged that in some spots you could see the skeleton underneath. Ricardo turned it face up. The creature's skull tilted so that it was looking at Hector. It seemed to smile. Underneath the body they found a dagger about eight inches long. Ricardo grasped it and examined it thoroughly. The blade was nicked and covered with a nasty layer of rust.

"It's not much," he mumbled, "but it may come in handy."

"Yeah, so you can get an infection when you cut yourself," said Natalia. "What kind of creature is this?"

Ricardo shrugged and began to strike the dagger against the wall. Iron dust rained down from the blade.

"A creature that shouldn't have been stuck in a closed room," he answered seconds later. "Something with wings like that isn't made to maneuver within four walls. It should have stayed outside."

He sat up, sheathed the dagger between his belt and pants, and looked around. He eyed the books on the ground, just as ruined as the one that Hector had picked up, and shook his head.

"We're done here," he said. "Let's go to the floor upstairs. If I'm right, it's the last one."

Natalia followed Ricardo out of the room; Hector, on the other hand, stayed where he was, his gaze fixed on the skeleton and its armor. He couldn't take his eyes off it. It was the closest he'd ever been to a dead body, but that wasn't what made an impression on him. What really had him paralyzed was witnessing the effects of an act of extreme violence. Something or someone had literally crushed that being against the wall of the house. Just like a fly.

Once more his eyes went to the window. He was able to see the remains of a half-destroyed tower and, a little farther off, the ruins of a burned house. Since he'd woken up, there hadn't been a single place he looked that wasn't marked by the hand of violence. Something terrible had ravaged this place.

"Are you coming or not?" Natalia asked from the doorway.

Hector nodded and followed her, stealing a last glance at the skeleton before leaving the room. The smile on the skull had an evil air to it, an air of arrogance and malice, as if it wanted you to know that it knew a secret you didn't.

The first thing he noticed when Ricardo opened the door was the room's lighting. Besides the light coming in through the windows, various torches held in censers halfway up the walls illuminated the surroundings. The fire burned with unusual vigor, throwing unsettling shadows on the walls from one end of the room to the other.

"I think we've finally found something," Ricardo announced.

They were in the foyer of a large library. Most of the furniture was empty, but there were still a fair number of books on some of the shelves.

Several tables surrounded by wooden chairs were spread out in the middle of the room. The place didn't look that damaged compared to the rest of the building: a crack here or there in the wall, a couple of shelves knocked over, and little else.

The three teenagers entered the room. The torch light multiplied their shadows over the walls and on the dusty ground. Ricardo looked at the censer to his left. It had the shape of an arm held upright, but in place of a hand was the base of the torch. The blazing fire tinted his face red, making him look like a demon.

"Someone must have been through here recently," said Hector, pointing to the lit torches.

"That can't be," Ricardo retorted. "Look at the layer of dust on the ground. Nobody's been through here in quite some time."

"They could have flown in, lit the torches, and left," offered Natalia.

Ricardo approached the censer.

"The fire doesn't give off any heat," he pointed out, and then placed his hand over the flame. Hector whistled through his teeth, startled by the gesture. "And it doesn't burn! It's magic fire!"

"Don't tell Adrian or he'll start clapping," said Natalia.

"Rocavarancolia, the kingdom of miracles and marvels," groaned Hector. He was still affected by the discovery of the skeleton in the room below. He couldn't get the image of that eternal smile out of his head. He felt his face and noticed the hardness of his own skull beneath his flesh. He removed his hand quickly. His thoughts were turning more and more dismal.

"Maybe we'll find a way to get home in one of these books," ventured Natalia. She didn't sound very convinced.

"We should be so lucky," whispered Ricardo. He shrugged his shoulders and sighed. "Well, we lose nothing by taking a look."

The girl walked over to a bookcase and grabbed the first book off the shelf. It was a large volume with a dyed leather cover, coated in dust. She blew on it to clear the cover. She squinted her eyes and shook her head.

"I don't understand any of it," she said. She propped the book up on the case and flipped through the pages. "Not a word."

Hector skimmed the spines of the half dozen books on the other shelf. The titles were written in characters that were foreign to him; they almost looked more like pictograms than letters.

"So they're not written in the language of the fountain," he said.

"What if we were only taught to speak it but not to read it?" asked Ricardo from another bookcase. His hands went from one book to another with dizzying speed.

Hector wrote his name in the dust that covered the bookshelf in front of him. His finger, like his tongue and his brain, could express itself in the new language with perfect fluency. And his eyes didn't have the slightest problem reading it.

"No. They gave us the full lesson."

"These are all written with strange letters. They look like Egyptian hieroglyphics. Or Chinese."

"Same as these."

"Meaningless gibberish," said Ricardo. "No . . . I don't understand it. Not a word—if they are words, that is." His voice betrayed an obvious despondency. He looked around with disdain. "This is a waste of time," he said. "Let's get out of here. There's still another room on this floor, let's go have a look."

Ricardo hurried out of the library. It almost seemed to Hector like he was fleeing the place.

The room next door was a communal dormitory. They counted fifteen beds lined up in a row against the wall. They were no more than empty frames, with nothing that could be taken for a blanket or a pillow. In front of each bed was a wardrobe, each in varying stages of decline. There was also a mountain of small dressers piled up against the wall. For a moment, Hector feared that someone had heaped them on top of another winged warrior, but when he saw a window just above he gathered that someone had piled the furniture to reach the skylight.

Ricardo climbed up the furniture and peered his head out of the open window. Dust and cobwebs rained down on his shoulders, but he didn't seem to mind.

"The roof's not in bad shape," he said from outside. "And there's something that looks like an attic a few feet away. Let's go up to take a look."

"I'm not going out on the roof, whether it's in good shape or not," Hector protested. The very idea of it made him feel faint. "I have vertigo and a tendency to fall. It's a bad combination."

"Fine. Natalia, stay with him. I'll go alone."

"No!" she replied. "Why do I have to babysit?"

"Hey!"

"I won't go too far, don't worry," said Ricardo. "If you need me, just yell. And if I yell, I want you out here right away, vertigo or not. Got it?"

He disappeared through the skylight so quickly that it looked like something sucked him through from above. For a while there was only silence, and Hector worried that maybe something had happened. But soon they heard his footsteps on the roof, slow and hesitant at first, then firm and confident.

"I hate this place," groaned Natalia, looking at Hector.

"All right, already!" he shouted, sick of the same old refrain. "I don't like it either, but I don't go on about it!"

"At least I'm trying to be useful! You're nothing more than a nuisance!"

"Oh, sure! I've seen how useful you are!" Hector said. He pointed to the bruise on his forehead. "You almost killed me with that blow!"

"Because you're a nuisance who doesn't look where he's going!"

"And you're crazy! And dangerous!"

Natalia shot him a look of such fury that he thought she'd hit him again. But what happened next took him by surprise: the girl burst into tears. It was a heartbreaking weeping that made her shake from head to toe. It was as if a sad Natalia burst like an explosion through the furious Natalia, as if something inside her just gave up. Hector took a hesitant step toward her, not knowing what to say or do.

"I'm not crazy," she stammered.

"I . . ." whispered Hector. "I'm sorry, I didn't mean to offend you . . ."

"No . . . you don't understand." Natalia shook her head. Her voice trembled. "Denestor tricked me!"

"He tricked all of us."

"No, no, no . . ." She shook her head more forcefully, if that was possible. Hector watched as a tear slid down, a shooting star of salt water. "He told me that my elves were here, and it's not true! He tricked me! He's a liar! He tricked me!"

Hector stared at the young girl, without understanding a thing. He would have preferred a thousand times over that she'd hit him with her stick—that wouldn't have been half as bewildering.

"Your . . . elves?"

"They gave me pills, you know? My parents gave me pills because they said I wasn't well, that my brain didn't work like it should." She ran her hand through her hair. It was so tangled that for a moment it seemed like her hand might get trapped there. "I'm not crazy. I see things, I've seen them forever, since I was little. I call them elves, although they don't look like elves from fairy tales. They're like shadows that bend and twist in on themselves. They always hide in places where only I can see them. Under my bed, in the wardrobe, or behind chairs . . . And they talk to me . . . They tell me things about people . . . Where they've been, what they've done . . . What they say about me. They also bring me things, things they found when no one was looking. They liked me," she confessed, her eyes bright with tears, "and I liked them. They were my friends. But my parents didn't . . . didn't understand. They thought that something happened to me, you know? They thought I was crazy! And when I showed them all the things that the elves gave me . . . all the rings, the necklaces, the pendants, the bracelets . . . they thought I stole them!"

Hector looked uncertainly toward the skylight, wishing that Ricardo would fall through it to free him from this embarrassing situation. But they could hear him no longer, not even his footsteps on the roof. Natalia clenched her fists and shook her head more and more forcefully. It was hard to understand her through her sobbing and wailing.

"And a stupid doctor gave me pills," she said, her eyes wide open. "And the elves left, you know? The pills made them go away. And since then the shadows have been nothing but shadows and it's the saddest thing that ever happened to me. I even thought . . . I thought . . . that they were right, that I was crazy and that the elves were a product of my imagination . . ." She swallowed. "And last night . . . Denestor came with his pipe and his stories . . . And I didn't know what to think . . . When he told me that I was special and that nobody realized it . . . I thought it was because of my elves! Do you know how relieved I felt? I asked him if the elves were in Rocavarancolia and he told me they were! How could I not want to go with him? He was going to reunite me with my friends! With my family! But they're not here! He lied to me!"

She fell to her knees, exhausted from crying. Hector approached her slowly. Natalia trembled; she was shivering out of control, almost convulsing. He knelt at her side and put a clumsy arm around her shoulder. She flung herself against his chest, crying her eyes out. Hector held her halfheartedly. He was very bad at consoling people.

"Don't tell the others, please," begged Natalia. "Don't tell them that I'm crazy. Please, please, please . . ."

He thought about the spider that stopped him from escaping, about Denestor and Lady Scar, about the rag birds that devoured his family's memories. He thought about the winged skeleton in the room below and its eternal smile. He held the young girl tight. She was warm and trembling in his hands, all bones and tears underneath the absurdly large sweatshirt she wore.

"You're not crazy," he assured her in a firm voice. And he really believed it. He really believed that Natalia's elves were real. "I believe you," he assured her.

She sniffed, and wiped her face with her sleeve.

"You don't believe me," she replied, and smiled a little. "You're saying that to make me feel better."

"No. I'm serious. I believe you. And you're right. Denestor tricked you. He said he wouldn't lie to us, and he lied to you. Your elves aren't here."

Natalia shook her head and buried her face deeper in Hector's sweatshirt.

"No, he didn't tell me the truth, but he didn't lie," she explained, and then looked around the room out of the corner of her eye. Something in her look and the tone of her voice told Hector he wasn't going to like what the girl was about to say. "Because there are shadows here too . . . They're hiding everywhere. But they're not mine; even though they look like them, they're not. They don't talk. They only watch us. They stalk us. My elves were nice, they liked me . . . These shadows . . . they want to hurt us, Hector. I know it. I'm sure of it." She separated from him and grabbed her stick tightly. "They don't like us."

"Is there an elf with us now?" He wanted to know, without really wanting to.

Natalia nodded. She raised her stick with a trembling hand and pointed at a fallen dresser close to the window.

"There are two crouched there, at one end. They keep looking at us. You don't see them because the wardrobe's hiding them. If you move, they'll retreat. They'll always stay just out of view. I'm the only one who can see them. Only me."

Hector didn't say anything. He could also see things that the others couldn't. Was Natalia under a spell herself? But, if that were the case, the spell must have been cast long before she came to Rocavarancolia.

He suddenly heard voices and thought it was Natalia's shadows, muttering out of sight. But the sounds came from the square.

"Do you hear that?" asked the girl.

Hector nodded. There was quite a commotion outside.

"It's Marco and the others. They're calling us."

They heard running footsteps above their heads. Ricardo climbed back down through the skylight, out of breath.

"They found the others!" he told them. He noticed that both were on the ground, sitting only inches apart, their cheeks red. "What are you doing?"

"Nothing!" Natalia exclaimed. She jumped up and wiped away her tears with her forearm.

Hector stood up too. He approached the window and looked out of the corner of his eye at the spot where Natalia said the elves were spying on them. He found nothing there, but he wasn't expecting to. He leaned out. The voices seemed to come from below, but he couldn't see anyone. They must be waiting for them at the building's entrance.

"She's terrified," he heard Marina say.

"Wouldn't you be?" asked a voice he didn't recognize.

"I already am," she answered. "But at least I understand what everyone's saying, and that helps."

Hector was moving away from the window when a sudden brightness in the distance stopped him in his tracks. It was a bronze glow, a spark of dusty light that hovered in front of the mountain citadel. He squinted his eyes and made out two other sparks, one on either side of the first. And they were moving. They moved much more slowly than Lady Serena's sphere, but it was obvious that they were flying toward the city.

"Are you coming down or what?" yelled Marco from the first floor. "We have visitors!"

"We're coming!" Ricardo answered. He was behind Hector, with his gaze fixed on the sparks in the sky. "What the heck is that?"

"Ships," announced Natalia from the other window. "They're ships."

And then Hector saw the sails stretched out in the wind. He could almost see the coordinated movement of the oars on both sides. There were three ships that cut through the air as if it were a calm sea. One came directly toward them, while the others turned to the left and right. In the bow of the first ship was the hazy shadow of a man.

"That's impossible," Ricardo whispered.

"Nothing's impossible over here," said Hector, impressed in spite of himself. "We're in Rocavarancolia. The kingdom of miracles and wonders." Denestor Tul hadn't lied about that.

THE HARVEST

There were four of them, three girls and a boy, all dressed in similar clothing: worn-out shorts and loose shirts made from dark fabric. Outfits that most likely weren't the ones they were wearing when they came to Rocavarancolia.

One of them, a skinny, lanky girl with long dark hair, sat on the ground with her back against the wall, her right foot bare. Her ankle was horribly swollen, and by the expression on her face even the breeze made it hurt. A robust, plain-looking girl sat next to her. She, too, had dark hair, and enormous, expressive dark eyes. Their hair was wet and disheveled.

The other two, to Hector's surprise, turned out to be twins, so beautiful that they outshone everyone around them. It was as if they absorbed all of the surrounding light to adorn themselves. The girl had red hair pulled back in a long, messy braid; the boy had short hairthat showed off his tall forehead. Their eyes were green. Their presence was so magnificent that even the old clothes they wore couldn't detract from their radiance. Hector felt insignificant next to them.

"And here we have four more of Denestor Tul's recruits," announced Marco. "The two siblings are Madeleine and Alexander."

The red-haired boy inclined his head in a gesture that was almost a bow.

"I'm Lizbeth Carroll, from Aberdeen, Scotland," said the plain girl, interrupting Marco's introductions. She spoke so quickly that it was hard to tell her words apart. "We don't know her name," she added, pointing to the wounded girl. "She still hasn't drunk from the fountain."

"You've done it already?" Ricardo seemed surprised.

"We were the first ones here," Alexander answered. He spoke with tremendous confidence, as if everything happening was perfectly normal. "And we were so thirsty that we almost dove head first into the fountain. You know how it works. As soon as we took a drink, we started talking in Rocavarancolian or whatever the heck it is, as if we'd been doing it all our lives."

Bruno knelt down next to the wounded girl while they finished the introductions. He brought water from the fountain in his cupped hands and offered her a drink. She shot a questioning glance at Lizbeth, who nodded her head. Only then did she drink, taking small sips like a bird.

"Well, I think we can give you an official welcome to Rocavarancolia," said Marco with a smile.

But the perplexed expression on the young girl's face didn't change, and when she spoke in a choppy, pained voice, all that came from her lips were unintelligible sounds. She looked around again, as bewildered as before.

"It doesn't work," said Bruno. By his toneless voice it was hard to tell if he was surprised or discouraged. "We obviously don't understand what she's saying, and she doesn't understand a word of what we're saying."

"You must have done something wrong," Natalia said.

"Giving someone a drink is a relatively simple task, Natalia. And I can assure you that, given the circumstances, I did it pretty well."

"Maybe she has to drink from the fountain herself," Marina commented. "It could be that the spell doesn't work if someone helps her."

"That sounds more reasonable."

Lizbeth and Natalia helped the injured girl to stand up, and they walked slowly toward the fountain, supporting her between them. Marco offered to carry her in his arms, but Lizbeth said that she didn't think it was necessary or a good idea.

"I wouldn't want someone I don't know carrying me around like a little girl," she said.

Hector thought Lizbeth looked exactly like that: a small, plump girl. She was shorter than Adrian and twice as round. Nature had given her rather coarse, blunt features, but there was something in her brown-eyed gaze that brought harmony to her face.

Adrian had climbed from snake to snake in order to get to the highest point of the fountain. From there, sitting astride the neck of the gigantic python at the top, he watched the trajectories of the flying ships. One of them slowly approached the square while the others moved in different directions, one to the right and the other to the left.

"What happened to her?" asked Hector, pointing his chin in the direction of the girl moving slowly across the square.

"It happened right after we got here," Madeleine explained. "We were all dazed by the change of language and everything else when we heard screams."

Her brother pointed to a building in the distance, a dilapidated shack between square and the large building where they'd woken up.

"They came from over there," he said. "And they got more and more desperate. We didn't understand a word, of course, but even so we took off running toward them."

"She was wandering around the house when the ground gave out beneath her, and she fell into the flooded basement below," his sister explained. "She could hardly keep herself afloat when we arrived." She touched her left cheek with her right hand, and then the right cheek with her left hand, as if she wanted to verify that they were still there. "Oh, Alex, I think I have a fever," she said. Then she let out a tired sigh and resumed the story. "We had a real hard time getting her out. We all ended up soaked," she said, although in comparison with the others, she was relatively dry. "Luckily we found some hampers with clothes right there in the house and we were able to change."

"Then you arrived, and shortly after came the green bubble with the Wicked Witch of the West."

"How odd," whispered Ricardo. "That you're sister and brother. Denestor brought you both at the same time?"

"Yes," Alex answered. "Although he appeared to me first. I was in the living room watching a movie and suddenly this gray character appeared in my chair out of nowhere. He almost gave me a heart attack, I swear." He laughed. "He made all of this sound so exciting that it didn't take him long to convince me. Then we both talked to Maddie and it was smooth sailing. Needless to say, it was 'Rocavarancolia, here we come!'"

"You realize that Denestor wasn't completely honest, right?" Hector asked. The redhead's enthusiasm was even more annoying than Adrian's; at least Adrian realized the gravity of the situation after Lady Scar's speech.

"He didn't say anything untrue," Alex maintained. "He clearly hid some things, but I don't think it's that big a deal. Okay, so he didn't tell us that it would be so dangerous, but what's life without a little excitement?"

"It's wonderful," Hector pointed out.

"It's boring," the other one said. "Look at us, kid. Yesterday we were living our dull, gray lives and now we're smack in the middle of a fantastic adventure. Isn't it fabulous?"

"My life wasn't dull or gray," Marina pointed out. "And I'm not here because I want to be, I assure you."

"Then why did you come?" asked Alexander, surprised.

"Because she didn't have a choice," Ricardo answered. "None of us did."

"You're wrong," the redhead answered, suddenly serious. "Denestor made it clear to me that the decision to come or not was mine alone to make, that no one else could make me do it."

"That's what he made you believe. Another one of his half-truths. No. Don't fool yourself: we didn't have a choice. He drugged us, Alexander. Denestor Tul drugged us."

"Excuse me?"

"The smoke from his pipe altered our senses," Marco explained. "He used it to dull our minds and make us not think too much about what we were doing."

Alex seemed surprised by the news, but then he smiled in disdain.

"Well, in my case he could have spared the pipe and the smoke." He spread his arms. "Please: look around you. We're in another world. In another world! How many people on Earth would kill for the opportunity to see something like this? Who in their right mind could say no to an opportunity like this?"

"Me," whispered Marina.

"And me," Hector hurried to say.

"Me too," answered Marco.

"I said, 'in their right mind'," pointed out Alexander.

Ricardo shook his head and started to stride toward the fountain. The rest of the group quickly followed. Halfway there he stopped suddenly and turned toward the redhead, who was watching him closely, as if he sensed that the conversation was far from over.

"We're not volunteers or anything close," Ricardo shot back. "We're not here by our own free will, no matter what the lady with the scars says or thinks. Didn't you hear her? She made it very clear: *The harvest.* That's what she called us. That's what we are to her. And that sums it up: they didn't bring us to Rocavarancolia, they harvested us. And there's a huge difference between the two."

"I guess it's a matter of perspective," whispered Alexander.

"I didn't like it at all when Denestor's pen pricked my finger when I signed," said Madeleine. "It was very unpleasant. Not to mention unsanitary. I wouldn't be surprised if I got an infection." She sighed as she touched her cheeks again. "I have a fever, I'm sure of it."

"It doesn't work," Natalia informed them when they reached the fountain. They'd set the injured girl on the ground for magic water fountain failure round two. "Either the fountain's spell has worn off, or it just doesn't have an effect on her. Who knows why."

"So how are we supposed to understand each other?" asked Adrian from up above. He'd contorted himself between the snakes till he ended up upside down, his forehead pressed against the intertwined tails of two vipers.

"We'll think of something, don't worry," Ricardo told him. "And stop acting like a monkey. The last thing we need now is another accident."

Marco crouched down next to the girl with no name, smiled, and showed her the palms of his hands. Then he indicated with a gesture that he wanted to examine her ankle. She shivered but nodded weakly and complied. Even though she had to clench her teeth more than once, she never complained while Marco palpated her ankle with a surprising gentleness for someone with such large hands.

"Nothing is broken," the German boy finally said. "It's only a sprain, although a pretty bad one. She'll need a good bandage and a lot of rest."

"Aren't you kind of young to be a doctor?" asked Madeleine.

"My father owns a gym in Berlin," he explained as he stood up. The young man's size once again made an impression on Hector: he must have been six feet two or taller. "And I spend so much time there that I've learned a lot about injuries."

"About causing them or curing them?" Ricardo inquired.

"I'm pretty good at both," Marco answered with a huge grin.

"Can you hear that?" asked Marina suddenly, tilting her head a little. "Like some strange music?"

Hector listened closely. She was right. He heard a distant humming; it sounded like a children's song carried by the wind.

"It's coming from the ship," Ricardo whispered.

"It's not a ship," Adrian said suddenly, now in an upright position among the snakes. "It looks like one, but it's not."

It wasn't until the ship entered their field of vision that Hector and the others discovered what he was talking about.

It wasn't really a ship, in the same way that Denestor Tul's birds weren't really birds. The hull of the flying ship turned out to be an enormous bronze bathtub, with feet shaped like the claws of a lion. The metal sides had holes through which various old brooms and mops stuck out, slicing through the sky like oars. Between the brooms and mops hung four giant wicker baskets, two on each side of the bathtub. The sails were fabricated from shirts and pants, all stitched together. And in the bow, steering the crazy thing, was a scarecrow dressed as a sailor.

"Eye of sturgeon and jellyfish soup," sang a strange voice, a voice that seemed made of weeds and hay. "It's time to fill our bellies! Come, come, come! I have rat pies and scurvy buns! Leprosy ice cream and scolopendra preserves!"

"Pinch me," Hector heard someone say. "This is a dream. It can only be a dream."

"It's our food."

"Disgusting!" Madeleine exclaimed. "He can't seriously be talking about leprosy ice cream! That's revolting!"

"If we take into account that our provisions are being delivered by a flying bathtub captained by a scarecrow, I don't think we should discount, at least not entirely, the possibility that he may be telling the truth." Bruno tapped his index finger to his chin several times. "Even considering the fact that, frankly, it must be very difficult to prepare leprosy ice cream."

"What's scolopendra?" asked Adrian from above. "A fruit?"

"A centipede. A bug."

"A type of myriapod, to be exact," corrected the Italian, in his tiresome voice.

The flying bathtub arrived at the square but showed no intention of landing or unloading the wicker baskets which supposedly held their provisions. They all looked up as it passed over their heads. The keel gleamed under the Rocavarancolia sun.

Hector was engrossed in studying the bathtub when someone jabbed him in the side. It was Natalia, who pointed at one of the dilapidated buildings in the square.

"There," she indicated in a whisper. "Can you see it?"

The boy shook his head at first, but then furrowed his brow when he detected a quick movement that he couldn't quite focus on. It could have been a silhouette that ducked around a corner of the building, or maybe just the wind blowing trash around.

"I don't know," he answered. He too lowered his voice. "I'm not sure. Could it be one of those shadows that's stalking us?"

"Are you stupid? I already told you that you can't see them. Only I can. No. It's something else."

Natalia moved to the left to get a better view. After a moment, she came back, shrugged, and shook her head.

"I've got ambrosias and delights!" sang the scarecrow. His head was an enormous brown sack, with two mismatched buttons for eyes and a poorly stitched slit for a mouth. Hector had never imagined that a scarecrow could look so sinister. "Follow me, follow me! Soon you can eat till you burst!"

The ship left them behind and continued its route, entering the city in a slow, wobbly fashion. The brooms and mops cut through the air, all in unison; the sail of stitched clothing swelled and deflated in a steady rhythm, as if an invisible being blew to inflate it and then needed to rest for an instant to catch its breath.

Ricardo and Marco held a quick conversation in a low voice. From time to time, one or the other glanced at the slow advance of the ship over the buildings.

"Follow me, follow me," sang the scarecrow.

"It would be best if we split up," Ricardo said to the group, after slapping Marco on the shoulder. "Lizbeth, Marina, and I will stay with the wounded girl. The rest will follow that thing. With a little luck it will land soon and you won't have to get too far away."

"I'm staying too," said Hector. "I don't feel very well." The idea of going into Rocavarancolia made his hair stand on end.

"No," said Ricardo. "You're going with the others." The tone of his voice was cutting, and left no room for a response. Hector looked at him with his mouth agape, surprised by the sudden abruptness. "Or does walking give you vertigo, too?" he asked. "Or don't you feel like expending energy on something as absurd as getting food?"

"Are you scolding me?" asked Hector in a low voice, so the others didn't hear.

"Yes, I'm scolding you," Ricardo confirmed, also in a whisper.

"So you're the boss then?" asked Alex, with a hint of sarcasm. "Did you take a vote before we arrived, or did you elect yourself?"

Ricardo looked him up and down.

"Boss? No, you're mistaken, I'm not the boss of anything," he assured him. They both smiled as if they were the best friends in the world, but it was clear by their tone and posture that they were testing one another. "It's just that Marco and I thought that the best thing right now is to split up. The injured girl can't walk, and someone needs to stay with her while the others go after . . . the bathtub of grub or whatever the hell it is . . . If you have a better idea, let's have it. We'll listen."

Alex shrugged without taking his eyes off Ricardo. The situation clearly amused him.

"Don't get me wrong, I don't have a problem with you being the boss," he said. "I was just surprised by how quickly you took command. That's all." He flashed a brilliant smile before saying, "I'll find a pretty conch shell for you to blow during our meetings."

"Don't bother us with your nonsense, Alex," his sister nagged. "It's always the same with you. Can we go after that thing, please? I'm starving."

The spyglasses from the balustrade fled in terror when Esmael swooped down on the terrace.

Lady Serena took a step back, startled also by the sudden arrival of the black angel. He was an expert at appearing unannounced; no less was expected of him, given his position as Lord of Assassins. He often boasted that nobody could see him if he didn't want them to. And it wasn't sorcery or alchemy or any other type of magic art, just skill and stealth at their finest. "Many who are now ghosts still wonder who killed them," he used to say.

The black angel crouched down on the balustrade, with his red wings stretched out to their fullest and his head inclined toward Lady Serena. The sunlight made the diamonds encrusted in his skin sparkle.

"A bow? Are you bowing to me?" asked the ghost. She felt flattered despite herself. Esmael might have been a despised assassin, but he was also a beautiful creature. And Lady Serena, despite being dead, was not immune to beauty. "What an undeserved honor!"

"I want to apologize for my lack of tact. I should not have sent Enoch. That stupid vampire has distorted my message."

"On the contrary. He couldn't have made it clearer: if I support your path to the regency, as recompense, you'll return my life to me."

"As I suspected." Esmael shook his head with remorse. "He conveyed the message in reverse. I never intended to buy you; I respect you too much for that. The only thing that idiot should have said is that there is a possibility that I can obtain for you a new . . . mortal casing, shall we say? I would do it right now if I could, I assure you. It doesn't matter in the least what your decision will be regarding Huryel's successor."

"But you need more power than you currently possess, isn't that right? You need the Jewels of the Iguana, and you can only get your hands on them if you're regent of Rocavarancolia."

Esmael sighed with poorly faked sadness.

"That is correct, my lady. Most of the book's spells require a wealth of energy that is far greater than that which I can generate."

"What book are you referring to?" she asked, in a casual tone.

Esmael remained silent for a moment, as if pondering whether it was advisable to respond to that question.

"It's a dark and bloody text," he finally answered. "Necromancy and black magic so monstrous that it scares even me. It's the grimoire that belonged to Hurza the Eye-Eater, the first Lord of Assassins of Rocavarancolia and one of the founders of the kingdom."

"Hurza's grimoire was lost centuries ago."

"And it remained lost for centuries, my lady. Until I found it."

"Where?"

"Does it matter? The book of spells of the first Lord of Assassins is in my power. And one of the spells that it contains is the Call to Reincarnation: the means by which I intend to restore your life to you."

"When and if you achieve your goal of attaining the regency and the Jewels of the Iguana."

"We just went in a lovely circle in our discussion, my lady. But yes. That's it exactly."

The ghost floated until she was level with the black angel.

"How do I know for certain that you have Hurza's grimoire?" she asked, dryly. "How do I know that you're not trying to trick me?

"Because I give you my word."

"And I wouldn't doubt it, Lord of Assassins, but I'd like to have something concrete to back it up. Call me suspicious, if you like, but I believe in actions more than oaths." She looked Esmael in the eye. The depth of his gaze was impenetrable; his eyes were two black wells of iniquity. "Show me the grimoire and put my doubts to rest."

The black angel fidgeted in discomfort. He turned his head to the left and right, and then looked beyond the balustrade, toward the city in ruins.

"I won't do it," he said. "It's not safe. The grimoire must remain where it is. But you will know that I have it, I promise. There are certain spells within it that I can perform. At midnight I'll give you the proof that you desire. I will execute one of the forgotten spells. Only for you, my sweet lady."

"I will wait impatiently for that proof," said the spirit. She turned her gaze also toward the city in ruins. "Old Belisarius claimed that the essence of one of the children is the essence of kings," she pointed out. "That would turn out to be paradoxical, right? So much time spent longing to be regent of Rocavarancolia and now that the chance of achieving it exists, there's also the chance that you won't enjoy much time in the position. There's no need for a regent when a king is seated on the throne."

"For that to happen the boy must survive," said Esmael.

"And that is a very remote possibility, but a real one. Unless, of course, you don't want him to survive. Then there's nothing and no one that can save him."

Esmael smiled.

"I'm amazed at how low an opinion you have of me." He straightened to his full height over the balustrade. "Are you insinuating that I would be capable of placing my ambition ahead of the good of the kingdom? Do I seem crazy enough to murder a legitimate king? Do you think me that heartless—that I could raise my hand against someone blessed with royal blood?"

Lady Serena sat silent and let her face provide the answer. A stony coldness spread across her features, freezing her expression in a grimace of contempt.

Esmael brought the palm of his hand to his mouth and opened his eyes in a bad imitation of innocence.

"How foolish. Such audacity . . ." he whispered. "I forgot that you, precisely you, ended the life of His Majesty, Maryalé. Who was not only your king, but also your beloved spouse. How could I have been so insensitive?"

"Because you're a swine, Esmael. Because you only exist to cause harm." If the wrath she felt had been fire, it would have turned an entire mountain to ash in an instant.

"Once again I have no choice other than to beg your forgiveness. But don't let your feelings about me blind you; don't let your hatred divert your attention from what really matters. Think about the book, my lady. Think of what we could both achieve if I gained the great honor of becoming regent."

And Esmael, the black angel, flew off. His wings, red as freshly spilled blood, shook in the air and carried him away. In his wake he left Lady Serena trembling with rage.

As they followed the strange ship, Hector was able to confirm that chaos was the natural state of Rocavarancolia. And it wasn't just because a large part of the city was in ruins: he got the impression that disorder was something innate to the city, even before disaster had ravaged it.

To begin with, the terrain on which the city was settled was so irregular that it seemed impossible that anyone in their right mind would build there. The ground was a succession of breaks, cracks, hills, and gullies which made it difficult to find a single yard of flat land.

The buildings were arranged as well as they could be over that geographic disarray, the foundations leaning against rocky hillocks or lurking in the bottoms of shallow ravines; the streets and alleyways, most of them narrow and winding, adapted to the geographical features with varying luck, like a dress made by a bad seamstress for an awkwardly shaped client.

And if the terrain was a marvel of rarities, the same could be said of the structures that made up the city. There was no pattern or cohesion; it looked as if it had been designed by a legion of architects from the most diverse styles. To walk through Rocavarancolia was to walk through a hundred different cities at the same time, all of them miraculous, while also sinister and absurd. The most ramshackle hovels shared a street with architectural works of art; dark and scary buildings crouched down in the shadow of towers so delicate that they appeared to be carved out of air. Everything was nonsense and madness.

To top off the chaos of such scenery was the black magic that Lady Serena had instilled in his brain. It floated in front of doors of buildings that seemed inoffensive, it stretched like a cat on rooftops and windows, it lurked in the entries to alleyways . . . It was a constant presence that Hector began to think of as a living being; the way that the dark ribbons contracted and extended reminded him of tired breathing. Shortly after they started out, he discovered a covered well over which floated a long thread of dark mist, and a little further away, a tower crowned by a hazy fence of mist, like a torch of black fire. In any case, the greatest concentration of darkness remained behind him, entirely surrounding the red cathedral on the outskirts of town. That hulking mass appeared more shrouded in darkness than anywhere else. Hector would not have approached the place for anything in the world.

"It's the most horrible thing I've ever seen," Natalia said when Hector turned toward the cathedral for the umpteenth time.

"I agree," he responded. "It looks like it's made to scare people, don't you think?"

"The whole city looks like it's made for that," she groaned.

The sun had reached its highest point in the sky and begun to descend behind the ruined city. There were puddles everywhere, reminders of the previous night's storm. The bronze bathtub, with the four baskets swaying at its sides, moved so slowly that they had no trouble following it. For the moment, it didn't look like it was about to land. By the stroke of mop and broom, it continued its stubborn course northeast. It was difficult to calculate how long they'd been following it, but for Hector, tired and hungry as he was, it felt like an eternity. Besides, he had to stop constantly to wrap his feet in the rags that he was using as makeshift shoes. He'd almost fallen to the ground twice.

"Arrr," the flamboyant helmsman yelled suddenly. He shook his straw head and began singing once again: "There are no cannons onboard, but we do have mulberries and tender bats! The hold is out of rum and full of ambrosia and bloody soup! Come one, come all!"

"Do you think he's serious about the tender bats?" asked Adrian as Hector tied the filthy rags around his feet again.

"They're probably hard as a rock," he answered. "I'm so hungry that soon I'll be gnawing on cobblestones."

As if to echo his sentiment, his stomach let out a long, loud growl.

Adrian broke out in laughter. The sound seemed as out of place in the city as his pajamas. Hector tied the two ends of the rags on his left foot together and kept walking.

They continued downhill on a narrow street. The buildings on the left looked as if they'd been knocked over one by one like dominoes. On the other side of the street, however, a row of decent three-story houses remained upright in perfect condition. From their dusty façades an army of deformed gargoyles and monsters made from stone watched them as they passed.

Marco had already reached the other end. Waiting on a rock, he saw something on the right that remained hidden from Hector's view. He kept so still that he seemed to have more in common with the stone sculptures adorning the buildings than with the rest of the group.

They gathered around once they caught up to him. Marco pointed to the east. Not very far from them stood a stone tower of a dirty greenish color; it was a massive structure four stories tall, situated on top of a hill. It was surrounded by a moat and a small creek that flowed mightily over the rocky ground. There were two bridges, one in front of the other: the first crossed the creek and the second, an ostentatious drawbridge, stretched across the moat.

"I don't know how much time we're going to spend in this city," said Marco, "but it's clear that we're going to need a place to stay while we're here. And I like this tower. It's in a good location, and besides, it has a moat around it. It gives me a good feeling. What do you say?"

"I like the color," said Alexander. The redhead wielded a white wooden stick that he'd taken from a mountain of rubble, and entertained himself by using it to whack a loose cobblestone. "But we have to consult with our fearless leader when we get back. He commands, we obey."

Hector scrutinized it in the distance. There was no trace of black mist in the area of the tower, and it truly was in an exceptional location. Besides, there were no buildings nearby and it could be assumed that someone situated on the battlements could keep watch over a great stretch of terrain.

When they started walking again, Alexander hung back a bit to walk next to Hector.

"Have you read *The Lord of the Flies*?" he asked. He had his left arm over his head and was rubbing his neck.

"What?" Hector looked at him blankly.

"*The Lord of the Flies*, the book. Have you read it?"

"No, I haven't read it."

"Well, do you know what it's about?"

He had a vague and distant recollection of starting to watch a movie based on that story. It was about a group of kids that ended up on a deserted island after a plane crash. There weren't any adults with them and they had to fend for themselves.

"I started to watch the movie when I was little, but I didn't finish it," he answered, as he tried to remember. "I don't remember it very well. I think that at some point something scared me and I changed the channel. Why do you ask?"

"You remind me a little of one of the characters in the book." He winked. "But you don't wear glasses."

Hector raised an eyebrow. He remembered that one of the main characters was a chubby kid that the others made fun of. And he was the only one who wore glasses.

"Are you trying to insult me or something?" he asked. "Because if that's what you're going for, you're doing a lousy job."

Alexander started to laugh. Somehow the redhead's laughter, unlike Adrian's, fit perfectly with Rocavarancolia. There was a hint of madness in it, of chaos.

"No, no, no," he said. "Don't take it the wrong way. Somehow all of this reminds me a little of the book, you know? Children lost in a savage place, with no adults . . . That's why I mentioned it. The book had some pretty rough parts. I haven't seen the movie, but I guess it could scare a sensitive person."

"I'm not sensitive."

"I didn't say you were."

Hector scowled at him. He didn't know where this conversation was going. He was tired and irritable, and although he had only just met Alexander, the boy was already proving to be unfriendly. He knelt down to check out the rags on his feet, more to end the absurd conversation than because he needed to. Alex kept walking, and when he saw Hector lagging behind, he turned to him, yelling, "Let's go, Fatty! The bathtub's getting away from us!"

Hector shook his head, puzzled.

"Did he just call me Fatty?" he asked Natalia, who was just passing him.

"Yes, he did call you that. Forget it. He's an idiot."

"No, he's not an idiot," Madeleine replied. "He never remembers anyone's name, and that's why he always gives people ridiculous nicknames. Would you believe that for years he called me Alexa?" She sighed. "Please don't take him seriously. Alex can be annoying, but he's harmless."

Hector snorted, gave a hard yank on the rag on his right foot, and kept walking. Something in the sky caught his attention for an instant, a fleeting light that flashed between two distant buildings. It didn't happen again, and Hector quickly directed his attention back to Alexander, his brow still furrowed. The redhead was now walking next to Marco, both chatting with excitement. The German kid pointed to the bathtub, and the other said something that Marco responded to with a laugh. Adrian walked behind them, his head down, absorbed in the movement of his feet; he looked even smaller in that pose. Bruno walked further back, a little apart from the others, very upright; he looked like he was stuffed into his checkered shirt and corduroy pants like a sausage. There was something old fashioned, even ancient, about Bruno, and not only because of his clothing, which could have emerged from the depths of an old man's wardrobe. It was something that showed in the way he trod, slow and methodical, and even in the way he expressed himself.

Madeleine and Natalia walked right in front of Hector, next to each other, but without speaking. Alex's sister moved as if the world belonged to her; Natalia, on the other hand, walked tensely, as if she expected an attack at any moment. From time to time he saw her look at the dark alleyways, her eyes narrowed, watching, perhaps, for the shadows that only she could see.

Four of them had stayed behind in the square. Ricardo, who from the first moment had placed himself at the helm; Marina, beautiful with her black dress, her blue eyes, and her languor; Lizbeth, whom he had yet to form an opinion on; and finally, the girl with no name, who nobody knew anything about. There were eleven of them. And they were still missing one to make the twelve that, according to the hideous Lady Scar, had been harvested by Denestor from the human world.

Why? Hector asked himself for the millionth time. *Why did they bring us to this hellish place? What do they want from us?*

THE SCAR OF ARAX

"Impressive," said Alexander.

Hector thought that word alone was enough to describe the newest wonder that Rocavarancolia had revealed to them.

Stretched out before them was something that at first glance looked like a dry riverbed. It was an enormous, twisting crevice which crossed a section of the city from one side to the other. The distance between its two edges varied, but rarely measured less than fifty feet. What shocked them, however, wasn't the crack itself—what truly impressed them was what it contained: hundreds and hundreds of skeletons, a vast number of bare bones piled atop one another, brimming over the walls of the pit in places, especially in the middle.

The teenagers were silent, astonished by the river of skeletons. And that sensation, the feeling of being overwhelmed, of contemplating something that they could never have imagined, was becoming all too familiar to Hector.

In that mass grave were skulls of monsters that were hard to describe, rib cages so vast that twelve men lying head to toe wouldn't reach from one end to the other, fearsome jawbones that jutted out among dozens of seemingly human skeletons . . . They saw a colossal skull, its jaw open in a threatening yawn that revealed two rows of long, twisted fangs; it could well be the remains of a dragon. There were more creatures than they could possibly identify. And all throughout, snaking through the bones and skulls, unfurled the black mist of Lady Serena's spell.

"This is not natural," said Bruno. Alexander let out a sarcastic burst of laughter at his comment. "I mean. . . it's not a riverbed." clarified the Italian. "See those houses?" He pointed to the left; about five hundred yards from where they stood was a mountain of debris that had fallen into the crevice, forming a bridge that joined one bank with the other. Whatever did this destroyed them too.

"Maybe it was an earthquake," ventured Natalia.

"Such a possibility exists, this is true," said Bruno as he stroked the frame of the right lens of his glasses in a mechanical manner, "although if I am to be honest, I do not consider it likely. I am no expert on earthquakes, but I suspect that if the earth shook with enough magnitude to cause that opening, it would have reduced all the buildings around it to rubble. Not to mention the entire city." His hand abandoned his glasses and began to stroke his chin. "Unless, of course, it was an unusually localized earthquake."

"Then what about all of the skeletons?" asked Adrian. "Where did they come from? Were they killed by the same thing that caused the crack?"

"I cannot answer that question," said Bruno.

"Sure you can," corrected Marco. "The answer's right under your nose. You've seen it before, flying from one side to another . . . And it snatched you from your own home to bring you here."

"Lady Scar? Denestor Tul?"

"No, dude, no. The same thing that destroyed this city is to blame: magic."

What you see before you is the Scar of Arax, Hector heard in his mind. The intruder's voice startled him so badly that he let out a strangled cry. Only Madeleine heard it. The redhead looked at him out of the corner of her eye, and although she didn't say a word, her expression of disdain said everything.

There was a great battle thirty years ago, the voice continued. *It was the last, the one that put an end to our dreams of conquest. For three long days the battle raged throughout the entire city. Street by street, house by house. They defeated us, of course, without mercy. But the end was a sight worth seeing. The stuff that legends are made of.*

The air boiled over with dragon's breath and enemy projectiles. The combat had reached as far as the mountain slopes. Rocavarancolia burned. Surges of pure magic consumed our spells. The enemy used brutal force. From the castle turrets we saw the vanguard of their army arriving, and we knew that all was lost.

It was then that His Majesty, Sardaurlar, left the castle on his black falcon, with his sword Arax in one hand and the reins of his mount in the other. He was alone. He wished for no one to accompany him in that last attack. The king plunged into the thick of the enemy army while the arrows, spells, and incantations depleted the magical as well as the physical protection of his shield. Two Yemei dragons pounced on him. With a single blow he decapitated one and sliced the other in two. The arrows pierced his armor, and the enemy spells tore into his flesh. Sardaurlar screamed, although not from pain. It was a scream of defiance, of pure rage. Another dragon bit off the wing of his falcon. But it didn't matter. The king leapt into the enemy armies while his dying mount fell in a spiral. He knew he was jumping to his death and he didn't care. He was always very dramatic, you know? However, there was nothing heroic in his action, make no mistake. Sardaurlar's last attack was pure cowardice: he couldn't admit to himself that he was defeated, so he undertook this suicide attack.

They killed him, of course. But his goal wasn't to survive; his goal was to unleash one last blow from Arax, his magic sword. The crack that you're looking at was caused by that blow. Sardaurlar died, but he brought over fifteen hundred of our enemies down with him. It wasn't enough to give us a chance at victory, but it gave us a legend to tell on the cold nights following our defeat.

Hector could hardly believe what he heard. It had been a man, a single man, who'd caused that crack in the earth. He looked at his companions, wanting to share the information with them and, at the same time, knowing that he couldn't. They talked in whispers, frightened by the Dante-esque spectacle and, of course, completely oblivious to the intruding voice in his head. In the sky above, the bathtub continued its slow voyage. Its shadow fell like lead over the river of bones, shifting over its surface like a ghost ship. When it passed over the areas of darkness marked by Lady Serena's spell, the shadow flickered and reappeared, reflecting the whiteness of the bones with terrible clarity.

The Scar of Arax crosses the city from east to west, the voice continued, and in it lie the remains of those who died in the battle of Rocavarancolia. It's a monument to our glorious past, to the legends that perished that day, to what might have been and was not. Here lie all our dead and many of the enemy's dead: their losses were so great that they couldn't take all the bodies back with them. And here, too, lie the bones of the children who preceded you.

Hector felt as if a frozen hand squeezed his heart. A gush of pure ice-water coursed through his veins.

And this is where you'll end up if Rocavarancolia has its way with you.

"Weapons?" Natalia said, hesitantly. She approached the edge of the gorge. "Those shiny things down there—could they be weapons?"

After a moment Alexander nodded vigorously.

"She's right! There are weapons in there with the bones! All kinds." He turned, smiling, toward Marco. "Swords, axes, spears . . . And armor! It's a whole arsenal!"

"Magic didn't put an end to Rocavarancolia," said Hector in a choked voice. His gaze was fixed on one sword, as large as a tree. "It was something much more human: it was war."

"That sounds real deep, Fatty," mocked Alexander. Hector looked at him, still stunned by Lady Serena's words; in light of all that death and destruction, who cared about a stupid nickname? "Magic. Earthquakes. It's all the same. What matters is that we have the answer to our prayers right in front of us: weapons."

"Congratulations, you just beat Hector in profound thoughts," commented Marco.

"Look, I'm hungry, and . . . well, I don't know much about these things, I admit, but something tells me that swords aren't edible," said Madeleine. "We better follow the bathtub, right? I don't think these weapons are going anywhere in the meantime."

Alex and Marco approached the edge of the crack and looked cautiously toward the bottom.

"It won't be difficult to climb down," said the redhead. Even though the wall was practically a vertical drop, it was full of crevices and notches that could be used to descend.

The voice in Hector's head returned:

One final warning about the Scar. There aren't just bones down there. So, talk your friend out of his idea or prepare to watch the first among you die.

Hector bit his lower lip. Alexander walked to the edge of the crack, looking for a good spot where he could start his descent. He turned his gaze toward the Scar of Arax. The threads of darkness stretched lazily between the piles of bones and skulls.

"I don't think it's a good idea to go down there," he warned. His voice trembled as he spoke.

"Fatty, Fatty, don't get nervous. You can stay here up above if you want." He winked at him. "I'll find something cool for you, don't worry."

Adrian was the only one who kept an eye on the bathtub's movement in the sky. The rest either watched Alexander or were still contemplating the impressive river of bones. Hector approached the edge, hesitant, not knowing how to stop Alex from climbing down into the pit. He wasn't fond of the redhead, but he didn't want anything bad to happen to him. And if he did go down there, something terrible would happen. He was convinced of it.

"Are you sure about what you're doing?" asked Madeleine. For a moment, Hector thought that she was talking to him and turned toward her, confused.

"Yes," Alex answered, and raised his head to flash her a dazzling smile. "I'm going to get weapons for all of us. That's what I'm going to do."

"We can climb down here, no problem." It was Marco who spoke, crouched next to an overhang, his forearms resting on his calves. The wall at his feet was filled with notches, so close to each other that anyone with a little agility could use them as footholds. "It's like they were made on purpose."

As Marco stood up, his right foot shifted some rocks near the edge of the crack. One of them dropped into the void and caused a small avalanche of bones. The sound made Hector's hair stand on end.

"Alex and I will climb down, and—"

"Marco," interrupted Natalia. She pointed at the pit with her stick. "You better stay up here."

"What?"

The calm of the Scar of Arax was broken. In several places the bones had begun to ripple and heave, pushed by something that slid under the surface and left in its wake a dismal wave of skulls and old weapons. The sound of the skeletons moving around made a delirious melody, a crazy, frightening rattle. Hector counted seven trails of bone, and they all moved toward the spot where the rock had fallen.

"I don't like this." Adrian took a step backward.

A set of armor gleamed as it shook in the pit. Hector saw a different whiteness emerge from among the bones: it was a milky white spine, covered with small pale bristles. It submerged again only seconds after appearing at the surface.

The scar worms, explained the voice. *Blind and deaf to everything except movement in the river of corpses where they live. They're like spiders waiting for prey to fall into their web.*

The waves of bones all converged, almost instantaneously, at the spot where the rock had fallen. Seven whirlwinds of bone and steel spun in a frenzy, some to the left and others to the right, in search of whatever had fallen from above.

Little by little calm returned, the clattering of the bones faded, and finally everything stopped. But the tranquility and silence weighed even heavier on Hector's mind than the maelstrom of shaking skeletons. Under that calm lurked the terrors of Arax, and without the telltale movement of the bones it would be impossible to know where they were. They could be anywhere. Lurking. Waiting.

It took a moment for the teenagers to react.

"There has to be another way to cross to the other side," Marco said, breaking the heavy silence that had fallen over them. "We have to go after the bathtub, remember?"

"You still want to cross this thing?" Adrian asked, horrified. He was pale and trembling. "I'm not doing it. No. No way. I want to go home. That's what I want. To go home."

"Hey, kiddo, hey!" Alex moved toward him, his arms open wide. "What are you afraid of?" he asked. "Do you really think we're going to let anything happen to you? Nonsense! We're here to protect each other, right?" He put his hands on Adrian's shoulders and adopted such a serious tone that for a second he seemed like a different person. "Forget about what the Wicked Witch of the West said, okay? No one is going to die. Nobody. Nothing is going to happen to us. And we're going to find a way to get home, I promise you. But in exchange you must promise me something: you have to swear that you won't be afraid anymore."

"I can't promise that," Adrian stammered.

"You're right. Nobody should be asked not to be afraid." He scratched his chin and was quiet for a moment, then he smiled with satisfaction, as if he'd just found the solution to a complicated problem. "You can be as scared as you want," he said, grinning, "but don't let it show, okay? Can you do that? Keep the fear inside, don't let it out."

Adrian nodded, dubious.

"Good boy." Alex tousled his head roughly. "And now let's see if we can figure out how to get ahold of that crazy bathtub."

"We can cross over the ruins," Bruno offered, pointing to the buildings that had fallen into the crevice.

Hector looked warily at the far-off bridge of rubble. Even from a distance he could see that the surface was irregular and dangerous. A slip or a loose stone would send them straight into the pit and its denizens.

"There's something before there," Natalia mumbled. "Can you see it? Halfway down the road, where the crack narrows. Another bridge."

"Yes!" Adrian exclaimed. "I see it too!"

The distance between the two rims of the scar was much smaller at the spot where Natalia pointed. A narrow rock terrace stretched from the opposite edge and stopped about fifteen feet short of the side they were on. Someone had improvised a bridge by laying what appeared to be a wooden plank across the gap between the tongue of rock and the ledge. The crossing looked even riskier to Hector than the mountain of rubble, but he said nothing as they walked toward it. He couldn't take his eyes off the bones and shadows that inhabited the Scar of Arax.

The bridge consisted of a long plank of dark wood, fairly thick, about three feet wide. It was placed on a slight incline.

"It appears to be sturdy," Bruno decided, after squatting down to examine it. He stood up and ventured a couple of steps forward. Hector bit his lip as he watched him near the center of the plank. "And so, it is. However, I suggest we take every precaution and cross one by one."

Bruno himself was the first to cross, walking like a robot or an old wind-up toy. Adrian came next, faster than a speeding bullet. Natalia took her time, rhythmically tapping her stick on the edge of the plank. Marco advanced with long, slow strides, his neck hunched between his shoulders, his gaze fixed straight ahead. Alex crossed in a carefree manner and even stopped halfway to sweep a splintered portion of the bridge with his foot. Then came Madeleine, with a walk full of grace, more suited to a ballroom than an old plank. Her red hair rippled in the breeze, more beautiful the more disheveled it became.

When his turn came, Hector didn't move.

"Come on, kid, you're up," said Marco from the other side.

He took a deep breath and tried to rouse his spirit, but it was no easy task. He had a hard time believing that bridge could hold his weight; besides, he couldn't erase from his mind the image of the clattering bones down below.

He went to take the first step, but then stopped. His legs trembled. Sweat drenched his back and the palms of his hands; it felt slick and unpleasant, as if he'd been slathered in oil.

Natalia snorted on the other side. She shook her head and started to walk back over the bridge in Hector's direction, so close to the edge of the plank that he felt sick.

"It's safe," she told him, once she reached his side. "Do you want me to hold your hand? I can do that. The bridge isn't going to fall."

Hector shook his head.

"I'll do it by myself," he stated, his voice wavering. "By myself, okay?" He bent down and retightened the rags that covered his feet. It wasn't necessary, but he didn't want Natalia to see his hands shaking.

"Well, do it in one go, come on. I'll stay here until you're across."

Hector stood up. He wiped the sweat from his forehead with his arm and took a hesitant step. Then another, this time onto the wood. The creaking plank sounded weak and fragile in his imagination. He continued nonetheless, aware of Natalia's gaze at his back and the group's impatience on the other side. When he left solid ground behind and realized that the only thing separating him from the river of bones and the monsters below was an inch of wood, he felt the impulse to get down and crawl the rest of the way. If the bridge hadn't been on an incline, he would have done it, but he was afraid of losing his balance.

"Look at me, Fatty, look right at me," Alex said from the other side, pointing to his own eyes with his index and middle fingers. "I am the center of the universe. There is nothing here but me. So look at me and keep going."

"Don't call me Fatty," he mumbled through clenched teeth, and took another step. And another.

Before he knew it he was on solid ground once more. Alex clapped him so hard on the back that he almost knocked him to the ground. He felt a mixture of relief over having crossed and great anger over having made a fool out of himself again. He felt like he'd been nothing but a fool since the moment he woke up.

"I don't like heights," he murmured, his brow furrowed. He needed to explain himself.

I'm not a nuisance, he thought, infuriated, as he looked sidelong at Natalia, who'd just crossed back.

The Russian girl ignored the group. All of her attention was focused on the flying bathtub.

"It's landing!" she said, picking up her pace.

The outrageous vessel had reached a small, rectangular plaza located about three hundred yards from the Scar of Arax and finally descended. The scarecrow maneuvered the ship as he lowered it, presumably in order to land in the square. It was a dismal place, surrounded by strange buildings, so narrow that there was only room for one door and one window on the façade of each. On top of that, none of the houses stood upright; they were all twisted to some degree, as if the foundations weren't capable of supporting their weight. Despite the sinister look of the place, there wasn't a trace of the dark mist.

The bathtub maneuvered slowly, lurching forward. Something that looked like an apple fell from a basket and split open against the ground with a sound that made Hector, now practically starving, crave something juicy. With one final jolt, the ship came to a stop about fifteen feet above the ground. All of the oars straightened out in unison with a resounding crack. The wicker baskets began to quiver and descend slowly, dangling from ropes tied to their handles. The scarecrow left the helm for the middle of the ship where he busied himself with something that the kids couldn't see, probably the mechanism that lowered the baskets.

"Come one, come all! Everything's ready!" sang the bizarre sailor. "Iguana brains and manticore juice! Essence of cockroach and newborn tongues! The juiciest meat from Rocavarancolia for Master Denestor's chosen ones!"

They hurried over, spurred on by their empty bellies. They hadn't gone even a hundred yards when Natalia stopped so suddenly that Adrian ran into her.

"No . . ." the Russian girl whispered. She held on tightly to her stick. "No! No! No!"

"What? What is it?"

Natalia pointed with the stick in the direction of one of the streets that joined up with the square. Something approached quickly from that spot. She turned her staff to point out another side street, where they saw more movement. A furry shadow emerged from the entrance of a ramshackle house, so quickly that it looked like the building spat it out. Another creature entered the square. And a third rushed in from an alleyway, growling and drooling.

"Rats!" Adrian cried, disgusted.

"No, they're not rats," Bruno murmured. There was no shock or surprise in his voice, only the usual flat coldness. "I don't know what they are. But they're not rats."

The furry creatures were larger than adult cats. They had flattened heads, with beady black eyes and elongated, toothy snouts. Their front paws were three times the size of their back ones and they had short claws that looked more bird-like than mammalian. Their tails were long and flexible, covered with clusters of bony spikes that were thicker at the end and made them look like prickly maces. They ran into the square, their heads raised in the direction of the floating ship. Hector counted at least twenty of them.

A small, nervous one with gray fur jumped toward the baskets, which were still six feet above the ground, clutched at the closest handle, and lifted itself up and into a hamper. The others ran here and there, their eyes locked on the ship.

"What do we do?" Natalia whispered. She looked at Marco first, then Alex.

"Let's go," Marco ordered. "We're leaving right now."

"But what about the food?" asked Adrian.

"If those things see us, we're going to be food," answered the boy, his gaze fixed on the frightening creatures that had taken over the square.

Once the baskets were within reach, the creatures leapt upon them, knocking them over and spilling their contents onto the rocky ground. In their eagerness to grab the contents, they lashed out at each other in fury. One of them smacked another in the face with the spiny end of his tail. The victim retreated and took revenge by sinking his teeth into the back of the closest beast.

Hector saw four more appear from a street perpendicular to the square, about a hundred yards from where he and the others pressed together against a wall for protection. The new arrivals ran toward the chaos that had broken out beneath the bathtub, when the leader stopped suddenly and turned its monstrous head in their direction. Its eyes bulged out of their sockets when it saw the teenagers. It let out a dry barking sound and, forgetting the baskets, took off toward them, even faster than before. The other three followed in unison, their heads lowered and their jaws half-open, while the rest stayed focused on the baskets in the square, still blind to the presence of Hector and his companions. On the floating bathtub, the scarecrow kept singing, not perturbed in the least by what happened down below.

Marco took a step forward, ready to confront the beasts frantically rushing toward them and snapping at the air.

"Get back . . . To the bridge, hurry." He gestured for them to retreat. He didn't raise his voice; he spoke almost in a whisper. "Run to the bridge. Come on."

Alexander and Natalia ignored his command and moved next to him, holding fast to their wooden sticks. The rest of the group moved away haltingly, without turning their backs on their companions, watching in terror as the beasts approached.

"I'm not afraid, I'm not afraid, I'm not afraid," Adrian repeated over and over, pale as a corpse. It hadn't taken him long to break the promise he'd made to Alex.

"Do you know how to use it?" Marco suddenly asked Natalia. The four animals were almost upon them.

She looked at him, perplexed, not knowing what he meant.

"Your stick! Do you know how to use it? Can you use it properly?" And since he didn't get an answer, he snatched it from her hands. In the same movement he sprung forward and intercepted the first of their attackers. He twirled the stick in the air as he leaned to the left, dodging a ferocious bite, and with a powerful smack he clubbed the creature in the head. The animal fell on its side and remained motionless at Marco's feet. The others kept coming. One of them, big as a German shepherd, feinted toward Marco and then jumped on Alex, probably figuring him for easier prey.

The redhead flexed his legs and swung his stick at the animal so forcefully that the smack in the jaw caused it to fly backward and flip through the air. It fell spread-eagle a few yards away and did not get back up.

The other two creatures pounced on Marco. He crouched to avoid the angry jaws of the first while he kicked the other right in the stomach. The two beasts recovered immediately and came at him again. Marco stood completely still, waiting for them with his eyes wide open, grasping the stick in both hands. Suddenly he seemed to dance between them. His movements were fluid, hypnotic, and the stick in his hands looked more like an extension of his body than a weapon. When the dance ended, the two creatures lay on the ground and Marco, without so much as a scratch, raised his eyes as if looking for more enemies to battle. It wasn't long before he found them.

One of the creatures in the square stuck its head out from inside a broken basket and discovered the teenagers. His growl alerted the others. Every last one of the vermin stopped to look in their direction. For a matter of seconds everything was quiet and calm; the animals seemed frozen, statues of flesh and bone that watched them with an expression of bleak hunger. Even the scarecrow ceased his singing. Without warning, the beasts ran at them. A stampede of claws, teeth, and bony spines flew in their direction.

"Back!" ordered Marco, now screaming, pointing urgently to the bridge. "Back! Everyone to the bridge! Run!"

Natalia grabbed Hector by the forearm and pulled him along so that he'd run faster. She let go when she realized that not only was he not moving faster, he was about to lose his balance. She stayed by his side until he managed to steady himself and then left him in the blink of an eye.

"Run! Run!"

Hector didn't blame her for abandoning him. The noise of the running and the howls of their attackers were deafening and, little by little, he was left behind.

The first to die, the first to die; Lady Scar said that I'd be the first to die, he thought. He felt a shooting pain in his side.

They ran at full speed onto the rock terrace. Only Marco and their attackers were behind him; the animals were closing in at an alarming rate. This time Hector didn't hesitate when he reached the bridge. The threat at his back made him forget his vertigo and what lurked below in the Scar of Arax. He practically flew over the plank and almost fell to his knees on the other side. Someone grabbed his arm to lift him up, but as nervous as he was, he couldn't tell who. Marco crossed the bridge behind him, so quickly that he almost mowed him down. Alexander met the recent arrival, panting. The two exchanged a quick glance and nodded in unison.

They crouched and grabbed the plank, one at each side. Natalia squatted next to them and stuck her fingers between the ground and the wood. The beasts still ran at them, froth and foam spraying from their mouths. When the first one reached the bridge, the boys pushed the plank on Marco's cue. The wood shook and the two animals on it fell into the void.

The others retreated in such a hurry that more than one almost followed their companions into the pit. The three teenagers gave the bridge a heave. The long plank collapsed with a rumble, and sank almost upright into the pile of bones.

The fallen creatures tried to stay atop the heap of skeletons. One howled pitifully, looking around in desperation. The other clung to one of the gigantic skulls and moved slowly to the top, whining and swinging its head from side to side.

"It's crying," Hector whispered. Seeing the terrified creature deeply disturbed him. In Rocavarancolia even the monsters had reason to be afraid.

At the bottom of the scar, the bones began to clatter once again. Skeletons and suits of armor here and there rose and fell. The waves of movement that aroused the horrors below dispelled the calm of the immense cemetery. Hector saw the milky spines appear among tibias, ribs, and skulls, all rushing toward their targets.

He wanted to look away, but something greater than his will stopped him, something primitive that until then had remained dormant inside him. A terrible crack resounded in the pit and a white shadow burst out of the bones, grabbing one of the unfortunate creatures by the neck and dragging it down into the depths, before he could even get a clear look at it. The trapped creature's howl was so horrifying that Hector covered his ears with his hands.

The beast who'd sought safety at the top of the giant skull staggered, panic-stricken. Suddenly the skull on which it stood was hit from below and burst into fragments. Hector caught a glimpse of the oversized jaws with their rows of fangs as they sliced through the flying splinters. They grabbed the animal by its hind legs and dragged it under. This time the victim didn't get a chance to scream.

Ahead of them, on the other edge of the crack, the beasts ran back and forth, without a thought for the fate of their companions in the pit.

"Let's go," Marco urged. "They're looking for another way to get across!"

"Just let them try! They'll get what's coming to them!" Alexander shook the stick that he'd used to take down one of the beasts. He was elated.

The beasts howled on the other side of the scar. One of them strutted at the edge of the crack, right across from the redhead. Its spiky tail stood straight up and shook back and forth, more and more frantically. The animal's eyes glittered with a terrifying intelligence.

"No!" Hector shouted as he realized what was about to happen. He took off running toward Alexander. "Get down! Get down on the ground!"

His warning came too late. The creature gave one last shake of its tail, and one of its spines shot out like an arrow. It sliced across the gap with a piercing whistle and struck Alex in the chest. The boy tilted backward, then forward in the direction of the pit, and finally fell to the ground in absolute silence, only inches from the edge.

"Alex!" Madeleine ran desperately toward her brother. Hector was the first to get there. He grabbed Alex under his arms and, not knowing if he were alive or dead, pulled him away from the edge. On the other side the creature began its dance over again, ready to fire another shot. Two others joined in, shaking their spiky tails with excitement. Soon more spines sliced through the air.

"Get away from the edge!" Marco yelled. He shoved Adrian, who was standing, stunned, looking at Alex on the ground.

"Let go of me!" Alex twisted in Hector's arms. The deathly stillness gave way to a terrible shaking. "Madeleine!" He was pale. What showed on his face wasn't fear: it was terror. "Where's my sister? Maddie!" he screamed, so out of his mind that he couldn't see she was right next to him, her hands clenched in fists at her mouth.

Alexander knocked Hector down in his desperation to get up. He tried to stand, wobbly, his face distorted in a mask. He still wasn't fully upright when Madeleine threw herself in his arms. The boy could hardly support the weight of another body and nearly fell again.

"I'm fine, I'm fine," he assured her. He turned to place himself between Madeleine and the creatures. His eyes shone with a fire that looked like madness, but also with relief. Alexander drew back from his sister and opened his shirt, and the bony spine fell at Hector's feet. It had managed to pierce his clothing, but lacked enough force to enter his flesh. Right over his heart was a tiny circle of reddened skin. If the creature had been even a few feet closer, Alex would be dead.

"Let's get out of here, quick!" yelled Marco frantically, though they were now outside the range of the spines, which barely reached their side of the scar. "They're crossing over the rubble!"

Several of the vermin jumped over the wreckage from the buildings that had fallen in the crack. Hector, still on the ground, counted eight making their way through façades, walls, and destroyed pillars. Natalia reached out a hand to help him up. He took it, but first decided to grab the bony spine that had almost killed Alex.

"They're coming after us!" Adrian yelled.

"Let them come," Alex whispered. His words were no longer boastful, but full of rage. He turned to face the bridge made of rubble. The leading animals were already reaching the other side. "Let them come and I'll give them what they deserve!"

"You're insane! We're leaving here right now!" Marco yelled again, grabbing him forcefully by the arm.

Alex pulled free and picked his stick up off the ground. He was out of control.

"Let them come!" he repeated, and before anyone could react, he ran toward the rubble bridge, brandishing his weapon and screaming like he was possessed.

"Alex!" his sister called.

"He's crazy! They're going to kill him!" Marco brought his hands to his head.

"Alex!" Madeleine screamed again, and fell to her knees.

Marco cursed and took off running after the redhead with Natalia's stick in hand. His yells were even louder than Alexander's.

"Hey! That's mine!" Natalia exclaimed. She looked around. She crouched down to pick up a rock off the ground, felt its heft, nodded, and ran screaming after the two boys.

Hector followed them. He acted on impulse, without thinking. Before he realized it, he was already running. In his right hand he clutched the bony spine. A sharp pain returned to his left side but that didn't matter; what mattered was the rhythmic beating of his heart and his temples, those war drums that had just awoken inside and pushed him after Alex, Natalia, and Marco, screaming like a madman. He no longer felt fear, insecurity, or even vertigo. The only thing that mattered, the only thing that was real, were the creatures that charged at them from the heaps of rubble.

And then, all of a sudden, just a couple of yards before the collision, one of the vermin stopped so abruptly that it slipped. It squeaked as if frightened, turned tail, and took off running in the opposite direction. The others followed suit, as terrified as the first. It was a full-on stampede. For a few seconds, the kids pursued the fleeing beasts.

"Come back!" Alexander yelled and swung at the air with his stick. "Come back here, you cowards! Come back!"

He stopped, panting. He let the stick fall to the ground and leaned over, his hands on his knees.

"Did you see that?" Natalia turned toward Hector, her eyes shining. "They fled from us! We scared them!"

"Yeah!" Hector was euphoric, almost about to jump for joy. "They ran away! They were afraid! Of us!"

"Yeeeesssssss!" Natalia came near and hugged him with all her might. Hector hesitated a moment, but finally hugged her back. The girl's hair tickled his face. They both smelled like sweat and dirt, but that didn't matter. They'd won. They'd chased the beasts away. There wasn't a trace of them. They couldn't even see them on the other side of the crack.

When Natalia released him to go find the others, Hector's knees gave out. The weight of what had just happened came crashing down on him like an avalanche. He didn't even want to think about what might have happened if those demons hadn't retreated.

And as if echoing his thought, that voice that wasn't his resounded once again in his head: *Don't be fooled. You had a bit of luck, that's all. Under normal circumstances, you all would have died. Every one of you. That attack was madness, complete madness.*

"It worked," he said. He got up and went toward the others. Marco hugged Natalia with such force that he lifted her off the ground. She laughed and slapped him on the shoulders, asking him to put her down.

Alex stood up straight and looked behind him. Madeleine, Adrian, and Bruno were approaching quickly. For an instant there was no expression on his face, just emptiness. It was only for a split second, but Hector was startled to see it. Then the sparkle returned to Alexander's green eyes, and his happiness returned with it.

"They ran like rabbits!" he howled and started thumping the ground. "What did I tell you, you little rascal?!" he asked, pointing his stick at Adrian. "Afraid? Who's afraid?"

Adrian broke out in laughter.

"Don't ever do anything like that again!" Madeleine punched her brother in the arm. "You're crazy! You almost scared me to death!"

Do you remember what I told you about the last king of Rocavarancolia? About how it wasn't courage or heroism that made him charge against a force that he couldn't defeat? Well, you just witnessed a reenactment of that scene. On a smaller scale, of course. And with a redheaded idiot playing the role of Sardaurlar. It wasn't bravery or heroism that made your friend run toward death. I wonder what it might have been . . . And most importantly, what made you follow him?

Hector couldn't answer the second question. But he did know what urged Alex to behave that way: it was fear, but pure fear, the kind that makes you irrational, makes you lose control. The two teenagers exchanged glances. Alex smiled and made the sign for victory. Hector returned the smile and then looked away, uncomfortable. In the sky, on the other side of the crack, the bathtub hoisted the ropes that were tied to the baskets and prepared to take off.

Hector lowered his eyes. He still held the bony spine in his hand.

"Incredible," Lady Serena managed to whisper, still astonished by how Denestor's pups had made the spinytails flee. "Truly incredible."

Through the silver spyglass she could see how they were now making their way over the bridge of ruins that connected both banks of the Scar of Arax. The black teenager was in the lead, guiding the group through the safest passages. He and the redheaded boy stopped to help the others when they had trouble on the route. Surprisingly, Hector didn't need any help at all. He continued determinedly, following the trail without difficulty.

The ghost heard a faint cough above her. Lady Spider, having made her presence known, lowered herself down from the top of the terrace with the help of the fine strand of silk secreted by her abdomen. She looked like a mess of limbs poorly attached to two shapeless sacks clumsily falling. But what seemed awkward at first glance was instead the most effective way for Lady Spider, given her peculiar anatomy, to get around.

She landed in front of Lady Serena and nodded her head several times, as if satisfied by a job well done. She had swapped out two of her monocles for a pair of reflecting binoculars.

"Everything's going as it should," she clucked, moving her monstrous head from left to right. Her voice vibrated. "All of the chicks are alive and well. And Huryel is asleep again, safe and sound in his bed."

"It's about time someone taught you how to use doors," said Lady Serena, and she dismissed the spyglass with a delicate gesture.

"Spiders never use ordinary paths. No, no, no. The steepest, most complicated tracks are where you find the juiciest flies."

"And have you found any?"

"A while ago I discovered a curious specimen wandering around the battlements, a fly with red wings and sparkling skin. I let it go. It was too big for me."

"You did well. It would have choked you."

There was a knock at the door and almost immediately, before any response, it was opened from the outside. Lady Scar entered the room with her wobbly, hesitant gait. With each step, it looked like she was tripping instead of walking, always just about to fall but stubbornly remaining on her feet. Lady Serena greeted her with a nod of her head and turned once again to the spider in the frock coat.

"How is Huryel?"

"Alive," she responded.

"Alive, he's alive." Lady Scar went out into the fresh air of the terrace. Where her left eye had once been was now just a grotesque empty socket. "Every day it takes more and more to keep him that way, but we don't give up on our task. Stubborn and uncompromising. That's how we are."

"Esmael has been here," the ghost announced.

"Where?" she asked, and as if she feared that the black angel might be behind her, she spun on her heels so quickly that her head separated from her neck, fell to the ground, and rolled down the slight incline of the terrace until it hit the balustrade.

The decapitated body approached the wall in two long strides, picked up the head, and returned it to its place. She clicked her tongue. She was used to the small inconveniences that from time to time arose due to her body's battered state, but it still displeased her greatly when her head fell off. It made her seem less than respectable. And besides, it made her dizzy.

"He came to make me an offer that was difficult to refuse. Maybe even impossible," explained the ghost.

"And what can Esmael offer you?" asked Lady Scar.

Lady Serena told them what Enoch the Dusty and then later the black angel himself had come to tell her.

"The Eye-Eater's grimoire, nothing more and nothing less," murmured Lady Scar after hearing her out. She laced her hands, pensive. "It's not the most powerful of the ancient books, but it's powerful enough to be a fearsome object. What a bother!" she griped. "We must deal with him. Nothing good can happen if that madman has such power at his fingertips."

"If he truly does have the grimoire, that is," Lady Spider pointed out, anxious to participate in the conversation. Although, at the end of the day, it didn't really matter to her who became regent or what happened with the book of spells. She just did what she was told, whoever was in command.

"We'll see what spell he surprises us with tonight," said Lady Scar. The thick aroma of the guardian of the Royal Pantheon and commander of the kingdom's armies wafted through the terrace. It smelled like forest decay, like mildew and dead flowers. "In Valcoburdo's compendiums there's a list of all known grimoires and their spells, and surely the Eye-Eater's book is among them," she said. "I'll consult them as soon as I can."

"As I'm sure you'll understand, my vote belongs to whoever has the book in their power," clarified Lady Serena.

"Of course, of course. That's only natural and understandable. What a mishap!" She stroked her empty socket, sulking, her hand riddled with scars. The movement of her finger frightened a small blue butterfly who'd taken refuge within. "But let's talk about more pleasant things: Denestor's harvest. Have you seen them? They scared off those pests with their squeals. Who would have thought? I just can't believe that they're all still alive."

"The Lexel brothers—" the arachnid began.

"Yes, yes," Lady Scar interrupted. "Placing bets on how many will die before nightfall. I know." Her face, ugly and deformed, so lined with marks and puckers that it looked like the map of a rugged country, twisted in what might have been a cunning expression. "Even I myself dared to bet some of my apples from Arfes. I say that not a single one will die today. Tomorrow, perhaps. But not today."

"And this outburst of optimism?" asked Lady Serena, shocked.

Lady Scar didn't answer. Instead she let out a cackle from her cavernous mouth and squinted her right eye.

One of Denestor's birds perched on the top of a tall building. Its shape and size were almost identical to the ones who'd flown to the human world the night before. But the demiurge had used very different materials to create this particular bird. Its body was made from wire twisted around itself, its head was a small, silver-plated cannonball, its eyes were steel ball bearings, and its beak was tanned leather coated with aluminum. It was a magnificent specimen, and it was built to last, unlike its fellow birds, who returned to the category of lifeless rags once their mission was completed.

At the urging of Lady Scar's will, it took a few steps toward the edge of the rooftop, moving its head from left to right, right to left. In its beak it carried with exquisite gentleness the left eye of the commander of the kingdom's armies. And it saw every last detail of what was happening with Hector and the others.

"I see them," Lady Scar murmured. Her words sounded slurred, as if they were sludge and her mouth was a swamp. "They've crossed to the other end of the bridge and they're walking toward the baskets. They won't find much, poor things. Hunger will be their bedfellow tonight. I see them, Lady Serena." A new grimace altered the features of the broken woman, a mix of contradictory emotions that not even she dared to name. "I see them," she repeated.

"What?" Lady Spider focused her binoculars on the square. "What do you see?"

"I see a team. Not yet fully formed, but in the making. I see two strong leaders, the robust teenager who remained in the square and the one with the dark skin. They've taken on the responsibility of looking after the others. And they did it immediately, without even thinking. And almost all of the harvest has rallied around them. Only one of Denestor's pups has opted for solitude."

"And what do you see in Hector?" asked Lady Serena.

"Dormant potential. He was the first to see what the spinytail was up to. And despite his fear, he followed the others into the fight. He's clumsy, foolish, and maybe even a little stupid . . . But he has what it takes, without a doubt."

"Do I detect pride in your voice?"

"Pride? No. I'm just saying what I see. Nothing more; may all heavens and hells forbid me from having an imagination." She clucked her tongue, disgusted. "Essence of kings? Who can determine that at this stage? The journey has just begun, and no one knows what awaits us at the end."

"But what if he survives? And if he really does have the essence of kings? Esmael assured me that he would let him take his place on the throne. Although even in my sickest delusions I can't picture him giving up the regency to put a little snot like that on the throne."

"I won't lie to you, my dear friend. Once this is all over, if the child is still alive and the possibility exists, small as it may be, of him becoming king, I will kill him," said Lady Scar, as she watched the kids search through the destroyed baskets. "Without a moment's hesitation, my hand will not tremble in the slightest. You know better than anyone the extent of the madness of the kings of Rocavarancolia. The essence gives power, but it also makes them go insane. Now is not the time for kings or madness. It's time to grow, to thrive, to open doors, to build . . ."

She watched in the distance as Hector took a break from gathering scraps to take a quick bite of a battered and bruised red fruit. Lady Scar penetrated his mind once again. She did it with the same ease with which she'd woken him up or linked their minds from Lady Serena's sphere. It was like penetrating an immense sea of dull lights.

The magic storm is letting up; I can't risk keeping in contact with you. And I don't know when I'll have the opportunity to talk to you again. That was what Lady Scar thought. Then she gathered her thoughts from the cavernous folds of her dusty brain and plunged them into the boy's mind.

Hector stiffened, straight as a rod, surprised anew by the voice that resounded in his head and that he thought belonged to Lady Serena. The fruit fell from his hand, and Natalia chewed him out for his clumsiness.

I've done everything that I can for you. Now you're alone. Don't let your guard down, child. Avoid the dark mist and always watch your back. And trust no one. Lady Scar slid her purple tongue through her broken teeth as she maintained contact with Hector. Her serrated fangs scratched her tongue, but not a single drop of blood fell from it. *Absolutely no one.*

THE EXPEDITIONARIES

They were the most beautiful eyes he'd ever seen. And it wasn't just because of their blue color with hints of violet; more than anything, it was the way they looked at things. There was poetry and sweetness in those eyes, and an overwhelming strength.

Marina sat across from Hector, and he couldn't take his eyes off her. Not overtly, of course; in the time since they'd returned to the square he'd found five different ways of observing her without being too obvious. Or so he thought. He felt stupid, but it was out of his control.

He nibbled at a rind of fruit even though there wasn't a scrap of flesh left on it. It was his last portion and he was still hungry. Another piece of fruit per head remained in the battered basket they'd brought back, but they'd decided that it would be wise to ration them. The fruit, a type of enormous dark green pear that didn't taste like anything they'd eaten before, was all they'd managed to salvage after the vermin's voracious attack; luckily for them, the pears weren't to the creatures' taste. Hector was so hungry that he still hadn't decided whether he liked them or not.

He noticed that the girl with the hurt ankle was watching him fixedly. Her long straight dark hair fell around her face like a dirty curtain. She leaned against the fountain, her leg fully extended, the ankle bandaged. Ricardo had learned that her name was Rachel and that Denestor brought her from Quebec; luckily he was able to communicate with her enough to calm her down and assure her that she was safe with them. Hector smiled. She returned the smile instantly, winked at him, and then looked mischievously at Marina, letting him know that he hadn't been as discreet as he thought. Hector blushed and focused on gnawing the pear rind as if the fate of the universe depended on it being completely clean.

The nine teenagers sat in a circle next to the fountain, waiting impatiently for Ricardo and Marco to return. They had decided, to most of the group's horror, to leave in search of more provisions. The young German thought he could find the area where one of the other bathtubs had landed. He'd seen it descend close to three tall towers located in the south, then it took off again, without its baskets, and headed to the castle. They'd insisted on going alone despite Natalia, Marina, and Bruno's offers to accompany them.

"We'll move faster if it's just the two of us," Ricardo said. "But don't worry, we won't take any stupid risks. No more hooting and hollering and pouncing on wild beasts. We'll be back as soon as we can." One glance at the sky exposed their concern. Hector realized that they didn't want to still be outside when night fell. Marco had mentioned the tower on top of the hill and Ricardo agreed that it might be a good place to take shelter.

Hector didn't like their plan, but he chose to keep his opinion to himself. Despite his hunger, he thought it was better to find shelter and wait for the following day to search for provisions. The sun was already well on its way down, and the strange blue of the sky turned murkier by the minute. He wasn't the only one worried about the approach of nightfall. The others' eyes were drawn more and more frequently to the heavens above. If Rocavarancolia was a fearful place during the day, Hector didn't want to imagine what it became once the sun went down.

A fierce and merciless wind began to wail through the ruins like a condemned soul. Hector wrapped himself as best he could in the loose gray shirt that he wore over his sweater. The fabric was unpleasant to the touch and gave off a smell of old, abandoned things, but it served to keep him warm. Alexander and Lizbeth had brought three large hampers full of clothing from the house where they'd rescued Rachel. Most of the items were identical to the garments they wore: smocks and pants made from sackcloth; rough burlap shirts, work shirts, jackets; baggy, long pants, all in dark colors. They'd been handed out to the group, and although few were willing at first to wear the ugly clothes, once the temperature began to drop they forgot their reluctance.

"The lost boys from *Peter Pan*," joked Alexander, when they were all cloaked in the dark shirts.

What Hector appreciated the most was a pair of sandals that he found in a basket. They were made of thick material with leather soles. They pinched a little at his heels, but were a huge improvement over the poorly tied rags.

They had no way of telling how long they'd been waiting for Ricardo and Marco. Bruno was the only one who wore a watch, and it had stopped the instant that Denestor Tul brought him to Rocavarancolia. It was an old, ugly watch on a chain that Bruno kept in the pocket of his shirt, with a hideous lion's face engraved on the gold cover.

"It's a gift from my grandfather," he explained. He stared at it with such focus that it seemed like he would make it work by sheer force of will.

"Well, he must not have liked you much," said Adrian. "It's very ugly."

Bruno raised his eyes to look directly at him. His icy glare was disturbing.

"How dare you say that something is ugly with those pajamas you're wearing?" asked Lizbeth, provoking peals of laughter from Alex.

"Leave it, it doesn't matter." Bruno got up and shoved his hands in the back pockets of his ancient corduroy pants. His baggy black shirt flapped in the wind. "And you're right about my grandfather," he said. "He's not very fond of me. Denestor could have spared himself the effort of erasing me from his memory. I'm sure that he would have been happy enough to do that on his own." He was quiet for a moment, his gaze lost in the buildings surrounding the square. He nodded toward a nearby alleyway and took off walking in that direction. "I need to use the bathroom. I'll be right back."

"Don't go too far," Lizbeth warned, looking at him worriedly.

They decided to pool whatever objects they had in their pockets, looking for anything that might be useful to them. The result was fairly depressing: their booty consisted of several sets of keys, three packets of tissues, coins, and two colored stones belonging to Natalia.

"We're doomed," Alexander murmured. "There's nothing here we can use."

"What did you expect, Alex?" asked his sister. "A gun?"

"I would have settled for a knife, smart aleck. That would have done the trick."

The memory of Alexander's panic was still fresh in Hector's mind. He'd recovered almost instantly, but for a moment all of his weakness and fear had been revealed. He remembered that the redhead had made Adrian promise that, no matter how scared he was, he wouldn't let panic take over, and he wondered if Alexander hadn't made a similar promise to himself.

He looked up again. To the west, twilight loomed between the jagged peaks of the mountain range. The mountaintops were surrounded by swirls of an intense dark blue; stains of purple and scarlet lit up the clouds' underbellies. Dusk, little by little, was overtaking the sky.

"Bruno! Ricardo told us not to go far!" Natalia screamed suddenly, jolting Hector out of his introspection. "Come back here right now!"

Bruno stood still in front of a tower located at the far end of the square. It was the brown stone structure surrounded by mist that Hector had noticed shortly after he regained consciousness. The Italian had gone through the courtyard gate and now stood at the door. The curtain of shadows floated just inches away from him, like an ill-fated aurora borealis.

Hector leapt to his feet.

"Bruno, come back!" he yelled, overwhelmed by seeing him so close to the mist. For a second he thought he saw an ethereal hand surge from the thick blackness, a dark claw that came dangerously close to the teenager's face.

"I think you should come see this!" Bruno yelled, and to Hector's horror most of them got up and headed over without a moment's hesitation. Only Lizbeth and Rachel stayed sitting down, side by side. Hector frowned, not sure what to do.

"Stay with her, okay?" he asked Lizbeth before hurrying off to reach the others.

The brick tower was four stories tall. The first three, built from small blocks of granite, were rectangular with narrow windows. The last story, on the other hand, was so different in form and material that it didn't fit in with the rest, as if it were a part of another building that someone placed there by mistake. The top floor looked like it was constructed from a single spherical piece, flat on top, with numerous wide oval windows with curved ledges. The first floors looked sturdy and solid, while the top floor seemed ethereal, as if instead of being anchored atop the others it just floated above them.

The garden that surrounded the building had been reduced to dust and barren soil. Here and there a tattered weed appeared that looked as if it were about to disintegrate.

"This place is horrible," Marina whispered as she contemplated a dead fern with disgust.

"And what are we supposed to see here?" Alexander asked. "It's another frightening house in the most frightening city in the universe."

"I believe this is a special building," Bruno told them. "Look: there were banners here at one time." He pointed to the flagpoles at the top of the gate. "And look closely at the symbol above the door. While we were following the bathtub I saw it on another building, very similar to this one."

They crowded around, so near the warning mist that Hector felt the need to push them away. Instead he got closer than the others to the gloomy darkness, placing himself in the way of anyone who might try to approach the front steps. He decided that if someone made a move to enter, he would knock them down at once. He'd make it look like an accident: just another stumble from the clumsy kid. He'd throw himself to the ground and pretend to be hurt, so they'd have no choice but to focus on him and forget about the tower. He was almost surprised by how quickly he devised his plan.

The symbol above the door was a ten-pointed star of a dirty red color. Its eight horizontal arms curved slightly outward, while the vertical arms stretched straight out from the long oval in the center. It looked like a strangely symmetrical insect perched on the wall of the tower.

"What does it mean?" asked Adrian.

"I don't know. Maybe it indicates what kind of building it is. A trade union symbol or something like that."

"Or maybe it's a warning," whispered Hector, eager to prevent them from getting the great idea to explore the tower. "The equivalent of 'Danger. Do not enter.'"

"There's only one way to find out," Alexander announced and took a step toward the stairs.

Hector looked at him, astonished, unable to believe that he was always the one who seemed eager to go through Lady Serena's mist. He was about to trip the redhead when they heard whistling from the square. They glanced over, startled. It was Rachel. She raised two fingers to her lips and produced a prolonged sound that amazed them with its high pitch and duration.

"Good lord!" Madeleine exclaimed. "What a set of lungs!"

"And what a bad idea to whistle like that in a place like this," said Bruno. "That whistle shall be heard in all of Rocavarancolia."

Lizbeth must have been thinking the same thing, because she hastily quieted Rachel, and then, once she saw that everyone's attention was focused on them, she pointed to one of the side streets that led to the square. Ricardo and Marco were approaching at a steady pace. They did not carry any baskets with them.

Hector breathed a sigh of relief when they left the tower garden to go meet the arrivals.

"This place is madness," Marco declared as he slumped to the rocky ground.

Ricardo did the same. He wore an absent expression. He brought his hand to his head and rubbed his hair vigorously, as if he wanted to dry it or erase some unpleasant thought from his mind. Then he huffed, raised his eyes, and looked at everyone around him as if it were the first time he'd seen them.

"It's not madness. It's a nightmare," he said, sounding as expressionless as Bruno. "That's what it is: a nightmare."

"What happened?" asked Adrian. "You didn't find any food?"

Marco shook his head. Ricardo looked up.

"What did you see?" Lizbeth asked. She raised her hand to her chest, as if trying to brace herself for a terrible shock.

Ricardo huffed again and ran his hand over his forehead. His chestnut hair fell in his eyes. When he talked, it wasn't to answer Lizbeth.

"No one will go in any building until we're convinced that it's a safe place," he said. His gaze had hardened. Not a trace of friendliness remained in his words or gestures. Hector gathered that the Ricardo before them was the same Ricardo who'd ordered him so sharply to follow the bathtub with the others. "No one goes anywhere alone; at the very minimum we go in pairs," he continued. "We won't go into the city unless it's necessary. We'll try to find the spots where those crazy people leave our provisions and that's it. No more adventures, explorations, or foolishness . . . This place is dangerous."

"We know, fearless leader." Alexander pounded his chest right over the spot where the vermin's spine had hit. "A nasty creature almost did me in."

"Believe me, those creatures are going to be the least of our worries," Marco cut in.

"What did you see?" Lizbeth insisted. She spoke very slowly and in such a serious tone that it almost sounded threatening. She stood in front of Ricardo and looked at him, scowling, with her hands on her hips. It reminded Hector of his mother's pose when she scolded him.

"I . . ." Ricardo avoided the girl's eyes. All of the confidence that he'd just displayed disappeared. He lowered his head as if he were extremely tired.

"It wasn't any one thing," explained Marco, in the absence of a response from his companion. "It was a series of . . . I don't know what to call it. This place is impossible, it's capable of anything. I don't even know where to begin." He looked around, as if searching for inspiration. Then he sighed and began to talk. "Right after we left we found a scaffold with a hanged body. There was nothing left but bones and . . . they were moving . . . They never stopped moving. We thought it was the wind, but it wasn't. It was something else. The skeleton was infested with insects; they'd made a nest out of the cadaver. They lived inside its bones. And they watched us, they watched us from the eye sockets. And that's not all." He swallowed and pointed behind him, although it was clear that as hard as they looked, they wouldn't be able to see what he was pointing at. "The city is burning, you know? About three miles from here a big section of it is on fire. But don't worry, the fire won't reach us here. It's not moving, you see? The flames are frozen. Motionless. There's not even smoke. And yet there it is, burning. The streets and buildings are engulfed in flames, halfway burned up. There are people screaming . . . And whatever it is that's keeping the flames from advancing is also keeping the people who are burning alive. They won't stop screaming. I don't know how long they've been in that hell, burning alive . . ."

"Shut up," said Adrian, tightly covering his ears. "Shut up. Shut up."

"Hey!" Alexander turned toward him. Despite the cold, the redhead's forehead was drenched with sweat. "What did you promise me, squirt? You can be as afraid as you like, but don't let it show. Okay?"

Adrian looked at him with bulging eyes.

"Well, tell him to shut up!" he exclaimed.

"Oh, did you think this was going to be a walk in the park? Now you know it's not! It's not a field trip, it's an adventure! And adventures are dangerous!"

"Shut up, both of you," Lizbeth yelled without taking her eyes off Ricardo. "What did you see?" she asked him.

The young man lowered his gaze. When he spoke, he spoke slowly, never raising his head.

"We couldn't find any supplies, although we didn't look that hard," he began. "We wanted to return as soon as possible, and, well . . . the burning neighborhood made our skin crawl. On our way back we passed a white brick house with a black roof, with three windows in the front." Ricardo's eyes shone wet with tears that did not fall. "There was a flowerpot with a twisted little tree on a window ledge, a dried-up bonsai." He touched his hand to his forehead, slowly. "It was my house . . . My mother gave me the bonsai two years ago and then it died. It was my fault, it was supposed to be outside and I insisted on keeping it in my room. It was a gift from my mother and I wanted to keep it close by, you know?" The tears still did not fall. Hector was amazed; he could see them quiver, but they remained attached to his lower eyelids. As frozen as the flames that Marco had just told them about. "When I brought it outside, it was too late."

"Your house? You saw your house?"

Marco requested silence with a gesture. Ricardo wasn't finished.

"The window of my room suddenly opened and my mom appeared. She yelled at me to quit playing and come inside, that that was enough, that it was getting very late and it was time to eat. And I was about to do it, you know? If Marco hadn't stopped me, I would have done it."

"I don't understand!" Natalia groaned.

"I didn't see Ricardo's house," said Marco. "I saw the entrance to my father's gym, with the usual posters about classes and the schedule of boxing matches for the weekend. And I saw *him* in the doorway, calling for me to finish mopping the hallway immediately. I believed it, too. I know now that it must seem impossible, but I swear to you I was about to go in . . . I approached the door, but then I noticed something else. My father and the gym seemed to flicker, and I could see what was projecting these illusions." He was quiet for a moment. "It's hard to describe . . . It looked like an enormous head that rose up from the ground, with a huge dislocated mouth and gigantic eyes. But it wasn't a head, it was a house: a house that was alive and hungry. The door was the mouth and the windows out front were the eyes that watched us . . . If we'd gone in, it would've devoured us, I'm sure of it."

"Like a pitcher plant," Bruno said suddenly. On seeing the others' expressions he added, "They're carnivorous plants that attract insects with their smell. Just like that house, but instead of an olfactory stimulus it used a visual one."

"Whatever," grumbled an ill-tempered Ricardo. "Marco had to throw me to the ground so that I wouldn't go in. And then a black tongue shot through the door and lashed out at us. We were out of its reach, but only by an inch or so. The cursed house let out a growl and finally I could see it for what it was . . . And my mother disappeared."

An uncomfortable silence hovered over the group. They all knew that something remained unsaid.

"She died two years ago," he murmured, "right after she gave me the bonsai. A stupid car accident: a drunk hit her and ended everything. And I had to come to this hellhole to see her again." The tears finally began to flow down his cheeks.

"That wasn't your mother, Ricardo," Marina said. "Only her reflection."

"I don't care!" he shouted, standing up violently. "They got inside my head! Who do they think they are, snooping around in my mind?!" He turned so that he was facing the castle in the mountains. "They tricked us to bring us to this horrible place. They made me forget all of the languages I knew, and now they dare to play games with my mother's memory. Damn them!" He clenched his teeth. Hector understood that his tears weren't tears of pain or sadness, but of rage. "I'd forgotten her face, you understand?" he shouted with fury. "I didn't remember her! I didn't remember my own mother! God . . . The pictures that we had of her don't do her justice. She was beautiful . . . and I've forgotten her. I've forgotten her." He made tight fists with his hands. "I'm going to make them pay for this. I swear it. I don't know how, but they will pay."

THE TOWER

There was a clock at the top of the tower. At least it looked a lot like a clock. It was a large glass sphere, located on the east face, just below the battlements. On the top part of the sphere was a small red circle and, in the spot where a sundial would indicate the time as ten after four, was the same scarlet star that they'd found on the brick tower in the square. "There's that symbol again," said Bruno.

"That mark up there . . ." Marco murmured, pensive. "Lady Scar mentioned something about a Red Moon, remember?"

"She said that in the last thirty years no one had lived to see it," Hector pointed out. And now that Marco had mentioned it, that circle did look like a moon. There were even traces of geographical features on its surface: deep cracks and fissures found mostly on its lower eastern side.

"Well, what do you think it is?" asked Adrian. "A clock or some kind of ornament?"

"Maybe it indicates when the Red Moon and that star will rise," Ricardo ventured. "Or when the next eclipse will be, or maybe it has nothing at all to do with moons or stars. What do I know."

The eleven teenagers were at the top of the hill, contemplating the building from the other side of the moat, at the foot of the drawbridge. It was a tower with a round floor plan, dark walls made from green sandstone, four stories tall. The only defect that they noticed was a powerful blow to the north face, which looked like it was caused by cannon fire. Although the blow hadn't penetrated the wall, it had certainly deformed it. Hector couldn't help but picture an enormous fist punching the wall.

The drawbridge was made of thick dark wood and measured about twenty feet long and thirteen wide. The chains, which descended from two openings situated on both sides of the tower gate, anchored the moorings at the end of the bridge.

They couldn't see to the bottom of the moat that surrounded the tower. Natalia started to lean over it, but Ricardo grabbed her by her shirt collar before she could go any further. Hector looked at the moat in apprehension. The memory of the Scar of Arax and what it contained was still too fresh in his mind. And although there wasn't a trace of the warning mist, he couldn't forget what the ghost had told him: the absence of darkness didn't mean that a place was safe.

At their backs they heard the continuous murmur of the river that flowed around the promontory. The water was more turbulent after the previous night's storm and carried pieces of wood and debris.

It didn't take them long to cover the distance between the square with the fountain and the tower. They'd moved quickly, spurred on by nightfall's imminent arrival. Marco had carried Rachel on his back, this time without the slightest objection from Lizbeth. Halfway there they came across a large black marble staircase. Its final step bridged over the torrent, but due to the rising waters it was almost submerged. Once they crossed to the other bank, it was easy to find the tower.

They stopped for a moment in front of the drawbridge. Everyone waited for Ricardo's signal to cross to the other side, but the chestnut-haired teenager remained still, watching the hulking tower suspiciously, as if he believed that building was also eager to devour them.

"What do we do, fearless leader?" Alexander asked. He carried the remaining fruit on his shoulder, bundled in a shirt with the sleeves tied together. "Do we stay here all night or do we cross already?"

Ricardo snorted. It was clear that he wasn't sure.

"Okay, let's go," he finally conceded. "But we take our time, and no one breaks away from the group. Wherever we go, we go together."

At that very second, they heard a dreadful howl. It came from the mountains, which at that point were nothing more than a dense area of shadows in the dusk. A second howl joined the first. A third was not far behind. Hector felt a pang of fear in the pit of his stomach. Those howls sounded like pure hunger, like bones gnawed with rage . . . Almost without realizing it, they drew closer to each other, searching for a sense of safety in numbers.

"They're not wolves," Lizbeth said. "Wolves don't howl like that."

They crossed the bridge quickly, glancing back from time to time, as if they feared that something might catch up to them before they could get through the tower gate. Hector walked down the middle of the drawbridge and didn't look once at the abyss that could be glimpsed below. The surge of adrenaline that he felt in the Scar of Arax was now a distant memory.

The howls continued, loud and terrifying. They easily drowned out the wail of the wind.

"Is it me, or do they sound closer?" Adrian asked.

"No," Lizbeth replied. "They sound the same as when they started. They haven't moved."

"I think they sound closer. I'm sure of it."

The gate led to a gloomy, vaulted corridor that led to a second door, much smaller than the large gate they'd just passed through. On the ceiling of the corridor they saw at regular intervals the sharp tines of three tall metal grilles, firmly embedded in the masonry.

It was Ricardo who opened the second door. The squeal that it made as it opened was perfectly in tune with the howls and the wailing wind.

It took their eyes a minute to adjust to the dense gloom that lay beyond the door, but little by little the shadows inside began to take form, becoming tables and chairs, floor candelabras and harmless shelves.

"Seems clear," whispered Ricardo, and crossed the threshold. The others followed close behind.

Staying within a yard of one another, they looked around. Natalia and Alexander held their sticks tightly.

The room was enormous. It took up the entirety of the first floor, and although it was completely disorganized, the chaos did not seem to be the result of any catastrophe. It looked more like someone had used the place as an improvised warehouse, without the least concern for preserving order as they piled things up. There were dressers, tables, chairs, and shelves packed full of various belongings everywhere. There were crystal lanterns, candelabras, an endless number of candles of all shapes and colors, bowls, ceramic plates, ladles, trays, and even a soup pot. Everything was covered with so much dust and cobwebs that it all appeared to be wrapped in a shroud.

"Look for matches, lighters . . . Anything that can start a fire," Ricardo said. "We need light."

"If you find weapons or food, let us know too," added Marco.

The teenagers spread out, opening drawers and examining shelves, looking through everything without getting too far from one another. They soon found themselves almost feeling their way in the semidarkness. In the center of the hall was a spiral staircase, with warped steps that led not only to the upper floors but also to a lower level. Hector approached it, with Adrian at his heels. He looked up and down through the stairwell. There only seemed to be one other floor below theirs.

Next to the staircase was a large wooden pail that contained several brooms, mops, and scrub brushes. Hector grabbed a broom and used it to dust off a nearby object so covered with cobwebs that it was impossible to guess what it was. It turned out to be a bulky wooden chest. He wondered whether he should open it, but finally curiosity got the better of him and he used the broom as a lever to raise the lid. The chest was full of clothing, mostly the same as what they wore. But he noticed a colorful T-shirt emblazoned with a cartoon character from a series that was popular some years back. In the middle of the shirt was a large tear surrounded by a dark stain that could very well have been dried blood. Hector hurried to hide the shirt among the other clothes.

"Did you find something?" Adrian asked.

"Nothing." He buried the bloodied T-shirt even deeper. "More clothing. That's all."

Adrian nodded and sneezed loudly. The kids wandering through the room stirred up clouds of dust.

"Ouch!" he heard someone exclaim in the dusty darkness.

"What happened?" Ricardo asked as he walked toward the sound.

"I'm an idiot!" exclaimed Madeleine. "That's what happened! I cut myself on a stupid crystal. It had a sharp edg—"

Her words were cut off by a surprised shout that coincided with a sudden glow in the darkness. It came from her hand. Madeleine still clutched the piece of glass that she'd cut herself on, a small light blue crystal in the shape of a rhomboid that was the source of the light. She seemed to be gripping a dazzling sphere, a foot and a half in diameter. The light wasn't enough to illuminate the whole room, but it did brighten the darkness.

"You did magic!" Adrian exclaimed, amazed.

"What I did is hurt myself," she replied dryly. "There are more crystals here, if you're interested."

"Let me see." Alexander approached his sister and looked at the cut on the girl's thumb with a frown. "It's nothing, only a scratch. It's hardly even bleeding."

"But it hurts . . . And I'm sure it's full of germs and bacteria. I'm going to get sick!" She gave the crystal to him to hold while she examined her wound. Not two seconds had passed after Alexander took it when the light went out.

"Well! I guess I broke it already? It usually takes me longer to wreck things."

Madeleine snatched the crystal from his hand and the light returned once again.

"It only works for me?"

Hector and Ricardo examined the other crystals. There were dozens of them heaped up on a tray made of polychrome painted wood. They were all identical in shape but not in color: there were blue, green, and orange pieces.

Ricardo took a blue one in his fingers and examined it with the light that shone from Madeleine's. Then he used it to make a quick cut on his fingertip. A silvery light appeared almost instantly around the rhomboid crystal. Ricardo handed the crystal to Hector and the moment it changed hands, the light went out.

"It appears that the crystals only work for those who activate them," Bruno commented. He selected a crystal from the shelf, and without thinking twice, plunged it into the palm of his hand. The expression on his face didn't change a bit. When the crystal lit up he raised it before his eyes to get a better look. "The blood seeps through the edges and circulates to the middle of the crystal. There's something here. A dark center . . . When the blood reaches it, the crystal lights up."

Ricardo took back the crystal that he'd given to Hector and once again light surrounded it.

"Well, we have light," he said. "Whoever wants some knows what they have to do. But be careful—it would be a pain if anyone bled out."

The light was now more than enough to illuminate the room clearly; even so Lizbeth and Marina each took one of the other crystals. Rachel said something that no one understood, but then she pointed vehemently to the shelf and the crystals. Marina brought her one, and the girl nodded contentedly before taking it. She then used it to make a cut on the back of her hand, and although the blood flowed and penetrated the crystal, there was no light this time.

"It must be broken," Marco guessed. He took the crystal and stuck it into his thumb. In a flash, a bubble of clear, pearly light surrounded his hand. Rachel groaned, upset.

Alex and Natalia were the next to activate crystals. The different points of light gave the objects in the room multiple changing shadows, like inky ghosts that stretched and shrank in time with the kids' movements. Hector took a crystal from the basket and brought it to the fingertip of his index finger, but he didn't have the courage to cut himself. The idea of hurting himself on purpose, even in exchange for light, repulsed him. He sighed and quickly returned the crystal to the basket. He looked at those who held the luminous spheres; the light gave them an almost nebulous quality, as if they weren't entirely there. Ricardo, with his own crystal in his hands, moved toward the spiral staircase and motioned for them to follow.

In the basement of the tower they found the dungeons. They took up the full southern half of the tower, and there were three cells that could be accessed through an enormous reinforced gate. In the keyhole was an iron key on a ring with other smaller keys.

The cells were large and damp, with thick steel bars with very little space in between. The stifling, enclosed feeling that bombarded Hector here was tremendous, so much so that he felt the impulse to take off running and not stop until he was outside the tower. From the walls of the main dungeon hung three sets of chains and shackles. There were scratch marks and dents in the masonry and dark, muddy stains everywhere.

"This place makes my hair stand on end," Marina said in a thin voice. "Can we get out of here, please?"

Hector agreed. The space reeked of evil. Terrible things had happened within these walls. And the dark echoes of those things had permeated even the stones themselves.

"Yes," Ricardo whispered. He, too, seemed overwhelmed by the cells. "There's nothing to see here. Let's go."

Opposite the dungeons, on the other side of the spiral staircase, were two more doors. Alexander opened the first and his face lit up when he saw what was inside.

"Finally," he mused, contemplating the large quantity of weapons that were heaped up in the room. "Finally, finally . . ." he repeated as he went in eagerly.

"The tower's armory," announced Bruno.

Weapons of all shapes and sizes were scattered everywhere. Swords, bows, shields, halberds, quivers full of arrows, axes, crossbows, daggers . . . They were lying on the floor, propped up in the corners, and hanging from rings on the walls. They practically covered everything. In the middle of the armory were two open trunks, full of pieces of armor. They went in one by one, in silence. The spherical light from the crystals that they carried sparkled on the steel and the decorated scabbards and handles. Hector looked from one side to the other, impressed by the number of weapons. All of them were designed to kill, he thought, awestruck: in every one of these weapons was a promise of violence waiting to be unleashed. He wondered how many had killed already.

Alexander walked over to an enormous, two-handed broadsword almost as tall as him. He tried to pick it up but couldn't even budge it from its place. He then settled on a much smaller sword that he grasped without removing it from its sheath. He managed to lift it, not without difficulty.

"Leave it, would you please?" Marco asked.

"What do you mean? This is what we're looking for! Weapons to protect ourselves!"

"Do you know how to handle a sword? Look how you hold it! The only thing you can do with that is break your wrist!"

"It's true, Alex," his sister said. "You look like a clown."

Alexander clenched his teeth and raised the sword so that the sheathed edge pointed at Marco's throat. His arm trembled, but its tremor was hardly reflected in the weapon that he wielded. The flaps of the sheath shook in the air like drowsy serpents.

"Maybe I don't know, but I'm a fast learner," he warned.

Marco half closed his eyes. He jumped forward and hit the sword with his forearm while he shoved Alexander. The weapon fell to the ground and the boy almost did too. Marco picked up the weapon and brandished it in a fluid and elegant motion.

"See? With a sword the only thing you'll do is cut yourself." He put it back in its sheath and adjusted the straps around his waist. Hector thought that if anyone was born to carry a sword, it was Marco. "Look for daggers and knives. And make sure they're not too big or too heavy. It shouldn't require any effort to hold them."

"My mother enrolled me in a fencing class, but I only went once. I didn't like it at all," said Adrian. He raised the open palm of his hand before his face and shook it from one side to the other. "They make you wear a horrible mask on your face. It felt like being inside a cheese grater. If only I'd stayed . . . If only I'd learned . . ." he added, dejectedly.

He bent down and rummaged through a mountain of weapons until he found a small knife to his liking. The handle was in the shape of a dragon with its wings spread wide. Adrian opened his shirt and slid the weapon into the waistband of his pajamas.

Marina went up to an elegant bow that stood against the wall; it was made of dark wood with red borders. She stroked its surface tenderly.

"My cousin has a competition bow," she said. "It's not like this, of course . . . It's full of pegs and weird stuff. Last summer he taught me to shoot."

"And did you do well?" Marco asked with interest.

"I didn't hit the bull's-eye once," she confessed. "I broke a window in the shed. And I killed a duck."

"Were you aiming at it?" asked Alexander.

"No!"

"Then look for a knife," Marco said.

Hector finally decided on a small dagger with a twisted handgrip. He didn't have a belt, but a clasp on the back of the sheath allowed it to hang inside his shirt.

Lizbeth took Ricardo by the wrist and made him turn toward her.

"Do you think it's a good idea for us to go around this place armed?" she asked. "Somebody's eventually going to get hurt, you know. It's reckless."

"We need weapons," he answered. "That much is obvious. This place is dangerous, and it isn't going to cut us any slack." He approached Marco, who was examining the dagger that Madeleine chose. "Did you learn how to use a sword in your father's gym?"

"Not exactly. . . I learned kendo. And basic tactics of other martial arts. But I'm no expert. Anyone with a certain amount of skill could give me a beating."

"Why don't you ask those beasts that attacked us!" Adrian exclaimed, and imitated hitting something with a stick. "Pow!"

"Well, we need to learn to defend ourselves and what little you know will be a godsend," Ricardo said. "Can you teach us?"

"Of course I can," Marco answered.

"How long do you think we're going to be here?" asked Natalia. She held a dagger with a curved blade, drawn halfway from its sheath.

"If we could get out of here tomorrow, that would be great," Ricardo said. "But maybe we should get used to the idea of spending a long time in this place."

"What? No way I'm thinking that!" said Adrian. "What I want is to go home, okay? I want my mom. I'm not having fun anymore."

"We all want to go home," said Lizbeth, in a comforting voice. "And we'll find a way. You'll see."

"No, we won't find it!" Marco shouted. Everyone looked shocked at his overblown reaction. "And the sooner you get that in your heads, the better! Thinking about going home is only going to hurt you."

"What do you mean?" Marina asked. "Since when does it hurt to have hope?"

Marco shook his head, as if preparing to explain something so obvious that it was inconceivable he had to put it in words.

"Denestor told us over and over that he couldn't lie to us, right?" he said. "That it was against the law for him to do so. And so far, everything he's told us is true. He told all of us that there wouldn't be a way to return home until a year had passed, when the doors to our world would open."

An uncomfortable silence loomed over the group. Adrian looked at Marco with his eyes wide open.

"Maybe he lied to us when he said he couldn't lie to us," he blurted out in a wavering voice. "Haven't you considered that? Huh?"

"No, no . . ." Marina shook her head, incredulous. "You can't trust what Denestor told us, Marco. It doesn't make sense for you to believe him! For heaven's sake, he's the bad guy!"

Ricardo sighed.

"If he could lie to us directly, he wouldn't have had to stage the spectacle with the pipe or the scroll with the contract," he said with a heavy heart. "Marco's right. Denestor manipulated us, but he didn't lie."

"I am afraid that's how it is," Bruno added. "Even in the contract that we signed there was a clause that specified that at the end of a year we would be given the opportunity to return home. Therefore, we must take as a fact that there will not be a possibility of returning home until that time has passed."

"A year," Lizbeth murmured.

A tense and terrible silence reentered the armory. The teenagers looked at one another. Hector saw bewilderment and despondency in their eyes, except for Bruno's expression, blank as usual, and Rachel's, confused once again by a conversation that she didn't understand in the least.

"A year," Alexander repeated. "A year isn't that long. You'll see. It will fly by."

As if to echo his words, more howling resounded outside. Hector shuddered. The idea of spending a year in such an atrocious place was terrifying. He frowned. True, Denestor had said that they'd be given the chance to return home when their year was up, but what world would they return to? A world where nobody remembered them? Speaking a language that nobody understood? Hector began to fear that the possibility of returning home was no more than another of Denestor Tul's half-truths.

Once they'd all chosen their weapons and Marco approved of each and every one, they left the armory. Lizbeth preferred to continue unarmed, and Ricardo didn't see the need to swap out the rusty dagger that he'd found under the winged corpse. The knife that Hector wore at his waist didn't make him feel any safer. The same went for Natalia and Alex, who hung on to their sticks. The redhead still couldn't take his eyes away from the armory's weapons; he looked like a kid who'd been forbidden from playing with his favorite toy.

It was Bruno who opened the last door in the tower's basement. The room that it opened into was the shape of a half-moon and it was so small that most of the group had to make do with peering into it from outside, since there wasn't room for all of them inside. In the curve of the wall there were several levers and wheels made from wood and metal. A foul odor of oil and grease filled the air.

"This must be where they control the drawbridge and the gates," said Ricardo, examining one of the levers. It was large and worm eaten around the edges. He pulled it down. Something creaked suddenly from within the tower walls, startling everyone.

"Raise the bridge! Raise the bridge!" Adrian cried. "That way the wolves can't get in!"

Ricardo turned one of the wheels and they heard more creaking in the distance.

"Maybe someone could take a look at the entrance?" Marco commented. "To see what we're doing . . ."

Hector intended to stay down below, but when he saw Marina head up with Adrian and Alexander, he decided to go too. The four of them quickly climbed the stairs and approached the tower gate after navigating through the chaos of furnishings on the main floor. Alex's and Marina's crystals illuminated the entryway. Absolute night lay beyond. Rocavarancolia was nothing more than a sea of shadows. From the gate, they relayed to those below what was happening.

"You've lowered the second gate!" they said when the grille descended. It happened abruptly, and the cracking sound of the serrated gate hitting the ground reverberated for a few seconds in the hallway.

After a moment the drawbridge gave a lurch. The rust from the metal supports and the dust that had gathered on the wood rose upward. A loud crack resounded inside the tower, followed by the continuous ringing of a metal chain being rolled up. The chains tensed and began to raise the bridge with a groaning and shaking of wood. It stopped halfway, on an angle like a gigantic, mocking tongue.

"Keep going!" Adrian encouraged. His cheeks were red with excitement. "The bridge is rising! Give it all you've got! Heeaaave!"

Another groan echoed from inside the tower and the bridge began moving again amid the ringing of chains and creaking wood. Hector knew it was a ridiculous feeling, but as soon as the bridge was raised up he felt safer, as if that moat could truly protect them from the horrors that lurked around Rocavarancolia.

"That's it! That's it!" Adrian yelled, jumping up and down, when the bridge closed off the main tower gate. He slapped Hector on the shoulder and smiled at Alexander. "Now we'll be safe, right?" he asked, and there was so much innocence and helplessness in his voice that Hector felt a knot in his throat.

"Of course we're safe," the redhead assured, his eyes fixed on the closed gate. The shadows in the hallway had grown darker.

When the bridge was raised and the three gates lowered, they went back to exploring the tower. The next two floors were divided into communal rooms, four on each floor, with eight coarse straw mattresses on the floor of each. The mattresses were little more than dirty covers made from worn burlap, sloppily filled with straw. There was no sign of furniture, and dust and cobwebs covered everything. There were three embrasures in each room, too narrow to keep the rooms ventilated.

"Where have you brought us?" Alex looked at Marco with a raised eyebrow. "To Motel Rocavarancolia?"

The teen shrugged his shoulders and flashed one of his incredible smiles.

"You have to admit, the place isn't bad, if you ignore the dust and grime, of course," said Ricardo. "We're probably not the first ones to take refuge here."

Hector thought of the bloody T-shirt from the chest, but said nothing.

Adrian walked over to a mattress and gave it a little kick, as if to test its consistency. Something moved instantly underneath the mattress. He made a face as he saw several spiders creep out through the tears in the fabric, disturbed by the quick movement.

Madeleine shouted and took a step back, raising her hands to her neck. "They're full of bugs!"

"They're not bugs, they're spiders," said Marina, and she crouched next to the mattress. She didn't seem to mind when one of the spiders, of a vibrant green color, ran over her shoe.

"Does it look like the one you saw last night, Hector?" Ricardo asked.

"There's a similarity. Although mine was a bit bigger and a snappier dresser."

"I wouldn't advise sleeping on those," Lizbeth commented, pointing to the grimy mattresses. "Unless you want to get eaten alive by bugs."

"I saw a chest full of clothing downstairs," Natalia said, and Hector prayed that it wasn't the same one he'd opened. "If we can't find anything better, we can spread clothes on the ground."

"Sleeping on the floor . . ." Madeleine said, as if the idea struck her as preposterous and absurd. She looked at her brother and shook her head. "This place gets worse by the minute."

"Nobody said it was going to be easy," Alex replied.

"And nobody said it was going to be as horrifying as it's turning out to be," she shot back at him icily. "And you got me into this, may I remind you. An adventure, you said. More like a nightmare, I say."

Alexander frowned but didn't respond.

"It's not your brother's fault that you're here," Hector chimed in. "It's Denestor's fault. He's the one who tricked all of us."

"Don't butt in where you're not wanted, Fatty," Alex said abruptly as he left the room without looking at Hector. He almost mowed down Marina and Rachel on his way.

"Your brother is kind of an idiot, isn't he?" Marina asked.

"He has his moments."

Hector snorted.

The last story of the tower was almost a reflection of the first: the whole floor consisted of one giant room. But while the one downstairs was crammed with furniture and belongings, this had just a solitary barrel located in the exact center of the room, which made it seem all the emptier. And right in the section of the roof located above the barrel was a rectangular hatch barred with a large metal bolt. Marco climbed up onto the barrel to try to slide back the latch, but all of his efforts were in vain.

"It's stuck," he said, jumping down. "It must lead to the roof and the battlements."

Lizbeth doodled with her foot in the dust on the floor as she looked around.

"This place is a little better than the rooms downstairs," she said. "We should stay here tonight, what do you think?"

"Dusty and ugly," Madeleine mumbled. "But you're right: less dusty and ugly than what we've seen until now."

Hector approached an embrasure. The air in the tower was quite heavy and he appreciated what little fresh air flowed in through the narrow openings. He looked outside and a panorama of the ruined city stretched wide before his eyes. The buildings, now nothing more than shapeless masses of darkness, were stacked in chaos over the broken terrain that rose as drastically as it fell.

He took a deep breath, and realized to his surprise that the air smelled intensely of the sea.

"A courtyard! There's a courtyard down below!" Adrian suddenly exclaimed. He was looking through a window on the opposite side of the tower. Everyone gathered around. The spheres of light that they carried in their hands created a curtain of moving shadows.

The courtyard was larger than the tower itself. Its surface was irregular, in keeping with the general tone of Rocavarancolia, and it was protected from the moat by a crenellated wall six feet high that could be crossed by a stairway situated in the middle. There were so many cobblestones missing from the ground that Hector felt like he was looking at a half-finished puzzle.

"There's a well on one side," Marina whispered. "And . . . what's that? A statue?"

"Now that's ugly!" Adrian exclaimed.

There was a purplish stone pedestal in the middle of the courtyard. On top, sculpted from the same type of rock, rose a statue of a spider-like creature standing on a mountain of skulls, with four of its eight extremities raised toward the sky in an act of prayer or challenge. It wore a complex suit of armor covered in thorns, hooks, and spikes, and although the helmet hid its head from view one could only assume that it was monstrous.

"That looks more like the spider I saw last night," said Hector.

Once they knew it was there, it wasn't hard to find the door to the courtyard. They'd overlooked it since it was half-hidden behind a shelf on the first floor. Lizbeth and Rachel stayed upstairs; Rachel was in no condition to keep going up and down that stairway, and Ricardo didn't think that they'd be in danger alone.

Between them they were able to move the shelf without too much difficulty. The door that was uncovered was identical to the first one.

As soon as they opened it, a pleasant breeze of cool air entered the tower; it had changed direction and there was no longer even a faint ocean scent.

The light from the crystals seemed to fade in the courtyard. While some of them headed for the well at one end, the others, with Hector in the lead, went toward the spider statue. At the base of the pedestal they found a deteriorated plaque that Marina read aloud by the light of the rhomboid crystal:

"In honor of the macabre glory of His Majesty"—she took a breath before continuing—"Arachnihentheradon, under whose prosperous and vicious rule was erected the Margalar Tower." There was more writing in smaller letters. It looked like something was added to the plaque at a later date. She squinted. "May the gods curse him a thousand times," she read.

"It looks like someone didn't like him much," whispered Hector.

"I'm not surprised. That bug is almost as ugly as his name," Alexander joked.

The statue measured six feet high and was carved with great care. The artist had even defined the scales of chain mail that could be seen through the holes in the armor, and had sculpted every last spine covering the armored plates. Such attention to detail included eight spine-chilling eyes that were visible behind the grille of the helmet's visor.

"Did you really meet a creature like this one?" Adrian asked, uneasy.

"It was the same species, but it didn't seem as dangerous," Hector answered.

"I swear I would have died of fright," Marina said.

"Didn't you like spiders?" Alexander asked.

"Only the ones that are smaller than me."

At the other end of the courtyard, Natalia, Bruno, and Ricardo had taken off the wooden lid that covered the well and were examining the pulley system. They were discussing whether it would be risky to drink the water.

Hector glanced at the wall that surrounded the courtyard. It was constructed from the same kind of rock as the tower. Throughout the length of the perimeter there were several flimsy wooden doors, most of them half-open. He counted five. Hector approached the closest one and opened it all the way. Inside he found a small room, dark and foul-smelling. On the ground was a hole that must have led directly to the moat.

"I think I found the bathroom," he announced, wincing.

Madeleine peered over his shoulder and wrinkled her nose, horrified by the discovery. Hector thought that the number of faces the girl could make was really astonishing.

"How disgusting!" she exclaimed, her very dignity offended. "I wouldn't dream of going in there, I promise you!"

"Well, that's up to you, darling," her brother said, as he placed his arm around her shoulders. "But something tells me that this pretty hole is going to be the best option we'll find round here." He winked at Hector. "And now, if you don't mind, I think I'll be the first to christen the restroom here at Motel Rocavarancolia."

"You're gross!" his sister said as she shoved him away.

Hector grimaced and backed up to let Alexander through. Then he began to walk aimlessly around the courtyard, unsure whether to return to the statue or visit the well. The wind had let up and he now breathed in a deep feeling of calm. He closed his eyes and let the peace envelop him. The others' voices sounded distant, foreign to him. He heard someone laugh, maybe Adrian, and for a moment he felt like he was at home, in the yard, listening to noises from the neighbor's house, and that everything that had happened was nothing more than a daydream, a flight of fancy that he could use to make Sarah laugh at dinner. Then he opened his eyes and Rocavarancolia stretched out before him, a world made of ruins and darkness, shadows and horrors. The wind chose that very instant to gather its strength and roar through the abandoned houses and rubble like a dying monster.

Hector shook his head and looked around. He glimpsed a subtle spark in the sky. He squinted his eyes. The spark of light fell vertically to the earth. For a second he thought it was a shooting star, until it changed direction and rose up again.

Little by little the sky was overtaken by unsettling flashes of light. Alexander, after coming out of the bathroom, was the first to figure out what it was.

"Oh my God!" he exclaimed. "They're bats with wings of fire! Isn't there a single thing that's normal in this madhouse?"

"Bats?"

Dozens of them appeared, dotting the darkness with the brilliance of their wings. They flew over rooftops, twirled in the air, or simply seemed to fly around aimlessly. Adrian let out a yell and took off running toward the tower, waving his arms over his head as if he feared that the bats might land on him. The rest stayed in the courtyard, watching the flying creatures in astonishment.

Hector watched one fly by, barely six feet from him, and he was shocked to confirm that it actually was a bat. It was only about four inches long, and its wings were two flashes of bright red. He stared at it, open mouthed.

"I can't believe it," Ricardo whispered.

"Can you see them? Can you see them?" Lizbeth yelled from the window on the top floor.

"Breathtaking," Bruno commented. "Look at them closely. The blaze from their wings attracts insects and then scorches them so they can eat them."

Hector saw one of the bats take a bite to capture the moth that it had just roasted. He was dazzled, like the first time his parents took him to see fireworks and he was unable to remove his gaze from the sprays of fire and gunpowder that flowered in the heavens.

The black angel flew over the ruined city. He glided through the air with an ethereal grace, magical, appearing aimless. Several blazing bats followed in his wake, squeaking with pleasure to be flying alongside the Lord of Assassins. Esmael could have easily left them behind, but for the moment he let them follow him, even though they made his movements visible to everyone. He was sure he was being watched from the castle. Lady Scar and her supporters must already know about his conversation with the ghost. And once he demonstrated that he truly had Hurza's grimoire in his power, they would do everything possible to snatch it from him. He grimaced as he admitted to himself that he could only demonstrate he had access to the book; having it "in his power" was another matter entirely.

He made no noise as he moved. The only sounds to be heard were the comings and goings of the wind and the occasional howl of the castle's wolf pack, excited by the presence of young blood in the city.

Esmael gazed at the metropolis that stretched out before him. Thirty years had passed, but he still hadn't gotten used to the devastation. He remembered Rocavarancolia as it was before the war, and the contrast between the city of his memory and the ruins down below weighed heavily on his mood. The Lord of Assassins sighed in the heavens and flapped his wings once to change direction. The horde of bats followed him like a trail of shooting stars.

In the night he distinguished the reddish silhouette of Rocavaragalago, the gigantic red building that rose up on the outskirts of the city. Neither the passing of the centuries nor the war had left the slightest mark on the structure. It remained exactly the same as it looked in the most ancient prints and paintings. Time seemed to stand still for the building. The fortress in the mountain might have been the kingdom's brain, the place where every course of action was decided, but that construction of lunar rock was the authentic heart of Rocavarancolia. A merciless heart that even the Lord of Assassins feared.

He turned to the north. Among the shadows he recognized the Scar of Arax, dividing the city into east and west. The whiteness of the thousands of skeletons piled up in the crevice emitted a dim glow, a slight phosphorescence that became clearer at night. Esmael looked away, repelled by such a nauseating vision. In that pit lay all those he once called friends; there was Dionysius and Coldmouth, Amarantus and Dorna the Dismal. And Lady Fiera . . . Esmael bit his tongue hard and the bolt of pain kept his mind from getting lost in thoughts that he didn't need right then. It wasn't the time to think about the past. It was the time to build the future.

He then turned his gaze to the Margalar Tower, where almost all of Denestor's kids had taken shelter. What was curious about the situation was that the tower's original purpose had been precisely that: to house the various specimens that came to Rocavarancolia on harvest nights. There had been fifteen other similar locations scattered throughout the city, but only this one had survived; the rest had been destroyed in the last battle. And now eleven of the twelve teenagers took refuge once again within its walls. Being of an optimistic nature, he had come to think that was a good omen. Along with the fact that not a single child had died during their first few hours in Rocavarancolia.

He suddenly flew faster, becoming a blur of darkness. The flaming bats disbanded, unable to keep pace with him. Esmael flew to the east, flapping his wings forcefully, quick as black lightning. He then swerved rapidly to the north. Nothing and no one would find him now. He quickly changed direction at random a dozen times before heading for his true destination: the brick tower in the square of the serpents.

In the blink of an eye, he entered through a window on the top floor. He folded his red wings and looked around. He stood in a large heptagonal room, decorated with endless rugs and tapestries. Torches lit up shelves full of books, long reading desks, and racks overflowing with vials, amulets, and the most diverse objects of a magical nature. There were two antique mounted Aldarkense warriors in the center of the room; they'd been immortalized in a military pose, their grooved sabers crossed in combat. Dust covered everything; swirls of it still hovered in the air from Esmael's arrival.

Enoch was leaning on the main table of the study. He had one hand on his neck, and his face was even more unsettled than usual; he was so pale that the shadow of bones showed underneath his skin. The vampire turned his head toward Esmael when he finally noticed he was there, and the simple movement distorted his face even more.

"The curse at the entrance messes me up inside, my lord," he explained, panting. "It's an entirely unpleasant sensation, as if my insides were shifting around and then settling back in their rightful place," he muttered. "Please give me a moment to recover."

And you're supposed to take my place as Lord of Assassins? Esmael thought. The servility of the creature made him sick. Until recently he'd never missed an opportunity to show his disdain, but circumstances had changed and now he had no choice but to treat the repugnant vampire with tact.

"Give thanks to the underworld that you're one of the undead, or right now you'd be so affected by the door's spell that you'd be howling in pain."

"I know, I know." A childish snicker escaped from the vampire's lips. His yellowish fangs flashed for an instant. "I pushed a lot of people into cursed doors during my youth. It was fun to watch them squirm and writhe and scream. It took them so long to die . . ."

The black angel looked at him with disgust.

"You warm my heart, Dusty One."

"Oh. I am not worthy of your praise, my lord," the vampire said, not recognizing Esmael's sarcasm. The expression on his face sweetened before he asked, "Do we have the support of our beloved phantom?"

"We will, as soon as I prove to her that we have the grimoire. That's why I called you here. We will need a small demonstration in her honor."

"Consider it done! With Lady Serena's support, everything will tip in our favor!" The vampire trembled with pleasure. "The regency will be ours!"

"Don't be so sure."

Esmael counted on the support of Ujthan the Warrior, Belisarius the babbling mummy, and Enoch himself. On her side, Lady Scar had the damned invisible alchemist, Lady Dream, and Mistral, that stupid, paranoid shapeshifter who remained hidden for fear that Esmael would kill him to tilt the balance in his favor. The Lexel twins also formed part of the council, but given their natural antagonism each one would vote for a different candidate, so their votes canceled each other out. Of the two council members who hadn't yet made their decisions public, Esmael was only sure of being able to convince Lady Serena, as long as Hurza's book remained in his possession. Denestor Tul would be much more difficult to win over to his side. The demiurge didn't like either of the two candidates, but Esmael feared that in the end he would support Lady Scar. It wouldn't surprise him. At the end of the day, their positions in Rocavarancolia were diametrically opposed: the demiurge was dedicated to giving life and the Lord of Assassins to snatching it away.

Esmael cursed Roallen's voracity for the hundredth time. The troll had been a part of the council until the previous year, when in a fit of madness he devoured the only two specimens that Denestor had harvested from the human world. Roallen had been exiled and Mistral took his place on the council. The troll had been the black angel's faithful follower, and with him on the council his election would have been simpler.

"Promise me you won't eat any of Denestor's kids," he said to Enoch, suddenly aware that the vampire's instincts rivaled those of the troll.

"Oh." He brought a hand to his chest. "I'd never place a finger on one of those tender creatures, I swear."

"It's not your fingers I'm afraid of, it's your fangs." Esmael smiled reluctantly. "Let's do what we came here to do, vampire: the book. The spell should take place at midnight. I don't want to make the lady wait. That wouldn't be very gentlemanly."

"Of course, of course," Enoch crooned. He moved away from the table and staggered over to a lectern half-hidden between two bookshelves. It was carved out of bone, varnished in yellow ocher, and stood four and a half feet tall. Hurza the Eye-Eater's grimoire was nestled securely in the eight skeletal fingers of the colossal hand that crowned the lectern.

The book was bound in eternally fresh blood. It flowed through the covers and the spine in slow spirals, like eddies in a turbulent lake; from time to time a bubble rose to the surface, only to burst a second later. The movement was as hypnotic as it was unwholesome. That wasn't the grimoire's original cover, but a later addition, a way of ensuring that no one who was not a vampire could use the book. Any other creature who touched it would be struck down in the act, assassinated by the magic of the bloody binding. There wasn't a spell capable of opening the book or disenchanting that cover.

It was Enoch who'd found it less than a month ago, during one of his usual nighttime hunts. The vampire spent whole nights wandering throughout the city, in search of anything with blood in its veins. Enoch had been hungry for thirty years, subsisting on vermin alone. He couldn't even remember what it was to be satiated. On the night in question, as he passed by a demolished tower, he was assaulted by a smell of blood so intense that he immediately lost all reason. There was something enormous under the rubble of that tower, something filled to bursting with delicious, fresh blood. Enoch moved aside the debris with such frenzy that he broke several fingers. The disillusionment that seized him when he discovered that the smell was coming from heaps and heaps of books bound with blood was indescribable. He broke into tears like a child. When he finally managed to calm down, he examined what he'd found.

Most of the books were not important: historical treaties, diaries of forgotten vampires, or grimoires with little power. But one in particular drew his attention powerfully. To the very last, every one of its pages was blank. There was something strange about that empty book; what vampire wanted to protect something that didn't contain anything? That very night he shared his discovery with Esmael.

The black angel thought he was the butt of some kind of joke, even though he knew that the vampire lacked the imagination to pull something like that off. Enoch turned page after page of the book while he repeated over and over that it didn't make sense that it was all blank, while to Esmael's eyes each page was full of drawings, diagrams, and handwritten text. Only when he discovered the traditional seal of the

Lord of Assassins in one of the book's margins did he understand what was happening.

There were two protections in place in that grimoire: one prevented anyone who was not a vampire from handling the book, and the other, more ancient, hid the text from the eyes of anyone who was not in the role of Lord of Assassins of Rocavarancolia. The final surprise was the revelation that the grimoire belonged to the very first of them: it was the book of spells of Hurza the Eye-Eater, one of the founders of the kingdom.

It became evident that at some point in Rocavarancolia's history, an ambitious vampire who had managed to move into the rank of Lord of Assassins had created the enchantment on Hurza's book and, most likely, all of the grimoires within his reach. Surely his intention was to establish the tradition that members of his species would occupy that high-ranking position in the kingdom.

To the black angel's chagrin, the curious nature of the grimoire made it so that he and Enoch were forced to become allies, although Esmael had been very careful not to share too much information about the book with the vampire. Enoch was evil, but his intelligence and creativity were limited; this made him terribly boring, yet easy to manipulate.

The vampire took Hurza's book in his hands. Whirlwinds of turbid blood shone in his red eyes. He opened the book with an affected manner, knowing the importance of what he'd obtained for Esmael. He allowed himself a smile while he showed the pages one by one to the black angel. Esmael rested a hand on Enoch's back. To access the power contained in the book he had to be in physical contact with the vampire, and that made the situation even more unpleasant.

"See anything you like?" asked Enoch after a while, with one hand raised, waiting to turn another page, when he saw a gleam of satisfaction in the black angel's gaze.

"Yes," Esmael answered. "I've found something that, without a doubt, will greatly surprise Lady Serena."

And at the top of the brick tower, the Lord of Assassins hunched over Hurza's grimoire with an evil smile on his lips.

THE FIRST NIGHT

The crystals went out one by one. Madeleine's was the first to go; the rest followed suit in the same order in which they'd lit up. Soon darkness gripped of the Margalar Tower. It was so thick that they could barely make out the faces of those right next to them. Natalia and Ricardo tried to relight their crystals, but the spilling of blood was in vain: not even the faintest light emerged this time. It seemed that the rhomboid crystals were single use only. Alexander and Natalia offered to go collect more, but Ricardo wouldn't allow it. According to him it was too risky to descend the spiral staircase in the dark.

They were on the top floor, lying in a circle on top of the clothing they'd scattered over the ground. In a wardrobe on the ground floor they'd found several blankets that they added to the improvised communal mattress, only after Ricardo and Marco, under Lizbeth's supervision, shook them out thoroughly in the courtyard.

Outside, the flaming bats continued to write characters in fire against the night sky. Their flight was even more erratic than before, as if the tremendous gusts of wind that cut through Rocavarancolia made it difficult to stay aloft. The sparse brightness that lit up the tower came from the bats whose frantic fluttering swerved near the building's façade. One of them came so close that it burst in through an embrasure, causing Adrian to panic. The bat left immediately through another opening, but this didn't stop Adrian from fleeing the room in terror, shouting and waving his arms in desperation. Ricardo chased after him and it took

him quite a while to bring him back. For once, Alexander didn't
reprimand him for breaking his promise to control his anxiety. Hector
guessed that the redhead had discovered that Adrian had a phobia when
it came to fire. And that was a fear that had nothing to do with
Rocavarancolia.

"I'm hungry," Alex mumbled. "I'm starving. I'll eat the first one of
you who goes to sleep, I swear it. Go to sleep, Fatty, hurry up."

Alex lay with his arms crossed to Hector's right; to his left was Natalia,
almost entirely covered up with a blanket. The girl had propped her stick
against the wall, still within reach, and she kept her knife in the rolled-up
shirt that she was using as a pillow.

Hector's stomach, echoing Alex's words, complained with a long growl.
They ate the last of the pears before they went to bed, but it wasn't
enough to assuage their hunger. It was evidently going to be a long night.

Once again, they heard howls in the distance, mixed with the
bellowing of the wind. Hector shook beneath the covers. Natalia's head,
a shadow among shadows, turned toward an embrasure. The sounds that
came from outside were enough to unsettle the bravest of them. No one
said a word for a long time. It was Lizbeth who broke the silence, speaking
so fast that, as usual, it was hard to understand her.

"I'd say this is a good time to think about what we're going to do
tomorrow, don't you?"

"Tomorrow," Madeleine whispered. The word sounded as horrible on
her lips as the howls coming from outside.

"We're not doing anything," Ricardo announced. "We're staying here,
that's it. This place seems safe and we've seen that wandering around the
city isn't a good idea."

"We have to be careful," Marco continued, "we can't just act without
a plan. Tomorrow we'll wait for the bathtubs to come out, we'll divide
into three groups to go after them, and we'll gather provisions, but only
if we're sure it's safe. Then we'll come straight back to the tower."

"We're not going to explore the city?" asked Alexander.

"No!" Ricardo and Marco exclaimed in unison. Hector was amazed
by how well the two teenagers worked together.

"I don't want to go out," whispered Adrian. His voice trembled. He
still hadn't recovered from the panic attack caused by the bat invasion.
"I'm never going out."

"I'm afraid my opinion may differ," Bruno declared. His manner of speaking, pompous and monotonous at the same time, blended perfectly with the dark environment. "I myself wish to explore the tower with the strange symbol in the square. That symbol holds meaning, and I suspect it might be worth investigating."

Hector sighed as he remembered the black mist that surrounded the structure. While he searched for something to say to dissuade Bruno, Ricardo jumped in:

"No exploring," he insisted harshly. "We will stay in the tower and only leave to gather provisions. At least for now, okay?"

"Remember what Lady Scar told us about sudden and fatal curses? And about the monsters that live among the ruins?" Marco asked. Hector heard Adrian stifle a cry under the blankets. "No. Our curiosity might be killing us, but we can't take stupid risks."

"The library," Bruno said. "You said you found a library. And we know for certain that the place is safe, since you already explored it and nothing occurred. Could I go there at least?"

"You won't understand a single word in those books," Hector said hurriedly. "They're not written in the language of the fountain." He was convinced that Bruno's real intention was to return to the square to enter the brick tower.

"But books don't only contain words," the other pointed out.

"I can take him if he insists on going," Natalia said. Hector looked at her, frowning, but said nothing. "And the square isn't far. It shouldn't be dangerous. We've gone there and back a couple of times already."

"I'd like to return to the square, too," announced Madeleine. "We left our wet clothes there, and I want to get them back. It's not a big deal, but at least I'll have something to wear besides these rags."

"If it's okay with you guys, let's leave this discussion for tomorrow," said Ricardo. "The first thing we have to do is find food. When our stomachs are full, we can think about whether we want to go to the damned library or not."

"We are completely ignorant regarding everything about this city." Bruno seemed unable to let the subject go. "If we want to survive, we need information; that is something that should be obvious to all of us."

"Tomorrow," Ricardo repeated, even more harshly.

"And the missing kid?" Natalia sat up on the mountain of clothing, causing a small landslide of blankets and covers.

"If he's alive, we'll find him."

"And how are we going to do that if we're not even looking?"

"He can come look for us too, right?"

"I don't know if he's alive or not," Ricardo replied. "I have no way of knowing. What I don't want is for something to happen to us while we're out looking for him."

"Maybe he prefers to go it alone," Lizbeth offered. "Maybe he thought he'd have a better chance at survival that way."

"Well, if that's what he thinks, he's wrong," Alexander was quick to point out. "The best option is to stay together. So we can protect one another." He stretched out toward Adrian and extended a hand in his direction. "Right, squirt?"

"Right," Adrian said, without much conviction.

"What I don't understand is what we're supposed to do here," Lizbeth said. "Why do you think they brought us?"

"To rebuild the kingdom, at least to the best of our abilities," answered Marco. "That's what it said in the contract we signed."

"So, what then?" Alexander sat on top of the pile of clothing. "We grab shovels, pails, and brooms, and start sweeping? We start building houses? Is that what they want? Street cleaners and carpenters?"

"They didn't give us any instructions," Ricardo pointed out. "Neither Denestor nor that scary lady told us anything about what we have to do."

"You're wrong," Natalia said. "They did tell us what we have to do: stay alive as long as we can."

"Did he talk to you about potential?" Marina asked next. "About the magic that we all have inside?"

There was a general murmur of agreement.

"He told me that I was special," Adrian whispered.

"At least in terms of pajamas, of course you are," commented Alexander.

"Special," Ricardo murmured. "But why? What makes us special?"

After talking for a while, the only thing they could establish was how little they had in common. They all came from different parts of the world, although most of them were European. Bruno thought that could just be a coincidence, or perhaps during the time the door between Rocavarancolia and Earth was open, it was easier for Denestor and his minions to reach Europe. The only kids from other continents were Hector, Rachel, and the twins, who came from a remote village in Australia.

"As in, there aren't even kangaroos there. It's probably the most boring place on the planet," Alex added.

They were also of different ages. They ranged from Adrian, the youngest, at thirteen years old, to Ricardo at sixteen. What surprised Hector most of all was finding out that Marco, tall and mature Marco, was only fourteen, the same age as Marina and Lizbeth and one year younger than most of the others.

Hector turned to Natalia. If there was someone special there it was her: she saw shadows that nobody else could see. She'd seen them on Earth and now she saw them in Rocavarancolia. The young girl tensed up when she realized he was looking at her.

"Don't say a word," she whispered, guessing his thoughts, and gave him a kick under the blankets.

"There has to be something that sets us apart from the rest," Ricardo continued. "Some reason that they brought us here. In my case I don't know what it could be . . . The only thing that makes me stand out is my skill with languages. I'm good at them. My dad's a translator, and ever since I was little, he encouraged me to learn other languages. But I don't think that makes me special."

"You're a born leader," Lizbeth pointed out. "You've taken charge of us. And although we hardly know each other, nobody argues with what you decide. Well, at least not much," she said, launching a rolled-up shirt at Alexander.

"I never argue," the redhead protested. "And I'm fine with him and Marco deciding what to do. It's always good to have someone to blame if things go wrong." He shrugged. "But I don't know . . . Is having a knack for leadership enough to get you into this mess? 'Cause I don't see Amanda Carter, my class president, here, and she, my friends, is a force to be reckoned with."

"Why do you think they brought you and your sister?" Lizbeth asked.

"For our beauty, wit, and charm—was there ever any doubt?" There was a loud guffaw in the darkness. Hector couldn't tell where it came from. Marco, perhaps. "No, seriously though. I don't have the faintest idea why Denestor chose me. I'm nothing special. But Maddie is; although she doesn't look like it, she's a real artist. She's a painter. She paints strange stuff, but she paints very well."

"Please!" she exclaimed. "Don't pay attention to him, he doesn't know what he's talking about. A few months ago I started taking a painting class," she explained. "From the first class I was using warm tones in my pictures: reds, browns, ochers, colors like that . . . I mix them almost at random and then I draw a bunch of lines on top so that it seems like you're looking at the canvas through a spiderweb or cracked glass. My teacher says they're powerful pictures, but I'm not sure myself if they're any good."

"They sound good," Marina offered.

Hector pulled the blanket up to his neck and changed position to avoid an uncomfortable lump in the clothing. Rachel was lying in front of him; fiery wings beat furiously outside the embrasure and he caught a brief glimpse of her face in their light. Hector wondered what was going through her head. Injured, far away from everything she knew, and surrounded by strangers she couldn't understand. Another bat flew close to the façade and by its light Hector could now see that she was sleeping soundly. The expression on her face was so tranquil that he envied her. He wasn't the only one who noticed.

"Okay," Ricardo said, "so we know what makes Rachel special: she's capable of sleeping anywhere, in any situation."

"Is she really asleep?" asked Adrian, surprised, as he peered out from among the blankets.

"Well, that's a talent," Alex commented. "Anyone have anything else to tell us?" he asked. "Anything you think makes you special? Singing, dancing, ventriloquism? We can use all of it! With a little luck we can start a circus!"

"Don't be an idiot," Lizbeth scolded, between giggles.

"Marco is strong and fast," Adrian said. It seemed like the conversation was starting to cheer him up. "He beat up the monsters that were stealing our food. Seeing him in action was incredible. It was like a movie."

"I'm going to teach you all to do that," said Marco. "Not a single creature will dare come near us, you'll see."

"That's right! He's going to teach us!"

The conversation lightened the mood. That and the fact that the howling had stopped. Now they only heard the wind, lurching and moaning; it sounded like there were giants battling outside.

"I'm special too," said Hector. "You've seen it: I spend more time rolling on the ground than standing up. My gym teacher says that he's never known anyone so clumsy in his entire life. In fact, he can't understand how I've survived these fifteen years . . ."

"You're exaggerating. You don't fall that much," Lizbeth pointed out.

"Last year the gym teacher had the bright idea to keep track of all of the accidents I had during his class. You heard me: he counted the number of times I tripped or ran into gym equipment, doors, walls, and classmates."

"No!"

"He did. I'm not lying," he lied.

"I'm afraid to ask . . ." said Alexander. "But I will. How many was it?"

"One thousand two hundred and twenty-eight," he answered. "During that class I destroyed two doors and a mat, I knocked a window out of its frame, and I put an exchange student into a coma, although, frankly, no one liked him much. I think he approved of that one."

The kids' laughter was so loud that several bats moved away from the embrasures, frightened by the sudden noise. Even the wind seemed to pause momentarily in its attack. Rachel half opened her eyes, mumbled something unintelligible, and then closed them again.

"I . . . I don't know if I should say this . . ." said Adrian, after a moment. His tone of voice was so cheerful that Hector almost laughed just to hear him talk. "I have a secret power. A special ability . . ."

He brought one hand to his armpit and flapped his arm up and down, producing a very unpleasant squelching sound.

"That's disgusting!" he heard Maddie say over the others' laughter. "Quit it!"

"I can't help it. I got bitten by a radioactive fart when I was little," Adrian said, very seriously, as he kept showing off his power. Hector laughed so hard that tears ran down his cheeks.

"Well, you know what they say," Alexander said. "With great power comes great—"

"That's enough! Stop it!" yelled Natalia. She sat atop the mountain of clothing and moved her arms excitedly. "This is not a joke! Can't you see how serious it is? When are you going to stop acting like children?!"

After a moment of uncomfortable silence, they heard Adrian say:

"But we are children."

"Speak for yourself!"

"Can you stop being so worried, please?" Alexander asked. "You can't be so tense all the time, you'll end up snapping! Just let go for a bit, come on, it's not a sin!"

"Could you please lower your voice and stop yelling?" Madeleine pleaded. "You'll make me go deaf."

"Are we really discussing whether or not we can make jokes?" Ricardo asked. "How riiculous."

Alexander climbed over Hector so that he could talk to Natalia in a low voice. For a second, Hector felt like he couldn't breathe under the redhead's weight, smothering in the confusion of clothing and blankets.

"Relax, worrywart." Alex put his hand on Natalia's. "The little guy finally settled down and you have to start up again. We are in a jam here, but you don't need to keep bringing it up over and over. That doesn't make anything better."

"I'm sorry," whispered Natalia, embarrassed.

Alex went back to his place, to Hector's relief. But the good mood that had prevailed till then dissipated. Once again, the threat of Rocavarancolia weighed upon them. And the sound of the wind became unbearable.

"Does anyone have anything else to say?" Ricardo asked.

Hector watched as Bruno sat up on the clothing. He thought that he was preparing to speak, but another voice spoke up first, and the Italian lay back down.

"Well . . ." Marina cleared her throat. "I don't think that what I do makes me special, but . . . I think there's something strange about it, especially considering what's been happening." She propped herself up in the darkness. "Here it is: I like to write. I've done it since I was little . . . stories and poems . . . nothing too long because I get bored too quickly. I'm not very disciplined. The thing is, a little while ago I started writing a kind of . . . saga? No, I wouldn't call it that . . . They're stories that all take place in the same city, you know what I mean? In a magical city."

"Oh!" Madeleine exclaimed. "Is it called Rocavarancolia?"

"No, no. It's called Delirium. Well . . . in my imagination it's very similar to Rocavarancolia, although it's not in ruins, of course. Thousands of strange creatures live there, some of them evil, but others peaceful and benevolent. It's, I don't know . . . the city where I'd like to live. Full of magic and fantasy and adventures and . . ." She sighed. "This could be my city, you know? And it makes me dizzy to think about it. Because I'm dying to get *out* of here."

"What type of stories did you write?" Marco asked.

"I didn't write that many," she answered. "I finished two stories, had another halfway completed, and I had the beginning of an idea for a new one. All fantasy. Just to give you an idea, in the one I haven't finished yet there's a cemetery where the dead are always talking to each other and to anyone who happens by."

"Can you tell us one?" Maddie asked.

"A story?" she said, surprised. "You want me to tell you a story?"

"Please," Lizbeth encouraged. "A bedtime story."

"Well, if nobody minds, I can try," she said, shyly. "Although I should warn you that I'm better at writing them than telling them."

"But not the one about the cemetery with the talking dead people," Adrian begged. "Please, not that one."

"Okay. I'll tell you another one then," she said. "It's the second story that I wrote about Delirium. Yes, that'll be good; besides, it's not too long." She made herself comfortable on the blankets and clothing, and after a moment of silence, she began the story. "It's called 'For Love,' and it's the story of the king and queen of Delirium," she explained. "They'd known each other since they were kids, and the moment they first saw each other they knew they were destined to be together. The first thing he said to her was 'When I grow up I'm going to marry you,' and she simply answered, 'I know.' They were seven years old."

"A love story!" Alex exclaimed, horrified. "No, for goodness' sake! I'll have nightmares if you tell us a love story now, my blood sugar will go up and I won't be able to—"

"Shut up!" Lizbeth, Madeleine, Natalia, and Marco cried at the same time. Adrian broke out in laughter at the coordinated response.

"I'll shut up," Alexander announced theatrically. "I know when I'm outnumbered. You may continue, charming duck murderer."

Marina continued the story:

"From the first moment, as I said, it was clear that the children were made for each other. Everyone insisted that it was practically as if they'd been born married. They were the perfect couple. Years later they became king and queen of Delirium and they both remained as in love as when they first met. Under their reign, the kingdom prospered like never before. They were magnificent years, splendid; everything was happy and joyful. Until an assassin came to court, an assassin from a neighboring country with orders to kill the king. But he made a mistake: instead of pouring the deadly poison into the king's cup, he poured it into the queen's."

Hector listened with rapt attention to Marina's story. The girl's voice had him as bewitched in that moment as her eyes had throughout the day.

"The queen fell deathly ill. As she lay dying, the king, who was out of his mind with grief, swore that not even death could separate them. He went to the tower of the most powerful wizard in the kingdom to ask for his help." She remained silent for an instant before continuing. "The wizard told him that he couldn't do anything to save her; the assassin's poison was so potent that there was no magic in Delirium or in any other world that could help her. But there was something he could do: an extremely dangerous spell, dangerous because it destabilized the very essence of magic. He would keep vigil over the dying woman, he explained, and at the exact moment of her death, when the woman's soul left her body, he would use all of his power to transform her into a ghost."

"That would happen anyway when she died, right?" Adrian asked. "The queen would become a ghost herself."

"No," Marina answered. "At least it doesn't work that way in the magical world that I invented. Very few of those who die are transformed into spirits. And that wasn't the queen's destiny; her soul would simply disappear forever. And since the king couldn't accept that idea, he asked the wizard to perform the spell, even though the wiard warned him about how complicated and dangerous it was. The king swore to give the wizard half of the kingdom if he was able to return his wife to him, even though she would be a ghost."

"How beautiful," Madeleine said. "That's true love."

"The wizard waited in the queen's chambers until the second she took her last breath. Then, when the woman's soul abandoned her body, he carried her to the tower, and performed the spell that transformed her into a ghost. But something happened that no one could have expected: the transformation made the queen go insane! She couldn't understand why, even if it was for love, the king had condemned her to be a ghost forever. 'I couldn't live without you,' he tried to explain. 'Don't you understand?

Life without you wasn't worth living.' She didn't listen. Rage consumed her. And blinded by it, she mortally wounded him. 'Send someone to find the wizard,' the king of Delirium begged as he lay dying at her feet. But she only watched him as he died. 'You've condemned me, fool,' she said. 'For love, you've condemned me to a life that's not life; for love, you've hurled me into a perpetual eternity of misery. I curse your love. Bring that with you to the darkness, bring it with you into oblivion. I will remain here forever, cursing your name and cursing the day I met you.'"

"The assassin knew that was going to happen," Ricardo said. "Surely he didn't make a mistake in poisoning the queen instead of the king. Sometimes the easiest way of doing away with someone is destroying what they love."

"And that's it?" Adrian asked. He looked disappointed. "That's the end of the story?"

"Yes," Marina answered. "It ends with him dead and her condemned to be a spirit for all eternity."

"What a sad story," Lizbeth murmured.

"All stories are sad," Bruno pointed out, and his dispassionate voice made his claim all the more emphatic.

"All of them? What do you mean?!" Lizbeth exclaimed. "No! There are happy stories! And lots of them have happy endings."

"No," he replied. "No, there aren't. There are no happy stories. Happy endings don't exist. It's a lie. They're illusions. Those stories you're talking about aren't finished. They don't tell the last part. They never tell you that every single time, in the end, everyone dies."

The infinite room was contained in a tiny emerald set in one of the walls of the main tower.

Lady Serena wandered through it, with a slow, weary step. As much as she tried, she would never find the end of the room. The walls and ceiling were lost in a grayish mist, while whirlwinds of thick fog covered the ground. Wherever she looked, Lady Serena saw only ghosts. Someone had told her that the room itself was a specter, the spirit of a city ravaged by the armies of Rocavarancolia.

The room had been built over five hundred years ago, when it grew evident that the proliferation of ghosts in the kingdom had become a serious problem. There were so many of them that it became impossible to take two steps without running into some bereaved spirit or experiencing some kind of paranormal phenomenon. The emerald was created for this reason: to keep as many spirits as possible contained within. The room attracted them like moths to a flame, and once inside, most of them could never leave. Only a few privileged specters could resist the emerald's spell and wander the streets of Rocavarancolia as they pleased. Lady Serena, given her peculiar circumstances, was one of them. Only on rare occasions did she allow herself to be lured by the emerald's call. Today she wandered through its interior, waiting for midnight to arrive, and with it, Esmael's spell. In her unsettled state, sparks appeared on her forearms, and her hands seemed to be sheathed in lightning.

The ghost of a hanged man walked before her, the noose still tied around his neck; at her left, a musician with his accordion, listlessly playing a song of love betrayed. To her right crouched the specter of a werewolf; death had surprised him in the midst of his transformation, and now he was an incongruous mix of man and beast, unclear where one ended and the other began. If she looked behind, Lady Serena could see a large, shapeless silhouette moving in her direction, the spirit of an immense being whose head was lost in the fog. Legions upon legions of wraiths surrounded her. Flocks of ghosts commanded the space up above, floating over her like a sea of restless clouds.

Midnight came and went, with no change inside the emerald. The ghosts continued their slow ambling throughout the infinite room, far from everything save themselves and their sorrows. Lady Serena stopped and looked around while the spirits passed through her as if she didn't exist.

"All right, Esmael," she whispered. "What do you have for me?"

She crossed the glass floor and appeared at the other end of the emerald, in an octagonal room located on the first floor of the castle. Lady Serena slid through the walls, looking from left to right as she entered each room or hallway.

"Esmael, Esmael . . . how are you going to persuade me?"

She poked her head through the wall to the outside. Even the night seemed to wait anxiously. She went back inside and kept exploring the fortress, passing through walls, rafters, and partitions.

She stopped suddenly in the middle of a hallway. She'd felt a strange, stabbing pain, a sting that somehow reminded her of forgotten sensations that she could no longer name. She looked at the door at the end of the hallway. It led to the throne room.

She went toward it, plagued by flashes of unease. She slipped through the wall.

The first thing she saw was that the cobwebs that had covered the Sacred Throne for years had come down. Now, for the first time, the lustrous seat itself was visible. And as grandiose as it was, it was dwarfed by the tangle of tentacles that surged from its arms and back. They were metallic pseudopods, each almost five feet long, that made the throne look like an insane, menacing starfish. Those tentacles would tear to shreds anyone who sat on the throne other than the legitimate sovereign of Rocavarancolia. Throughout history, many had died, torn apart in its embrace. Some of these had tried to demonstrate that they themselves should wear the crown, and others were seated against their will.

Lady Serena watched as they waved restlessly in the air. They looked bewildered.

Then she saw a man.

He stood at one of the room's windows contemplating Rocavarancolia, his shoulders hunched, stooped over as if a great sorrow weighed upon him. He wore his finest armor, covered in changing tattoos. His long blond hair nearly reached his waist. The ends of his locks were jet black. Lady Serena had brushed that hair hundreds of times.

She felt lost, even more damned than before. No tears came to her eyes, because ghosts weren't capable of crying, but pain, suffering, and intense guilt tore at her from inside. And now she knew: Esmael had the grimoire of the first Lord of Assassins in his power. She was convinced that Lady Scar would find the spell within Hurza's book when she consulted the lists and compendiums of all known grimoires.

"Maryalé," she called. Her voice trembled as she spoke the name of her husband, the man whom she had killed over six hundred years ago.

He turned around. The face that she'd kissed and caressed so often was lined with tears. Maryalé wasn't a ghost, he was real. Esmael had revived him. The black eyes, the fine line of his eyelashes, the noble and proud wrinkles that lined his forehead, his sharp chin . . . It was him. Just as she remembered him, just as she'd seen him for the last time in life. There were tears in his eyes then; they spilled while Lady Serena lay dying in her bed, poisoned. But now she understood that Maryalé didn't cry for her. He cried for what he'd just seen through the window: he cried for Rocavarancolia.

"Serena," said the ancient dead king. He reached out a trembling hand in her direction. "My kingdom . . . What happened to my kingdom?"

The night brought with it the heavy darkness of a shrouded coffin. In the castle in the mountains, no monsters slept. Even Lady Dream stayed awake in her room, with her dry eyes open wide, looking with the fixed gaze of a reptile at the cracks in the wall, as if something there irrevocably drew her attention. On the other side of that same wall, in the room next door, Old Belisarius, wrapped in his numerous bandages, sat at a table covered with the most curious belongings. Next to him, standing morosely, one of the pale servants of the fortress would pick the objects from the table and then bring them, one by one, to the old man's face, so that he could see them better. Belisarius trembled with every keepsake that passed before his cataract-clouded eyes. The servant showed him a music box, a gift from an old lover. Then, a horn made of gray bone, a promise yet unfulfilled. Then, a string of beads that he'd stolen from a girl that he himself had murdered. Remembering the past was the closest thing to dreaming that Belisarius knew.

The Lexel brothers sat face to face in their quarters in the north tower. They looked at each other continuously. They had removed their masks and contemplated each other with a sick, all-consuming hatred. Many in the castle were convinced that the twins lived on nothing but the hatred that they professed for one another. They spent long nights in vigil, watching each other with murderous eyes. On the ground under the table was an empty basket that not too long ago had contained several apples from Arfes.

In the throne room, a revived king vanished into nothingness when the spell that resurrected him came to an end. Lady Serena remained there for a long time, looking at emptiness, floating several inches above the ground. The ghost trembled.

Rorcual, the alchemist, stood before the large mirror on the wardrobe in his room, observing his nonexistent reflection. It had been so many years since he'd seen his face that he'd forgotten what it was like; he couldn't even remember what color his eyes were. He stroked his unshaven, cracked chin. Then he poured himself another cup of wine, tottered over to his bed, and fell in.

On one of the castle ceilings, Lady Spider carefully prepared the new batch of provisions that would be sent out the next day over the ruined city. Salted meat, replicated fruits, sausages, hard bread; all of it passed through her four arms as she arranged the baskets. When she was finished, she would visit the regent, who lay prostrate on the top floor of the main tower. She would make him drink one of her fortifying potions, and then she would finally retire to rest in her web. The scarecrows stood at attention as they watched her progress, their straw-filled hands clutching determinedly at the helms of their ships.

Outside, the pack meandered through the destroyed gardens of the courtyard. Their eyes remained fixed on the ruined city. They felt the call of fresh blood. The leader of the pack, a large dark male with an enormous scar across his right eye, raised his head in the dead of night and howled. The others were not far behind.

In Highlowtower, Denestor Tul slept a deep sleep, so deep that he might have been taken for dead. Around him wandered a multitude of his most absurd creations, together keeping watch over their creator's sleep. Most of them blindly loved the demiurge. For Denestor Tul, they would have given away their lives—lives that he gave them—without a moment's hesitation. An antique gunpowder rifle with a dozen scissors for limbs climbed into the hammock where the demiurge slept and curled into a ball at his side.

Beyond the castle and the mountains, among the ruins of Rocavarancolia, roamed Enoch the Dusty, sniffing the air in search of some prey that he could bleed dry. On the way he passed near the cemetery hollow. The Royal Pantheon, a structure made of black marble with a large cupola and four pyramidal outbuildings, occupied the center of the graveyard. The rest of the land was covered with hundreds of tombs and mausoleums. Enoch stopped for a second to listen to the conversation of the dead. They were restless. They too had been disrupted by the arrival of the new harvest. Their conversations were an incongruous din.

The main gate of the Royal Pantheon opened to let Lady Scar through, furious and even more disheveled than usual.

"Will you be quiet?!" she yelled to the talkative cemetery inhabitants. "I want to sleep! Shut up, or I swear that I'll come down there tomb by tomb and cut out your damned worm-eaten tongues!"

"Sleep, my lady, sleep," answered one of them, the cadaver of an ancient wizard with little power. The voice was muffled by the coffin and the ground that covered it. "And forgive our audacity. Let us right our affront by helping you get to sleep."

And the dead began to sing a lullaby, so off key that even Enoch ground his teeth. Lady Scar let out a curse, ripped off her ears, put them in the pockets of her threadbare shirt, and went back inside the Royal Pantheon, shaking her disgruntled head. Underground, hundreds of dead mouths broke out in laughter.

Enoch continued his journey, with the wind flapping the folds of his dusty cape. After a while, a trace of hot blood reached his nasal passages. It came from the second floor of a half-collapsed building. There was Denestor's last kid, the only one who hadn't taken refuge in the Margalar Tower.

The vampire climbed through the house's entrance like an incongruous lizard. Squinting, Enoch spied the young boy through a window. He was crouched in front of a fire, concentrating on the task of roasting a rat skewered on his sword. On the ground next to his bare feet there was already a sizable pile of gnawed bones.

Enoch licked his lips. It would be so easy to open his throat and drink his blood, his delicious and marvelous blood.

Suddenly, the teenager looked up in his direction. The fire's flames were reflected with a frightening intensity in his eyes. The vampire, startled, dropped to the pavement and began to walk away rapidly, almost running, glancing behind him now and then, as if he feared that the boy was in pursuit. He laughed, aware of how absurd his fear was. He was a mere child, one of Denestor's pups. What caused this absurd panic? Enoch shook his head, laughed again, and kept walking, now more slowly.

He only looked behind him one more time.

At the top of the lighthouse sat Esmael, the black angel. He sat with his back to Rocavarancolia, his gaze lost in the shifting horizon of the sea. From time to time the lighthouse beam shone over the ocean to the east, reflecting in its passage the precious stones that covered the black angel's skin. Among the reefs at the foot of the cliffs floated the remains of dozens of ships that had been wrecked, deceived by the betraying light of the Rocavarancolia lighthouse.

The lighthouse's dome had recently become one of Esmael's favorite places. He liked to sit there and let his eyes wander over the restless surface of the water. It calmed him to hear the waves crashing against the rocks and the shipwrecked vessels. Sometimes he wondered how far he'd be able to fly out to sea before exhaustion overtook him. On more than one occasion he'd been tempted to do it: take flight one final time and go toward the distant horizon on a one-way journey. Throughout the centuries there had been more than a few Lords of Assassins who'd taken their own lives, sometimes out of dishonor, sometimes simply out of boredom. In fact, his first impulse after the defeat that put an end to Rocavarancolia's aspirations had been just that: to plunge deep into the sea and never return.

Esmael sighed, his gaze lost in the horizon. Then he turned his eyes in the direction of the Margalar Tower.

There, most of the teenagers slept.

Hector was surprised that the others had been able to fall asleep, but the even sound of their breathing assured him of their slumber. He, on the other hand, had resigned himself to spending the night awake. His mind was abuzz with all that he'd lived through in the last few hours. It was as if a poorly filmed movie of what had occurred were playing in fast forward in his brain. Denestor, Lady Scar, the human spider, the Scar of Arax, the darkness that Lady Serena had inserted into his mind . . .

Every so often the sounds from outside made him turn his head toward the embrasure. The wind howled in a thousand different voices. He also heard the beating on the tiles, the noise of rocks clashing together, and occasionally the sinister howls coming from the mountain. Rocavarancolia was noisier at night than during the day. And scarier. Sometimes he thought he heard footsteps and his imagination was filled with creatures lurking and hordes of terrors that climbed the walls.

The wolves, if that's what they were, resumed their howling, and he stretched out again in the darkness.

"Are you asleep?" he heard Natalia ask.

"No," he whispered. Someone muttered something in their sleep. "I can't sleep. I tried counting sheep, but the wolves came and ate them."

"You're silly," she said. And although he couldn't see her face, Hector guessed that Natalia was smiling. "You can hold my hand if you want," she offered. "If you're afraid, I mean."

Hector smiled. A flash from one of the flaming bats circling around the tower suddenly lit up the dark room. He reached out his hand, searching for Natalia's. When he found it their fingers intertwined tightly. Feeling the warmth of the girl's hand in his was a comfort, a respite. They remained quiet, without letting go, each of them lost in their own thoughts. And to Hector's surprise, he, too, began slipping into sleep; despite the sounds outside and all the tension, exhaustion finally took its toll.

The last thing he thought before he fell asleep was that he would have preferred to squeeze Marina's hand. The thought instantly embarrassed him, but he neither could nor wanted to avoid it. Marina had the most beautiful eyes in the world.

STONE, FIRE, AND MAGIC

Hector woke up abruptly.

He sat up with the sleeve of his sweatshirt stuck to his cheek, so dazed that for a couple of seconds he didn't know his name or where he was. He felt a deep, heavy feeling in his left temple, as if a good portion of his brain refused to awaken and was tugging him back to sleep.

Natalia was next to him, and by her expression it seemed that she'd woken up as disoriented as he was. Her dark hair stood up in messy crests and peaks, making her look like a stupefied bird. She seemed surprised to find him next to her.

"Get up, slackers! Let's go!"

Alex and Ricardo stood on the spiral staircase; they were the ones who'd woken them with their yelling. Hector grumbled and slapped at his face to free himself from the sweatshirt sleeve. Warm daylight came in through the small windows and lit up the room. Its caress, though weak, was comforting. He saw Adrian drowsily rubbing his eyes within the heap of clothing, and Rachel, against all logic, still sleeping despite the shouts from the two teenagers. There was nobody else around.

"Come on, sleepyheads!" Alex insisted. "They brought us a gift! Get out from under the blankets already!"

It wasn't his words that made Hector give him his full attention, but the sound of a juicy bite that woke him up, as well as his empty stomach. Ricardo was eating an apple of an intense gold color, so succulent looking that it made Hector drool. Alexander swung a small wicker basket in his hand.

"The bathtubs?" Natalia guessed. She slid out from under the covers and crawled over the pile of clothing. "Did the bathtubs come by?"

"No. The basket was in the courtyard, next to the statue of Hector's friend. They must have left it for us last night."

"She's not my friend," he mumbled, without taking his eyes off Ricardo's apple. When the teenager took another bite, Hector unconsciously imitated his action.

Alexander took an apple from the basket and threw it to him. Hector missed, and it fell onto the clothes. When he picked it up, he was amazed by how smooth it felt, as delicate as silk. The sun's rays made its golden skin sparkle.

"What if they're poisoned?" Adrian asked as he looked reluctantly at the apple Alex had just tossed.

"Well, if they are, they are, Snow White," answered the redhead. "It's the most delicious thing I've ever tasted in my life. If I die, I'll die happy. Give it back if you don't trust me."

Adrian shook his head and took an exploratory bite out of the apple. Hector did the same. He only took a tiny nibble of skin and pulp, but that was enough to understand what Alex was talking about. He gasped when he tasted the juice of the fruit in his mouth. To say it was delicious was an understatement. He'd never tasted anything so marvelous; he'd never imagined a flavor like that could even exist.

"Oh my God!" he exclaimed, and looked at Alexander and Ricardo with his eyes open wide. They both nodded and broke out laughing at the same time. "It's like eating a little piece of heaven."

"Be careful and don't choke!" Ricardo told them. "Marco almost had an attack when he ate it. It brought tears to his eyes."

"It's so good!" Adrian got up suddenly and started jumping on the blankets.

Natalia finally managed to wake Rachel by shaking her shoulder. Alexander took out the two apples that were left and threw them to the girls. They both caught them in the air, with admirable skill. Natalia was the first to try it, and no sooner had she tasted it than she let out an outrageous moan and fell backward. Rachel looked at her, surprised, yawned several times, and took a huge bite out of hers. Her eyes opened at once to the size of dinner plates. She looked at everyone, astonished, said something in her incomprehensible language, and proceeded to devour the fruit at top speed.

Hector, on the other hand, did everything he could to make it last. Every mouthful was a direct explosion of paradise on his palate, but also, with every bite he noticed his hunger disappearing. When he finished the apple, he felt completely satisfied.

They reunited with the others among the chaos of furniture and belongings on the first floor, which seemed even more jam-packed in daylight. The sun filtered in through several small openings halfway up the wall, so narrow that they hadn't even noticed them the night before. They were all disheveled and dirty, all except Alex and Maddie, who looked as radiant as they had before they went to sleep.

"How do they do it?" Natalia asked Hector in a low voice once they'd helped Rachel into a large armchair. "I smell like cat vomit."

"I feel like cat vomit," he said.

He looked at Marina. She was leaning against a tall nightstand. The night had made a mess of her hair and she looked sleepy, but she was still beautiful. The young girl rubbed her eyes and stifled a yawn with the back of her hand.

Natalia finally managed to wake Rachel by shaking her shoulder. Alexander took out the two apples that were left and threw them to the girls. They both caught them in the air, with admirable skill. Natalia was the first to try it, and no sooner had she tasted it than she let out an outrageous moan and fell backward. Rachel looked at her, surprised, yawned several times, and took a huge bite out of hers. Her eyes opened at once to the size of dinner plates. She looked at everyone, astonished, said something in her incomprehensible language, and proceeded to devour the fruit at top speed.

Hector, on the other hand, did everything he could to make it last. Every mouthful was a direct explosion of paradise on his palate, but also, with every bite he noticed his hunger disappearing. When he finished the apple, he felt completely satisfied.Even Rachel seemed shocked by the verbal feat that Lizbeth had just displayed, and she couldn't understand a single word of it. Alexander slapped Ricardo on the back and whispered in his ear:

"Now we know who's really in charge here."

"Do we have to start cleaning now?" Adrian asked. "I mean, we just got up!"

"It seems like we don't have a choice," Natalia commented, making a face. "But I hope you let us go to the bathroom first, or you'll have more to clean than you think."

The Margalar Tower soon became a hive of frenzied activity. Marco, Lizbeth, and Ricardo took charge of taking the mattresses out to the courtyard while the others, armed with brooms, rags, and pails filled with well water, battled the dust and filth on the top floor. When they finished there, they moved on to the chaos of the ground floor, moving furniture and junk to the first floor and the basement in an effort to clear the place. Whatever was too big to maneuver down the stairs ended up in the courtyard.

In a short while there were two clearly defined groups. Those who truly did their best, Hector among them, and those who devoted themselves to snooping around in wardrobes and avoiding hard work, with varying degrees of subtlety. In the latter group were the twins and Adrian, and although Lizbeth called them out on more than one occasion, there wasn't much they could do to make them focus on the work. The only one with an excuse to be lazy was Rachel, who spent most of the time sitting where she wouldn't be in the way. Ricardo had improvised a pair of crutches for her from two old brooms. First he pulled out all of the bristles, and then he wrapped both ends in rags so they wouldn't slide on the ground or poke into her arms when she used them.

While they tidied up the ground floor, they made a conscious effort to search for anything that could be useful, revealing, or simply interesting.

Madeleine found a polished wooden cabinet full of medallions and necklaces. They were all in a sorry state, faded, rusty, blackened, or all three at once. And it looked like even when they were in good condition, they wouldn't have been considered pretty. Quite the opposite, in fact.

"Human spiders? Horrible women covered in scars? Lying little gray imps?"

In a wooden box covered by an old rug they discovered another pile of objects, in much better shape. There were toys, baubles, string, key chains, and a bunch of other trinkets of uncertain usefulness.

"They must have belonged to the kids they brought here before us," Marina said.

They all put their chores aside to sort through the box. Natalia took out a curious rectangular wooden chest that let out strange, vaguely animalistic sounds when shaken. They saw rings of all sizes and types of metal, bracelets and necklaces, toys so crude that they were nothing more than poorly carved wood. Alexander took a clumsy rendering of an animal that looked like a horse; it had six feet and a long tail that ended in a curved stinger.

"Look at this!" Hector exclaimed. He'd found a card made of a metallic looking plastic. It had unintelligible characters printed on it, and a strange photograph seemed to float several millimeters above the surface of the top left-hand corner.

"It must be some sort of hologram," said Bruno.

The creature whose full-body portrait appeared in the floating image was not human. It was a chubby being, with short, thick legs and arms so flat they almost resembled wings. It had a flattened head, four oval eyes, and a type of blunt beak in the middle of its face. It was hard to tell if its body was covered in plumage or in some kind of clothing.

"They don't only bring people from Earth," Hector said. The hologram flickered as he moved it, showing a close-up of the creature's face. He had the feeling that it was smiling. He wondered if its bones had also ended up in the Scar of Arax.

As they moved several boards leaning against the western wall, they discovered an odd stove. It was a small stone platform, maybe three feet tall, with several metal tracks on top. The platform's surface was separated from the rails by a gap an inch or two deep in which they saw the remains of charred wood. Next to the stove was a cupboard brimming with pots, pans, and jugs full of thick oil.

Alex grabbed one of the jugs and went up to the top floor of the tower. Ricardo and Hector followed him. The redhead climbed onto the barrel under the ceiling trapdoor and greased the joints of the enormous latch with a rag smeared in oil. Then he managed to pull it loose without difficulty. The hatch opened toward him and the light of day burst in through the hole. For a few seconds, the teenager was surrounded by an aura of golden light and dust suspended in the air.

There were horizontal grooves on the trapdoor that would help them up to the battlement. Alexander scrambled up and peered through the opening.

"It looks safe," he announced. "Permission to ascend, fearless leader?"

"Only if you jump afterward."

Alexander let out a guffaw and pulled himself up. Hector felt a pang of worry as he watched him disappear through the trapdoor.

"It's filthy, but there's no danger of anyone falling from the tower," they heard him say after a couple of seconds. "Oh . . . the view is magnificent. Come on up! You have to see this!"

Before they went, Ricardo called to the rest of the group. Lizbeth and Rachel stayed on the ground floor, but the others didn't hesitate to crowd around the barrel, their faces raised to the open trapdoor. They went up one by one. Hector would have preferred to wait down below, and when he finally followed them it was more out of worry over what they'd think of him than true conviction. The idea of being on the roof of the tower made his hair stand on end.

Natalia gave him her hand when he peeked his head through the trapdoor, and she helped him up the last step. For a moment he stayed on all fours on the ground, his hands and knees buried in a small, gross island of dried bird and bat excrement. He stood up, disgusted, wiping the palms of his hands on his pants.

The rooftop was surrounded by a wall five feet tall from which the battlements rose up at regular intervals. Rocavarancolia lay beyond the wall, with the mountains and castle to the west. But everyone's attention was focused in the opposite direction.

"The sea," murmured Natalia, excited. Her eyes sparkled. "I've never seen the sea."

The immaculate blanket of blue appeared sharply beyond the last line of buildings, as if separated from the city by a cliff, a dike, or something similar, then it extended in the distance until it merged with the sky at the horizon. It was a monumental sight. The shifting surface of the ocean was sprinkled with glimmering flashes and dark patches, with twinkling shadows and streaks of foam. They almost thought they could hear the distant crashing of the waves.

"Maybe we can escape by sea?" Adrian whispered, not fully convinced. "We could build a raft or something . . ."

"Lady Scar said that the city was surrounded by mountains and cliffs," Marco reminded him. "I don't think we'll find a way to the sea. And even if we did . . . where would we go? And how?"

Adrian shrugged his shoulders.

"My dad let me take the helm of his yacht once . . ."

"Yacht? You have a yacht?"

"Actually, we have two."

From the tower's battlement they had a privileged view of the city. Rooftops and terraces were scattered haphazardly in every direction, like pieces of a construction set strewn about by a mischievous child in a frenzy of arcades, bridges, staircases, and plazas.

"There's not a single blade of grass," Marina murmured, leaning out between two merlons. The wind rustled through her messy hair. "I can't see a drop of green. Has anyone seen a tree or any other plant?"

"Scrawny reeds in the river and dead ferns on a couple of patios," answered Ricardo. "Nothing else so far."

"What an awful place." She took a step back.

The red cathedral was the largest structure in Rocavarancolia; it rose up in the southeast, ill-fated and terrible, surrounded by Lady Serena's dense curtain of shadows. It wasn't the only large building in the city. To the three towers that Ricardo and Marco had approached the day before, they could add another dozen buildings that reached higher than the others by far. Near the cathedral itself was an obelisk almost as tall as it was.

"The sky outside the castle is full of lights," Adrian commented. "Can you see them?"

They all moved to the western face of the tower for a better view of the mountains. Around the castle they saw an endless number of unsettling flashes of light, most of them centered around the entrance. They reminded Hector of the typical reflective glint you'd see in a movie when someone was looking through a spyglass or aiming a weapon, although he doubted that was the case in this instance. There were too many flashes, and besides, they were constantly moving.

"Well, what are those things?" Alexander murmured. "Flying lamps? Glass vultures?"

At that precise moment, as if the redhead had invoked them, a flock of black birds flew over their heads; their deafening squawks cut through the air like laughter mixed with the rattling of a machine gun. They watched them vanish among the ruins, like a long, chaotic black braid.

Shortly after, they decided to resume their cleaning chores. Adrian stayed on the battlement, on the lookout for bathtubs. The teenager was so enthralled by his new assignment that not two minutes would go by without him announcing loudly that everything was clear and calm. He only shut up when Alexander threatened to throw him off the battlement if he heard him yell again.

Down below, the battle against clutter and dust continued under Lizbeth's command. Fulfilling her orders, Hector stacked up candelabras, battled spiderwebs, swept, and helped transport furniture up and down stairs. And whenever possible, he glanced at Marina, who was as busy as he was. He couldn't help it. Maybe Madeleine surpassed her in looks, but Marina's beauty had something that transcended the redhead's: a calm, spiritual touch that somehow took hold of Hector. And he was unable to resist the growing attraction. The only thing he knew was that he couldn't stop looking at her: he needed to know if she was still there, that she hadn't vanished without a trace, that she wasn't a dream or just another marvel of the bewitched city.

He suddenly realized that he hadn't spoken to Marina even once. He'd participated in group conversations, yes, but he'd never spoken directly to her. He wandered near, gathering courage to say something, anything. A simple exchange of a few harmless words, nothing more. But he just couldn't manage it. The palms of his hands were sweating, and a knot formed in his throat. Sometimes he moved to the other side of the tower, aware that his behavior was absurd, but it never took him long to return to her orbit.

When he saw her approach a bookshelf that Ricardo had already gone through and cleaned, he saw his chance: he would tell her that it was already clean, and then, casually, he would tell her how much he liked the story about the phantom queen. He felt stupid planning the development of a conversation, but he could see no other way of gathering up the courage to talk to her.

When he finally reached Marina, with his heart thumping and the feeling of frozen fingers squeezing his insides, from the top of the Margalar Tower came the voice of Adrian, yelling at the top of his lungs:

"The bathtubs! They're leaving the castle! They're leaving the castle!"

Hector and the twins rushed out, clinging to the façades of the ruined buildings in an alleyway, alert to the slightest noise or movement.

They headed for the towers where Marco thought he'd seen a bathtub land the day before. And it indeed looked like one of them was heading straight for that spot. Although they were still far away, they could already hear the pilot's songs. Marco had pointed out which street to avoid so they wouldn't encounter the house that had tried to eat him; but that hardly eased Hector's mind. Maybe they could escape that threat, but many others lay in wait. The black mist was everywhere. He chose to walk in the lead, but not because of bravery. He wanted to prevent the twins from taking paths that came too close to a shadowy area.

Hector felt ridiculous. The act of walking in rags, with a dagger sheathed in his belt and a round shield at his back, seemed almost as unreal to him as most of what was happening. The shield had been a last-minute inspiration of Marco's. Before leaving the tower, he made them all go to the armory and select shields, most of them small and manageable. "If the creatures with the spiny tails appear, cover yourselves well with them," he advised.

The three teenagers arrived at the street corner. They stopped to check that the street was clear. When they deemed that it was, they resumed their march, almost at a run, until they found shelter against a courtyard wall.

At the same time, Natalia and Marco were heading toward the north, toward the area where they'd encountered the vermin the day before. Ricardo, Bruno, and Marina followed the trail of the third ship, whose path also seemed to lead to the other side of the Scar of Arax.

Lizbeth, Rachel, and Adrian had remained in the tower. They'd tried to convince the boy to accompany Marco and Natalia, but it was all in vain. He didn't want to so much as hear about leaving the tower; he didn't even want to be around when they lowered the drawbridge. He'd hidden in a room on the second floor and said he'd only come out when the bridge was raised again. Even Alexander seemed to think his was an impossible case. Lizbeth had offered to go in his place, but they all agreed that it was better for her to stay and take care of Rachel.

Hector wasn't happy about sharing his venture with the twins. Alexander didn't bother him now as much as he did at first, despite his insistence on calling him Fatty, but he couldn't forget his unhinged behavior at the Scar of Arax. Hector was sure that he could lose control again at any moment. And he didn't like the idea of being nearby when that happened.

The three towers that they walked toward were identical, at least in height and structure; the base and the first two floors were pentagons, although the rest of the building was rectangular. All the façades were dotted with large, arched windows with hardly any space between them, which lent them a curiously lightweight appearance.

The towers differed in the materials used in their construction. One of them had been erected in light marble, another seemed to be made from glass and mirrors, and the third was made from a greenish wood. The white tower and the glass tower were significantly damaged; the rooftop of the first looked like it had exploded outward, whereas the north façade of the second was in such bad shape that most of its surface was a tangled mess of cracks. The top floors of the green tower were completely enveloped in Lady Serena's black mist.

The towers differed in the materials used in their construction. One of them had been erected in light marble, another seemed to be made from glass and mirrors, and the third was made from greenish wood. The white tower and the glass tower were significantly damaged; the rooftop of the first looked like it had exploded outward, whereas the north façade of the second was in such bad shape that most of its surface was a tangled mess of cracks. The top floors of the green tower were completely enveloped in Lady Serena's black mist.

As they approached, they saw in the distance the glow coming from the neighborhood in flames. They couldn't make out the entire area, but they could glimpse parts of it through the buildings that crowded together to the southeast and the houses in ruins. Now, alone, Hector felt overwhelmed for the thousandth time by the city that was as abhorrent as it was marvelous. Tall columns of fire rose up as high as the buildings they consumed; intense red blazes licked at the façades, rooftops, and overhangs, unraveling in endless spirals, piercing the void; rivers of still flames collapsed the streets into coal and embers that unfurled into the air like miraculous flowers; and all of it, of course, appeared stained and spotted before his eyes by Lady Serena's black mist. Even so, Hector had to agree that it was a beautiful sight. Instead of fire, it looked like cut glass. The glow of the unmoving flares dyed the keel of the bathtub red as it approached the towers.

"We must never let the fire go out," Alex quoted.

"Again with *Lord of the Flies*?" Hector asked.

Alexander nodded, cold and distant.

"Can you hear them?" he asked.

Hector was about to shake his head when suddenly he, too, could hear *them*. The wind carried with it the shrieks of those who burned in the neighborhood in flames. All the apparent beauty of the place vanished at once: such beauty was no more than a trick, another murderous illusion. There were people there, people being consumed by flames without dying, their death delayed perhaps by the same magic that prevented the fire from spreading throughout the city. Hector shuddered. As they approached the towers, the shouting became a persistent murmur, a hair-raising hum that was impossible to iwgnore. At least, as they advanced, they lost sight of that cursed neighborhood.

There was a fourth tower next to the others, but all that remained was the first floor. The rest of the building had vanished without a trace, barely leaving any rubble; from where they were it was difficult to guess what material it was made of. What was left of it looked like dirty ice.

Between the three towers and the remains of the fourth stretched an enormous square full of white statues, most of them in good shape, although a good many lay in pieces. To the very last, those that remained standing were immersed in an impressive, motionless battle royal.

Everywhere they looked, they saw warriors striking each other, monsters in threatening poses or fallen on the ground. Hector found stone representations of two winged creatures similar to the one they'd found the day before; both straddled a giant whose arms and head were disproportionately large in comparison to its body, and savagely stabbed its back. The giant was turning and trying to reach the attackers with its mace, but they were out of reach.

The most impressive of all the statues in the square was an enormous dragon, raised on its hindquarters, that swiped at a group of soldiers on horseback who taunted it with their lances. For a short while, Hector was unable to tear his eyes away from the open jaws of the beast, with its rows of sharp fangs as long as his dagger. He almost thought he saw a flutter of air in its throat, as if it could hurl a blaze of fire at any moment.

The sailboat approached slowly from the west, leaving behind the burning neighborhood and turning to avoid the glass tower.

"And if the critters with the spines appear?" asked Madeleine.

"Then we turn around and leave without making a sound," Alex answered. Hector breathed a sigh of relief. "Our leader said that we can't take risks and we're going to listen to him. He's wise and brave," he grumbled before adding, "and these shields are very small."

"Come! I bring owl gullet and Gorgon breath! Snake fingers and swordfish wings!"

The ship began its maneuvering above the square. The pilot was identical to the one from the day before; even the voice sounded the same. He left the helm and began to lower the baskets very close to an odd group of tree statues near the ruined tower; they were more than sixty feet tall and sculpted from the same stone as the combatants. They had irregular trunks, much thicker at the bottom than up high, and the treetops were completely horizontal.

Hector stared at them, puzzled, while the scarecrow lowered the baskets. Those trees were out of place there, in the midst of a still battle. There was something about the square that really bothered him, although there was no trace of mist around.

One basket tipped over as it hit the ground and a piece of meat wrapped in mesh rolled on the pavement until it came to a stop at the warriors' feet. The teenagers, who'd waited motionless while the baskets were being lowered, now took off running toward them.

There were statue fragments scattered everywhere. They ran past a gigantic torso dropped among a set of limbs. It was then, looking at the pieces of white stone, that Hector realized what had happened in the square.

He stopped, horrified by what he'd just discovered. He took a bad step, trippled and fell to the ground. His left elbow hit the pavement and a shooting pain made him first grit his teeth and then cry out.

The two siblings ran at full speed to him.

"Look, he's being clumsy," Madeleine muttered with disdain when they reached his side.

"Don't pay any attention to her. You know what they say about redheads: they're bad, very bad." Alexander stretched out his hand as he looked cautiously around him. "Are you okay?"

Hector shook his head. But his gesture had nothing to do with his physical state.

"They're not statues," he whispered, as he pointed at a piece of white stone. It was hollow, and inside part of a tibia and a fibula were visible, cut off where the stone was cut. "They were real. They were alive. They must have been battling in the plaza, and something turned them to stone."

Madeleine stifled a cry with the palm of her hand. Alex looked one way and then the other, and after a slight hesitation, he shrugged, his gaze fixed on the decapitated warrior.

"Better them than us," he pointed out. His voice only shook a little. He ran his hand over his hair before looking at Hector again. "If you're going to fall every time we find something shocking, soon you won't have an unbroken bone left in your body."

"How can you act that way?" he asked, ignoring Alexander's coolness. "They were alive!" Hector stood up without taking the redhead's outstretched hand. His leg hurt and his elbow was numb.

"Okay. They were alive, Fatty, *were*. You can't do anything for them, and truthfully, none of these guys seemed all that friendly," he pointed out. "Or is it that you'd rather run into that thing in the flesh?" he asked, gesturing with his head to a frightening being on his left.

The creature was nearly nine feet tall, thin and sinewy, with enormous hands and long fingers jutting out from the mop of fur that covered its forearms; its head was almost spherical, half-covered in hair that looked like it was braided with a nest of vipers. Its open mouth revealed two rows of razor-sharp fangs. That monster wasn't any more horrifying than much of what they'd seen thus far in Rocavarancolia, but there was still something startling about it.

"You see?" Alex smiled and started toward the baskets. "Let's go get some food. I'm dying to try eye of skunk and squirrel kidney."

Alexander placed the provisions on the table that was behind the main gate of the Margalar Tower. They were the first to return and now, in the others' absence, the place seemed strangely deserted. Lizbeth had lit several candles and candelabras, and the combination of the flickering lights and the melancholy daylight that entered through the cracks in the walls made the tower seem emptier still.

Hector fell back in a chair, exhausted and still sore from his fall in the square. Adrian sat on one of the steps of the staircase, silent and gloomy; not even Alexander's jokes could make him smile. Hector suspected that he felt embarrassed by not wanting to leave the tower.

Lizbeth took a quick inventory of the supplies that they'd brought. Luckily, the scarecrow's songs had little to do with the baskets' contents.

There was fresh and salted meat, slices of hard bread with moldy crust, cold cuts, various vegetables, cheese, fruits, and what seemed to be some type of fish covered in a gelatinous substance.

"It all looks revolting," Madeleine complained.

"Maybe you'd prefer monkey brains and all the other delicacies those nutjobs sang about."

"If I ever do feel like monkey brains, all I'll have to do is stick a spoon in your ear."

Marco and Natalia were the next to return. They carried two baskets apiece. They hadn't had any problems crossing the Scar or gathering the supplies.

"Those creatures from the other day were spying on us from afar," Natalia commented as she sat in a chair next to Hector. "But they didn't come close. They're afraid of us! Can you believe it?"

She stretched her arms as far as she could to loosen them up. Hector was astonished by the girl's strength, especially since at first glance her thinness made her look so fragile. He, in pain and bruised as he was, could only pick up one basket, but he knew that even if he'd been in perfect condition there wasn't a chance that he could have carried two. He touched his forehead. The blow that Natalia had given him still hurt.

Although the sun remained high, the sparse rays that managed to reach the tower began to wane. Lizbeth lit several more candelabras to fight the growing darkness. The young girl had found several lighters inside a pot. They were flute-like, almost a foot in length, and made from carved wood. A piece of metal in the shape of the head of a fantastic beast, a type of spiked lizard with round, bulging eyes, was fitted at one end. On pressing a small horn on the opposite end, the mouth opened, and a small blue flame shot out. Hector couldn't help but recall the petrified dragon from the square.

As time passed, they grew more and more worried about their missing companions.

"What time do you think it is?" Adrian asked.

"By the sun, I'd say late afternoon," Natalia said. "We spent a lot of time straightening up the tower."

"They're really late."

"Our leader is with them. Nothing will happen to them, you'll see."

"But what if they don't come back?"

"They'll come back, worrywart, they'll come back," the redhead answered decisively.

Hector fidgeted uneasily in his seat. He and Marco exchanged glances. The German was as tense and worried as he was. The enormous teenager got up out of the armchair he was sitting in, with a determined expression.

"I'm going to look for them," he announced. "And I don't want anyone leaving here while I'm gone, understand?"

"I'll go with you," Alexander said.

"No, you're not coming," he said bluntly as he felt for his sword. "You'll stay here and wait with the others. And if you get the slightest notion of following me, I'll throw you in the dungeon and lock it, is that clear?"

Before Alexander had a chance to reply, they heard Ricardo's voice from the moat, asking them to lower the drawbridge. Hector breathed a sigh of relief. Lizbeth and Alexander ran to the basement to let them in, and a few minutes later Ricardo, Marina, and Bruno came through the tower gate.

They weren't carrying baskets, but they did have three books, so huge and heavy that Marina seemed to need some help with the one she'd taken. Bruno, on the other hand, walked with his book open, so focused on its pages that it looked like he was in a trance. He paid attention to no one, offered not a single glance at the baskets or the candles and candelabras—just found an empty chair, sat down, and continued to immerse himself in the book.

"Books?" Alex asked. "Aren't they a bit hard to digest? Or did you bring them for the fiber?"

Ricardo explained that as they followed the third ship beyond the crack and its skeletons, they came across a second fissure in the earth, a seemingly bottomless trench almost fifty yards across. The bathtub had stopped right in the middle and lowered the baskets into the void.

"There's no way to reach them," he said. "We went to the edge, but they were out of our grasp. The captain dropped them in the hole and started on his way back to the castle." He pointed to Bruno. The Italian remained buried in the book; his eyes, small behind his glasses, moved at dizzying speed. More than just looking at the pages, he seemed to be ingesting them. "Since it was on our way, we passed by the library to keep the kid happy. That's why we were so late. It was really hard for him to decide which books he wanted."

"Well, he must have picked them by weight," Lizbeth said. "What a couple of monsters."

"You shouldn't have done that, Ricardo," Marco scolded. His voice took on a tone of dire seriousness. "We all agreed that anything outside of our plans is a risk that we can't afford."

"I saw no danger." Ricardo shrugged. "It was in and out. And we'd already been there before."

"It doesn't matter: you shouldn't have done it," Marco repeated.

Hector hobbled over to the table to take a look at Marina's and Ricardo's books. Out of the corner of his eye he saw that two identical symbols were engraved on the binding of Bruno's book, located in the middle of each cover. It was the same ten-pointed star that they'd found on the brick tower and the strange clock. The stars on the book were embossed with silver, so cracked that the one on the back cover was barely visible.

"Have you found anything interesting?" he asked Bruno, who gave no sign of having heard him.

"Don't even try," Marina warned. And on hearing her voice, Hector felt a blaze in the pit of his stomach. "As soon as he grabbed the book, he checked out. He's been reading it since we left the library."

"Reading?" he asked. An insidious little voice inside his head wouldn't stop saying, *You're talking to her. You did it. You're talking to her.* It was hard to ignore it. "Can he understand it?"

"No. At least I don't think so . . . But it's full of drawings and engravings. Like the other two—that's why we brought them."

Ricardo approached a basket to examine its contents.

"That's too bad about the third bathtub," Lizbeth commented. "At any rate, I think we'll be okay with the food from the other two. At least we won't go hungry."

"Can we write to them to ask them to leave the provisions in another spot?" Adrian piped up. He remained somewhat apart from the others.

"They said that they couldn't interfere, for good or for bad," Lizbeth answered. "What I don't understand is why they would leave the food in the middle of a pit. What sense does that make? Can someone explain that to me?"

"The spots where the provisions are dropped must have been decided a long time ago, before that trench existed," Marco said. "And the idiots either haven't realized it or don't care."

Hector opened one of the books. It was a thick volume with a dark cover, adorned with a drawing of two crossed swords. The smell of dust and neglect coming from the pages made him wrinkle his nose. A drawing of a weapon appeared on each page, surrounded by annotations in a foreign language. At least Hector guessed it was a language; the words looked more like a parade of insects than real words.

"A weapon catalog?" Natalia asked.

"Bruno wanted to bring it. I don't know why, it doesn't seem interesting to me in the least," said Marina. She was so close to Hector that their bodies nearly brushed against one another. "But look at this other one." She took the second book and opened it on the table. The binding, which bore not a single mark or drawing, creaked. "It's a kind of atlas, but not of countries or continents. They're entire planets."

Hector had to make a considerable effort to divert his gaze from the girl's tangled hair and focus it on the open book. Most of the others came over to investigate. The volume was divided into chapters eight pages long; each one, as Marina said, was dedicated to a different world.

The first two pages of each chapter included a general map of the planet in question: a rough sketch of its continents and seas, complete with annotations. On the next three pages were tables and more tables of incomprehensible text. Next appeared a second map: a city map this time, maybe the most important or most representative city of that world. And finally, the last two pages were illustrated with pictures of its inhabitants. In most cases they were beings identical to humans or with minimal differences, but in others they didn't resemble humans at all. In a world that was predominantly forest and jungle lived a race of humanoids with long extremities and pointy ears; in another in which there was hardly a visible speck of land, the dominant species was a type of greenish siren, their city built among submerged reefs and jungles of seaweed and coral. There were lands inhabited by centaurs and unicorns, whole planets infested with reptiles and draconic creatures, worlds of minuscule winged critters who lived in palaces built from wood and petals . . .

"Our legends," Bruno whispered. He'd left his book on the chair and now contemplated the atlas with his usual empty expression. "Gathered in this book are many of the myths and legends of our planet. Sirens, elves, fairies . . .

"Earth is here too, in the exact center of the book, although the map representation looks like it's pretty old." Bruno pointed out several places while Ricardo studied the annotations written next to them, as if he were trying to decipher the names of the cities written in those strange characters. There was Rome, London, Moscow, Berlin, Prague . . .

The drawings on the last few pages dedicated to Earth also showed archaic individuals, women and men dressed in medieval clothing, long robes or appalling rags. One of them was mounted on horseback, and horse and rider alike were squeezed into heavy suits of armor.

"The maps and drawings show what our world was like centuries ago," Bruno said.

"So how long have these nutjobs been kidnapping people?"

The last section of the book was dedicated to Rocavarancolia itself. The map of the city wouldn't be of any use helping them navigate, since it was more an artistic representation than a true map. The perspective in the drawing changed and the size of some buildings looked exaggerated in order to convey their importance. There were the mountains, dark and steep, the castle, and the magnificent red cathedral on the outskirts. But what got the group's attention more than anything were the buildings they could see floating in the air, mostly towers and minarets. The tallest among them seemed to rise up directly over the square that Hector and the twins had just visited.

"Did anyone see a building floating around there?" Alexander asked.

"I think I would have realized if I had," Ricardo muttered.

"In Delirium . . . the city I invented in my stories, there were flying buildings," said Marina. "They were built of lightweight stone and, although most of the time they stayed fixed above the city, they could be moved around here and there."

"Delirium is Rocavarancolia," Natalia said. "You wrote stories about this city."

"Before I knew about it?" Marina shook her head. "No, it has to be a coincidence, nothing more."

"And where are those flying buildings now?" Adrian asked.

"They must have flown away," Marco said. "Or something destroyed them."

The map of the planet where Rocavarancolia was located showed three large continents. One of them occupied almost the entirety of the northern hemisphere. The other two, much smaller, were located to the south, separated by an ocean painted with violent blue tones and replete with maelstroms and drawings of sea monsters. At first they were unable to find a city there. It was Ricardo who finally spotted it, after comparing the text that surrounded the map of Rocavarancolia with the annotations from the general map. The city was located at the westernmost part of one of the southern continents.

On the last two pages pertaining to that world, there were no drawings of its inhabitants. Instead, both pages were filled with an immense red moon, drawn so perfectly that it looked more like a photograph than an illustration. The markings and fault lines on its surface formed a complex net of scars in the eastern area of the celestial body's equator. That moon was practically identical to the one they'd seen on the tower clock. They were silent for a few seconds.

"I don't like the look of that thing at all," Natalia whispered. "Not one bit."

Bruno seemed to share her opinion, because he turned the page back to the map of Rocavarancolia. He pointed at a tower with his finger. It was small in comparison to the cathedral and the mountains, but it was clear that the artist had wanted it to stand out among the buildings surrounding it. On its rounded top was a ten-pointed star. By its location, Hector understood that it was the brick tower from the square with the fountain. Bruno pointed out four other identical towers scattered throughout the city, three on the surface and one hovering above it. The same symbol appeared on all of them.

"That star also appears on the binding of the book I brought. And I already figured out what it means." He grabbed the book that he'd left on the chair and placed it next to the atlas as he announced in a voice devoid of emotion: "It means magic."

"Magic!" Adrian finally came over to the group. His eyes shone.

"What are you talking about, Gandalf? Magic wands, top hats, and rabbits?" Alexander asked. "Or sleight of hand and card tricks?"

"I'm talking about real magic, Alexander. Not joke magic or parlor tricks. And I have a hunch that this book teaches how to use it."

Bruno turned pages at random. In the weathered volume there were pages of diagrams and illustrations interspersed with pages full of unreadable text. The Italian pointed out a sequence of vignettes that depicted in a crude and caricatured manner a leggy devil being split open from his chest to his belly button, but there was no way of knowing what caused it. Each box had a second drawing above it: a human hand with ringed fingers posed in different positions. In one of the drawings it was horizontal with the palm half-open and two fingers extended; in another it was shown in a vertical position with the fingers flexed at different heights. Bruno was right. The book taught magic. Those hands explained the movements necessary to inflict a mortal wound on an adversary.

"The steps are explained perfectly," Bruno commented. "You can see that every picture has several lines of text. I suspect that these are the words that must be recited when the corresponding hand movement is performed."

"And with that you can split someone in half?" Lizbeth was frightened. "By just moving your hands and saying a few words?"

"I don't know for sure, but everything seems to point in that direction."

"Well, thank heavens we can't understand what it says, or we'd all end up disemboweled."

Many of the pages contained the same layout with the sequence of drawings, the position and posturing of hands, and above them, the text to be recited. But there were other illustrations that were much less explanatory. On one page was a complicated diagram formed by octagons and pentagons of different colors and sizes, located in different positions among an endless number of strange sketches that seemed to represent spirals, eyes half-closed or bulging open, scratch marks, both lit and extinguished candles . . . Another page was entirely covered in the drawing of a skull that bore the marks of multiple incisions and on top of which was placed what was likely a human heart.

"The ten-pointed star signifies magic," Bruno repeated after a pause. "I'm sure of it."

"Then . . . the tower in the square . . ." Adrian began.

"A magic tower?" ventured Alex.

"Or maybe a wizard's tower," Natalia murmured.

"Whatever it is, we should have—"

"No!" Hector exclaimed, interrupting Bruno in such a surprising and violent manner that Madeleine and Marina stepped back, startled. "You want to go to a magician's tower, if that's what it is? Is that what you were going to say? And what if that symbol means it's a cursed tower? You can't be sure! You don't know what's inside!"

"It looks like abracadabras make Fatty nervous."

"Hector's right," Ricardo said. "Going into those towers could be dangerous. We're better off just forgetting about them."

"But . . ." Bruno began.

"At least for the time being," Ricardo added.

"Look, look at this drawing," said Adrian. He pointed at what looked like a spell explained in a single sketch. It was composed of a dark sphere that floated halfway up against a white background. The hand movement related to this enchantment was described in a single vignette and consisted of only two positions. "There's no text. Maybe it's a spell that works without magic words?"

"And what's it for? To make balls float in the air?"

Bruno executed the hand movements just as they were explained in the book. He did it quickly and with incredible skill. Nothing happened. Adrian wasted no time in mimicking him, although in a slower, clumsier way, but with the same result.

"What did you expect?" Madeleine asked. "Did you really think it was going to be that easy? That's dumb!"

In that same instant they heard a loud bite. Everyone looked at the baskets. There was Rachel, propped up on her crutches and with an enormous pear in her hands. She looked at everyone, smiled, and said with her mouth full:

"Abracadabra."

Esmael walked among the dead.

He walked at a steady pace, his eyes half-closed and his wings respectfully folded against his back. The Royal Pantheon was sacred ground and even he needed to mind his manners there. The mausoleum contained the majority of the kings and queens of Rocavarancolia, and at their sides, those who, by their service to the kingdom, had earned the high honor of accompanying them. The monarchs were buried in majestic tombs, adorned with seated statues that represented them with such fidelity that it was as if they had come back to life and stopped to rest atop the heads of their own tombstones. The rest of the deceased in the pantheon rested in large niches in the walls, each one with a corresponding plaque that listed their name as well as their principal achievements.

The black angel also had a spot reserved in those walls, although, of course, he was in no hurry to occupy it. And besides, he hoped that upon his death it wouldn't be a simple mortuary niche that awaited him here, as magnificent as they were. His intention was to earn the privilege of being buried in a king's tomb, with his own statue keeping watch over his eternal sleep. That was his greatest desire, what he longed for above all else: to become king of Rocavarancolia. But he wasn't deceiving himself; he knew that his ambition was almost impossible to attain. Never had a black angel been seated on the Sacred Throne and lived to tell the tale. Nonetheless, that wouldn't stop him from trying.

In all his life, he'd only dared to confess his ambition to one person, Lady Fiera. She was a black angel like himself, who died in the battle that led to the kingdom's ruin. More than fifty years had passed since the night when he, on an impulse, told her about his dream.

"Forget it," Lady Fiera advised him, as she sat up in the bed that they had shared. "Many of our kind have tried, and they have always ended the same way: carved up in the throne room."

Esmael was familiar with the bloody list of black angels who thought they deserved the throne. Dentrelar, the best of them all, was a commander who led the armies of Rocavarancolia during twenty glorious years and who never knew defeat. He decided that the time had come for him to take command of the kingdom when Jeremiah the Unfinished died. There wasn't a soul in Rocavarancolia who deserved it more, he said. Unfortunately for him, the Sacred Throne didn't share his opinion, and he ended up in pieces. A hundred years later, Molev, hero of a thousand battles, was the black angel who brought the head of Leviathan the Cyclops and the entrails of the Duke of the Underworld to Rocavarancolia. In a fit of madness, he decided that the throne should belong to him and not to the coward who occupied it at that time. He also ended up in pieces. Dronte and Verones shared the same fate. So did Kanchal and Lady Stiletto. And many, many others . The list was endless.

"Many have tried and none have succeeded, Esmael," Lady Fiera told him on that evening long ago. "And that's the way it should be. We black angels aren't made to wear the crown; we are what we are, savage creatures, made for blood and killing, not for government, with all its intrigues and subtleties. Our kingdom is the battlefield, and that," she emphasized, "is how it should be."

Never again did he talk with her about the subject. He was so sure that Lady Fiera was wrong that he didn't see the sense in discussing it. And now, almost fifty years after their conversation, he was more convinced than ever that he could be the first of his species to sit on the Sacred Throne without being ripped apart. It was true that a black angel had never been king of Rocavarancolia, but a black angel had never been regent before, and he was close to attaining that position.

Esmael went even further into the intricate labyrinth formed by the hallways of the Royal Pantheon. He felt the weight of history with every step he took, in every breath of air that penetrated his lungs. As he advanced through the heart of the Pantheon, the names of the heroes of yesteryear leapt out at him from the white-gold plates next to their niches: Rufus the Worthy, Lady Scum, Verban Dolomite, Dentro the Dragonslayer, all remembered, but not venerated like the kings and queens of Rocavarancolia. The black angel passed them as well on his path, jealous of their grandeur, hungry for their legend. Esmael walked in the shadow of His Majesty, Boronte Glaco, the first giant king of Rocavarancolia, whose magnificent statue reached sixty feet tall; before that he passed King Ronces the Decapitator, who gripped the two axes that he was famous for; he contemplated anew the fierce majesty of Castel, the eighth troll king of Rocavarancolia, the bloodthirsty destroyer of worlds. Yes, history surrounded him.

History is made up of the dead, thought the Lord of Assassins. Suddenly he heard approaching footsteps, and an instant later he smelled the odor of rot that could only belong to Lady Scar. Esmael had put stealth aside on this occasion. He didn't need it in the Royal Pantheon and, in fact, he wanted to be discovered. Victory wasn't enough for him: he needed to gloat. He smiled with malevolence and continued walking, purposefully ignoring the clumsy trot of the woman trying to catch up to him. It took Lady Scar several minutes to reach him.

"Did you come to harvest the evil that you sowed, black angel?" she asked. Something in the voice of the guardian of the Royal Pantheon disturbed him, a touch of barely concealed sarcasm that cast a shadow upon the excellent mood with which he'd entered the mausoleum. He turned slowly toward her with a look of contempt.

"I've come to talk to a member of the Royal Council who I know can be found here. And to pay my respects to the dead, of course," he added, with a malicious smile. It was clear that by this point Lady Scar should be aware of what had happened the night before. And in case there remained any doubt, the scarred woman's next comment completely resolved the issue.

"Of course, of course. We both know how respectful you can be with them." He again detected the same tone of mockery in her voice.

"Is there something you want to tell me?" he asked her unenthusiastically. "I'm in a hurry and I have no desire to waste my time with you."

"No, Esmael, I won't detain you any further. Do what you need to do." The black angel grimaced faintly and continued his walk. Shortly after, he found what he was looking for. Lady Serena stood in the middle of an intersection of hallways, floating six feet in the air before the seated statue of the twenty-sixth monarch of Rocavarancolia, His Majesty, Maryalé. The phantom's expression was indecipherable.

Esmael smiled on seeing her, the unease provoked by his encounter with Lady Scar already forgotten. He was aware of having made a mistake in bringing back the little crybaby king; he was convinced that in doing so he'd predisposed the phantom to being more against him than she had been before. And even so it was a mistake that he didn't mind having made. It had been so tempting that it would have gone against his very nature not to give in. Besides, he was toying with the advantage of having Hurza's book in his power. The aversion that Lady Serena must feel for him wouldn't let her forget that detail. He was sure of it.

She turned her gaze toward him for a fraction of a second before returning, lost in thought, to contemplating Maryalé's tomb.

"Yes, Esmael? What do you want?" she asked, her voice devoid of interest.

"What I've been after all day, my dear friend: to have a small chat with you. I don't know why, but I have the strange sensation that you've been avoiding me. I hope I'm wrong."

"You're not wrong, Esmael. It's been a long day. If it's any consolation, I haven't been avoiding only you, I've been avoiding all of Rocavarancolia. I've had a lot to think about and I've been seeking solitude to do it."

"I suppose so." Esmael smiled. His fangs gleamed in his dark face. He resisted the urge to lick his lips. "I'm sure that the demonstration I did last night in your honor was more than enough to convince you that I truly possess Hurza's grimoire."

"It was, it was. Without a doubt."

Lady Serena turned toward him once again and looked at him from above. Words didn't exist to describe the hatred that she felt for the despicable creature in front of her. To bring back the man that she had loved and killed for the purpose of demonstrating that he had the cursed book was such a vile act that she didn't have a name for it. But what bothered her more than anything was the fact that, after all the time that had transpired since Maryalé's death, she still hated him for what he had done. If he hadn't disappeared shortly after she saw him, she would have killed him all over again. And that made her despise Esmael even more: he had shown her what kind of being she'd become.

"It's one of the book's lesser spells," explained the black angel, ignoring the ghost's furious glare. "The Brief Resurrection, it's called. And even being a minor spell it took the better part of my power to perform it."

"I know all about it. The Brief Resurrection, yes . . . Hurza the Eye-Eater's necromancy can resurrect anyone for a brief span of time, provided that someone nearby can remember the person in detail."

"That was you, of course."

"Of course."

"So, do you think it's possible to have that little chat that I mentioned before?" asked the black angel. "Maybe this isn't the best place for it. I don't know whose ears might be listening." In fact, he knew with certainty that Lady Scar wasn't far, paying close attention to their conversation.

Lady Serena looked him up and down before responding. Her tone of voice was one of deceiving amiability. Each word dripped with venom.

"No. It won't be necessary to go anywhere else," she said. Her lips formed a sarcastic smile. "In fact, our conversation is going to be much shorter than you think." Her smile grew as she spoke. "It's surprising the amount of information one can find in the magic compendiums, you know, Esmael?" she commented with feigned indifference. "Valcoburdo's, for example, contains not only spells from the majority of known grimoires, but also a large number of curiosities related to them."

Esmael squinted his eyes. Now he understood the reason for Lady Scar's mocking tone. He cursed his stupidity. He hadn't even bothered to verify what information about the Eye-Eater's grimoire was available in the compendiums.

"You can only use Hurza's book if you remain Lord of Assassins," the ghost continued. "As regent you can't fulfill your promise of giving me life. What use will the Jewels of the Iguana be to you if you won't even be capable of reading the spell? And we both know that no one can cast a spell written in a grimoire without reading from the book itself; there's no way of copying them, nor does there exist a mind capable of memorizing them. Therefore, my dear friend, what truly benefits me now is that you remain in your present position. Who knows? Maybe in time you'll manage to amass enough power for the spell that you so kindly offered to cast on me."

"You're a hag, Lady Serena," Esmael growled. They exchanged glances overflowing with rage. They were on sacred ground, in the one place in Rocavarancolia where violence was forbidden. The magic that protected the Royal Pantheon prevented anyone who passed through its doors from being harmed, but it didn't stop the two of them from taking threatening stances, eager to pounce.

"And you're a fool," the ghost spat. "And a fool should never take control of a kingdom, even a kingdom as doomed as this one," she added before she took flight and, without looking back, passed through the walls of the Royal Pantheon.

Lady Scar, who had observed everything from a distance, with arms crossed and a smile on her battered lips, could not help but applaud the ghost's stage exit.

Esmael shot her a black look. He burned with fury. He clenched his fists tight. If it weren't for his leathery skin, his nails would have cut into the palms of his hands.

"Table," she repeated. She grabbed the fork that she'd just used to eat an assortment of fruit and she turned it around in the air, pointing to Alexander with it. "Abracadabra!" she exclaimed.

The redhead lowered his head and began to croak very softly, opening and closing his eyes in time with the sound.

"That's the most sensible thing I've heard you say since I've known you," Lizbeth said.

Only a few minutes had passed since they'd finished eating, and they sat around one of the tables that they'd brought out to the courtyard.

They hadn't found anything as delicious as the golden apples, but they were all more or less satisfied with the food, all except Madeleine, of course, who naturally protested with every mouthful. Hector had liked the cheese more than anything else; it had a flavor that reminded him of honey without being overly sweet.

Bruno sat at one of the heads of the table. He'd eaten meagerly, with the book of magic open in his lap. Every so often they saw him practice the hand movements; they were almost always the same as the ones that appeared above the drawing of the floating sphere, but sometimes he took on long and complicated movements that corresponded to other spells.

The wind began to blow again, softly at first, but later picking up speed and fury, exactly like the day before. And like the day before, as the hours passed the temperature began to drop. Many of those who'd taken off shirts and jackets wrapped up once more in layer after layer of clothing. Only Marco remained dressed in a thin, sleeveless shirt.

After dinner they dispersed into small groups in the courtyard. Only Marco, Bruno and his book remained at the table, along with Ricardo and Rachel, who kept taking turns teaching each other words. Adrian sat on the steps at the tower's entrance, constantly watching the sky. Hector guessed that at the slightest sign of flaming bats he would flee inside. Night fell over Rocavarancolia, their second one in the city. Hector found himself walking alone atop the wall that surrounded the courtyard. He stopped to look at the gloomy silhouettes of the buildings beyond the moat, leaning against the crenellated defensive wall. The encroaching night was like an ocean of ink that spilled little by little outside, creating patches of dim blackness among reefs of an even deeper darkness. Marina, Alexander, and Lizbeth were at the other end of the wall. From time to time he heard the girls' laughter. The redhead's charm was overwhelming, and Hector had to admit that without him and his deranged sense of humor, the last two days would have been much worse. Alexander took an exaggerated bow in front of the girls and said something that made them laugh again.

He could have joined them, but preferred to remain alone. He looked toward the city enveloped in night, although his mind floated far away. He thought of his home, his family. He wondered if in the time he'd been in Rocavarancolia they'd thought about him even for a moment. He knew there was no memory of his existence in their minds, but even so . . . Was there any point at which they missed something without knowing exactly what? An absence that they couldn't put a name to?

He sighed. He felt small and lost. Right there, as he contemplated the shadowed city, he realized how much he missed his family. He remembered that the last time he'd talked to his mother had been a shouting match, with his nerves on edge after she chewed him out for being late. He shook his head, unable to believe that he'd gotten mad over such a trivial thing, over such foolishness. It couldn't be real. It couldn't be true that the last image his mother had of him was him yelling hysterically.

"And what does it matter if they don't remember me anymore?" he thought, on the verge of tears.

"There aren't any stars," someone whispered to his left. Natalia was leaning against the battlement wall, looking up. He hadn't heard her arrive.

Hector raised his eyes. The sky was clear, but he couldn't see a single star. The night was an unfathomable depth, a hungry abyss that seemed to descend on their heads. The emptiness made him even sadder.

"I miss my family," he said.

"Not me." The girl shrugged her shoulders. "I liked them and all that, but I never really felt like I was a part of them, you know? I always had the feeling that I wasn't where I was supposed to be. And no, don't even say it, I don't think that this horrible place is, either."

"And they took them away with pills."

"You should have told the others."

Natalia firmly shook her head.

"They won't think that you're crazy," Hector insisted. "How can they think that after all that's happened?"

"I know that they won't think I'm crazy. But I'd rather not tell them, okay?"

"Well, I don't understand. It doesn't make sense for you not to. Maybe if we find out why they brought us here, we'll know what they want from us. And maybe those elv—"

"You're a nuisance," she cut him off. "You're a fool and a nuisance."

"And clumsy, and I have vertigo. And a thousand other defects. But we're not talking about me, we're talking about—"

"I'm not going to tell them!"

"But why not?"

Natalia snorted and looked daggers at him.

"Because ever since I told you, you've had one of those shadows behind you, okay? Are you happy? Now you know! It follows you everywhere. And I don't want that to happen to the others."

Hector swallowed, astonished. He was tempted to look behind him out of the corner of his eye.

"You're saying that one of those things is following me?" he managed to ask in a feeble voice.

"Aren't you listening? That's what I just said. Yes. It's following you. When you went after the food, it was behind you."

Hector gasped. He was about to ask her where the shadow was now when, suddenly and without being able to help it, he started to laugh. It was absurd. Taken as a whole it was all absurd: shadows that followed them, terrible darkness that infiltrated his mind by magic, flying bathtubs steered by singing scarecrows, flaming bats, birds made of rags . . . None of it made sense. It was like being in the dark underbelly of an amusement park. Tears sprang to his eyes.

Natalia looked at him, perplexed.

"Holy moly, Fatty's gone insane!" Alexander exclaimed. "Save yourselves! Run! Run!"

Hector looked at him, doubled over with laughter. And the sight of the redhead, covered in black rags with his dagger at his side, like he just stepped out of a low-budget film, made him laugh even harder.

The sky filled with flaming bats. From the mountains came the first howl of the night. And Hector kept laughing.

They were all heading back to the tower together when they saw Bruno jump up from his chair, drop the magic book to the ground, and take off running inside the building like the devil was at his back.

"What happened to him?" Alex asked Marco when they caught up to him.

"I think it was my fault," Marco confessed. "He went crazy when I told him that the hand in that strange drawing wore a bracelet with a crystal like the ones we lit up last night."

Hector picked up the book and looked at the page in question. Marco was right. A bracelet adorned the hand in the drawing, and from it hung a rhomboid crystal that could have been an exact replica of the ones they'd used for light the night before. From within the tower came the sound of hurried footsteps and of drawers opening and closing. They heard Bruno ask Adrian about the crystals, since, as Hector had guessed, he'd run to take refuge in the tower as soon as the first bat appeared. A few minutes later, Bruno came through the door with a fistful of rhomboid crystals.

"Something was missing. That's why the spell didn't work." His eyes shone, not a very vivid shine, but enough to be disturbing when compared with his usual cold indifference. Hector had the impression that someone or something far from the Bruno they knew was peering out from behind that inexpressive mask. "Maybe it's a catalyst, or some way of amplifying the spell. I don't know. I don't know . . ." He cut one of the crystals so forcefully into the back of his left hand that a streak of blood immediately ran down his wrist and stained the sleeve of his shirt.

"Gross!" Madeleine shrieked.

The sphere of light flared up around the crystal before Bruno even withdrew it, spraying a light red mist on the pavement. He grabbed the book from Hector unceremoniously and performed the movements with his right hand while the left, bathed in blood, clutched both the tome and the glowing crystal. Nothing happened. He even repeated it three times.

"It can't be," he whispered.

"You're a brute," Lizbeth said as she moved toward him. She took a white handkerchief from her skirt pocket. "Just look at that gash. Let me see . . ."

"That won't be necessary," Bruno replied as he took a step back to move away from her, the sphere of light projecting his shadow against the tower's façade in a grotesque shape. "There be a mistake. I must have missed something." The Italian's glance went back and forth between the crystal and the open book. Suddenly the gleam in his eyes returned. "I know, I know: we confused the sign with the function. That's what it is." He looked at them with his customary stare and Hector shuddered. "The purpose of these crystals isn't to provide light; the light's nothing more than a side effect, a sign that the crystal is working. Don't you get it? It's an indicator. When we activated them with our blood, we started some sort of process inside, and when that was completed, the light went out."

"My cell phone has a red light that comes on when you plug it in to charge," said Adrian. "And it goes out when it's charged again."

"Charge," murmured Bruno. "That's a possibility. Yes. That's feasible. The crystals act like batteries and this one is charging right now." He shook the hand that held the sphere of light. More drops of blood fell in the courtyard. "Does anyone have one of the crystals that we lit last night?" he asked.

Marco pulled his out immediately.

"Yes, yes, yes," Bruno repeated, Marco's crystal already in his hand. "That's it. The spell needs an energy source in order to work."

His right hand made the two movements just as they were depicted in the book. And once again nothing happened. Bruno wasn't even fazed. He repeated the movement twice more, but with the same result. He tried it again, and again. The expression on his face didn't change, but something in his posture revealed a tremendous frustration.

"It's useless," Lizbeth said. "Forget about it for now and let me treat that."

"Maybe you broke your wand," Alexander commented.

"I don't know what happened," Bruno said, as he repeated the two gestures for the thousandth time. "It should work. I'm sure that this is the correct procedure. Maybe there are factors that I didn't take into account, or maybe one crystal isn't enough," he conjectured. He left the book and the crystal on the table and allowed Lizbeth to take his wounded hand. The sparkle that had appeared in his gaze was beginning to fade. "I don't understand," he repeated. "I was sure that I could get it to work."

Marco went toward the book and glanced at it while Lizbeth bandaged Bruno's wound with her handkerchief.

"In my father's gym we had several books in Japanese about martial arts," he said. "And you don't read them like we do in the West, from left to right, you read them in reverse: from right to left. We got the exercises wrong two out of every three times. Why don't you try that?"

Bruno looked at him for a long time, without blinking. He seemed to be processing the information that he'd just received. Then he nodded slowly, moved his hand out of Lizbeth's grasp even more slowly, grabbed the crystal once again, and repeated the gestures that they'd seen so many times over the last few minutes, this time in reverse order. As soon as the second was completed they all noticed a sudden crackling in the air.

An empty area in the courtyard, five feet tall, became a vortex of darkness. The air, now black, cracked and rustled. Everyone stepped back—everyone but Bruno, who remained still, watching the phenomenon that tinted his face with shadowy reflections. Suddenly the black area hatched. In its place appeared a scarlet sphere, over a foot in diameter, that turned slowly in the void.

They all watched, stupefied, as the sphere appeared out of nothing. Its surface looked fleshy and was covered with creases. As they watched, three orifices opened in the middle of the sphere, two small parallel ones at the top and a longer, horizontal one below them. A grotesque and gurgling voice surged from the fleshy sphere.

"It's alive," Madeleine whispered. "That thing is alive."

No one understood a word that the sphere said, but by its tone it seemed to be asking a question.

"What did it say? What was that?" Adrian asked from the door frame where he'd taken refuge.

In the upper slots of the sphere two murky sparks appeared. It turned to Adrian and moved at great speed toward him, repeating the words over and over. The boy screamed and fled inside the tower. The sphere stopped at the door, turned around once more, and looked at Bruno. It spoke again.

"I don't understand you," the Italian said. "I do not know what you are saying."

The creature thrust itself toward him. It stopped just half an inch from Bruno's face, but he hardly blinked at the living sphere's charge. It spoke again, more slowly, in that incomprehensible language. By its tone of voice, Hector understood that the thing was furious. The sphere began to tremble, an exaggerated movement from left to right and then from back to front. For a moment it seemed like it was about to explode. And then, it disappeared. It simply vanished. Bruno recoiled, surprised, and had to lean against the table to keep from falling.

Everyone looked at each other, shocked by what had just occurred.

"Abracadabra," Alexander said.

"Abracadabra," Hector repeated. He groped for the back of a chair and then sat down, very slowly. His legs were shaking.

MISTRAL

Denestor Tul slept on the first floor of Highlowtower, stretched out in the hammock where Ujthan the Warrior had carelessly tossed him five days ago. The demiurge had remained in the same position since then, with one arm stretched out over his head and the other folded over his stomach.

Anyone who passed through the gate of Highlowtower and looked up would soon discover that this was no ordinary building. Although it measured more than a hundred feet tall, the tower only had a single floor, that shot upward, with no roof or any visible divisions, like a gigantic cannon that pointed to the heavens.

A veritable chaos of cords, ropes, and ladders dropped from the rafters, slid down the walls, or seemed to hang from the void by magic. Wardrobes, ledges, and shelves were nailed to the walls at different heights or tied firmly with cords. The demiurge's creations wandered everywhere: unusual birds of a thousand colors, papier-mâché insects, kites with movable joints, automata and other beings so surreal that they looked nothing like anything that had ever existed. They all had free rein in that vertical territory. The rest of the space was packed with dollhouses, hangers, bird boxes, hat racks . . . And up above, beyond all the disorder of rope, shelves, and moving creatures, the clear sky of Rocavarancolia was visible.

As soon as Denestor's breathing began to change, as he grew closer to waking, an hourglass dressed in a sequined waistcoat grabbed one of the cords, hung on with the spoons it had for hands, and pulled downward. The demiurge opened his eyes and yawned.

Soon after, a dark hunchbacked silhouette fell from the nonexistent ceiling of Highlowtower. It was Lady Spider, sliding down a fine strand of silk, answering the hourglass's call. She descended headfirst and in a wondrous balancing act she carried in her hands two jugs, one teapot, and one large mug.

Denestor watched her descent from where he lay in the hammock. An infinity of dire, urgent thoughts swam in his head, but he chose to ignore them. He'd have time to worry later. Around him several of his creatures celebrated his awakening from a long sleep. Denestor allowed himself another yawn and stroked a lizard made from thimbles and colored glass.

"Good morning, good morning," crooned Lady Spider as she maneuvered in her web to land right side up at the foot of the hammock. While changing her position, she inverted her vessels at the same time, so she didn't spill a single drop. "It's a pleasure to have you among us once again, demiurge. And nothing like an invigorating potion to fine-tune the mind and body after such a long, well-earned rest." She poured the contents of the jars in the teapot, and as soon as the lid closed there came the sound of a small detonation inside. Then Lady Spider filled the mug with the translucent liquid that poured from the teapot and handed it to Denestor.

"Thank you," he murmured, his voice harsh. He noticed that his muscles were stiff, his throat scratchy, and there was a tremendous weight on his spirit that he refused to acknowledge. The heat from the ceramic mug in his hands was comforting. Almost as much as the first sip of the potion. He savored this last moment of tranquility, and reluctantly asked the question he was so afraid to voice: "Are any of the children still alive?"

"Any? All of them! Most of them are happy and content in the Margalar Tower! They play with sticks and eat everything I prepare for them!"

"How long have I slept?" he asked, surprised. He must have been mistaken. Maybe only a couple of hours had passed since he passed out at the council table. No, that wasn't possible. He was almost recovered, and from the arachnid's words he deduced that some time had passed since he'd lost consciousness.

"Five days have passed since the night of Samhein," she informed him. "You were in a very deep sleep, demiurge."

"Five days," he murmured, incredulous. He got out of the hammock. He didn't put his foot on the ground, but rather grabbed with one hand one of the cords hanging from above while he coiled his foot in the other. "Five days and not a single dead child?" He couldn't get over his shock. He didn't know how to take this news. It was too good to be true.

"Isn't it fabulous? They've surpassed everyone's expectations! Some even placed bets on how many would die before the first night." Lady Spider let out a sinister little chuckle. Her chelicerae moved to and fro like knives poorly affixed to her face. "Lady Scar was the only one who said that not a single child would die, can you believe that? And to celebrate she gave an apple from Arfes to each of them."

The demiurge furrowed his brow. That wasn't like the commander of the armies and the guardian of the Royal Pantheon. And it was definitely hard to believe that not a single teenager had died yet. Denestor began to climb from rope to rope while Lady Spider followed on her thread, always keeping level with him. The demiurge's creations that were capable of flying or climbing up the walls followed them.

"Which reminds me of something . . ." the spider continued. "Lady Scar as well as the black angel have requested to see you as soon as you wake up. They say they have extremely urgent matters to discuss with you."

"They can wait," Denestor mumbled. Their interest in seeing him could only mean one thing: the regent was still alive. And that made him glad. Huryel was one of the few residents of Rocavarancolia for whom he felt real affection.

They soon arrived at the tower's battlement and the narrow overhang that bordered it. The light of day blinded the demiurge after such a long time immersed in the darkness of sleep. He rubbed his eyes. A winged spyglass approached them and after a gesture from Denestor it alighted in front of his face. He blinked, trying to focus his gaze as best he could, and searched for the teenagers in the ruined city. The first one he found was the one that he'd brought from São Paulo. He was on a rooftop, napping in the shelter of a chimney. And despite being asleep, his posture betrayed an alert tension, as if he could wake at any moment. His right arm and the short sword that it clutched were the only things that stuck out from beneath the gray cape wrapped around him. The demiurge noticed the sword with interest; if he was correct, it was an enchanted weapon, albeit with lesser magic. He couldn't help but wonder where he'd gotten it from.

Denestor looked away from the sleeping boy to fix his attention on the Margalar Tower. There, most of the teenagers slept as well, together on the top floor. Only three were awake. The Italian was focused on a book in a room on the second floor, while the other two battled with wooden sticks in the courtyard.

Indeed, all twelve remained alive. Denestor frowned; even seeing it with his own eyes, he couldn't believe it. And just as he looked away from the tower, he realized that something was not as it should be. He looked again, more carefully. And this time it only took him a second to understand what had happened. Shocked by his discovery, his hands immediately groped for the support of the battlement. He cursed in a low voice.

"Is something wrong?" Lady Spider asked, aware of the demiurge's sudden bewilderment.

Denestor looked at her for a moment and then shook his head.

"Nothing," he lied. "Nothing is wrong. A bout of weakness, my dear Lady Spider. Nothing more."

He sent the spyglass away with a hand signal and turned from the ruined city to go back into Highlowtower. He knew it couldn't be true. By tradition, the first thing Rocavarancolia demanded after the night of Samhein was a blood sacrifice. This time was no different. Lady Scar hadn't won the bet: one of the twelve teenagers had died shortly after arriving in Rocavarancolia. And Mistral, the shapeshifter, had taken their place.

Hector stretched out in bed. The light of a brand-new day filtered in through the embrasures. From the courtyard came the sound of quick footsteps and clashing wood. Apparently, someone had woken up early to train.

He looked both ways as he rubbed one eye and considered the possibility of going back to sleep. The mattresses were arranged against the curve of the wall, with nightstands and wardrobes between them. Five of them were empty, but as sleepy as he was, he couldn't see who they belonged to. One was probably Bruno's; that strange boy hardly slept. Hector yawned again and when he closed his eyes to try to get back to sleep, he realized that he had to go to the bathroom. He propped himself up on the mattress, put on his slippers, and slowly left the room. Around him, the peacefulness of the Margalar Tower was comforting.

It was hard for him to believe that five days had already gone by, and it was even more difficult to process the fact that he was getting used to all of it. And that feeling bothered him. He was aware that if things went on like this, he'd soon come to consider the tower as his home, and he wasn't convinced that was good news.

The city remained a mystery to them. For the time being, their outings had been limited to gathering provisions from the ships and, on one occasion, a quick visit to the square with the fountain so that Madeleine could get her clothes and Bruno could take another look at the library. The trip had been in vain; the Italian hadn't found any more books to his liking and neither did they find a trace of Maddie's or the others' clothing.

The noise from the fighting outside became muffled when Hector started down the stairs. As that sound diminished, another became audible: two voices whispering on the second floor. When he arrived he found that they came from the room right in front of him. The door was half-ajar and through the gap in the door frame Hector could see Madeleine and Marina. They'd placed a huge washtub in the middle of the room and Marina, her back to the door, was emptying a bucket of hot water into it. They were both naked from the waist up.

Hector gulped, unsure whether he should walk along or stay there. His mind urged him to leave and yet his legs refused to obey. Madeleine was beautiful in a devastating way. It was a delight to see her naked body, like looking at a splendid work of art that had just come to life. But looking at Marina awoke a different sensation inside of him, similar to what he felt when he bit into the golden apple, as if he'd just discovered a new and magnificent world that until now had remained hidden.

The steam that arose from the washtub dissipated into lingering white clouds around them. The water made their bodies sparkle and the torches and candles tinted them with a soft, rose-colored glow. The whole scene radiated warmth. Marina bent over the bathtub, soaked a sponge in the water, and scrubbed her side, from the curve of her waist to her armpit. Hector remained hypnotized in the doorway. He wasn't even paying attention to what the girls were saying. His eyes went from one to the other and he couldn't help thinking that he'd die on the spot if Marina turned around and discovered him spying. And in spite of that, he desired with all his might that the girl would turn around so he could see her better.

Maddie stretched toward the other side of the bathtub and untied the knot in her skirt, and with a quick movement of her hips it slid down to her ankles. Hector felt the air go out of him. He groped at the wall for support, his hand flapping in the void just inches from its goal. He turned to orient himself, lost his footing, and tumbled down the stairs. The whole tower woke with the racket of thuds and shouts. He heard footsteps running on the upper and lower floors.

Hector lay aching halfway down the last flight of stairs. Nothing was broken, but his entire body hurt.

"Ow," he moaned.

"This issue of yours is getting to be a problem, Fatty." Alexander looked at him from above with his arms akimbo. He had a stick in one hand and a shield in the other. "Gravity must really hate you."

"I tripped, you stupid red-haired idiot," he said, dazed and embarrassed. From where he was he could see Madeleine and Marina, already covered up, looking at him worriedly. He glanced away instantly when he noticed the redheaded girl's legs, still pearly with moisture.

"Are you okay?" Marco stretched out a hand to help him up. Hector grimaced and stood. He felt like he'd spent his whole life rolling on the floor. And for once he deserved it.

"What happened?" they asked from above.

"Nothing! Hector fell again!"

The aforementioned huffed and limped out with what little dignity he had left.

Adrian charged him on the left flank after feinting an attack to the right. Hector barely managed to deflect the blow with his shield. The impact caught him off guard and was so forceful that it almost knocked him over. He thrust desperately at his opponent while he recovered his balance. Adrian deflected him easily and, not content with just that, disarmed him with a well-aimed blow from his sword. Hector's stick went flying, turning in circles in the air.

"You're dead!" Adrian exclaimed, and leaned the end of the stick on his chest.

Hector panted. Adrian had already killed him five times this morning. Too high of a mortality rate, even for him. Marco halted his combat with Alexander, grabbed Hector's stick, and returned it to him.

"Don't try to anticipate his movements," he said. "Just defend yourself from what you see. Starting out, that will be more than enough. And raise your shield a bit more."

Hector shrugged. He wasn't paying much attention, and Adrian took advantage of that. He still had his head in the scene that he'd glimpsed in that room. For most of the morning he hadn't been able to avoid blushing every time Madeleine or Marina crossed his path. And his gaze was drawn to them again and again.

Natalia and Ricardo, on the other hand, seemed so focused on their combat that it looked like the outside world had ceased to exist for them. Their movements betrayed a certain clumsiness and naivety, but he had to admit that they far surpassed the others. Hector had been Natalia's opponent the first morning and he'd received so many blows that he ended up covered in a constellation of bruises. The next day, Marco paired the Russian with Ricardo and Hector with Adrian, in an attempt to even out the pairs. Hector found himself with a less dangerous opponent but a more enthusiastic one, so much so that the number of blows he took hardly changed. At least he had the satisfaction of hitting his opponent from time to time, which was enough to keep his pride more or less intact.

But of all of them, Alexander was the one who put forth the greatest effort in learning how to fight. He spent most of his time in the courtyard, and if he couldn't persuade anyone to train with him, he dedicated himself to fighting invisible enemies with his stick and his shield. He wanted a sword, a real sword. He repeated it over and over as many times as Ricardo and Marco repeated that he wasn't ready yet. The morning before, as he rummaged around in the armory for the thousandth time, Alex found in a chest what he said was going to be his sword. It was a single-handed sword with a green blade and a black hilt, perfectly balanced. The redhead brandished it right away, still in its sheath. That sword seemed tailor-made for him.

"Not yet, kiddo," Marco had said. "If you can beat me just once, I'll let you carry it. Until then, you're staying with the stick and dagger."

"The first thing I'm going to do with my sword is skewer you like a turkey, you old spoilsport."

Next to the weapon he'd found a rectangular shield, also green and black, with the image of a salamander enveloped in a blazing emerald flame, and a matching helmet. Adrian was smitten with them, and although they matched the sword, Alex had no difficulty whatsoever giving them to him. The shield was too light for his size, and although the helmet was a bit big, from that moment Adrian wore it constantly.

"Defend yourself, you coward!" he yelled at Hector, before pouncing on him again. Hector sighed, deflected the blow, and aimed another one straight at the helmet. Adrian stopped it almost reflexively, raising his shield. It was Hector's most repeated attack. He couldn't help it. He loved the sound the stick made as it struck the helmet.

He was surprised by the change that had come over Adrian in the last three days. He seemed excited again to be involved in this adventure, so much so that the day before he'd finally dared to leave the tower to search for provisions.

He'd gone with his shield at the ready, his dagger unsheathed, and his helmet tilted to one side, looking around in all directions in a state of permanent alertness that was more an act than real. But for all of the bravery he'd gained, when night fell he was the first to seek refuge in the tower, even before the first flaming bat streaked across the sky. Hector wasn't fooled: the change in attitude was just a result of the boy's fickleness. Once more, for him, all of this was nothing more than a game, and he'd carry on in that spirit until something else caused fear to take hold of him again.

He deflected another attack from Adrian with some difficulty and tried to extend the movement into a blow to his side. But he was too slow, and his stick sliced into the void more than five inches from its target. Suddenly, the crack of an arrow sinking into wood resounded through the morning with extraordinary clarity, most of all because no one expected to hear it.

"I did it!" Marina announced excitedly. She raised her bow in a sign of victory. "I finally did it! Ha! I hit it! Did you see that?"

It was the first time in three days that she'd managed to land an arrow—maybe not in the bull's-eye, but at least on the enormous plank where it was drawn. The other projectiles either were lost beyond the wall or ended up broken or stuck in the rocks.

Marina had opted for the bow as soon as it was clear to her that hand-to-hand combat wasn't her thing. She'd chosen a beautiful longbow from the armory, made of wood painted black with gold trim, but she had to return it once she found out how difficult it was to draw back. She had to settle for a short bow, much easier to handle.

"I did it!" she repeated. Then she nocked another arrow on the bow. She drew back, aimed, and let go. This time the arrow whizzed over the wall.

"Well done, Hawkeye," said Alexander.

Marco had placed the wooden board with the target far away from the place where he taught the classes that he called "basic weapons training," to prevent the possibility of Marina's poor aim accidentally finding one of her companions. She wasn't the only one who didn't participate in the half-training, half-game combat. Rachel would have liked to join in, but her ankle still wasn't in good shape, so she contented herself with the role of spectator. She tried to shoot the bow, and although it seemed impossible, her aim was even worse than Marina's—so bad that Marco forbade her from getting within two feet of an arrow.

As far as the others went, Lizbeth and Madeleine made it clear that they didn't have the slightest intention of wielding a sword or anything that resembled a weapon; Maddie, moreover, conveyed her displeasure over the whole display of savage violence. Bruno was much more reserved in his refusal: when Marco handed out the wooden staffs on the first day, he just shook his head and sat down in a chair with the book of magic.

Hector's dislike for Bruno grew with each passing day. His coldness and his behavior made him nervous. He tried to avoid him whenever he could. And he wasn't the only one; almost all of the others avoided him as well. Bruno not only didn't seem to mind, but he, too, did whatever he could to keep away from the rest. At that moment, he was probably in some room or other with his nose buried in his dusty book. He was hardly ever away from it, despite the fact that, from what he said, he had learnt nothing from its pages other than the invocation of the sinister sphere. Ricardo had asked him not to repeat the spell, and Bruno had assured him that he wouldn't.

"It was obvious that the sphere was annoyed by having been conjured, and the language barrier made any communication with it impossible," he said. "To conjure it again would be foolish and meaningless."

Hector repelled yet another attack from Adrian. Exhausted, he felt a tired pang in his side and raised his hands to signal his surrender.

"Okay, I'm finished," he said, leaning forward. "I can't take any more, I'm worn out."

He couldn't remember having exercised so much in all his life. He retreated to the only table that remained outside and fell back in a chair. Ricardo and Marco had turned the rest of the furniture that they'd removed from the tower into firewood, clearing up the place and gaining several sacks of wood that they could use to feed the fire in the stove.

Marco paired Adrian with Alexander and continued to give advice while he watched the two fights unfolding in the courtyard. Hector followed them with his gaze. Little by little, his life in Rocavarancolia was taking on the air of monotony and calm that went with any routine. Maybe spending most of their time cloistered away in the tower wasn't too exciting, but if that was what it took to stay alive, he wasn't about to complain. He didn't want to live through adventures; he just wanted to live. And to go home.

When they spotted the ships, they split up once again into two groups to gather provisions. Hector went with Ricardo, Natalia, Lizbeth, and Adrian, who was even more excited to leave than the day before. He wore his helmet and clutched the salamander shield with all his might. He looked even smaller all wrapped up in the gray and black rags that they all wore.

Leaving the Margalar Tower always made them nervous. It was inevitable. They'd come to think of it as a type of sanctuary where nothing bad could happen, whereas beyond the gate stretched the hostile territory of the city. Despite not having had any dangerous encounters over the past few days, when they left the tower they felt a constant sensation of threat. And the mere act of lowering the drawbridge made them a part of that unsettling landscape, that land of lurking shadows.

They met at the tower's entrance, chatting in a lively manner to hide their nervousness. More than once their glances went toward the strange clock that crowned the entrance. In the five days they'd spent there, the star had barely moved past four twenty. The symbol of the Red Moon, on the other hand, remained fixed on the top of the sphere. The day before, Bruno had calculated that, at the rate that the star moved, it would take over two hundred days for both symbols to line up.

"And what will happen when they do?" Adrian asked.

"It is impossible to know for sure," Bruno had answered. "But if I had to place a bet on it, I would say that will be the moment when the Red Moon comes out or when it becomes full."

"Maybe that's when they'll let us go home."

"I doubt it. The contract stipulated a year as the minimum time in Rocavarancolia, and, like I said, the convergence of the two symbols will take place several months before that time frame ends."

A dozen blue butterflies circled around the tower in a frenzy of zigzags and pirouettes. Alex joked around with Adrian while he tried to tickle his sister. She twisted and turned and tried to escape his attempts, but she couldn't help giggling.

Natalia was a little further along on the drawbridge with an empty basket in her hand. She brushed her dark hair off her forehead and frowned. She wore baggy pants of a dirty red color and a long black jacket over a gray shirt. She looked toward a spot in the city that Hector couldn't see, probably watching for the legion of shadows that, according to her, were lying in wait for them.

Hector looked around, wondering, as he often did, where he might find the shadow which followed him everywhere. In his imagination, it was a creature very similar to the smudges of darkness that Lady Serena had implanted in his mind, only with a pair of legs and two long arms. He imagined it moving like an unusually stretchy quadruped, capable of fitting into the tiniest nooks and crannies and walking on ceilings like an insect. When he asked what they were really like, Natalia shrugged.

"They're all different. Some look like gobs of tar and others are like clouds that sweep over the ground."

Two days before, Natalia had gone with the group in charge of gathering provisions to the square with the towers. When she returned, she told him that the wooden tower was completely overflowing with black shadows.

"They were piled up in the windows and the doorways. And they never stopped watching me . . . It made me want to scream, I swear. There were dozens of them, all staring at me."

"That place gives me the creeps," he said. He couldn't forget that the top floors of the building were surrounded by Lady Serena's mist.

"Everything gives you the creeps."

"That's true."

The two groups walked across the drawbridge. Alexander was still harassing his sister, tickling her waist every time he walked by. She turned around, sick of it, and tried to hit him with the basket. He avoided it with a jump and took a bow between Marina and Ricardo. They exchanged a complicit look, then fell upon him and returned in spades all the tickling that he'd put his sister through. On the verge of tears, Alex squirmed and stumbled forward as his friends attacked him.

Hector smiled, shook his head, and quickened his step to reach Natalia, who looked over her shoulder at the erratic flight of the blue butterflies. Beyond the bridge Rocavarancolia waited. The echoes of Alexander's laughter followed them, frenzied, joyful, full of life. Hector would remember that laugh for a long time. From that day forward there would be little reason to laugh.

Denestor Tul, demiurge of Rocavarancolia and guardian of Highlowtower, spent two hours flying around the Margalar Tower.

To all appearances he was just another blue butterfly flying among the rest; one had to look very closely to realize that he wasn't a real insect. His wings were made of paper, his body was made of colored dough, and his legs were made of rat hair. Denestor had created it hastily and even so it turned out to be one of his most perfect works, as if his anxiety had refined his natural talent. It took him a great deal of effort to transfer his consciousness to the creature. Although this was a common spell among demiurges, Denestor still wasn't completely recovered from the night of the harvest, and accomplishing it took more concentration than usual.

He now flew around the tower, waiting for the moment when he could safely approach Mistral. He saw his chance when the children finally left to go after the ships and the shapeshifter remained in the tower, next to the injured girl. The butterfly in which the demiurge's consciousness traveled fluttered above the children as they crossed the drawbridge. Natalia looked up and focused on him for a second. Denestor feared he'd been discovered, but in the end they'd continued on their way, chatting, joking, and laughing. In that respect they didn't look like the groups from years before; they weren't as somber or sad as the others.

They still haven't tasted the true flavor of Rocavarancolia, the demiurge thought. *They still don't know what awaits them.*

The butterfly that was Denestor Tul waited for Mistral to raise the drawbridge, then flapped his paper wings, caught a current of air, and let himself be carried toward the embrasures of the tower. He went through one of them and came to a stop in a room on the second floor. There was the injured girl, paging through an antique atlas of related worlds with a bored expression. The girl spied him fluttering on the ceiling and smiled maliciously. She rolled an old piece of parchment into a ball and threw it forcefully. Denestor had to swerve rapidly to avoid it; he descended and flew through the half-open door just as a new projectile passed by him.

He didn't find Mistral on that floor. He flew up the spiral staircase toward the top of the tower and found the trapdoor that led to the battlement open. He went through it. There was the shapeshifter, leaning against a crenel and scanning the ruins of Rocavarancolia with an absent air.

"Mistral," Denestor said through the butterfly. The demiurge's voice was barely a whisper, but the shapeshifter had no trouble hearing it. He smiled. The smile was halfway between bitterness and melancholy.

"You were starting to worry me, Denestor. You don't usually take so long to wake up," Marco said.

"What have you done, you fool?"

Mistral shrugged.

"Isn't it obvious? The night of Samhein I killed one of your pups in the dungeons, I threw his body into the Scar of Arax, and then I took on his appearance." He raised his hand before his face, and the butterfly landed instantly on the tip of his middle finger. "That's what I did, demiurge." Denestor thought he perceived a trace of sadness in his voice.

"You're mad, Mistral. I didn't expect this from you. From anyone else, sure. But from you?"

"I did it for the kingdom. There was no other way." He raised his hand with the butterfly on his finger to look at it closely. "There are times when it's necessary to forget law and tradition and act according to common sense."

"The council will find out about this. They'll exile you to the Malyadar Desert just like they exiled Roallen. It will be the end of you."

"Are you going to give me up, Denestor?" Mistral asked. For a moment his features seemed to bubble and a vestige of his true face peered through. "Is that what you're going to do?"

"I don't have a choice. You know that."

"True, true. You're Denestor Tul, demiurge of Rocavarancolia and guardian of Highlowtower. Loyal defender of the law and tradition of this dying kingdom. Do it, Denestor, do it. Turn me in and condemn us once and for all. But what an absurd paradox that you'll be the one to put the last nail in our coffin."

And suddenly Denestor Tul understood the dilemma that Mistral had placed him in. It was something so obvious that it had gone right over his head. The council, by law, wouldn't only exile the shapeshifter. The council was obligated to kill all the teenagers that he'd helped. Mistral had interfered in the harvest and now they were all contaminated.

"You see?" Mistral asked. "It's not as easy as it seems. I kept them alive, demiurge. If it hadn't been for me, the spinytails would have devoured them the first day. They ran toward them, for hell's sake! Can you believe it? Screaming and shouting, as if that would be enough to scare them off." He lowered his voice to a whisper. "If those damned vermin hadn't sensed my true self, they would all be dead. And look where I brought them: the Margalar Tower, the safest place for them in all of Rocavarancolia. Would you say I influenced the course of events? Would you say I interfered in the culling process?

Denestor sighed. Ten of the eleven surviving teenagers would be executed if the council found out about Mistral's recklessness.

"You're crazy, shapeshifter" was the only thing he could think of to say. "Crazy."

"I am, I know. As crazy as that troll Roallen, I admit it. But at least my madness isn't harmful to the kingdom."

"You can't keep up this deceit forever. Someone will find out."

"I have it all planned out. As soon as they can make it on their own, I'll disappear. I'll fake my death. I'll fall into the Scar of Arax, and I'll slip away through the underground passageways. Everyone will believe that I was turned into worm fodder." Mistral smiled bitterly on realizing the paradox that represented. The boy that he killed had met the same end. "Trust me, please. Your loyalty to the kingdom is blind, I know; I understand that and I accept it. But you don't owe loyalty to the laws that will mean our extinction. Let me keep them alive. Let me save them."

The blue butterfly sighed. Mistral appeared to have thought it all through. And what could he do? He shook his wings and took off flying around Marco's face.

"If they find out . . ."

"They won't," the shapeshifter assured him. "As soon as I finish teaching them the basics of sword fighting, I'll leave them to their fate. Look at them now. They walk through the city without fear and this time I'm not with them. Soon I'll let them fly solo, I promise."

"The spinytails . . ." Denestor suddenly remembered. Without Mistral in the group going to the square, the vermin would attack without a doubt.

"Dead. Last night I left the tower while everyone slept, I found their nest, and I killed them to the very last one. One less danger for the harvest. One more interference."

"You can't keep them all alive, you know that, right?"

"I'm not trying to. Only as many of them as possible. And I'll be gone long before the Red Moon comes out. I promise, Denestor. Will you keep my secret?"

"It looks like I don't have another choice."

Mistral smiled. The ancient demiurge couldn't help but remember the teenager he'd brought with him and whom the shapeshifter had killed before he even had a chance to wake up in Rocavarancolia. In appearance he was very similar to the kid who stood before him, although Mistral was somewhat bulkier. And the other boy gave off a special shine. It was easy to convince him to come to Rocavarancolia. He was a dreamer, eager to learn and live. His smile was open and joyous, and his eyes vibrated with an inner strength that was beyond measure.

"Why did you choose this one?" asked the blue butterfly. "Why not one of the others?"

"It was because of his appearance," answered the shapeshifter. He shrugged. "He looked beautiful to me. I couldn't help it."

"He didn't deserve it," Denestor said. The butterfly's voice was clearer than if it had surged from the demiurge's own throat, who, back in Highlowtower, was tormented by grief. "He didn't deserve it."

"None of them deserve it. But what else can we do?" He sighed, his gaze fixed on the teenagers as they neared the Scar of Arax. "We're monsters."

Later, Hector was unable to remember what had made him go searching for the third bathtub, the one that left provisions in the pit to the northeast.

As he watched it, he saw a figure suddenly appear on one of the rooftops and take off running toward it at top speed. At his back flapped what looked like a short gray cape and an empty sack. Despite how quickly he moved and how far away he was, Hector was able to see that it was a kid roughly his own age. The boy reached the end of the rooftop without slowing his pace and leapt with an astonishing agility, sailed over the gap between him and the bathtub, and fell inside. The ship wobbled from side to side from the sudden invasion, but regained its balance promptly. The pilot was unperturbed; the new passenger's arrival had caught him mid verse and he continued as if nothing had happened.

"Did you see that?"

"What? What?" Adrian asked, looking around in all directions.

Hector pointed to the ship and explained what he'd just witnessed.

"It has to be him! The missing boy!" Lizbeth said. "We found him!"

"She's right! There he is!" Adrian yelled, throwing back the emerald helmet. They all looked in the direction of the bathtub. There was the teenager, standing on the deck, calmly regarding the baskets.

"What do we do? Should we call him?"

Ricardo shook his head.

"He won't be able to hear us from this distance," he said. Hector knew that wasn't the reason. The issue wasn't whether he could hear them, but rather what other things they might alert to their presence if they started yelling.

"So what do we do?" Adrian repeated.

Ricardo considered the distance between themselves and the bathtub. Then he turned his gaze toward the Margalar Tower. They were halfway to the Scar of Arax, and the bathtub that they needed to collect supplies from hadn't even arrived yet. He ran his hand through his chestnut hair, making it stand on end. He looked unsure.

"Hector, come with me," he said at last. "The rest of you will gather provisions, and be careful, all right? We're going to see if we can talk to that acrobat."

Natalia frowned when they separated, as if she didn't think it was such a good idea, but she said nothing.

Ricardo and Hector moved quickly through the twisted streets, in the direction of the flying bathtub. They tried to always keep it in their sight, but occasionally the buildings hid it from their view. The teenager remained onboard, rummaging through the baskets and placing the foods that he liked in his sack.

They heard running footsteps behind them and turned around in unison, Ricardo with his dagger already half-unsheathed. It was Adrian. He came running after them, panting and red in the face.

"I want to go with you, not with the girls!" he said.

Ricardo cursed under his breath. He looked back at the bathtub, then cursed again.

"Let's go," he said. And by the tone of his voice, Hector guessed that he was already starting to regret having separated the group. "But don't leave my side by even an inch or you're gonna get it, understand?"

The three of them walked through the ruined city. When they came to the Scar of Arax, the flying bathtub and its stowaway were only about two hundred yards away. The teenager was still onboard, dedicated to his task with exasperating calm. It was obvious that it wasn't the first time he'd been aboard one of those ships. Hector wondered what reasons he had for not joining the group or why he hadn't at least introduced himself, even if he didn't want to stay with them in the tower. He didn't have to risk his life raiding bathtubs on the run; they would have happily shared their provisions with him. His actions didn't make any sense.

The second ship, the one that was headed in Lizbeth and Natalia's direction, flew overhead just as they were crossing the gap. They marched over a heap of rubble that formed a dam between the piles of skeletons. The sailboat's keel was blinding under the rays of Rocavarancolia's tiny sun.

"He's making a move," whispered Adrian when they reached the other side.

He was right. The teenager had closed his sack and now leaned against the bathtub's edge, glancing to the left. He looked just like someone on a bus waiting for his stop. At that moment the ship entered a wide street.

There were only buildings on one side of the street: narrow houses six stories high. Practically the entire façade of one of them had come down and left a clear view of the rooms inside, just like a dollhouse. They understood what he was considering even before they saw him gather momentum on the bathtub. He jumped onto the nearby building with impeccable precision. In the stillness of the afternoon they heard the soft sound of his landing, straight into one of the rooms on the fifth floor. He spun around and saw them running up the street. He looked at them indecisively, shook his head, and disappeared inside the structure.

"Wait!" Ricardo yelled. "We just want to talk to you!"

They ran to the entrance. There wasn't a trace of Lady Serena's mist, and that calmed Hector somewhat. A tall stairway led to the building's door. Ricardo went up first, with the other two not far behind. Hector gripped the iron handrail as he advanced and avoided looking down with every step: that stairway was too steep for his liking.

Then everything happened at a dizzying speed. Ricardo pushed on the door, but from the other side it was snatched from his hands and then shoved forward with such force that he couldn't step away. The door hit Ricardo in the face and knocked him down. Hector and Adrian jumped aside to avoid falling with their friend, who tumbled down the stairs. Ricardo managed to grab the handrail and came to a stop a few steps from the ground.

In the door frame, a sinewy dark-haired boy appeared, with a bronzed complexion, aquiline nose, and dark eyes.

"Get out! Out! Out of my way! Out!" he shrieked frantically. He brandished a short sword, waving it back and forth.

In their hurry to get away from him, Adrian and Hector collided, hindering him even further. The boy jumped forward just as Ricardo, a few steps below, stood up. Hector put one hand on his dagger, but before he could unsheathe it, his attacker's fist caught him in the chin. The last thing he saw before falling was Adrian, protecting his face with his shield, and a brief flash of metal at waist level. The boy passed by Hector in a flash, grabbed the rundown handrail, and vaulted into the street.

"Idiot!" Ricardo took off running after him, clearing the steps in one leap. But the other had such a head start that he gave up the chase after a few strides. He clutched his side and knelt on the ground, aching and out of breath.

Hector grasped the handrail and stood up. He felt his chin. *He had a sword*, he thought, dazed. *He could have killed me, he could have killed me . . .*

"Hec . . ." he heard behind him. A current of ice-cold fire ran down his vertebrae, one by one. "Hector . . ."

Adrian was down, his back against the handrail, a terrible pallor appearing on his contorted face. He gripped his stomach with both hands, although his efforts were in vain: blood seeped through his fingers, slow and steady. A visible stain appeared on the ground, an unstoppable red tide that traced arabesque patterns in the fissures and irregularities of the staircase. Hector took a step toward him, and when he saw his own reflection in the puddle of blood, he felt like he was drowning.

"Hector?" Adrian repeated. His mouth opened and closed. Hector thought of a fish out of water, suffocating. "The shield . . ." he whispered, his voice growing weaker and weaker. He moved one hand away from his stomach to point to the shield that had fallen out of his reach, a couple of steps down. The blood flowed more quickly now. "Please . . . I dropped . . . my shield . . ." He looked at him with heartbreaking urgency.

Hector felt his knees give way.

"Ricardo!" he yelled.

Adrian blinked several times. He looked about, as if he didn't recognize the reality that surrounded him, as if it were completely foreign. Then his eyes closed. Slowly, very slowly. A teardrop with a bloodstained reflection rolled down his cheek.

THE AGONY

Hector had a scream caught in his throat. He felt it rise as Adrian slipped away in front of the door. And although he wanted to let it out, he couldn't; the scream stayed tangled up in his vocal cords, refusing to leave. It was like a stubborn yawn, like a sneeze that he just couldn't get out.

He was about to release it when Ricardo ran up the stairs. Hector saw the look of horror on his face when he discovered Adrian in a pool of blood, and almost screamed out of sheer reflex. But then he heard a moan, a soft whimper that signified that life remained in the stabbed body, and the moment passed.

Ricardo carried Adrian to the Margalar Tower. It was a nightmarish journey through the ruined city. Hector walked by his side, never taking his eyes off the unconscious kid. Ricardo had torn his shirt into shreds to bandage the wound, but even so he left a trail of blood behind them. Every few steps another drop would spill onto the pavement, sometimes as small as a coin, sometimes so big that it reminded Hector of the red moon from the atlas and the sphere on the tower. For a second, he was tempted to tell Ricardo that they'd made a mistake, that they weren't heading in the right direction. That they should turn around and return to the Scar of Arax to throw Adrian in. His place was in that ossuary, not in the tower.

And now he felt that monstrous scream again, moving around in his throat as he looked at the fire that burned in the stove. The smoke rose only to fall again and dissipate through the ventilation holes in the tray of firewood. The flames tinged of red the sword blade that Marco heated over the fire. And Hector felt he wouldn't be able to contain this damned scream much longer. He had to let it out or it would eat him alive.

"He's afraid of fire," he managed to say. That red blaze looked like blood, a hemorrhage transformed into flames. "You can't do that, he's afraid of fire . . . Don't you remember?"

"This will cauterize the wound," Marco said. "So it will stop bleeding."

"But he's afraid of fire!" he insisted.

"Hector, if you don't shut up, I'll smack you," Marco warned. The reflection of the flames in his pupils made him look like a deranged demon.

"But . . ."

"Hector!"

Natalia put an arm around his waist and led him out of the kitchen. Large, dark drops remained on the floor of the tower and on the stairs, marking the path of the wounded boy. Hector shook his head, dazed, when he saw them. He broke away from Natalia and went to the basement. He looked in the baskets of clothing until he found the cartoon character T-shirt stained with blood that he'd found their first day in the tower. He went back upstairs and used the shirt to clean the bloodstains. He bit his lower lip. The idea of wiping up Adrian's blood with that T-shirt had seemed like a good idea at first, but now that he was doing it he felt horribly stupid. He started to cry, still scrubbing the floor mightily, obscuring the old blood on the torn shirt with freshly spilled blood.

Alexander approached him.

"Get up, Hector," he said, stretching out his hand. After a moment's hesitation, Hector accepted it and stood up slowly.

The mood in the tower had never been so dismal. In one of the rooms upstairs, Ricardo and Lizbeth took care of Adrian. The others were scattered throughout the ground floor. Marco heatedthe sword to cauterize the wound; Natalia leaned against the wall, her arms crossed, an expression of great helplessness and rage on her face; Madeleine, Marina, and Rachel sat together at the main table, each sadder and more devastated than the last; Bruno, at the other end of the tower, away from everyone, rested his hands on the cover of the book that sat in his lap. He looked eager to open it, but he restrained himself, as if he realized that this wasn't the right time.

Alex and Natalia exchanged glances.

"Let's go find him," the redhead said. She nodded and decisively stepped away from the wall. "He has to pay for what he's done."

"No one is doing anything of the sort," Marco warned, not taking his eyes from the fire.

"He stabbed Adrian! You want us to let it go, just like that? He's a murderer!"

"And how do you expect to find him?" Marco asked. "If you hadn't noticed, Rocavarancolia is enormous. And besides, the problem isn't tracking him down, it's keeping the things that lurk in this city from finding you while you look for him."

"We know how to defend ourselves!"

"No! You don't know! If you go out alone, the only thing you'll manage to do is get yourselves killed! Is that how you think you can help Adrian? By getting yourselves killed?"

Alex grunted and sank into a chair, furious. Natalia looked daggers at Marco and climbed the stairs as fast as she could.

"Why did he do it?" Marina asked. "Why did he attack you? I don't understand."

"Maybe he was afraid," Madeleine murmured. The two girls held hands on the table.

"No," Hector said. He trembled to think of it. "I saw him. And he wasn't afraid. He was enraged. That's why he attacked us."

"This is almost ready." Marco turned the sword over. Hector looked away while the scream in his throat fought to escape.

"It won't do any good," Bruno said. "You'll cauterize the wound, but there's also internal damage. Adrian is going to die. The best thing we can do is start to accept it."

"I'm not going to accept it, smartass!" Alexander shouted. He jumped out of his chair and rushed toward Bruno. "I promised him that I'd get him home and I'm going to do just that! Do you hear me?"

"I hear you perfectly, Alexander," he answered, not the least upset. "But let me tell you that I don't see any way that you can help him, much less bring him home." As always, the tone of his voice didn't vary one bit. Hector snorted, so furious with the Italian that he could have slapped him right then and there. In fact, he hoped that Alex would do it. "If the loss of blood doesn't kill him, the infection will, without a doubt. The question is how much time he has left. Several hours or, at the most, a little more than a day. It all depends on which internal organs were damaged. With the pain he's going to suffer the best thing for him would be for it to happen as soon as possible. The most merciful thing would be to help him d—"

"Shut up!" Alex yelled. For a second he looked like he was ready to hit him, but instead he turned his back and walked away abruptly.

Mistral turned back to the sword. Soon the time would come to burn the wound. He wasn't fooled: Bruno was right. There was no way to save him, at least no natural way of achieving it. The quick look he'd had at the wound was enough to give him an idea of its seriousness. The damage was so great that only magic could help him. Healing spells weren't too complex; even he, as little versed as he was in witchcraft, would be able to perform one. But this would mean being completely exposed. He couldn't save Adrian without being discovered. And if he were, neither his life nor the children's lives would mean anything. It would be the end.

He changed position in the kitchen. The heat was infernal, but even so he had to force his pores to exude the sweat that otherwise would not have appeared on his skin. He had to pay attention to so many details to avoid suspicion among both the harvest and the residents of Rocavarancolia; he lived in constant fear of being found out. More and more frequently he believed he'd made a mistake, that he should have let things happen naturally and not interfered. But it was too late for regrets; he had to stay here, despite the risk. For the kingdom, yes, and for that child he'd killed to take his place. If he disappeared now, the kid's death would have been for nothing; helping the others at least gave it some value.

Death for life, thought Mistral, his eyes fixed on the sword blade. Sometimes everything was that straightforward: sometimes the best way to face problems was to simplify them. He hadn't attended the Royal Council's meeting, for obvious reasons, and he hadn't seen Lady Spider's measuring of the children's essence, but he didn't need to. He knew which kids had the most potential. In the five days that he'd spent with them, he'd formed a rough idea. And Adrian's potential was enormous.

It would be a shame for Rocavarancolia to lose such a wealth of power. Mistral gritted his teeth and turned the sword again. Saving him was easy—he only had to point in the right direction—but he knew that to do so meant that another one of the children would die. Life for life:

there was no other way. And although in itself that would be a just and rational exchange, there was yet another advantage: if all turned out well, he wouldn't just save Adrian, he'd put a power in the group's hands that no other harvest had held, at least not so quickly. Their chances of survival would multiply enormously. Then why did he hesitate? He couldn't comprehend it, especially considering that sooner or later one of the teenagers would head in the same direction. And he couldn't allow that, because if he did, if he didn't have control of the situation, the risk of a real tragedy occurring would be tremendous.

"It's done." He took the sword out of the fire. The blade shone.

Hector averted his eyes when Marco went up the stairs, sword in hand. He looked around, worried, suffocating. The weapon's gleam was burned in his retina. He blinked to erase it, but it remained, shining red hot against his closed eyelids. He needed fresh air. He escaped to the courtyard, almost at a run. Alexander followed him shortly after. The two walked side by side, in silence. The redhead bit his lower lip and hit the pedestal of the spider king with his fist as they passed it.

Just then they heard a scream of pain coming from the Margalar Tower. It only lasted a couple of seconds, but it was enough to make them shudder from head to toe. Hector felt his own scream rising to finally escape his throat, but right at that moment Alexander grasped his arm and the scream withdrew, returning once again to a knot stuck in his windpipe. He turned to the redhead. Alex's eyes shone with animal ferocity.

"Over there . . ." he growled.

Hector followed the direction of his gaze. Beyond the wall and the moat, on the first line of rooftops that they could see from where they stood, was the boy who'd stabbed Adrian, crouching down, looking toward the tower. He rose when he was discovered, watched them for a couple of seconds, and then disappeared at a run, his gray cape flapping frantically behind him.

When it got dark, the pack howled as they'd only done during their first night. Mistral frowned. They smelled death and blood, and it made them frenzied. And they weren't the only creatures who were affected by the smell of human blood. He hoped he was wrong, but it was likely that more than one scavenger now circled the vicinity of the Margalar Tower. He should take extra precautions. He should probably make sure the kids were never out in the courtyard alone. There were vermin in Rocavarancolia capable of jumping over the moat or attacking from the air.

Lizbeth appeared on the stairs, her countenance one of terrible gravity. She carried a washbasin with a heap of dirty bandages. The others waited below, seated around the table. They sat in silence, staring at nothing, each lost in their own thoughts.

"He has a high fever," Lizbeth said as she sat at the table, throwing the used bandages aside and leaving the washbasin next to the stove.

"So what do we do?" Marina asked.

Ricardo shrugged. His nose was swollen and bruised from the door hitting him.

"I wish I knew," he said. He was devastated. No one blamed him for what had happened, although it was clear that didn't make him feel any less guilty. After all, it had been his idea to go after that kid. Hector felt sorry for him, but he knew that if he tried to console him it would only make things worse.

"Let's go to the castle," Natalia suggested. "They can't be so cruel as to let him die, right? Surely they have a doctor there or something. Someone who can heal him."

"It's too dangerous," Marco said.

"Besides, the castle is one of the forbidden places," Bruno reminded him. "And we must not fool ourselves with false hopes: Lady Scar made it abundantly clear that they will not intervene even if our lives are in danger. They cannot interfere. It's the law."

"We could try, at least," Madeleine said. "We have nothing to lose. And yes, they forbade us from going to the castle. But that doesn't mean that we can't send them a message, right?"

"And how do we do that?"

"Tomorrow, in the bathtubs. We can leave notes in the baskets explaining what happened. Someone will read them, I'm sure. Maybe they can help us."

Hector sighed and leaned on the table. It was all useless. First, because it was very possible that Adrian would die overnight, and second, because Lady Serena had made it clear that they were alone, abandoned to their fate in the ruined city. Besides, he was certain that the castle's inhabitants were aware of what had happened. They must be watching them somehow; maybe Natalia's shadows were in charge of informing them.

He didn't share his thoughts with the rest of the group; despite what Bruno had just said, he felt that right now it was better to embrace any hope whatsoever, even if false.

"I'll stay with him through the night," Lizbeth said.

"We can take turns," Marina offered.

The other shook her head.

"Don't worry, there's no need. I won't be able to sleep anyway. I'll do it. I'll let you know if anything changes . . ." Her voice broke. Everyone knew what kind of change she was referring to.

"It's weird, you know?" Marina began. "We've been warned constantly about this city. They told us that it's full of monsters and dangers, of enchantments and who knows what else . . . But it wasn't Rocavarancolia that stabbed Adrian. It was a boy, a kid like us."

"And you think that's strange?" Marco asked. "Human beings have been slaughtering each other since the beginning of time."

"The most horrible monsters are the ones that don't look the part," Hector said quietly.

Mistral glanced at the teenager. It took a great effort for him not to betray the impression Hector's words had made. For a second he was convinced Hector was on to him.

It was still a while before dawn, early hours of the morning. Inside the tower most of the teenagers tossed and turned on their mattresses, unable to fall asleep. In a room on the second floor Adrian lay unconscious; next to his bed sat Lizbeth, half-asleep in her chair, but attentive always to the wounded boy's state. Silence reigned in Rocavarancolia. The pack had finally quieted.

A cloud of black dust, recently arrived from the west, flew over the moat. It was dark and compact and although it was carried by the wind it didn't seem to submit to its whims, but rather used it to advance toward its target. For a few seconds it turned and danced over the moat, jumping from air current to air current until it met with one that traveled in its desired direction: toward the tower's embrasures. The black cloud of dust slipped through one on the second floor, and once inside it compressed and twisted: it acquired a vaguely humanoid form, something between a shadow, a ghost, and an illusion. It gained definition as it walked toward the door of the empty room.

Little by little, one by one, the features of Enoch the Dusty began taking shape on the creature's face. The vampire was thirsty. An eager light shone in his red eyes. When he left the room, he was almost solid. Only the soles of his feet still had the consistency of dust, so that they could cushion the sound of his footsteps on the ground.

He sniffed around the spiral staircase. The smell of blood made him lick his lips. He hurried on, so greedily that he almost slipped. He tried to calm down. He must be careful now. He couldn't risk being discovered or he'd share the same fate as Roallen, the troll who was exiled to the desert far beyond the mountains.

He's going to die, the vampire thought, as he followed the trail of the scent of blood to Adrian's room. *The child's going to die. So what does it matter if I drink a little? No one will ever know. And I'm so, so thirsty . . .*

He approached the door, rested his hands on it, and listened carefully. The boy wasn't alone; there was someone with him. The vampire could hear their breathing, full of life, and the rhythmic hum of blood coursing through their veins.

Black dust swirled around the wrinkles in his face. He'd made the mistake of changing back too quickly; he should have waited to make sure that no one else was with the wounded child. Now he had no choice but to transform back, with the risk that implied. Given the extreme weakness that he found himself in after so many years, he was better off not abusing the power of metamorphosis, or he could end up scattered forever, with no chance of coming back together again. But he had no choice, not if he wanted to keep going. And he wanted to. There was nothing he wanted more.

Enoch blew. From his cracked lips surged dark dust, spirals of grainy darkness. As the dusty, hovering cloud grew, Enoch's size diminished. The old vampire blew himself away, until all that remained were two lips covered in sores, floating in the void. Then that horrifying mouth disintegrated as well. And once more, Enoch was nothing but black dust.

He slipped through the fissures and cracks in the door, carefully, just a little bit at a time. He didn't want to draw attention to himself. Soon most of him was on the other side of the threshold. He slithered along the floor while he took stock of the situation.

The chubby girl was nodding off in a chair. On the mattress lay the wounded boy, his face pearly with sweat. The blanket they'd covered him with had shifted and his torso was exposed. Although they must have just recently changed the bandages, the vampire could still smell the blood that stained them. On an old wooden table on the other side of the bed were two washbasins filled with water, one of them cloudy with blood. The flood of dust snaked behind Lizbeth's chair.

She opened her eyes suddenly. She looked behind her, confused, but in the dim light from the oil lamp she saw nothing but shadow. She got up to feel Adrian's temperature. She sighed, removed the wet rag from his forehead, soaked it once again in the washbasin of clean water, moistened his lips and cheeks with it, and then placed it back over the boy's eyes. She then sat back down in the chair. Behind her, in disturbing silence, the figure of Enoch began to materialize once more.

The vampire had a moment of doubt once he was completely transformed. His first impulse was to pounce on Adrian, rip his throat open, and drink until there was nothing left.

I'm not an animal, he reminded himself. *I'm hungry. That's all. I'm hungry. And the poor boy is suffering. I'll give him the rest he deserves, and in exchange I'll slake this cursed thirst of mine. That's not interfering. We're doing each other a favor. That's all. Yes. That's all. But I won't behave like an animal. I have my dignity . . .*

Saliva glistened at the corners of his mouth and slid down his chin. He approached the back of the chair. He raised his right hand, leaned over toward Lizbeth, and stroked her hair with his fingertips. The young girl shivered, but the touch was so subtle that she didn't turn around.

"Sleep, my dear, full of blood and life. May nothing disturb your sleep," whispered Enoch. Then he recited the seventeen ancient words that composed the sleep spell. Lizbeth appeared to sink into her chair. Her breathing became slow and heavy.

Next the vampire went to the mattress. His eyes shone, fixed on Adrian's exposed bandages. The smell of blood grew stronger and stronger. It tugged at him, compelled him toward the stretched-out body like an invisible claw that seized his entrails.

I just want to remember what it means to be sated. Just that.

Enoch the Dusty loomed over Adrian: a dark shadow surrounded by suspended dust. His hands shook. He leaned over, slowly, above the bandage that covered the wound. He felt a pulsation underneath the bandages, as if it too were eager to meet with his lips. At that moment,

Adrian awoke. The vampire stood up at once when he noticed the change in the wounded boy's breathing. The boy's clear eyes saw him rise up before him like a vision from a nightmare, a dark shadow with a half-open mouth lined with fangs, and two smoldering eyes. He tried to scream but the only thing that left his mouth was a terrified gasp.

"Be still," Enoch ordered. And then he uttered the only ancient word that he needed to consummate the spell. Adrian's body was instantly paralyzed: his mouth half-open, his eyes bulging with panic.

Enoch scrutinized his face, unsure. The child's eyes remained fixed on him. Despite being immobilized, he could still see him. And at the same time the vampire could see the extraordinary terror that was revealed in those eyes.

"I'm hungry," he said, in a pathetic attempt to justify his action. "Do you understand?"

He whimpered. He'd been starving for so long that it had been years since he'd been able to think clearly . . . In his head there was hardly room for coherent thoughts; everything was imbued with hunger and voraciousness. He hissed and took a step backward, his gaze on the black bandages. The vampire shuddered.

I'm not an animal, he repeated to himself. I'm Enoch. And once I was respected and feared. Once my name meant something, it inspired terror and was uttered with dread in over twenty worlds. And I didn't have to lower myself to visiting deathbeds to obtain my sustenance. What happened to me? When did I become a scavenger?

But the temptation was too great . . .

The vampire growled, violently grabbed the washbasin full of bloody water, and drank it down in one single gulp. The watery blood washed down his dry throat, taking the dust that had stuck to his gullet with it.

Enoch stepped back, sobbed desperately, and turned to dust before the dying boy's terrified gaze.

Adrian's scream woke the whole tower. It was brief but dreadful, a shriek cut short by pain and agony. They rushed en masse to his room to find him half falling out of bed, his face shaken by fear, pointing to an empty space between the bed and the table. Despite the racket, Lizbeth remained in a deep sleep. Hector was the only one who didn't enter the room. He stayed in the doorway with one hand on the door frame. He felt as if a grainy current brushed against his bare feet. He looked at the ground, puzzled, but saw nothing more than shadows upon shadows.

Adrian shivered. His hand became a claw that clutched at Alexander by the front of his shirt and pulled him down. Despite his weakened state he almost pulled the redhead onto the bed. He said something in a voice so quiet that only Alex could hear him. Then he collapsed back on the bed, unconscious. And still he was trembling, as if fear had seeped into his subconscious.

"He says that a vampire made of dust wanted to drink his blood," the redhead announced, confused.

Mistral looked around. Enoch the Dusty had been there, attracted without a doubt by the child's blood. In a way it was a shame that he hadn't finished Adrian off; if he had, that would have put an end to his own hesitation. And as an added benefit, Rocavarancolia would finally be rid of that loathsome vampire once the council exiled him.

No one was in the mood to try to sleep. They didn't even return to their mattresses. They ate breakfast without an appetite and scattered throughout the ground floor of the tower, waiting for dawn.

"His fever has gone up," Lizbeth said. The boy didn't look good. She couldn't understand why she hadn't woken up during Adrian's attack. She sat down with a hand on her chest and an absent expression. She still seemed dazed.

"Do you think he really saw that?" Hector asked. "A vampire made of dust?"

"Maybe it was delirium caused by the fever," Bruno interjected. "But taking into account the nature of this place, nothing is impossible."

Hector nodded. For a moment he'd forgotten where he was. In Rocavarancolia, anything was possible. Absolutely anything.

When dawn arrived, Adrian was plunged into a state of feverish semiconsciousness. He hardly seemed aware of his surroundings. There was always someone at his side, although it was Lizbeth and Rachel who spent the most time with him: they had both taken the responsibility of caring for him upon themselves.

Hector was the only one who still hadn't gone to see him; he hadn't set foot in that room even once, nor did he have any intention of doing so. Every time he passed by the door he felt a cutting bite in his gut, a stabbing pain made up of anguish, sorrow, and fear that made him rush to get away. When Natalia told him that Adrian had asked for him in one of his rare moments of lucidity, he only shrugged his shoulders. He refused to watch his friend die. He wasn't brave enough to enter that room to say goodbye. And although that was destroying him, he couldn't help it.

Mistral looked up. A vague and unidentifiable sound reached him. Too subtle for the others to hear, but not subtle enough to escape his keen perception. It came from inside the tower, from a spot on the first floor. The shapeshifter got up from the table and started walking toward the stairway, without hurrying or showing any sign of concern. He didn't want to alarm Madeleine and Marina, who were with him at the time. That same morning, he'd seen scavengers meandering beyond the moat, most likely attracted by Adrian's impending death, and although he strongly doubted that any of them had found a way to enter the tower without being seen, he had no choice but to take every precaution. Now on the first floor, he followed the sound until he arrived at the door where it originated. There was someone crying on the other side. It was such a soft cry that whoever was there obviously was making sure that come hell or high water, no one would hear it. Mistral retreated, uneasy. This wasn't his business; he had no desire to get involved in anyone else's intimate affairs. If someone wanted to cry without being seen, they were well within their right to do so. And he was just about to leave when the crying stopped abruptly. Next, he heard footsteps. Whoever was inside was about to come out. The shapeshifter retreated quickly but didn't have time to reach the staircase.

To Mistral's astonishment, it was Alexander who opened the door. He came out rubbing his eyes on his shirtsleeve. Alex stopped when he saw him standing still in the middle of the hallway.

"What are you doing here?" he asked abruptly. Despite his efforts to hide it, it was obvious that he'd been crying and that he knew he'd been found out.

"I was looking for you," Mistral lied, and on seeing the alarm on the boy's face he rushed to add, "No! He's still alive, Adrian's still alive . . . I only wanted to know where you'd gone off to, that's all." He was so bewildered by the situation that he couldn't come up with a better excuse. "Hey, are you okay?" he asked.

Alex nodded and started walking briskly to the staircase.

"Are you sure?" Mistral prodded, when he passed by him.

"Do you not have eyes in your head or what?" he asked in anger. "Of course I'm not okay. I'm not okay at all. Nothing about this is okay." He bit his lower lip hard before continuing: "He's going to die, Marco. And there's nothing we can do to stop it. Nothing."

"But we're trying," he said.

"Trying? Oh, please." Alex made a face. "And what are we supposed to do? Is sitting and watching him die useful? Damn it, can't you see? We're stuck in a situation we can't beat." He looked at Mistral with rage. The shapeshifter had only seen him this way on one other occasion, when he took off running after the spinytails in the Scar of Arax. But now the redhead had nothing to fight against, nothing to fight back. "Adrian will be the first to die," he said in a whisper, a thin voice that held back a scream. "And he won't be the last. You know it as well as I do. We're all going to die. We can't survive this."

The shapeshifter shook his head.

"If that's what you think, then we're already lost," he said. "Don't give the city that advantage. We can't surrender. No, no, we can't. We have to keep fighting."

Alex's gaze regained its clarity. He stepped back and brought a hand to his forehead. His rage seemed to slip away. He nodded.

"I know, I know . . . God . . . You don't know how difficult this is for me."

"For all of us."

"For all of us, yes," he murmured, "but you guys didn't get your own sister involved in this mess. That makes it even worse, you know? I can't stop thinking about it. I can't stop thinking that it's my fault that she's here. It wasn't even Denestor Tul who convinced her to come, you understand? It was me. Me alone."

"You can't blame yourself for that," he said. "Denestor would have ended up convincing her sooner or later, either with his mumbo jumbo or with the smoke from his pipe."

Alexander shook his head.

"You're wrong. She's as stubborn as can be. If she says no, it's no. Believe me. There's no twisting her arm." He smiled sadly. "I don't know if it's a virtue or a flaw, but that's how my little sister is. No. Denestor wouldn't have convinced her if she'd said no." All the same, Mistral knew that wasn't true: the girl's will would have bent to the demiurge's arts regardless. "She's here because of me," Alex insisted. "And if something happens to her, I won't be able to handle it." He leaned back against the wall. "And every day here is torture because all I do is pretend to be someone I'm not. I act like everything is fine, like I'm strong and can handle anything . . ." His eyes teared up, but Mistral knew that he wouldn't see him cry. "I guess it's not that bad. I stay strong and keep going. But . . ." He bit his lower lip again, then looked Mistral in the eye. "But sometimes I can't take any more," he confessed. "Sometimes I can't take it, because I'm tired of always being strong, of always being here for everyone, intact, relentless . . . I'm tired of swallowing this need to scream my head off and beat up anything that moves." He sighed pitifully. "Sometimes I just want to surrender."

"Even so, you don't. And that's what matters."

Alexander looked like he was going to laugh, but instead he pointed with his head toward the room he'd just left.

"You're wrong. What do you think I was just doing in there? What do you think I do in there a dozen times a day? Surrender. That's what I do. I go in and I surrender. Over and over again. When no one's watching me, when I know that you're all far away in that damned room I come down here. And then I put a smile on my face, walk out, and pretend to be a hero."

"And what's the difference?" Mistral asked. "The result is the same, isn't it? What does it matter if you're a hero or just pretending?"

"I know I'm lying," he said.

Like every day, the sailboats with their provisions left the castle in the late afternoon. Marina and Madeleine had prepared eight notes, one for each basket in the bathtubs. They had little hope of receiving help from the castle, but they needed to feel like they were doing something for Adrian. The alternative was to keep twiddling their thumbs and waiting for it to all be over, and that was even more frustrating.

This time, Hector, Marco, Bruno, and Madeleine were in charge of going after the provisions that the ships left beyond the Scar of Arax. The whole way they were more focused on the third bathtub, and the buildings it flew over, than on the boat they were supposed to be waiting for. But the boy never showed up. For the first time on their ventures into the city, Marco carried a bow and a quiver full of arrows. He seemed more alert than ever, as if he expected an attack at any moment. Even so, nothing happened. They gathered the provisions, left the notes in the handles of the baskets before hoisting them up again with the cords, and returned to the tower safely, without a single encounter.

Lizbeth lowered the drawbridge and went out to meet them at the gate.

"He's the same," she told them. She'd pulled her disheveled hair back in a messy braid. "Now all he does is call out for his mother. Rachel's with him."

"My brother's not back yet?" Madeleine asked as she set a basket on the table. Lizbeth shook her head. The red-haired girl frowned. The square with the petrified statues was much closer than the Scar of Arax. The group that was in charge of gathering supplies in that area always returned before the other one. She approached Marco, who was about to close the gate.

"Leave it open, please," she said, and she stood on the threshold, as if waiting there would speed Alexander's return.

Bruno placed his basket on the table and went straight to the chair where he'd left the book of magic. He sat with his legs crossed and the book open in his lap. Soon he heard a drawn-out wail coming from the spiral staircase. A shiver ran down Hector's spine. The scream stirred in his throat.

"He will die soon," Bruno said, without lifting his eyes from the book. "It is for the best. He won't suffer anymore."

"Could you stop being so morbid for just a minute, please? Or is that too much to expect?" Madeleine asked from the gate. "I've never known anyone as strange and bitter as you. I'm sure that's why Denestor brought you. He knew you'd feel right at home in this city."

"I am home," he agreed. "I am where I should be. Just like you. The only difference is that I know the reason why Denestor brought me, and you don't."

There was a long silence. Everyone looked at Bruno, perplexed. Behind the dirty lenses of his glasses his eyes looked small and distant.

"You know why they brought you?" Hector finally asked. "Is that what you just said?"

The Italian's impassive gaze broke from the book to look at him with a disinterested stare.

"I'm here because where I go, people die," he explained. "That's why Denestor brought me. I bring bad luck."

"What does that mean?" Madeleine asked, after another long silence.

"I suppose that some might say that I am jinxed. My grandfather is a little more extreme. He insists that I am cursed."

"You're not telling me you believe in that nonsense?" Lizbeth said.

"It is not nonsense; it is real, and it is hard to argue with. I bring bad luck. And it has been that way since the moment I was born: my mother died in childbirth and my father shortly after. My grandfather says he died from sorrow."

"But it wasn't your fault!" Lizbeth seemed shocked by Bruno's words. "Pardon me if I say that I don't believe that Denestor brought you here because you're jinxed." She put her hands on her hips and leaned forward. "That's just silly. Do you hear me? Silly."

"Do not rush to judgment. You still do not know the rest of the story," Bruno warned. "When I became an orphan my aunt and uncle took me in. They both died before long in a car accident: lightning struck them in the middle of the highway and my uncle lost control of the car. His two children also died in the accident. Up until then it might have been nothing more than a tragic chain of coincidences, I admit. But there's more.

"My maternal grandparents took me in after my aunt and uncle died. They lived in a mansion on the outskirts of Rome. Death followed me even there. My grandmother died of a heart attack right after I arrived at their house, and as for my grandfather, already a superstitious man, well, that was the straw that broke the proverbial camel's back. If it hadn't been for the fact that I was the last descendant of his bloodline, I'm sure he would have found a way to get rid of me. Instead, he let me stay at the mansion and placed the servants in charge of my care. Two of the five servants who worked in the house at that time died in the following months, one from a sudden lethal illness and the other in a household accident. The others left their posts: they thought I was cursed as well."

Hector listened to the story in amazement. There wasn't the slightest inflection in Bruno's voice, nor the faintest trace of emotion. His narration was in a monotone, a constant droning that peeled off layer by layer the strange story of his life and the deaths that surrounded him.

"Three children in my nursery school died of different illnesses my first month there. My grandfather took me out of the school and the deaths stopped. From then on, for the first half of my life, my education and care were delegated to various tutors, nannies, and maids. He invariably let them go after several weeks, in an attempt to protect them from my harmful influence. I hardly ever saw him. We lived in different wings of the mansion, separated by doors that were always locked.

"When I turned seven, there were no more nannies or tutors for me, just one servant and one cook, who, of course, my grandfather replaced frequently. The mansion's great library was my tutor from then on. It was enormous and so well stocked that I had plenty to read for years and years. That's where I spent most of my life. The entire north wing of the mansion was my refuge, my home; I left the house only on rare occasion, and when I did it was always under the supervision of a servant who had orders not to let me approach anyone.

"The last time I saw my grandfather was three years ago, on my twelfth birthday. It was then that he gave me the watch. I suspected that he was trying to prove something with that present; maybe that he had defeated me, that my curse had not managed to reach him . . . I do not know. I do not care."

"Good lord!" Lizbeth exclaimed when it seemed like Bruno was finished talking. "You didn't ever have any friends? Kids your age to play with? To talk to?" She took a step toward the Italian and stretched out her hand as if she meant to touch him, but she didn't actually do it. "No one to love you?"

Bruno shrugged.

"From my first memories my world was reduced to the mansion and its library. I had no contact with anyone besides my childhood tutors and governesses. I hardly saw the servants or the cooks. I guess my grandfather ordered them to limit their interactions with me to a minimum." He looked at all of them with his empty stare, with that expression that was more a mask than an actual face. "But that phase of my life is in the past. Denestor came and brought me to the place where I am supposed to be. I will be happy here."

"Even so . . ." murmured Lizbeth. "Even so . . . I don't believe it, I just can't believe it. I mean, your life has been very strange, I admit. But I don't believe that Denestor brought you here because you're . . . bad luck."

"I asked him," the Italian answered. "I asked him if the fact that people died around me was connected to the reasons why they wanted me in

Rocavarancolia. And he answered yes. And he could not lie to us, remember, Lizbeth. He could not lie to us."

Hector gulped. Natalia and her shadows. Bruno and his bad luck. And the others? What made them special? Madeleine's drawings? The stories about the enchanted city that Marina invented, that so closely resembled Rocavarancolia? And him? Why did Denestor bring him? And what for?

He studied the Italian teenager, trying to imagine what it must have been like to live in such isolation. That made almost as much of an impression on him as the rest of Bruno's confession. Most of his life he'd been a prisoner in his own home and, from what he said, he'd never known affection or even the most simple and essential human contact. Was that what had turned him into such a cold and dispassionate creature? Or was his behavior related to the curse that appeared to follow him?

"They're coming!" Maddie announced, snapping him out of his reverie. There was concern instead of relief in the girl's voice. "Something happened! Someone's injured!" she said, and left the tower at a run.

They all followed her outside. Alexander's group was nearing the drawbridge after crossing the stream. And it was clear that they'd suffered some kind of mishap. Ricardo limped and was using a staff as a crutch. Marina was in the rear, with her bow in hand and her step uneasy. But the only one Hector had eyes for was Natalia: Alexander carried her in his arms, and the sight, joined with the memory of Ricardo struggling to carry Adrian, made his heart sink.

"No," he whispered, and quickened his step. "No, no, no, no . . ."

With every word of denial the scream trapped in his throat grew stronger and stronger. With every step he took toward his friend he felt that it would finally come out, he felt it in his mouth, hot and dense, wrestling furiously against his lips, anxious to finally explode. He was convinced that if it happened, he would never be able to stop screaming. He would become a scream himself.

"What's wrong with her? What happened?" he asked when he reached them. The girl in the redhead's arms opened her eyes and murmured something incomprehensible. Hector felt so relieved to see she was alive that the scream was cut off. The girl's left shirtsleeve was soaked with blood.

"We were attacked by a damn iguana the size of a horse; can you believe that?" Alex said. He had a cut on his cheek and a bruise on his forehead.

Once inside they cleared off a table and placed Natalia on top of it. The girl was strangely rigid. Marco carefully tore off the soaked sleeve and then did the same with the two shirts she wore underneath. They could all see the savage bite marks outlined in blood on her skin. A constellation of wounds in the shape of a crescent moon covered her arm from her wrist to her elbow. They were deep incisions, and a dirty greenish color was visible around them.

Mistral sighed. He already knew what had attacked the group. It had been a chimera dragon. They were hybrid beings created by the gene magicians of the world of Alais. They were part harmless native dragon and part venomous chimera. The cavalry of that world had used them as mounts in the war against Rocavarancolia, and in the chaos of battle many specimens had been lost in the city. Most of them died out, but a rare few survived as best they could among the ruins. The venom from their bite wasn't fatal, but it caused a strong paralysis which the victim couldn't escape on their own. They needed the right antidote or a healing spell. Without either of these things, Natalia would die. It would take a while, but she would die.

Mistral cursed in a low voice and watched the rest of the group. Alexander drank water, his eyes fixed on Natalia. Bruno was further away, closer to the book of magic than to his companions.

The shapeshifter shook his head and lowered his eyes. He had to do it. There was no other way. If he didn't act quickly, he ran the risk of Bruno taking the initiative. And if that took place and something happened to the Italian, all was lost.

Rachel appeared in the stairway, supporting herself on her crutches. When she saw the scene taking place down below, she hurried down the stairs.

"Bandages and clean water," Lizbeth ordered. "I want to clean this mess up. Then we'll bring her upstairs. Let's go! Move it!"

They gradually formed an idea of what had happened. It seemed that the creature, an enormous lizard that looked part alligator, part iguana, had surprised them in the square. Ricardo was the first one struck down, with a swipe of its tail that left him out of action for the rest of the skirmish. The others didn't take long to react. Alexander and Natalia leapt upon the beast, stabbing it furiously, but their weapons weren't enough to fight against the monster. Alexander was struck in the face when the beast turned in response to the attack. Then it was Natalia's turn.

"It bit into her arm and shook her like a doll. It knocked Alexander down with a kick and retreated with Natalia in its teeth," Marina recounted. "I didn't know whether to shoot or not, I was afraid I'd hit her . . . But then something strange happened. I saw something like a shadow . . . it descended on the animal and covered it completely. It left so fast that I couldn't see what it was, if it really was anything, or if it was just an illusion. That lizard thing trumpeted like an elephant, tossed Natalia against one of those stone creatures, and took off running. I shot an arrow, but I didn't hit it."

Hector studied Natalia's paralyzed body. One of her shadows had defended her from the monster's attack. The revelation surprised him. She thought that those beings hated her, but they'd come to her rescue.

"Swords and spears!" Alexander shouted. "That's what we need to tackle things like that!" He threw his cup against the wall. The ceramic shattered to pieces. "If we'd killed it right from the start this wouldn't have happened! Damn it!"

Once they had washed and bandaged her arm, they brought Natalia up to the second floor. Her mobility was becoming more and more limited, and they had to proceed with immense caution on the narrow stairway to carry her upstairs. Marina and Lizbeth had arranged another bed in Adrian's room, and they laid Natalia in it.

Adrian barely moved. He remained lying on his side, his eyes half-open, staring at nothing. Hector stayed outside. Even now he still didn't have the strength to cross the threshold. The smell of death that emanated from the room was too intense. No, he wasn't brave enough.

"Did you see the green marks around the wounds?" Marina asked.

"It's venom," he answered without looking at her. "That thing poisoned her."

"What's going to happen to her?"

"I don't know. I just don't know . . ."

Mistral watched as Alexander ran down the stairs. He waited a few seconds and then went after him. The redhead didn't stop when he reached the ground floor and kept going toward the basement. The shapeshifter soon lost sight of him, but it was clear that he was heading to the armory. He quickened his pace.

Now was the time. The others were all upstairs. He went over to the book of magic that Bruno had left on the chair. It wasn't a real grimoire, of course; no one would have risked leaving an object with so much power within reach of the harvest. The book that Bruno found in the library was nothing more than a treatise on the evolution of the magic arts during the reign of the spider kings. It contained examples of various spells. The particular one that Bruno had managed to perform was a spell that conjured grotesque lackeys, of a sort. The living sphere came from another dimension, ready to fulfill whatever the magician asked of it. The sphere became frantic when Bruno didn't respond to the traditional greeting, and had vanished in a matter of seconds, beside itself, back to its own reality.

Mistral flipped through the pages of the book, searching for one specific spell; in the process he came upon an illustration that made him turn the page so hastily that he tore a corner of the parchment. He heard Alex return from the basement. He looked out of the corner of his eye in his direction and then turned his gaze back to the spiral staircase, to make sure that no one would suddenly appear. He didn't want to risk implicating anyone else. He shifted his focus back to Alexander, who was adjusting the buckle on the sheath of the green sword in his belt.

"I found something," he said quietly. Alex shrugged and kept walking toward the staircase. "You should see it. It might be important . . ." The redhead looked at him with a furrowed brow, but made no move to approach. "The book can't be read like ours are, from left to right, remember? It's the reverse, from right to left."

"And what's that got to do with me?" Alex asked, rudely.

"Can't you see? What goes for text also goes for pictures." He held up the book in front of him, open to the page that showed a wound opening, picture by picture, in the stomach of a demonic creature. He pointed to the first illustration with his index finger. "The spell detailed here isn't about hurting the demon, you see? It's about curing the wound! It closes it! It's a healing spell!"

Alex approached the book and studied the drawings carefully.

"But that doesn't get us anywhere," he said after a few seconds. "We still don't understand a single word of it, so reading from left to right or the reverse doesn't mean anything . . ." His gaze moved from the book to Marco. His face lit up. "The tower in the square! We have to get in there. If it's a tower of sorcery, there should be more books, maybe we'll find one we understand . . ."

"It's too risky, Alex." Mistral shook his head. "Ricardo wouldn't even hear of it. We can't risk anything bad happening to—"

"I don't care what he thinks," Alexander broke in. "We've done everything that he's said up until now, and Adrian and Natalia are dying up there."

"That's not fair. He's not responsible for what happened."

"No," he sighed. "You're right, you're right . . ." He passed a hand over his forehead, messing up his hair. When he looked back a determined fire blazed in his eyes. "Let's go now," he said. "You and me. There's no need to tell anyone else. If we run into danger, it'll just be us."

The shapeshifter looked him up and down. He made the face that didn't belong to him look doubtful, but then he made it nod decisively.

"Let's go then," he said. His voice did not falter.

REQUIEM

Although Mistral knew what was going to happen before Alexander tried to cross the tower gate, he couldn't help but be startled by it. The defense spell activated the moment the redhead stepped foot on the threshold, and literally lifted him up off the ground.

Mistral pretended to stammer in astonishment on the stairs and then stepped back, with his hand over his mouth. The surprise on his face was fake, but the horror was sincere. A flock of black birds took off in flight, frightened by the terrible scream that Alex uttered when he became trapped in the gate's spell.

Mistral pretended to stammer in bewilderment on the stairs and then stepped back, with his hand over his mouth. The surprise on his face was fake, but the horror was sincere. A flock of black birds took off in flight, frightened by the terrible scream that Alex uttered when he became trapped in the gate's spell.

The echoes of his cry spread through Rocavarancolia at magnificent speed, like ripples in a pond after someone's tossed a stone into it. It resounded past the ruined façades, through the arcades over the narrow streets, shot through the avenues like an invisible wave that carried in its trough the news of the tragedy that was unfolding.

The scavenging beasts that wandered near the plaza raised their heads and sniffed eagerly when they heard the scream. The air smelled of death, which was their sustenance. But they soon detected the burnt-silver odor of sorcery and knew very well that they should stay clear of it.

Beyond the Scar of Arax, the boy with the black eyes stood up on the rooftop where he rested and looked down toward the sound, astonished that it could come from a human throat. Further to the northeast, in the cemetery, the dead fell silent for a moment and focused their attention on the scream.

"A spider spell," said a low voice underground, slow and wise. "Only they can cause so much pain."

The scream reached as far as the Margalar Tower.

Madeleine was the first to hear it. She left the sickroom without a word, but was so tense she seemed to be at breaking point. She looked for something, something that wasn't in the room or in the hallway of the second floor.

"Are you okay?" Hector asked nervously. Just from the look of her he knew that something bad had happened.

"Have you seen my brother?" she asked.

Before he could answer, he heard Ricardo from inside the room.

"Did you hear that?" he asked.

Hector concentrated. He heard a distant murmur, a vibrating sound that he couldn't place or identify. Lizbeth walked over to an embrasure and peered out.

"It's a scream. Someone is screaming."

"My brother? Has anyone seen him?"

Hector shook his head, startled. The sound continued endlessly, without pause.

"Marco? Where's Marco?" Ricardo left the room. He was still using a staff as a crutch, although that didn't slow him down one bit as he went down the stairs. He almost flew. "Marco?!"

Madeleine was at his heels, yelling her brother's name, but the only response was that interminable cry. Hector looked at the stairs, hesitant. This couldn't be real. This couldn't be happening. He turned back toward the room. He saw Bruno, motionless between the two beds, with his face turned toward an embrasure. He almost thought he saw an aura of bad luck surrounding him. He almost yelled at him to leave, to stop ruining the place with his disastrous influence. Lizbeth and Rachel stayed together, looking through another embrasure. Marina was sitting on Natalia's bed. She got up slowly and looked at Hector. She was crying.

"It's Alex," she said, her voice breaking.

Hector brought a hand to his throat. The scream was no longer there. It had disappeared without a trace, as if that shriek had made it obsolete. Or as if he'd been robbed of it.

Lizbeth and Rachel stayed with the wounded in the tower. The others took to the ruined streets, following the trail of the incessant scream. They ran. Ricardo, despite his improvised crutch, did not fall behind. The further they went the clearer and more terrible the scream became. Hector didn't need the sound to guide him. He already knew where it was coming from.

Madeleine was the first to enter the square with the fountain. When she reached the brick tower, she gave a shout and took off running toward the courtyard gate. Marco ran out to meet her and stopped her from going any further. She tried to break free, but he held her effortlessly.

The others arrived just seconds later. What they saw left them stunned.

Alexander was trapped in an opening in the tower gate. He twisted and screamed, wrapped in a curtain of pearly light flecked with purple sparks. His feet floated in the air, a couple of inches off the ground. It seemed as if the pain itself kept him there, suspended in that atrocious way, pinned in the air. His green sword was on the ground, still in its sheath.

"What happened?" Ricardo asked, panting. He looked at Marco, dismayed. "What the hell happened?!"

"The tower . . ." Marco managed to utter. His voice trembled. "We wanted to help Natalia and Adrian . . . We thought that . . ."

"Alex!" Madeleine yelled, twisting and turning in Marco's arms. She was the embodiment of despair.

Mistral held her tightly against his chest. The shapeshifter couldn't take his eyes off the trapped boy. The pain the cursed gates caused was infamous. After a long, drawn-out death the body collapsed, devoured by the spell's dreadful magic. There wasn't anything or anyone who could save Alexander now, absolutely nothing. And Mistral was as responsible for his death as he was for the death of the boy whose appearance he'd taken. It had been his hands that strangled the sleeping teenager. And it had been his hand that prodded Alexander here. The irony of the self-proclaimed protector of the last harvest of Samhein being the one who caused the first two deaths in the group wasn't lost on him.

Alexander still screamed. The mask of suffering and agony that his face had become turned toward them, but he showed no sign of recognition: in those eyes there was room for nothing but pain.

Ricardo went into the courtyard.

"Don't touch him!" Marco warned. "The spell still surrounds him! Can't you see? If you touch him, you'll be trapped too!"

"We have to get him out of there!" Ricardo exclaimed. The sight was terrifying. Alexander writhed in the air, howling with pain. The warning mist tightened around him like a moving shroud. And then there was the scream, brutal and prolonged, that resounded in the depths of his being like some sick prank that Hector couldn't manage to escape.

Ricardo carefully climbed the stairs that led to the gate. He raised his staff when he got to the last step and reached it out to him, but as soon as he touched Alex, the sparks began making their way up the wood. Ricardo cursed and threw the staff before the spell could reach him. He hopped back on his good leg.

Mistral searched for Bruno with his gaze. He trusted that the Italian would figure out how to get Alexander down. If he were left with no other choice, Mistral himself would reveal the answer. However, since he'd given Alex the idea of entering the tower and swiftly prevented the others from approaching the gate, he preferred that someone else made the discovery. He was calling too much attention to himself, and he couldn't take any more risks.

Bruno looked at Alexander with his hands in the pockets of his black jacket. There was no curiosity in his eyes. There wasn't anything, not even the slightest spark of compassion. He'd been so isolated his whole life that it appeared he'd lost the ability to feel empathy for his fellow man.

"It's impossible," whispered the shapeshifter. He still held Madeleine fast, even though she no longer tried to escape. What strength the girl had left was used for crying. "Whoever touches Alex will suffer the same fate."

To Mistral's surprise, it wasn't Bruno who figured it out.

"Rachel," Hector murmured. The teenager looked at Ricardo, who nodded with enthusiasm when he realized what his friend was referring to.

"Magic doesn't affect her!" he yelled. "Neither the water from the fountain nor the energy crystals worked on her!" He hobbled toward the gate. "Bruno, Hector! Go find her! Quickly! Run!"

Hector nodded determinedly and took off running at full speed back toward the tower. Bruno, after a moment's hesitation, went after him.

They left Lizbeth more worried than she'd been when they arrived. Hector didn't have the presence of mind to reassure anyone. Alexander's scream had followed them all the way back to the tower and now it escorted them back to the square, so desperate and terrible that it saturated everything.

Rachel went as fast as she could, but the uneven ground in Rocavarancolia wasn't ideal for walking on crutches, and neither Hector nor Bruno were strong enough to carry her on their backs. The Italian had grabbed the book of magic from the tower and clutched it against his chest, leading the charge with his robotic step.

"I saw the spell that's keeping Alexander captive in the book," he muttered when Hector asked, not very politely, why he brought it. And he hurried him along even more rudely when Bruno stopped in the middle of the stairway crossing the stream to try to show him the spell.

"Are you an idiot or what?" Hector shouted. "We have to go back now! Can't you hear that? That's Alexander!"

Nothing had changed while they were gone. Alex kept screaming, with the same force and the same agony. Madeleine cried on Marco's shoulder, with Marina by her side.

Rachel yelled something unintelligible when she saw her friend trapped in the gate and covered her mouth with her hand, horrified. Ricardo wasted no time and immediately made her understand what they wanted.

"And if we're wrong?" Marina asked. "And the spell traps her, too?"

No one answered. Mistral knew that Rachel's immunity to magic was almost complete. Only the most primordial sorcery could affect her, but any other spells and enchantments didn't work on her, either for good or for bad. The shapeshifter had only seen one similar case in all his life. It had been thirty-five years ago, when a native of Tramora died only days after arriving in Rocavarancolia, devoured by a manticore. The gift or curse of the impermeability to magic hadn't served him very well.

Rachel climbed the stairs slowly. Ricardo waited below, while the rest guarded the entrance to the courtyard; the only one who remained apart from the group was Bruno. Hector held his breath when Rachel reached the last step. The girl handed one crutch to Ricardo and then, leaning on the other, stretched out a hand to Alexander. The girl's fingers passed first through Lady Serena's dark mist before plunging into the glittering web that held the redhead prisoner. The sparks immediately leapt onto her hand. She pulled it back hastily, as if she'd been bitten.

She scratched her arm vigorously and looked at Ricardo, embarrassed. The magic sparks had vanished the instant they touched her.

She said a single word in her language as she scratched frantically, as if she had a terrible itch. Then she stretched her arm out again toward her friend, grabbed him by the waist, and pulled him out. Alex fell forward in such a way that he was left with his torso leaning out of the magic web and his legs still caught in it. Rachel pulled again and the boy landed on top of her. The girl managed to keep her balance for a moment, then toppled down the stairs and landed in the courtyard.

Ricardo hurried over to help them, but Marco, again, stopped him with a shout.

"He still has the spell on him! Don't touch him!"

Alexander didn't stop screaming or writhing; his body contorted on the ground in the courtyard in the same way that it had in the gate. Although the magic web from the threshold had disappeared, he remained surrounded by an abundance of sparks. And they could now see how the spell had ravaged his body. Against the pallor of his skin, black cracks and intense red scratch marks were opening. And Hector discovered something that had until now been hidden beneath the dark mist: smoke surged from Alexander, pouring out in small wisps through the wounds and sores that covered him. He was burning from the inside.

Rachel continued scratching frantically, sitting on the ground not far from Alex. Ricardo approached her to make sure that she was all right. The girl cried, but not from pain. She dried her tears with her hand and crawled over to Alexander. She put an arm around his shoulders and another around his waist and pulled him toward her, halting the convulsions with her own body. Despite everything, the screams continued.

"Now what do we do?" Hector asked. The madness seemed to never end; the nightmare seemed like it had no intention of ever stopping.

Mistral exhaled. The only way of helping Alexander was to kill him. A swift death would be a gift from the gods compared to the agony that awaited. But he couldn't tell them that—not without revealing himself, anyway, not without hinting that he knew the spell.

"We can't make Rachel carry him to the tower. She couldn't even if she was in good shape, much less on one leg," Ricardo said. He rubbed his hair constantly, as if an idea might come to him from doing so. "And we can't touch him . . ."

"How long will this last?" Marina asked. She was crying as well. "We already took him down from the gate. What else do we need to do?"

"Someone make it stop, please, please . . ." Madeleine moaned.

"It's in the book," Bruno muttered suddenly. He held it open for the group to see. "The spell is in the book."

This time Hector did look at it. The drawing that Bruno pointed to took up an entire page of the tome, with a torn corner. In it he saw a large stone arcade with a web of sparks floating in its midst, identical to the ones that surrounded Alexander. A horrible creature, half human, half monkey, writhed in the center. The drawing's perspective showed the arcade from inside a building, and on the inside face of the masonry was a series of engravings so mixed up with one another that it was hard to distinguish the individual patterns.

"Do you see how to stop it?" Marina asked. Madeleine looked hopefully at the Italian.

Bruno shook his head.

"I don't think so. The only text accompanying the drawing is too short to explain anything. And the illustrations on the pages before and after don't seem to relate to this spell at all."

Mistral didn't need to see them to know that. That section of the book was limited to compiling a series of illustrations of the most important spells created in the time of the spider kings. And the cursed seals were among them. There was nothing there that could save Alexander, but he trusted that thanks to the drawing, Bruno could deduce how to deactivate the gate's spell. Of course, that wouldn't save Alex. It would be like trying to save the life of a gunshot wound victim by smashing the gun that shot him.

The redheaded boy kept screaming in Rachel's arms. That scream overtook everything. And suddenly, so unexpectedly that they all jumped, another scream joined Alexander's.

"Stop! Just stop it!" A burbling, cruel voice reached them from a nearby alleyway. "By the venom of the bastard dog of the Seventh Hell, stop it!"

Lady Scar appeared from a side street, scowling, tottering in her grotesque way. She covered her ears with her hands and shook her head from side to side. She was dressed in the same filthy sack that she'd worn when they saw her less than a week before. She smelled like dead forest.

"By the archangels of Skull City and the death rattle of the last wolf," she growled as she quickly stumbled toward them. "Not even the two thousand dead in the cemetery make as much ruckus as that dimwitted redhead of yours!"

Ricardo unsheathed his knife and took a step toward the bloated woman. Hector stepped back, disgusted by the presence of such a monstrosity. Lady Scar was only a few yards from the courtyard gate, and up close she was even more revolting. She was covered in scars and ulcers, wounds and marks. Most of her lower lip was missing, revealing twisted, decaying teeth that made her look perpetually ill humored.

"What are you trying to do, child?" she clucked. "Do you think you can frighten me with that knife? Is that what you think?"

At that very instant, an arrow sank halfway into Lady Scar's forehead, the tip sticking out from her broken skull, stained with black blood. The creature stopped in her tracks. She grunted. She shot a furious glance at Marina, who was standing motionless after shooting her bow, and yanked the arrow out. The projectile came out easily, smudged with blood and brains. Then Lady Scar broke it into two pieces, which she threw far away.

"I'll overlook this stupidity." The flesh on her forehead closed quickly over the wound, leaving a new white scar on that cadaver-like skin. "But no more of this, I'm warning you."

"Please!" Madeleine fought with the arms that held her prisoner. "Save him! I beg you! He's my brother!"

Mistral frowned. He hadn't expected to be in such close proximity with another member of the council. It was one thing to be observed through the demiurge's spyglasses, but it was another thing entirely to be right under their noses. If Lady Scar recognized him, he was lost. And with him, the children of the Margalar Tower and, most importantly, the kingdom. He stooped behind Madeline as best he could. He was tempted to shrink his muscle mass to make himself less visible, but that maneuver was almost as risky as stepping right in front of Lady Scar. The only thing he could do was try to pass unnoticed.

"Save him? It's too late for that. No one can save him. The only thing I can do is shut him up, before he makes the whole city go mad."

Madeleine screamed.

Lady Scar continued her path toward the courtyard gate.

"Not another step, you monstrous old hag," Ricardo warned, as he crossed the gate to cut her off.

She raised her arms in a gesture that could have been feigned surprise or surrender, before saying:

"You win, rude little boy: not another step."

Suddenly, her monstrous hands broke off at the wrists and fell to the ground, like grotesque, mutilated spiders. The left fell palm up, and with a jump it righted itself and took off running toward the courtyard next to its companion. Madeleine screamed again. They were all too shocked to do anything other than contemplate the abhorrent appendages in terror.

They passed under Ricardo's legs at full speed and entered the courtyard. They reached Alexander, still writhing in Rachel's arms. The young girl was desperate; tears ran in torrents down her cheeks. She stiffened as the hands climbed up her skirt and jumped onto Alexander's twitching body, but even then she didn't let him go. One of the hands went around to the boy's back. The other searched for his neck. Hector couldn't see what they were doing, but suddenly all went quiet, in such an abrupt and total way that he thought he'd gone deaf.

The redhead blinked, moved a hand in the direction of his sister, said something unintelligible, and raised his head, just to let it fall again. His breathing was ragged.

Lady Scar's hands, each leaving a trail of purple sparks, hurried back to their owner, climbed up her legs, and reattached to her wrists at dizzying speed.

"But you said you couldn't . . ." Marina began.

"I know what I said. Don't be fooled: I didn't save him. He's going to die and he's going to die soon. All I did was disconnect his pain receptors so that he does it without suffering. And no, don't thank me. I didn't do it out of compassion. I did it so he wouldn't afflict us with his screams any longer." The tone of her voice was one of unpleasant apathy. "Say your goodbyes sooner rather than later. He won't last long."

Madeleine's cry intensified. Mistral held her, trying to console her while attempting to hide from the commander of the Rocavarancolian armies at the same time.

Lady Scar began walking again, with that gait that was halfway between tripping and falling. Bruno took off at a run from the tower courtyard and intercepted her before she could reach the covered alleyway, still clutching the book. "Why are we here?" he asked her. "Why did Denestor Tul bring us here? What do we have to do?"

"Get out of my way right now, little boy, that's what you have to do," she said. "You want answers?" She pointed with her sore-covered hand to the brick tower. "Go there. You might find something if you survive the gate's spell. Or better yet . . ." Her index finger left the tower and pointed at the buildings located at the other end of the square. "Ask your friend on the rooftop. He already knows more about this city than all of you put together." And having uttered this, she disappeared into the alley.

They looked in the direction that the scarred woman had indicated.

On the rooftop of a two-story mansion, crouching next to a gargoyle with a horse's head, they saw the boy who'd stabbed Adrian. The short cape that he wore seemed woven from ashen sand.

On seeing himself discovered, he stood up, placed one hand on the gargoyle, and took a step backward, neither taking his eyes off them nor making a move to flee, not even when Marina took aim with her bow. He remained upright next to the stone monster, defiant. The wind rustled through his black hair. His dark eyes looked like living shadows.

"Did you come to laugh at us?!" Ricardo asked. "Is that why you came, murderer?!"

Marina took a step sideways, to better center her target.

"Shoot him," urged Mistral. All of the fury that he felt toward himself was transferred to the boy on the rooftop. If he hadn't stabbed Adrian, none of this would have happened. He let Maddie go to grab her bow. "Shoot him!"

Marina flinched when she heard his shout and took the shot, more out of surprise than out of any real intention of doing it. The arrow passed between the boy and the stone statue, a few inches from his chest. The teenager jumped over the gargoyle and disappeared among the terraces and rooftops.

"You're getting a lot better, Hawkeye," Alexander coughed. They all turned toward him. He spoke in a low, raspy voice, but they understood him perfectly. It was hard to believe that only a few seconds before he was screaming in pain. "I'm sure that if you keep practicing, one day you'll hit something . . ."

Alex hadn't seen the arrow that hit Lady Scar's forehead, but no one said anything. They watched him as if he'd come back from the dead.

"This is so strange." He lifted his right hand. A new crack was opening on the back of it, from his wrist to his thumb; it was an intense red scratch with a black line down the center. "I don't feel a thing. Not cold, or hot. It doesn't hurt. I've never felt so calm."

"Alex . . ." Madeleine fell to her knees beside him. Marco put his hand on her shoulder.

"Don't touch him," he pleaded. "As much as you want to, don't touch him."

"But I—"

"You heard him. Don't even think about putting a hand on me," Alexander warned. Another zigzag crack opened above his right eye. From the left side surged a thread of gray smoke. "Do you want the smelly sack lady to come back or what? No. Leave it, okay? It's not worth it."

"You're going to die," Madeleine sobbed.

For an instant there was a glimpse of real fear in Alexander's eyes. But it was only for a second, a flash that vanished as quickly as it had appeared. Exactly the same as what had happened at the Scar of Arax.

"And you're going to live," he told his sister. The sudden resolve in his voice made Hector shudder. "It's not . . . Oh, damn." He raised his hand to his head and then pulled it back, a smoldering reddish lock of hair in his fingers.

"I'm sorry, I'm so sorry . . ." For a second Maddie looked ready to hug him and Alex jerked back violently, climbing up Rachel so suddenly that he almost knocked her over.

"You're sorry? For what? For having an idiot brother?" he panted. The effort of moving out of the way had left him out of breath. "I'm the one who should ask forgiveness. I'm sorry I got you mixed up in this, Maddie. I brought you to this nightmare. Please forgive me."

"No, no, no . . ." Madeleine shook her head. She swiped at her tears to brush them away. "It wasn't your fault," she said. "Forget about that, because it's not true. I didn't come here because you persuaded me. I came because I wanted to. You should have seen your face; you should have seen the sparkle in your eyes when you came to my bedroom with that horrible creature . . . 'An adventure,' you said. 'How can you let it get away? How many people get a chance like this in their entire lives?' you asked me. You thought it was going to be like one of those crazy stories that you like to read so much. That's why I came, Alex, that's why I came. Because I knew that nothing would have kept you from coming. I came to protect you, because I know you, because I know you're a mess and you need someone looking out for you so that nothing happens to you." She clenched her fists and hung her head. "I'm sorry, Alex . . . I didn't know how, I didn't know how to protect you . . ."

"Nobody could have done it," he said. "Because you're right, I am a mess." He smiled and the corners of his mouth filled with smoke. "Nobody could have saved me." He raised his head to look at the group huddled together in the courtyard. "You won't let anything happen to her, right?"

"We'll protect her," Ricardo said. "We'll take care of her. I promise."

"You promise me too," Alex said, looking straight at Marco. "Promise me you'll take care of her."

Mistral trembled. What did Alexander suspect? What had he seen? In the brief moment it took him to respond he searched the redhead's gaze, but didn't see anything to confirm his fears.

"I promise," he assured him, without thinking for a moment about the potential consequences of that promise.

Alex nodded contentedly, as if that were all he needed to hear. Then he looked at them one by one.

"I'm glad I met you," he said. "We didn't spend that much time together, but it was enough to know that you're all worth it. You're all worthy. Don't let this city destroy you, understand? Defeat it. Give it what it deserves. Show it what you're made of." He leaned back and gave Rachel a smile. She brushed his hair away from his forehead and his smile grew, grateful for the touch.

Madeleine sobbed.

"My sister," Alex whispered. Rachel held him more tightly, if that was possible. Their hands were intertwined. "I'd like to talk to her. I don't know how much time I have left. You understand, right? You'll be fine. But she . . . I . . ." For the first time he didn't know what to say. He made a strange gesture with his hand. Fine strands of smoke arose from his nails. "I want to say goodbye."

Marco watched him with wide-open eyes, as if he were looking at something that was terribly mistaken, out of place. He nodded and left the courtyard. Bruno went after him, after taking one last look at the tower gate. Marina took Hector and Ricardo's hands and they started walking, the three of them huddled together.

"Hector," Alex called before he'd gone two steps. All three of them stopped. "You really never read *Lord of the Flies*?" he asked, in a feeble voice. Embers of fire glowed on his face. Hector looked at him, confused.

"No . . . I never read it."

"But do you know how it ends? Do you know what happens to the chubby kid?"

Hector swallowed. Another line of crimson radiance opened on Alexander's cheek. He shook his head. It was hard for him to talk, hard for him to fight the tears that burned in his eyes, in his throat: they beat inside his chest with the thunderous fury of an evil that couldn't be exorcised, of pain that couldn't be escaped.

The redhead smiled.

"He saves them," he announced in a raspy voice. "He saves them all. He keeps them together and makes them survive on the damned island . . ." From between his lips wafted a flower of smoke. "Save them, Hector. You can do it."

He shook his head. He couldn't save anyone. Not even himself. He should have been the first to die. Not Alexander. The redhead couldn't be destined to die here, in this dirty courtyard, this lifeless garden. What sense did that make? Alexander should have learned how to use that sword which seemed tailor made just for him. He was the one who should have saved them all, because he knew fear and knew how to conquer it.

Ricardo put a hand on his shoulder and gently urged him forward. Hector nodded and let himself be led away, never taking his eyes off Alexander, who lay in Rachel's arms, with his sister kneeling just inches away from him, yet untouchable.

Alex was shining.

Marina sobbed into his shoulder. Hector held her tightly while he wondered how he could feel so cold. He had the sensation of being frozen from the inside out. They sat far from the courtyard, in the heart of the square. Ricardo was next to them, his pale face making his bruised nose stand out. A little further back, Marco and Bruno leant against the fountain. The Italian, impassive as always, had the book open in front of him and only occasionally looked up to glance toward the tower courtyard.

They were too far to hear the siblings' conversation. Rachel was there as a mute witness, stroking Alexander, imparting the comfort of her touch. They couldn't say how long it lasted. Perhaps an hour, maybe two. Time had come to a standstill in the square. Maddie never told them what they talked about in the tower courtyard; she didn't tell them what it was that made her smile or what caused her to be on the verge of breaking out in laughter.

Little by little the silences between them grew longer. It took more and more effort for Alexander to talk. His face and body were peppered with red and black cracks, crimson stains that opened on his skin like flowers in a trampled snowfield. A ray of scarlet light surged from one of the marks on his face, a prolonged, luminous beam that reached beyond the gate. In some places his clothing began to burn up. The end was here, and although Mistral felt a compelling need to look away, he forbade himself from doing so.

Alex lifted a hand to Maddie's face. Rachel followed his movement with her own hand to keep him from touching her directly. Alex caressed the hand that caressed his sister's face. Another beam of light shone from the boy's forearm and extended to the tower's second floor.

And although until then they hadn't been able to hear anything that was said, Alexander's last words reached them all with unexpected clarity.

"Here it comes," he said. "Here it is . . . And it's huge and white, and it shines and dances and turns . . . Stars! Maddie! It's full of stars! I see them! There are hundreds! Oh! Here . . . next to me . . . There's someone next to me . . . Maddie? Is it you?"

A single, dazzling red tear rolled down his cheek; it looked more like magma than blood. Alexander was still smiling.

"I can see it," he said, and his hoarse, ragged voice gave the impression that he was looking at something marvelous. "I can see everything from here. The whole world. It's all here before me . . . I . . ." A cloud of embers arose from his incandescent lips. "I love you, Maddie."

Suddenly, he stiffened in Rachel's arms. He raised his head, tense, as if every last one of the cells in his body were being pulled upward at the same time. The cracks in his flesh opened wider and wider and the pallor disappeared, devoured by bright red. The rays of light that surged from his body multiplied. Alex appeared to have been forged in the middle of a red sun that had fallen into the tower's courtyard. His silhouette was a blistering, scarlet glow.

Hector moaned. Marina had lifted her head off his shoulder and was watching Alexander's last moments of life, too, biting her right fist. The red radiance and the arrows of light finally collapsed, the sun went out, and where there had been brightness only darkness remained. For a moment, Rachel held in her arms a statue of ashes identical to Alexander. Then a gust of wind kicked up and carried him away, out of her reach. It was like watching a giant dandelion seed head being scattered in the breeze.

"The light . . ." Marina stammered. She held Hector so tightly that it hurt. It was hard to understand her words. "It shouldn't have been so beautiful. Death shouldn't be so beautiful."

"He's dead, that's for sure." Ujthan the Warrior sternly nodded his gigantic head. "Deader than Radibinarantorius, murdered fifteen times over."

The body still lay on its side at the table, halfway falling off the chair, its head buried in a mountain of parchment. The first thing Denestor thought when he entered the office was that Belisarius had fallen asleep while he was studying. Then he saw the horn bone, plunged deep between the elder's shoulder blades. Outside, lying in a corner in a pool of blood, he found a servant's decapitated body. There was no trace of the head.

The room seemed more crowded than it actually was due to the presence of Denestor himself, the trembling servant who accompanied them, and, above all else, the colossal hulk of tattooed flesh that was Ujthan. The immense fellow maneuvered like a huge ship among coral reefs, amid the chaos of furniture, shelves, and different objects that filled the study. With every movement the tattoos on his body contracted and relaxed. He took Belisarius by the shoulders and sat him up in the chair. He held him there, placing one hand on his chest without ceremony or respect, as he unwrapped the bandages covering his head. Denestor nodded when the ashen features came into view. It was Belisarius, without a doubt.

Ujthan released the body, which fell back down onto the table. The bandages cushioned the impact on the scrolls and belongings covering its surface. A music box fell to the ground and sprung open. The only melody that issued forth was a prolonged shriek of terror.

Denestor looked at Belisarius's lifeless body. He stroked his pointed beard, pensive. It was a surprising coincidence: one of the children died in the city, and at the same time, someone was assassinated in the castle. If it really was a coincidence.

"Tell me again," he ordered the shaken servant.

"Master Belisarius sent for us for the evening reading session. When we came he was still alive . . ." he said in a quivering voice. He was shocked and trembling, and with good reason. All of the servants were mentally linked, in such an extreme way that you could say they shared one brain. That union made them more efficient, but in this tragic case, it also made them experience firsthand the death of their comrade. "He asked us to light the candelabras, and as we began to fulfill his wish someone attacked us," he continued. "It was quick, Master Denestor, very quick. The pain that we feel . . ." He shook his head, as if there were no words to describe it. The demiurge couldn't help but think of the teenager who'd died that same afternoon. "It took a while for us to get over the shock. As soon as we recovered, we rushed here to try to catch the assassin. But they'd already escaped."

"Who else lives in this part of the castle?"

"Only Lady Dream. She occupies the rooms next to these. Her butler was the first to appear. He didn't see or hear anything. And the dreamer stayed asleep the whole time."

Denestor sniffed the air in the study. Although he didn't detect an odor of sorcery, that didn't mean there was none involved in the murder; it could have been covered up with some type of distortion spell. That would be somewhat difficult, given the protections that prevailed in the castle, but not impossible. As soon as he returned to Highlowtower he would create a magic detector to analyze the room and its surroundings.

"Lady Scar has decided to get rid of everyone who supports Esmael," Ujthan growled. "That's obvious. She wants to be regent at any cost."

Denestor shook his head. Belisarius's seat on the council would be taken by Solberinus, another loyal follower of the black angel. And the next two on the list to join the council were also supporters of Esmael, so Ujthan's theory didn't make sense. Unless Lady Scar was preparing to massacre all the Lord of Assassins' followers, which, despite the animosity that the woman felt for Esmael, was highly unlikely.

No, Belisarius's death had nothing to do with their power struggle. Then, who killed him? And what was the motive? He let his gaze wander around the room. The chaos of belongings, ornaments, and books was overwhelming. They could have taken out half of the study's contents and it would still look like a peddler's shed. The only thing that was missing for sure was the servant's head.

The demiurge thought about the two cadavers. If there were a necromancer in Rocavarancolia, verifying the assassin's identity would be simple; those wizards had ways of making the dead talk. But there were no longer any necromancers. The last, Annais Greenpearl, had died in defense of the kingdom, while protecting Rocavaragalago. He would have to resort to other magic arts, and for the moment, all the spells that he could think of required some time to perform. He had no choice but to consult with the regent and with Lady Serena, more versed than he in matters of magic. Or with the Lord of Assassins himself, if he had no other alternative.

The music box kept shrieking on the ground. Denestor crouched down, picked it up, and shut it with a snap. He straightened up, his fingers tapping on his beard.

"And you said that Lady Dream's chamber is next to this one?" he asked the servant.

"On the other side of the wall, Master Denestor."

"I think it would be a good idea to pay her a visit."

"Visit that crazy woman?" Ujthan fidgeted uncomfortably. "I wouldn't go into the room of a sleeping dreamer if my life depended on it!"

Denestor shrugged. He wasn't just thinking of entering the room of a sleeping dreamer: he was going to enter her dreams.

The wind howled like a beast who'd just broken free. It reared its head furiously on the balconies, jumped from moat to crevice, toppled stones and tree trunks, shook the bones in the Scar of Arax, making the worms that resided within them go mad. Its frenzy was even greater than usual, as if it strained to scatter Alexander's ashes throughout all of Rocavarancolia.

Some still maintained the heat from what had been a living body and shone with a soft, rosy brightness, but most of them were nothing more than gray strands, dead matter which had forgotten that it was once alive.

At the top of the lighthouse in Rocavarancolia, Esmael grabbed a fistful of ashes as they flew past him. They shone like embers. He looked at them for an instant in his outstretched palm, then shook them off his hand and let them resumetheir journey to the sea.

The wind continued howling its requiem throughout the enchanted city.

Hector slowly climbed the stairs of the Margalar Tower. He felt as if he were outside his own body, like a spectator who watched, without much interest, as a despondent teenager climbed the stairs with difficulty. It was strange, but he couldn't recognize himself as the same person who only days before had walked through snowy streets with his costumed sister on his back. In a way, that boy was as dead as Alexander.

When he arrived on the second floor, he entered Adrian and Natalia's room without hesitation. He couldn't even remember what had kept him from doing so until now. He had forgotten, if he ever even knew.

Adrian was talking in his sleep, lost in delirium.

"The horses are burning," he whispered, in a voice so soft that Hector had to lean in to hear him. "They're burning, Mommy . . . Mommy!" He opened his eyes and groped for Hector's hand with his own. Agony and fever shone in his eyes. "It's so cold in the stable . . . So cold . . . Forgive me, Mommy . . . But the horses were cold and I . . . I . . . Forgive me, please, please . . ."

He then slipped back into a restless sleep. Hector let go of his hand, and after brushing his hair out of his forehead, he approached Natalia's bed. The young girl slept deeply, lying on her good side, her wounded arm extended.

Hector touched his face and discovered, to his surprise, that he was crying. The curious thing was that he didn't feel any sadness. He found himself submerged in an unpleasant calm, an empty tranquility. He closed his eyes and sighed. He could hear the sobs and desolation coming from the ground floor, followed by comforting words uttered in a broken voice. Those sounds came from another world, as strange to him as the boy disguised as a vampire who went from house to house asking for candy, as foreign as the tears that wet his face.

The room smelled of blood and sweat. It smelled of sickness, of poison, of pain . . . But it also smelled of life. That was the main smell. Life that refused to surrender, life that clung with tooth and nail to the light.

He opened his eyes and watched Natalia. As he looked at her, he became aware for the first time of how precious, magical, and fragile life really was. He was moved by this revelation, so simple and so majestic at once. He spent a long time at his friend's bedside, watching her in her stupor. Her lips moved now and again, as if she were about to speak in her dreams.

"Everyone dies," Bruno had said their first night there. And it was true, but it wasn't the only truth.

"It's going to get worse," he heard suddenly. Ricardo was in the doorway. His demeanor was devastatingly serious. With his swollen nose he looked like a boxer about to fall to the ground, senseless.

Hector knew he wasn't referring to Natalia or Adrian's condition. He was referring to all of them, to Rocavarancolia, to everything that was happening. He nodded. He was right: it was going to get worse.

"We're going back to the tower," Ricardo said. "Bruno says that he can deactivate the gate's spell. He'll need Rachel to help him from within, but he thinks it will work . . ." He sighed. "You can come, or stay here with the girls and Adrian."

"I'm going with you," he said. He dried his tears and walked to the door, still feeling alienated from himself. When he reached Ricardo he asked, "Have you read *The Lord of the Flies?*"

Ricardo nodded without looking at him.

"What happens to the fat kid at the end?" he asked. He had a knot in his throat but his voice was firm.

"Do you really want to know?" Ricardo asked. Hector sighed. Did it even matter?

"No . . . I guess not."

It was an enormous bed, with a showy canopy from which fell a black curtain adorned with silver thread. It was thirteen feet long and ten wide, and in the very center, dwarfed among the piles of sheets and endless pillows and cushions, lay Lady Dream.

Denestor Tul, demiurge of Rocavarancolia and guardian of Highlowtower, sat in a comfortable red armchair situated to the right of the bed. Next to him was another servant. He held a steaming chalice prepared by Lady Spider.

The face of the sleeping old woman appeared chiseled in stone. Denestor looked at the intricate web of wrinkles that covered her face and sighed. He gestured to the servant, who handed him the enormous goblet. The demiurge held it in his hands, hesitant. Then he drank its contents in two gulps. He instantly felt a profound drowsiness overtake him, a languid warmth that made its way down his arms and legs, dragging him into oblivion. He opened his mouth to yawn. When he closed it, he was already asleep. The empty goblet fell from his hands and rolled onto the rug.

Denestor began to dream inside a dream that wasn't his. He dreamed in the sleeping old woman's dream. He saw himself in a gigantic hall of blue marble, with large rectangular columns arranged among pools of clear water placed at different heights. He walked along the mosaic floor, listening to the echo of his footsteps and the melodious trickle of the water. He heard a child's laugh and then a little girl with light-colored hair and blue eyes appeared before him, dressed in a white and gold nightdress. It was Lady Dream, as she'd looked fifteen decades before.

"Denestor Tul, demiurge of Rocavarancolia and guardian of Highlowtower!" the child announced, taking a graceful bow in front of him. "He's come to see us! He's still alive, and smells of mint and patience! Come! Everyone, come!"

A crowd of women walked toward him. They came out of the pools or from behind the blue columns, or they appeared directly before him out of nowhere.

The demiurge was soon surrounded by a multitude of little girls, young women of different ages, mature adult women, and old ladies in varying stages of decrepitude. They all had light-colored hair and blue eyes.

They were all Lady Dream. And they were all insane. Denestor gulped in his dream. He was already regretting his visit to the old woman.

He's still alive? he thought, with a shudder. Dreamers were disturbing beings, creatures with immense power but so detached from reality that they were difficult to deal with. All dream sorcerers ended up crazy sooner or later; spending the majority of one's life in direct contact with one's own subconscious and those of others made them hopelessly mad. And that madness, fused with their control over dreams, made them all the more powerful. And all the more unpredictable.

But Denestor hadn't called on the old woman to take advantage of her powers as a dreamer. He only wanted to ask a simple question, and he wanted to do it as soon as possible. The alternative of waiting for Lady Dream to wake up was a risk that he didn't want to take; it could be days or even weeks before that happened, and the more time that passed the less chance he'd have of obtaining a coherent answer.

"What brings you to our world, demiurge?" asked a beautiful Lady Dream, dressed in her finest. Her blond hair fell to her waist in two elaborate braids.

"A trivial matter, my beautiful ladies," he assured her. "I've only come to ask if in the last few hours you heard any sound that caught your attention." There was the possibility that she may have heard something that her servant didn't.

"We heard the sound that a drop of fire makes when it calls for its mother," answered one of them.

"We heard the cry of a stone that doesn't want to be a stone, and of a violin that screams because it can't fly any faster," said another.

"A howl beyond time and a broken song . . ." said a third. "That's what we heard, demiurge. And the silence of the dead, and the footsteps of the forgotten . . . The chatting of the butterfl—"

"My dear ladies," Denestor hurriedly interrupted. "I'm referring to a sound outside of the dream. I find myself in the difficult position of informing you that just a few hours ago, Old Belisarius was murdered. I thought that perhaps you might have—"

"Belisarius? He wasn't dead yet?" said a girl of scarcely eight years old. She made a face and kicked at the ground. "Consternation, curses, and hexes for all! Have we been asleep for such a short time?"

Denestor furrowed his brow. He didn't like the turn that this conversation was taking, at all.

"Your butler informed me that you told him two days ago that you were going to sink into a long slumber, but he didn't tell me how long you'd decided to sleep," he answered.

"Until it's all over! Yes, yes, yes!" they all answered at once. "It's for the best. We won't draw any attention if we're as small as mice. We live among the strands of dreams and maybe we can survive that way . . . Oh, Denestor! Poor Denestor! We wish we could take you with us! We wish we could save you!"

A glacial chill spread through the demiurge's dreaming body and extended to his real body in the armchair.

"Until what's over? What's going to happen?"

They all looked at him with the same expression of devastated sadness, but no one made a move to answer. One by one, they exploded into tiny, brilliant particles, explosions of water and crystal that sprinkled over everything. And as they vanished, they never stopped looking at him with sorrow. When there were no Lady Dreams left in the great hall, the pools and columns disappeared as well into a slow drizzle. And suddenly Denestor Tul found himself floating in a void.

He was floating above Rocavarancolia.

The city burned. Hordes of terrors surrounded Rocavaragalago, the monstrous building constructed from pieces of the Red Moon. Seen from the sky, the building had the shape of a ten-pointed star. A myriad of creatures hit and scratched its walls. The sounds of war echoed everywhere. Army formations, barely visible at such a height, were like rivers that chased one another through the streets of Rocavarancolia. There were trumpets and battle cries. Explosions and the clashing of weaponry. The pack howled as they only did during battle.

Denestor Tul, demiurge of Rocavarancolia, heard the roar of a dragon for the first time in thirty years. He felt such relief that he was on the verge of laughter. Dreamers sometimes mixed present, past, and future, and telling them apart wasn't easy.

"You're wrong, Lady Dream! That's not going to happen! It already did! It's been thirty years since the battle that destroyed the city!"

"You're not looking at yesteryear, demiurge." Lady Dream's voice resounded over the clamor of combat. "It's the near tomorrow that you see before you. War will return to Rocavarancolia, Denestor. A new battle is gestating in the womb of the kingdom, and it will break out very soon."

"That's impossible. We're not ready for another war." He shook his head. It didn't make any sense. No, it couldn't be. Besides . . . who was going to fight? And with what armies would they defend themselves?

He was trapped in one of Lady Dream's deliriums. That was the only explanation: deliriums of a mad dreamer.

"The word *impossible* means nothing here, Denestor." Her voice softened to the tone of an old woman who's proud of her grandchildren. "And even less now that the harvest dances with us: look at them, look, aren't they lovely?"

The scene changed.

He no longer flew over the battle; now he floated just a few yards above the spherical floor of the brick tower. The city was quiet. It was nighttime and he was surprised to see the teenagers there, since it was already getting dark. Was this a vision of the future to come? Had it happened already or was it another of Lady Dream's deliriums?

"It's today," said the old woman in a dream-like voice. "It's now."

The girl who was impervious to magic stood immobile on the doorstep. The itching the protective spell caused was so intense that she couldn't stop scratching herself. The others crowded at the foot of the stairs, all with torches and weapons at the ready. Mistral was among them, his back turned to keep watch as the black night surrounded them, his bow ready, an alert expression on his face.

The neutral girl followed the instructions that the eerie boy with the glasses gave her. She looked for loose stones in the door's archway, any element that could be pulled out of the magic circuit. They were trying to deactivate the doorway's spell, Denestor realized, and he didn't know if he should feel admiration or fear in the face of such daring. No harvest had ever gained access to the towers of sorcery in their first week in Rocavarancolia. He looked at Mistral with rage. How far did he plan on going to protect them? How many more crazy stunts would he pull?

The girl left the tower, ceaselessly scratching her shoulder. She carried a small skull in her hand that had been embedded in the stone. She handed it to Bruno and then went in and out through the gate several times, looking around with a furrowed brow. She nodded. The spell had disappeared.

Denestor saw them enter the tower one by one. The Italian was the last to go in; when he crossed the threshold the demiurge saw his lips draw apart in a strange expression he didn't quite manage to pull off: the smile of someone who had never smiled before.

"Denestor. My dear Denestor . . ." Lady Dream's voice surrounded him like a caress, like an exhalation of warm air. "You can't hear it, can you? Roaring, death, battle. Blood, fire, and dragons. Don't you hear them? Oh, my marvelous demiurge. You still don't know what you've brought us from the human realm . . .

"You've brought us the end."

BONUS CHAPTER: THAT NIGHT

That night Denestor Tul, demiurge of Rocavarancolia and guardian of Highlowtower, made eleven trips to the human world. On eleven occasions the rag birds emerged from the vortex that linked the kingdom with Earth and allowed them to venture on their quest, bursting into shrieks to announce that they'd found a trace of promising essence on the other side of the portal. They then flew to meet their creator, surrounded him with the maddening beating of their wings, and carried him off with them.

Eleven times they brought Denestor Tul to the human world.

The first time, the birds carried him to the room of a boy with chestnut-colored hair, an athletic teenager who slept soundly. Denestor watched him for a long time, with a bitter heaviness that grew in his chest. The harvest had begun. The night of Samhein was upon them. The teenager woke up, swaying from the green smoke that unfurled from Denestor's pipe.

"It's a dream," Ricardo said when Denestor Tul introduced himself. It wasn't a question. "I'm dreaming . . ."

The demiurge smiled and made a gesture with his head that didn't mean anything, but that he hoped the boy would take as agreement. Then he spoke of Rocavarancolia, he described the city's lost grandeur, he talked of the adventures that awaited if he agreed to accompany him. He told him he was special.

"Special . . ." the boy murmured, his senses muddled from the pipe smoke. "In my dreams I'm always special," he confessed, a shy smile on his lips. "A hero able to perform the most amazing feats . . ." He nodded clumsily. He'd made his decision. And could it be any other way? What made this new dream any different from all those he'd dreamed before? "I'll go to Rocavarancolia," he accepted. "I'll save your kingdom, demiurge. And then I'll wake up."

"And if I go, who'll take care of my sisters and brothers?" asked the girl with the large brown eyes. Denestor greatly admired Lizbeth's attitude. Even convinced she was dreaming, she thought of her family. "There are seven of us, you know? My father died soon after the youngest, Tobias, was born, and my mom did nothing but work and work to raise us." She talked rapidly, so much so that at times it was hard to understand her. "And my brothers and sisters get sick a lot."

"But not you?" the demiurge asked, curious.

"I've never been sick," she answered proudly. Her pupils were very wide, affected by the pipe smoke. "Never in my life . . ." She shook her head. Her movements were slow, almost languid, in contrast with her words, quick and sure. "My mother says that I got all of the good health and my siblings the bad . . . They get sick . . . And I take care of them. I sing to them . . . I give them medicine . . ."

"Don't worry about them," Denestor said. "Before we go we'll visit each one of your sisters and brothers. I know the right magic to make them stronger. I can't promise you that they'll never get sick, but it will be a lot harder for them to." The girl smiled, content with the prospect, and tried to catch a spiral of green smoke. "Are you coming then?" asked the demiurge. "Will you accompany me to Rocavarancolia?"

"Oh. Rocavarancolia . . ." she murmured. "Yes, I'll go with you," she said. "I'll go in my dreams . . . My sisters and brothers never get sick when I'm dreaming."

"They took my elves away!" the Russian girl complained, her fists clenched tight, a helpless expression on her face. She had woken up to find Denestor sitting at the foot of her bed, and for a moment, the demiurge was afraid she'd attack him. Luckily, the smoke took effect before she could get close enough. "They stole them from me . . ." Natalia said, studying the palms of her hands, as if she might find a clue there regarding the whereabouts of the creatures she referred to. "The pills took them from inside of me." She raised her head suddenly to look at him. "Are you an elf?" she asked, and Denestor shook his head. "No, you couldn't be, of course . . . You're too big. And too ugly."

"I'm the demiurge of Rocavarancolia. The city from which I came to talk to you, the city of miracles and marvels . . . the—"

"Are there elves there?" she asked eagerly.

Denestor Tul looked at the girl and nodded, very slowly.

"There are elves there," he assured her.

The teenager looked at him with alarming apathy. His voice was monotonous, without the least trace of emotion. The only thing the demiurge could think about as they talked was that the boy was empty, no more than a hollow body, with nothing inside to sustain him.

"Rocavarancolia," Bruno said, and in his mouth that name lost all its magic and musicality. "I do not remember ever reading any mention of that city." He made a vague gesture toward the library around them. "Which contributes to my suspicion that this is nothing more than a dream. Although there is also the possibility, of course, that in some way the smoke from your pipe is altering my senses and perceptions so that I think precisely that."

"The city that I'm telling you about doesn't belong to your world," Denestor hurriedly said, passing over the boy's last comment. "You won't find mention of it on this planet. There couldn't be. But that doesn't mean that it doesn't exist, I assure you. Rocavarancolia is real. And it needs you."

"Interesting," he said in a tone of voice that seemed to indicate that nothing interested him. "There's something I would like to ask. Since I was born, I have had the sense that bad luck consumes those around me. People close to me die and everything seems to indicate that their deaths are related to me. Could that be one of the reasons why I am special? One of the reasons why I am necessary to this kingdom that you are telling me about?"

Denestor squinted his eyes and looked beyond the young boy's strangeness. Bruno was marked. He could see it clearly. And by all appearances, he had been since he was born.

"That is, without a doubt, one of the things that makes you special to Rocavarancolia," he assured him.

★★★

Marina woke from a curious dream. She'd been dreaming that she was writing a new story. It started out simply: a stranger appeared in a teenager's bedroom to take him to Delirium, the enchanted city which had, for some time, taken center stage in her stories.

She sat up in bed, dazed and disoriented. Her room had taken on a greenish tone; a light fog hung in the air. Sitting at the foot of her bed, calmly smoking a pipe, sat a gray man. Exactly the same as the one she'd been writing about in her dreams.

"Oh," she said. "I'm still asleep. Did you escape from my story?"

"A story?" the stranger asked. "About me?"

"Yes." She shook her head sleepily. She began to raise her hands to rub her eyes, but halfway there she forgot what she was doing. "A story about a man who kidnaps children to take them to an enchanted city. Only he can't tell lies . . ." She frowned. She'd forgotten the rest. The beginning of her story dissolved into thin air. She was dreaming now, she told herself. A dream within a dream . . . Who knows? Maybe a good story could come out of it. "You're here to take me to Delirium?" she asked.

"No," Denestor answered. "I'm here to take you to Rocavarancolia."

"Take me where?" Dario narrowed his eyes, suspicious.

He'd never heard of the city this weird guy had mentioned. He wasn't even sure if he could pronounce the name correctly, even though he'd just heard it. He shook his hand to wave away the smoke that the little man insisted on blowing in his face. He almost broke out laughing when the man told him that he was special.

"To Rocavarancolia," the stranger repeated. "A glorious place that unfortunately is now just a shadow of what it—"

"Is it better than this?" Dario interrupted, as he made a gesture that took in not just the alleyway and the three homeless kids who slept in boxes, but also all of the misery, desperation, and horror that had lately been pursuing him. "Is your city better than this wreck of a life?" he said. "Is it better than living among trash? Is it better than getting drunk to celebrate your father's death?"

Denestor studied the face of the young man before him. His eyes shone, full of bottled-up rage, anguish, desire to flee . . .

"I can't answer those questions," he confessed. "The only thing I can assure you is that your life in Rocavarancolia will be very different than it is here."

"Then you don't need to say another word," Dario said. "Whoever you are, whatever it is you want, get me out of here."

The room of the young man named Marco was crammed with photographs of landscapes and postcards from the most exotic places. Next to the window was a telescope and dozens of travel magazines piled upon the shelves.

"Another world?" he asked eagerly. "A city from another world? It can't be true. It can't be . . ." His voice trembled with pure and simple excitement.

"But it is, I assure you," said Denestor Tul. He leaned toward him. "And it's not just any city: it's Rocavarancolia. The wonder capital, the place where miracles and marvels reign."

"Marvels . . ." the boy repeated, attuned to every one of his words and gestures.

"Even the longest of lives wouldn't be enough to take them all in, boy," the demiurge promised. "Will you come with me to a place like that? Do you dare?"

"Yes. I want to go," said Marco, breathless, stumbling in his rush to get out of bed, as if it was necessary to set off as soon as possible. "I want to go to Rocavarancolia."

Denestor smiled, moved in spite of himself by the boy's naivety. He suspected that he might not even have needed the smoke from his pipe to convince him to go along.

"An adventure!" the boy with the blond hair yelled. He seemed ready to jump for joy on the bed. The pajamas he wore were ridiculous, clouds and little lambs, pajamas meant for a toddler. "I love dreaming about adventures. It's so fun!" He fell to his knees among the blankets and looked at him fixedly. "Will there be magic? Can I do magic? I want to do magic!"

Denestor smiled.

"There is a chance that you might be capable of doing it, yes."

"Are you a wizard?"

"Something like that," he answered.

He raised one hand, and with a snap of his fingers he made a small flame spring up from his knuckles. The young boy turned pale. His eyes bulged in their sockets, and from his expression alone Denestor realized that he was about to start screaming. With a quick flick of his wrist he turned the flame into a block of ice that began to sparkle. An ocean of light and color lit up the room through the smoky green haze.

The boy's panic was cut short even before it began. A smile returned to his lips.

"Magic," he whispered, in a state between shock and trance. His eyes flashed, and in them Denestor saw, far off, the reflection of the flame that he had hurried to put out.

The girl named Rachel crawled across the bed and pressed her nose up to Denestor's wrinkled face. She blinked several times, without taking her eyes off the stranger's parchment-like skin. Then, as if she wanted to test whether such a person was real, she pulled on his cheeks.

The demiurge looked at the girl, shocked, not knowing how to react to her scrutiny.

"You're real," Rachel pronounced. And she backed her pronouncement with such vigorous nodding that Denestor was surprised her head didn't detach from her neck. "And even though it seems like a dream, it's not . . . Denestor Tul, demiurge of Rocavaralala, it is my pleasure to announce that you are real. Congratulations." She broke out in laughter and, surprised by the sound of her laugh, covered her mouth with her hands.

"I am real, yes," he confirmed. "And Rocavarancolia is real, too. That's the city where I want to take you. A magical place full of—"

"The only problem is that if you're real, I can't be . . ." she interrupted. The smoke of Morpheus had plunged her into a confused state. "We can't both be real. That would be so strange! Maybe you're the one who's dreaming me . . . This is fun! If I go will you let me smoke your pipe?" she asked, her eyes glued to its bowl. She sniffed the greenish smoke.

"It's not suitable for you to—"

"Oh, it doesn't matter. I'll go with you. I want to see what Rocavaralala is like! With a name like that it must be a fantastic place!"

"How many people ever get a chance like this?" Alex asked her. "An adventure, Maddie! That's what this old guy is offering us! An adventure in another world!"

Madeleine looked at her brother with a furrowed brow. Seeing him appear in her room, followed by that little gray man, had really scared her. But suddenly, just after breathing a mouthful of the green smoke that hovered around the stranger, she had calmed down. It was a dream. It couldn't be anything else. But at the same time she was certain that it wasn't. The feeling of reality was emphatic, tremendous, terrible, so much so that for a second she had the absurd idea that that was the first real thing she'd experienced, as if everything that came before was nothing but a dream.

The redheaded girl took a step back to try to escape the cloud of smoke that swirled around the strange man. Its odor was dizzying. The window in her room was open, and when she went over to it, the fresh air instantly cleared her head.

"That is what I offered your brother," the man Alex had introduced as Denestor was saying. "An adventure that few have ever even dreamed of. Rocavarancolia needs you. It needs both of you to rise from its ashes, to recover the glory that made it great."

Maddie took another step back. She was barely a yard from the window. And the air kept her safe from that suffocating emerald smoke that staggered her mind. She thought about jumping. The window was on the first floor and it was scarcely five feet to the ground. She would flee and then go in search of help.

"Do you want to stay here forever?" Alexander asked her. "Living a boring and empty life? I don't want to be like the others, I refuse to be. We're special, Maddie, and in that city we can prove it."

"This isn't a dream . . ." she murmured.

"Maybe you're right," he answered. "Maybe it's real." He looked at her tenderly. "If you don't want to go, I'll go by myself. I'm not going to miss this chance."

Madeleine looked at her brother, her heart beating rapidly in her chest. She was certain that if she fled, she would never see him again. Alex would go off with the stranger. He'd do it without a moment's hesitation. She shook her head. Threads of green smoke seeped into her lungs. Once again she was tangled in unreality. Even so she had one last opportunity—she was still capable of taking one last look at the open window.

Then she took a step forward and entered the green mist.

The last time that Denestor went to the human world was to visit a snowy city where a chubby teenager slept in his bed, still wearing his street clothes. The demiurge of Rocavarancolia sighed, tired, as he carried his weary bones over to the brown-haired boy's desk. The harvest was already, by far, the most numerous that he'd gathered in recent years. And many of them seemed to be remarkable specimens. He wanted to believe in them. He needed to believe that there was still some hope for the kingdom. He closed his eyes for a second. Exhaustion, despite the potions that Lady Spider had provided for him throughout the night, began to take its toll upon him.

Suddenly, the boy woke up.

"Who are you?" he asked. In spite of himself, Denestor shuddered. The young man's voice carried an authority and strength at odds with the body it came from. For a moment he thought it was Esmael who was talking to him. "How did you get in my room?"

The demiurge of Rocavarancolia and guardian of Highlowtower collected himself, improvised a smile, and hastened to answer:

"You startled me, boy. I thought you were asleep."

And that's how the story began.

Character Glossary

The Harvest of Samhein

The name given to the group of twelve teenagers that Denestor Tul brought to Rocavarancolia from Earth.

HECTOR: a slightly overweight teenager from the United States, introverted and kind of clumsy.

NATALIA: a reserved and ill-humored Russian girl.

RICARDO: a noble and athletic Spaniard who takes charge of mediating between the harvested teens.

BRUNO: a native of Rome. Intelligent, with a cold, antisocial, almost robotic demeanor.

ADRIAN: a resident of Copenhagen, he's the youngest of the group. He's spontaneous, childlike, and fearful at the same time.

MARCO: a hardy German teenager, with a talent for leadership. He knows the basics of boxing and several martial arts.

MARINA: a pretty French girl with blue eyes and an active imagination.

ALEXANDER: an Australian whose peculiar sense of humor at times borders on inappropriate. He's Madeleine's brother, and red-haired like her.

MADELEINE: a frivolous, superficial beauty. She's Alexander's sister.

LIZBETH: a strong, somewhat plain Scottish girl from Aberdeen. She's very warm and maternal.

RACHEL: Although she's unable to communicate with the others, her cheerful, lively personality shines through.

THE ROYAL COUNCIL

DENESTOR TUL: demiurge of Rocavarancolia and guardian of Highlowtower. He's in charge of bringing the harvest to the kingdom.

LADY SERENA: once a beautiful woman and now a ghost, green from her clothing to her hair.

LADY SCAR: a woman riddled with numerous wounds and scars. She's the commander of the kingdom's armies and the guardian of the Royal Pantheon.

ESMAEL: black angel and Lord of Assassins. He's a beautiful, unscrupulous creature.

UJTHAN: an enormous, belligerent warrior. His body is completely covered in tattoos.

BELISARIUS: an ancient wizard, wrapped in thousands of bandages due to the decrepit state of his body.

ENOCH THE DUSTY: a vampire who's gone thirsty for thirty years, able to transform into dust.

RORCUAL: an alchemist, invisible for several years after trying a potion on himself whose effect he still has not been able to reverse.

LADY DREAM: a sorceress of extraordinary powers who sleeps continuously.

MISTRAL, THE SHAPESHIFTER: a missing member of the council.

THE LEXEL TWINS: two mysterious wizards who hate each other to death. One dresses in black with a white mask, the other in white with a black mask.

HURYEL: the kingdom's regent. He has been on his deathbed for some time.

LADY SPIDER: not a member of the council, but she takes care of Huryel. She's an arachnid creature of considerable size.

ACKNOWLEDGEMENTS

A big thank you to Natalia Stengel, Lucía Molatore, Michael Santorum, Leticia Mahieu, Rubén De Miguel, Santiago García, Carmen Pila, Ignacio Illarregui, Seve Fernández, Marc R. Soto, Bruno Valderrey, Jon Burguera and of course, to Vanesa Pérez Sauquillo. Thank you for making this story better than I could have done on my own.

For this new edition, a huge thanks to Fiona for her beautiful covers, and to all the lovely people at Dark Horse who have worked on this book. Special thanks go to Ervin Rustemagić, my favorite sorcerer, and to Gabriella, the best companion and partner to be had in any adventure, project, or delirium.

About The Author

José Antonio Cotrina was born in Vitoria (Spain) in 1972. He started publishing short stories and novelettes at the beginning of the nineties, and his first full-length novel, *Las fuentes perdidas* (*The Lost Sources*), appeared in 2003. *Las fuentes*, a dark fantasy piece with a road movie premise, showed his inclination toward stories that mix the fantastic with the macabre.

Since then he's published fantasy, horror and science fiction for all ages. *The Cycle of the Red Moon* trilogy is his best known YA work, as well as the later *La canción secreta del mundo* (*The Secret Song of the World*). Among his many accolades he holds a Kelvin (one of Spain's biggest fantasy awards) for *Las puertas del infinito* (*The Gates of Infinity*), which Cotrina co-wrote with Víctor Conde. He also writes and publishes with Gabriella Campbell. *Crónicas del fin* (*Chronicles of the End*) is one of their joint works.